THE BOMB MAKER'S SON

ALSO BY ROBERT ROTSTEIN

Corrupt Practices

Reckless Disregard

THE BOMB MAKER'S SON

A
Parker Stern
Novel

ROBERT ROTSTEIN

SEVENTH STREET BOOKS®
AN IMPRINT OF PROMETHEUS BOOKS
59 JOHN GLENN DRIVE • AMHERST, NY 14228
www.seventhstreetbooks.com

Published 2015 by Seventh Street Books®, an imprint of Prometheus Books

This is a work of fiction. Characters, organizations, products, locales, and events portrayed in this novel either are products of the author's imagination or are used fictitiously.

Cover image © Media Bakery
Cover design by Nicole Sommer-Lecht

Inquiries should be addressed to
Seventh Street Books
59 John Glenn Drive
Amherst, New York 14228
VOICE: 716–691–0133
FAX: 716–691–0137
WWW.SEVENTHSTREETBOOKS.COM

19 18 17 16 15   5 4 3 2 1

Library of Congress Cataloging-in-Publication Data

Rotstein, Robert, 1951-
    The bomb maker's son : a Parker Stern novel / by Robert Rotstein.
        pages ; cm
    ISBN 978-1-63388-044-3 (pbk.) — ISBN 978-1-63388-045-0 (ebook)
    I. Title.

PS3618.O8688B66 2015
813'.6—dc23

2015000886

Printed in the United States of America

Sweet savior from moribund winter,
rescuer from blank, incessant December,
defying cruel probability . . .

CHAPTER ONE

I get out of my sagging old Lexus, brace myself against the open car door, and take a reflexive look around the underground parking garage. I always check the shadows—I've been assaulted in here before. The familiar smells of motor oil, dust, and moldy damp concrete provide solace. I walk into the courtyard. The night is warm, the garden lush with banana plants, tree ferns, and gardenias. The dim solar lanterns along the winding flagstone path provide scant light between here and the stairwell leading to my condo unit.

A woman who seems to coalesce from molecules of darkness is suddenly blocking my way. Despite the balmy August night, she's wearing sunglasses, a heavy black coat, and a scarf—perhaps a Muslim hijab—that covers her head and the lower half of her face. Her hands are concealed in her pockets.

I clench my fists to prevent tremors and walk forward, trying to mask my trepidation with a confident façade. As I'm about to pass her, she says in a barely audible whisper, "Parky."

So she's looking for child star Parky Gerald. Six months ago, during a highly publicized trial, a witness let slip that I was the former kid actor, revealing a secret that I'd kept hidden for twenty-five years. Since then, I've been hounded by obsessed fans seeking autographs and attention. I don't sign autographs, not because, as some celebrities claim, they're meaningless, but because I refuse to commit forgery. I'm no longer that kid actor. I'm Parker Stern, attorney at law.

Although I now understand why the woman is here, I'm no less cautious. What sane person stalks a forty-year-old has-been? When she takes her hands out of her pockets, I recoil, but she only reaches up and lowers the scarf.

"Heavens, Parky, you actually don't recognize your own mother?" she says.

Of course I don't recognize her. It's dark, and she's in disguise. Not only that—she's *here*. She's never been to my home, and I never expected her to be.

"Jesus, Harriet, what the fuck?"

She shakes her head in disapproval of my language. When I was a child, every other word that came out of Harriet Stern's mouth was a profanity. But that was when she was a promiscuous, drug-abusing stage mother, before she became Quiana Gottschalk, the elusive, mythical elder of the cult that calls itself the Church of the Sanctified Assembly. She and the Assembly's founder tried to embezzle millions from my movie earnings to finance the organization. At age fifteen, I became an emancipated minor and sued to get my money back. My mother and I don't speak unless we have to.

"I need to talk with you, Parky," she says. "Can we go up to your place?" She checks her surroundings like a wary bird and reties the scarf around her brown hair.

"What are you doing here, Harriet? They finally excommunicate you, too?"

"Your condominium unit, Parker!" She says this in the imperious tone that I grew up with, the tone she must use with intransigent Assembly underlings.

"I don't think so."

As I pass her, she grabs the sleeve of my cotton workout shirt. "I'm sorry. Please. I need your help."

Something's off. The Quiana Gottschalk I know doesn't apologize and doesn't beg anyone for favors, especially me. The Quiana I know travels with an entourage of Assembly thugs and would never show up at my condo alone. The Quiana I know doesn't wear blue jeans. Why is she wearing blue jeans?

More out of curiosity than filial concern, I say, "Fine, come on up. But make it quick. I have an appellate argument tomorrow."

We climb the stairs to my condominium unit. My mother is fifty-

nine, petite, and elegant, but usually also commanding and intimidating. Tonight, she looks as skittish as the moths flitting around the
amber floodlights.

I open the door and let her inside, looking behind me one last time to
make absolutely sure that her Assembly henchmen aren't lurking in dark
crevices or under rocks. She walks into the living room and takes stock.

"Very nice," she says, "though I'd think that someone with your
talents and success could afford something larger. And your furniture
is rather stark. You could use some more color in this room. The sanctified colors of the Celestial Rainbow are dazzling."

It's true that the place lacks color: the wicker chair, love seat, and
area rug are all black and white. The glass cocktail table is just black.

"I prefer it this way," I say.

She raises a tattooed eyebrow. "Yes, you've always seen things in
black and white, Parky."

We stare at each other until she sits down on the wicker chair. I
sit across from her on the sofa. When she leans forward with uncharacteristically rounded shoulders, I wonder if her posture indicates the
first stage of osteoporosis. The Assembly has bizarre theories about
nutrition and modern medicine. They insist upon a low-alkaline,
unbalanced diet, deny the germ theory of disease, and believe that the
government has poisoned the public water supply. Even a powerful
elder like Quiana is vulnerable to their quackery.

"Aren't you going to offer your mother some herbal tea?" she asks.

"What's this about?"

She looks down at her hands, obviously disappointed at my refusal
to brew her some tea. "I have a friend who needs a lawyer. I'd like you
to represent him. I'll pay you your normal fee, of course. I'll pay you a
premium if that's what it takes."

"I'll never represent anyone who has anything to do with your so-
called church."

"He isn't a devotee of the Assembly. He's . . ." Her voice quavers,
and she has to take a breath and start over. "He's got nothing to do with
my present life. I knew him before."

"What's he charged with?"

She kneads her hands, like she did back in the day when apologizing for a drinking-and-drug binge or when crying because the latest movie producer she was screwing dumped her.

"I asked you what he's charged with, Mother." I rarely call her that, but my response echoes her own regressive behavior.

"He wants to turn himself in. I don't know why after all these years. He'll need a lawyer." Her eyes glisten. Are her tears real? My mother always wanted to be an actress, but she had neither the talent nor the temperament. That's why she lived her dream through me, her only child. "He's been a fugitive since nineteen seventy-five."

"You expect me to believe that someone wants to turn himself in after almost forty years?"

She shakes her head and shrugs simultaneously. My mother has taken advantage of the best cosmetic surgery that the tithes of Assembly devotees can buy. Yet the skin on her face has softened and drooped; gravity and time have avenged her attempt to defy them. "I'd feel better if you got me some tea."

I don't move.

"Will you take on his case, Parky? Please."

"Harriet, what's he charged with?"

"Multiple murder and acts of domestic terrorism." The words are spoken, not by my mother, but by a man standing in the dark hallway leading to my bedroom.

My peripheral vision flashes red with rage and fear. Fists clenched, I get out of my chair and approach the man slowly. He's in his mid-sixties, five-eight or -nine, wiry, so not a physical threat—unless he's carrying a weapon. He has a receding hairline, but still enough wavy gray hair that you wouldn't call him bald. He's clean-shaven, wearing a gray T-shirt with a maroon ring at the neck, a stylish windbreaker with a matching maroon pocket logo, and blue jeans. There's a small gold earring in his left ear. Fortunately, his hands are at his sides, empty.

"Sanctified Assembly?" I ask, glowering back at Harriet.

"Your building security isn't very good," she says. I expect her to assault me with a triumphant smirk, but she's staring somberly at the coffee table.

"My name is Ian Holzner," the man says. "In nineteen seventy-five, I was charged with a crime I didn't commit." There's a gentle richness to his voice. "The press has unfairly referred to me as the Playa Delta Bomber. I assume you've heard of me."

I shake my head. "History has obviously passed your ego by."

"Parky, please," Harriet says.

The man purses his lips, not quite a grimace. "I'm thinking of turning myself in to stand trial."

"In my opinion, it's suicidal," my mother says. "These days, the government is even more oppressive than—"

This Holzner character gives my mother a laser-sharp look, one that would usually bring her ever-simmering temper to a boil, but improbably, she stops talking. I'm glad, for no other reason than I don't want to hear a diatribe about how the United States government oppresses the Sanctified Assembly.

"*If* I decide to turn myself in, I want you to represent me," the man says. "Harriet tells me you're the best."

Interesting that he calls my mother *Harriet*, a name she's disavowed and purports to despise.

"I do very little trial work these days," I say. "I'm an appellate lawyer now. Less stressful." What I don't say is that, for the past few years, I've suffered from severe stage fright every time I walk into a courtroom. *Glossophobia* is the technical term. With a mix of powerful antianxiety medications, I've been able to manage to get through the more highbrow, and so more civil, appellate-court arguments.

"Nonsense," my mother says. "You were born to perform. If not on stage, then in a courtroom. You're going to take Ian's case."

"I don't think so, Harriet," I say.

She stands up, walks over to Holzner, and loops her arm in his. She's beaming like a grimy street lamp in a littered alley. "Parker Stern, I'd like to introduce you to your father, Ian Holzner. Ian, this is our son, Parky."

I'd think this was one of my mother's cruel, manipulative games, that Ian Holzner couldn't possibly be my father, except for one thing. When I look at him, really look, I realize that I resemble him as only a son can resemble a father.

CHAPTER TWO

As a kid, I often asked my mother to tell me about my father. Among her stories, she told me that he was a fallen war hero, a spy, a musician, an anti–Vietnam War radical, and a famous actor. As a four-year-old, I once, between takes on a sound stage, asked the actor I was working with whether he was my father. After he said "no," I went on to pose the same question to every male member of the crew. When my mother realized what I was doing, she dragged me away by the arm and slapped me. By the time I reached eight, I'd figured out that everything she'd told me about my father was a lie. After that, when I asked about my father, she'd tell me that his identity was none of my concern. Later, when I understood what *sleeping around* meant, I concluded that she probably didn't know herself who my father was. It turns out that he really *was* an antiwar radical. What better way to conceal the truth than to slip it among a bunch of lies?

But now I know why she lied, because how could she tell me the truth? In the space of five seconds, her revelation has rewritten my past the way a well-placed footnote can change the meaning of an entire book. I've always believed that if I met my father, I'd feel rage or confusion or joy or resentment. This awkward reunion has left me numb. I thought I'd have a million questions. I can't think of one.

Holzner deftly disengages his arm from my mother and looks down at the floor as if embarrassed. At least he's exhibiting the right emotion.

"Don't worry, I'm not here to play daddy," he says.

I don't know whether I'm relieved or disappointed.

"I'm here because I need a lawyer. You've gone against powerful adversaries, and nothing is more powerful than the United States government. You've taken on tough cases, and my case couldn't be tougher.

That's why I want to hire you." He speaks in the cadence of an evange-list. I know where I got my acting and lawyering chops.

"Can you pay my legal fees?" I ask. I don't really care about the finances, but talking money is the best way to stay detached.

"I told you that I'd make sure you got paid," Harriet says.

My eyes stay on Holzner.

"I can't afford to pay you anything," he says. "I've been an auto mechanic for the past twenty-seven years. If you won't take your moth-er's money, then I'm afraid you'll have to take the case pro bono."

My mother was always attracted to dissemblers, the worst being an evil hack actor named Bradley Kelly, the founder of the Sanctified Assembly. She trained me to be an actor, thrust a toddler into a bogus world. People think the legal profession is built on lies, but the fact is that a lawyer has a state-sanctioned obligation to search for the truth. That's one reason I became an attorney. At least this Holzner fellow is forthright, or so it seems.

"What are you accused of," I ask.

He walks over to me slowly, in a relaxed stride that seems calcu-lated to appear unthreatening. "On Tuesday, December seventeenth, nineteen seventy-five, at around three thirty in the afternoon, a bomb exploded at the Veterans Administration in Playa Delta, California. Four people died and nineteen were injured. I had a history of blowing things up in the name of revolution. The Playa Delta bomb bore my sig-nature. I didn't do it."

"Who did?"

"That's the problem with being innocent," he says. "You don't know what really happened."

I look at my mother. "Is that who you were, back then, too? A kid playing guerilla soldier?"

As always when I ask about her past, she glares at me but doesn't respond.

"Your mother was never political," Holzner says.

Harriet turns her back on us and goes to the window overlooking the ocean.

"Tell me more," I say.

"I was a radical guerrilla soldier committed to ending the Vietnam War. We did that. After the war ended, it was our goal to foment a violent revolution that would bring down the racist, imperialistic American capitalist system." He smiles sardonically. "Grandiose, wasn't it? The other principal leader of our collective, Rachel O'Brien, was tried and convicted for conspiracy. At her trial, she blamed me for the bombing. She lied."

"Can you prove that she lied?"

"No."

"Then how do you propose I defend you?"

"Do you know what the FBI's COINTELPRO was?"

"Why don't you tell me about it."

"Short for *Counter Intelligence Program.* J. Edgar Hoover's attempt at destroying revolutionary organizations like the Weather Underground, the Black Panthers, and my group. A covert operation, and completely illegal."

Harriet walks back over to us. "The government still uses illegal tactics to spy on law-abiding citizens, to trample on constitutional rights."

"So say the Sanctified Assembly propagandists," I reply.

Ordinarily, she'd snap back, but now she crosses her arms and looks to Holzner almost deferentially.

"COINTELPRO's investigation of the Weather Underground was so dirty that no one went to jail," Holzner says. "You could use the same defense."

"There's a difference," I say. "If I'm not mistaken, their bombs never killed or injured anyone. You're charged with multiple murders, and we live in a post-9/11 world."

"I didn't harm anyone, either. The cops set me up, illegally seized evidence. Fabricated it."

"I need specifics."

"Three COINTELPRO agents picked up my brother, Jerry, by the ankles, dangled him off a third-floor landing, and threatened to drop him headfirst if he didn't tell them my whereabouts. They repeatedly broke into my parents' home and conducted illegal searches, trying to make it look like burglary. I believe they illegally taped conversations of people I knew."

There's a sharp rapping from the faux-brass door knocker, followed immediately by four knocks with pounding fists. Another breach of building security. Holzner and my mother glance at each other, two people who share a secret and a plan. More pounding, so hard that I fear the wood will splinter. Holzner dashes toward the glass door that leads to my balcony, slides it open, and, like some 1960s-movie cat burglar, vaults over the concrete wall—a remarkable feat for anyone, and especially a man his age. I hurry after him and look down, expecting to see him lying injured after a drop from the second floor. He's gone.

Before I can stop her, my mother goes over and opens the door to two men dressed in black suits and red ties, the uniform worn by enforcers for the Church of the Sanctified Assembly. With them is a tall, angular woman with Eurasian features. She's dressed in a black pantsuit and red business blouse. She wears no makeup, and yet her round face, wide eyes, and tapered nose make her beautiful, if any human who shows no emotion can truly be beautiful.

Maybe it's my mother's straighter posture or her harsh gaze, but she's Quiana again, and only now do I truly notice that she hasn't been Quiana since she showed up at my condo.

"What are you doing here, Heim?" my mother says in a condescending tone.

"We were concerned about you, ma'am," the woman says unctuously. "And we obviously had reason to be." She deigns to let her icy brown eyes drift over to me. "We didn't expect to find you in the presence of this apostate." Her tone has changed to mildly disdainful, unheard of for an Assembly functionary. Harriet starts to speak but doesn't say a word. This Heim is either risking harsh punishment or isn't the low-level functionary I took her to be.

"And I didn't expect the Sanctified Assembly gestapo to trespass on my property," I say. "Get out." I walk over and interpose myself between the trio and my mother. The two thugs close ranks and come forward.

"You're impertinent," my mother says to me. "Just remember what I've told you and heed my words. You're to back off, Parker." She turns to the Assembly devotees. "I have no obligation to explain myself to you, Mariko. But if you had a brain in your head, you'd realize that this person was *once* related to me and that he spends his life blaspheming. I can get him to stop." She motions with her fingers and walks out the door. The two men follow immediately, but the woman lingers, regarding me with scorn, until she, too, walks out the door.

Only then do I consciously understand what just happened. I tried to protect my mother. I haven't done that since I was eleven years old. These people are supposed to obey her every command. What is it about Ian Holzner that would make Harriet risk her exalted position? It can't just be that forty years ago, he saddled her with me.

CHAPTER THREE

One of the selling points of my condo unit is the ability to stand outside on the balcony and watch the sailboats, tour crafts, and speedboats maneuver through the Marina Del Rey jetty and out into the Pacific's vastness. The sun-dappled surface, the sharp horizon, the wispy cirrus clouds leave the false impression that the sea has discernible boundaries. Only at night, facing the dense black, can one conjure the true ocean and begin to understand that its apparent contours, like the apparent contours of life, are products of deficient imagination.

I look out into the void and try to process what just happened. My mother is apparently jeopardizing her position in the Assembly to help a man who's an alleged murderer. For all I know, Ian Holzner is some Sanctified Assembly elder involved in a byzantine scheme that only he and Harriet understand. Harriet claims he isn't. But she's lied to manipulate others for at least as long as I've had memory.

Still, I'm curious, both as a lawyer presented with a singular case and as a son who's discovered his long-lost father. I power up my computer and search the name *Ian Holzner*. The *Wikipedia* article shows a black-and-white news photograph of him taken during a protest over the 1970 National Guard killing of four students at Kent State University. Despite his Fu Manchu moustache and shoulder-length dark hair, he bears a striking resemblance to how I looked when I was that age. I find myself irrationally staring at the photo to confirm that that young man is *not* me, mystically transported back in time. He's wearing a military camouflage jacket and work shirt, like you see in movies and TV shows about that era. A cliché. He's holding a megaphone, his lips parted midspeech. His right arm is raised in the air, fist clenched.

Another cliché. But clichés begin as powerful symbols, and these particular symbols started with guys like Holzner.

I scroll down to the "Early Life" section. He was born on January
22, 1949, in Playa Delta, California, the adopted son of former vaude-
villians. His father, a tightrope walker and juggler, was of Irish descent.
His mother, who was Jewish, was one of the record-breaking acrobats
depicted in a famous picture on the top of San Francisco's Coit Tower
in 1946.

The article contains a link to a YouTube video of the stunt. The men
are shirtless, and the woman is dressed in a gymnast's leotard and a tutu.
One of the men is stretched out in a backbend on the building's ledge.
A second man is doing a handstand on the prone man's chest. Holzner's
mother is doing a handstand by holding onto the second man's feet.
Only the acrobats' collective ability to maintain their balance keeps her
from tumbling off the building to certain death. My insides flutter and
dip not only because I don't like heights but also because I realize the
woman in this video is my grandmother.

I return to the *Wikipedia* entry. Holzner's parents encouraged him
to take up gymnastics. In 1967, UC Berkeley awarded him a full athletic scholarship. Upon enrolling, he majored in engineering but later
switched to philosophy. As a freshman member of the gymnastics
team, he was named an All American for the floor exercise. He narrowly missed qualifying for the 1968 US Olympic team. So that's how a
sixty-five-year-old man was able to vault over my second-story balcony
and disappear into the night. The man is a stranger, and yet I feel irrational pride in his early accomplishments.

The article goes on to describe how Holzner, deeply affected by
the police beatings of protestors at the 1968 Democratic National
Convention in Chicago, gave up gymnastics for anti–Vietnam War,
and later, antigovernment, politics. He dropped out of college midway
through his sophomore year. Over time, he became involved in increasingly violent confrontations with the police. He was arrested and jailed
for disturbing the peace, trespassing, destruction of property, and criminal conspiracy.

The end of the Vietnam War in 1973 didn't diminish his radicalism. That same year, he and a woman named Rachel O'Brien formed a collective that law enforcement dubbed the Holzner-O'Brien Gang, which claimed responsibility for bombing several federal facilities and businesses throughout the western United States, causing only property damage but no bodily injury. The reasons for the continued violence were unfocused: a corporation's support of South African apartheid; another's support of a coup in Chile; the Oregon Health Department's alleged sterilization of poor women; the Los Angeles Police Department's involvement in the deaths of six members of the Symbionese Liberation Army. It seems that, once the Vietnam War was over, Holzner and his ilk were aspiring revolutionaries in search of a cause. Or maybe he just enjoyed making bombs and setting them off.

As Holzner told me, the 1975 bombing of the Playa Delta Veterans Administration killed four and injured nineteen. Although no one took credit for the act of terror, forensic analysis identified Holzner as the bomb maker. After a manhunt that lasted days, and in which he was supposedly holed up in a house in the South Central ghetto, he somehow evaded capture, spending years on the FBI's most-wanted list until more contemporary criminals and terrorists supplanted him. His partner, Rachel O'Brien, was arrested in 1976 during a raid on an Oregon commune. She was tried for murder but avoided the rap by implicating Holzner in the bombing. The jury did convict her on the lesser charge of conspiracy. She served seven years in prison before winning parole in 1983.

At the end of the article is a collection of quotations attributed to Holzner. I only have to read one to know how misguided my father was: *It's time for privileged white kids to join our black brothers and sisters and take up arms against the racist American war machine; it's time for us to build the bombs that will reduce our hometowns and the bourgeois values they represent to rubble. Long live revolution!*

I close the article, clicking the mouse aggressively, surprised at my level of agitation—or is it disgust? My mother is a domineering, abusive stage mother turned religious charlatan who preys on the vulnerability of others for profit and self-aggrandizement. My father was an immature, privileged kid who was playing war and might have murdered innocent people. I've spent my professional life trying to see that justice is done, and when that's impossible, to represent my clients zealously. As for my private life, I've tried to lay low and not hurt the people around me. Reading about Holzner, I feel that I'm not the person I thought I was, that somehow I'm complicit in his crimes. Once revealed, long-suppressed truth can be so disappointing.

If the Law Offices of Parker Stern exist, they're located at my back table in The Barrista Coffee House in West Hollywood. The staff and I jointly own the place. Now, it's the day following the visit from my "parents," and the last of the late-afternoon caffeine freaks have just left the shop. I'm reading a memoir by Bill Ayers, one of the founders of the Weather Underground. The book is self-indulgent and defensive, but what I care about is that Ayers seems to ignore the Holzner-O'Brien Gang entirely. At least I'm getting a sense of these 1970s radicals, seen through the prism of old-age rationalization. They were educated, well-off, good-looking, popular kids who formed their own deadly fraternity and played at guerilla warfare. They were so condescending and narcissistic that they actually believed they could lead the oppressed masses in armed rebellion against the United States government, when all the masses wanted was their share of the American dream. The Weather Underground, the SLA, the Holzner O'Brien Gang—they didn't have any idea which way the winds were blowing.

Someone approaches my table and hovers over me. I look up to see my mother, dressed in a black peacoat, white blouse, black beret tilted on her head at a forty-five-degree angle, Jackie-O sunglasses, and a fuchsia silk scarf. If she thinks she's incognito, she's wrong. Her outlandish outfit is only drawing attention. Once again, she's alone.

She sits across from me, removes the sunglasses, and like a Vegas blackjack dealer satisfying a hit, slides a manila folder toward me. She turns around and motions toward Romulo, The Barista's manager, who's doing double duty busing tables.

"Fetch me a black coffee in a paper cup," Harriet says to him. It's a command, not a request.

"I thought caffeine is off limits for Assembly devotees," I say.

"Just this once." She flutters a hand toward Romulo. "I'm with your boss. He says it's on the house."

"Romulo is my partner and The Barrista's manager," I say. "The real boss. And he doesn't give out freebies."

"It cuts into the profits," Romulo says with a straight face, though he's a man who laughs easily.

Harriet blinks once but shows no embarrassment. "You mean I have to pay for my drink?"

"It's Romulo's call."

He makes a mock show of contemplation. "Okay, on the house this one time."

Harriet turns away, frowning as if she were the one who'd been put upon. She and I stare at each other in silence. Thirty seconds later, Romulo returns with the coffee. She doesn't even thank him.

"What can I do for you, Mother?"

She slaps her hand on the table hard, rattling my coffee cup. "Open the envelope."

Inside, I find a black-and-white photograph of a young Ian Holzner holding a toddler in his arms. The boy has a Band-Aid on his left knee and streaks of blood on his shin. He's grasping the man's neck with both arms. Holzner looks like he did in the *Wikipedia* photo, though he's shaved off the Fu Manchu mustache. He's grinning slightly, but the expression might only be an involuntary contraction of the risorius muscle, because there's no joy in his face. Standing to his right is a petite woman in a dark tank top and bell-bottom jeans—Harriet Stern. She's wearing aviator sunglasses, and she's barefoot. Her straight, dark hair flows down to her waist. She, too, is smiling, but there's something downcast in her expression. She's holding a cigarette between the index and middle fingers of her right hand. I started acting in commercials at age three, so I've seen photos of myself as a toddler, but no pictures like this. I can't remember seeing any photos of my mother and me together taken before I turned seven years old. By that time, I was already an established actor. I stare at the photo for a long time. We were in the woods somewhere.

"I don't remember this," I say. But I've always had a blurry memory of scraping my knee in the forest and of a nice man holding me. It's my only recollection of a father, a fragment of memory that I've clung to all my life while fearing that I imagined it. The pain from learning that it's real is excruciating. I toss the photo back to my mother.

"What's the point of all this, Harriet? It's too late, too sordid."

"If you represent him, I'll answer your questions. After the case is over."

"What questions?"

"The ones you've been asking ever since you were a child. About your history."

"As if I'd believe what you'd tell me."

We stare at each other for a long time.

"Why would you want to hire me?" I say. "Why not get a lawyer who's objective? A lawyer who's more qualified? I'm not even a criminal lawyer."

"We want you because you're his son. No one else will believe in his innocence."

"I don't know if I'll believe in his innocence."

"But you'll want to. Besides, you're good. And I know you. You want the information I'm offering." Everything has always been a commodity for my mother—patience, compassion, her own child. Especially her own child.

"Even if I wanted to take the case—"

"Of course you want to, Parky."

"Even if I wanted to take the case, I couldn't. If Holzner turns himself in, the feds are going to seek the death penalty, and I don't qualify as competent counsel."

"You've tried a death-penalty case before."

So she's been following my career for a long time, because I was involved in that capital homicide case after only five years on the job. I don't know whether I'm pleased or annoyed that she observed my life like a lurker on an Internet bulletin board.

"I handled one capital case when I was an associate," I say. "I was third chair. It was pro bono, and I was working with two experienced death-penalty experts. Under the rules of court, to serve as lead counsel in a capital case, you have to have practiced criminal law for ten years, including, I don't know, two or three murder cases."

"You've handled other pro bono cases involving serious crimes. The woman who killed her husband because he beat her, that bank robbery."

"I'm mostly a civil lawyer, Harriet."

"There's an alternative. You can do it if you consult with an experienced death-penalty lawyer. I already arranged it."

"What do you mean you arranged it?"

"Louis Frantz can act as consulting attorney." Lou Frantz is one of the top trial lawyers in the country, a person who inspires awe in even the smug TV legal commentators and the litigation wonks. Frantz and I have been adversaries in two brutal lawsuits and don't like each other.

"That's absurd."

"It's perfect."

"Why don't you just hire Frantz to represent Holzner? He'll definitely take Assembly money."

"Because Ian and I want you."

"Frantz would never agree to help me even if I were willing."

"He's already agreed."

Of course. The Church of the Sanctified Assembly is one of Lou Frantz's biggest clients.

"Your girlfriend will assist you in the trial, if that makes a difference," she says.

"By my *girlfriend*, you're talking about Lovely Diamond?"

"Yes. I can't get over that silly name."

Lovely Diamond is a lawyer who works for Lou Frantz. She's also my former law student, a budding superstar trial lawyer, and the woman

I can't have but can't live without. At age nineteen, she spent a year or two performing in hardcore pornographic videos, a fact that many in the media won't let her forget. About a year ago, she regained custody of the son that she'd given up at birth, and soon after she broke off our relationship because I wasn't father material. She also thought that I courted danger. Since then, I've tried to win her back, but it's mostly been a war of attrition.

"It's agreed?" Harriet says. "You'll help your father?"

So my mother is offering yet another version of my family history— the truth, finally?—and a chance to be near Lovely Diamond again. I crave both of those things. But at the moment, there's something else I want even more, and that's a chance to get to know my father.

"If Holzner turns himself in, which I can't believe he'll really do, I'll take on the case."

She actually smiles, which she rarely does, at least around me. The smile fades as abruptly as it appears. She reaches across the table, picks up the photo, and puts it back in the envelope. "You have to get to the jail. Ian is surrendering to the FBI as we speak. He needs you."

CHAPTER FOUR

I fear that the news media will already have picked up on Holzner's surrender before I get to the Metropolitan Detention Center, the fancy name for the jail that houses federal inmates. But when I arrive, the building's entrance is clear. As I walk toward security, I hear a clacking of heels on linoleum. Lovely Diamond moves across the room with the determined walk of someone who's displeased and looking for someone to blame. She's wearing a white cotton blouse and black pants. Her blonde hair is pulled back behind her ears, and she wears only a bit of lipstick and eyeliner. No matter how plain she tries to appear, no matter how hard she tries to flatten out her body's curves, people stare at her when she walks into a room. It's been more than a year since she broke up with me, and the acute pain has faded into an occasional unspecified ache I only later recognize as longing. Sometimes, I'll sit outside on my balcony, let the soft Pacific breeze caress my face, and pretend that it's Lovely who's stroking my cheek.

"What the hell, Parker?" she says, in a tone so strident that she's probably dashed my daydreams forever.

"Good to see you, too."

"Lou ordered me down here. Why?"

"He didn't tell you?"

"Why else would I ask you?"

I explain in a hushed tone that Holzner is accused of being the Playa Delta Bomber. She's only thirty-one, so she's never heard of him.

"This is going to be a cool case," she says when I finish. She views the law and trial work as grand theater, just as I did before the stage fright hit and all my assumptions about the practice of law evaporated. Then I reveal that Holzner is my father.

She audibly gasps. "Omigod, Parker, I'm sorry."

"It's fine. It's just a case."

A jailer escorts us into the cramped attorney meeting room, which is painted in a shade of green the color of bread mold. Sitting on the other side of a conference table is Ian Holzner, already dressed in a loose-fitting khaki jumpsuit, standard issue for recent arrestees.

"We meet again, Parker," he says. "Harriet said you'd take my case. I'm glad." He regards us with a relaxed frown that somehow conveys amusement, not distress—odd for a fugitive who's just been incarcerated after forty years on the run. He's sitting with his legs crossed upon the chair and his hands folded on the table in prayer pose, making him look more like a guru in an ashram than an inmate in a jail lockup. I introduce him to Lovely.

Without waiting for us to ask a question, he says, "There are two reasons why I turned myself in. The first is that I'm pretty sure the feds were onto me, anyway. Or would be soon."

"What made you think that?" I ask.

He tenses and then deflates, losing his Zen-like demeanor. "Because of Dylan. He's . . . he was my son. Your half brother. Eight months ago, he was killed by a rocket-propelled grenade while on patrol in Afghanistan. My picture appeared in the local throwaway paper, and there were people from the military trying to contact me about death benefits. I think the government got suspicious about my identity. There were people asking questions of the neighbors, showing up at work." He inhales deeply. "Dylan was a good boy, a good son."

"Jesus," I say, under my breath. A young man died needlessly, a father grieves, and I'm truly sorry about that. But I also envy my dead half brother because he wasn't abandoned. You can't reason emotion away. But a lawyer learns to hide it.

"Tell us your story," I say. "All of it."

He says that Martin Lansing was the name of a baby who was born and died on January 22, 1949, the same day he was born. One of the radical "underground railroads" forged the baby's birth certificate and made a duplicate, which Holzner used to apply for a Social Secu-

rity number. Holzner appropriated the name *Martin Lansing* and hid
himself in the humdrum of anonymity. He spent years in tedious isola-
tion, continually on the move and working at various low-level jobs. He
often survived on a diet of dry cereal and boiled noodles seasoned with
salt and garlic. It was an unremarkable existence except for the constant
fear and paranoia. He ended up in Utah, working as a ski instructor,
where he met his wife, Jenny, who knew nothing of his past. They kept
moving, leading an itinerant life, but Jenny wanted to settle down and
have children. He got a job in Orange County as an auto mechanic
and has been there ever since. Jenny died in 2011 from non-Hodgkin's
lymphoma.

"Tell me about Dylan," Lovely says.

"That's irrelevant," I say.

"Everything's relevant," Lovely says.

"There's no need to hear about this man's son."

"Dylan looks like . . . looked like you," Holzner says.

"And that's supposed to make me feel more like your son? I'm your
lawyer and only that." Maybe I'm not really interested in knowing my
father. Maybe I've taken the case to ensure that the only thing between
us is professional. No rational attorney would defend his parent in a
murder case.

"Mr. Lansing, once you learned that you were suspected of the
bombing, how did you elude the FBI?" I ask. "Who helped you?"

"I won't answer that," he says in a flat tone.

"Everything you tell us is privileged. Answer my question."

"Doesn't matter. There are people who could still be hurt, charged
as accessories to murder. There's no statute of limitations on that, right?"

"Rachel O'Brien, Charles Sedgwick, Belinda Hayes were the other
principals in your collective. Can they exonerate you?"

"They wouldn't help me."

"At her trial, O'Brien said you assembled the bomb and planted it."

"She lied."

"Did she lie when she testified that you planted explosive devices
in buildings where people were?"

He puffs up, sheds years, and now resembles the radical orator I saw on *Wikipedia*. "I'm not ashamed of what we did. We waged a just war against the government that even Martin Luther King called the greatest purveyor of violence in the world. Our collective was responsible for nine bombings of federal facilities and corporations in the western United States that supported American imperialism and oppression of the poor and minorities. No one was ever injured as a result of those operations. Not even a scratch. That was intentional. Other than the one that exploded at Playa Delta, I built every one of those bombs. I was good at it. My actions were noble. I don't apologize for them. But I did not bomb the Playa Delta VA."

How convenient that he admits only to the crimes for which the statute of limitations has expired.

"If you didn't, then who did?" I ask.

"No idea."

"So you want us to get you off on a legal technicality, right? COINTELPRO's illegal activities? Who cares about the facts so long as the system failed you, huh? Or maybe you don't want the truth to come out because you're guilty of murder."

Lovely starts to say something but catches herself.

"Grow up, Parker," Holzner says. "So you had a tough childhood. How tough could it have really been? You were a pampered actor making millions and having a bunch of people cater to your every whim. And now you live in a million-dollar condo on the Silver Strand and work when you feel like it. Not such a bad life. Open your eyes and take a look at people who're really struggling."

I study his face and see a past that never was, a rescuer who never came, and possibly a murderer.

"You said there was a second reason you were going to turn yourself in," I say.

"Because of my past, because of my fear, when I became Martin Lansing I never discussed my true political beliefs with anyone, not even my family. I posed as a middle-of-the-roader, the apathetic workingman. I didn't teach my son to question a government that fabricates justifications for senseless wars. I didn't teach him to question a government that spies on its citizens." Though the steel-tough quality to his voice remains, his eyes shine with moisture, but only that, as if he can control the amount of tears that will flow.

"I behaved like my Orange County neighbors would if their children had joined up," he continues. "Flag-waving, patriotic. Anything to fit in, to make sure I didn't blow my cover. When Dylan told me he was joining up, I said I was proud of him. I even boasted to people at the shop that my son was going to be an officer in the Marines. I talked about how when he got out he'd be a member of an exclusive club that spawns CEOs and successful politicians. I'd lived a lie so long, I forgot who I really was. The selfishness . . ." He grimaces in disgust. "Because I was a coward, because I ran from Ian Holzner, I killed my own son. So, I *am* a murderer of sorts, just not the kind you think. And now it's time to atone."

We're quiet for a long time.

"There's something else, Parker," he says. "You have a sister. Her name's Emily. She's seventeen. A senior in high school. By doing this, I've essentially made her an orphan. Unless you can get me off."

Lovely places her hand on my forearm. "Where's Emily now?" she says.

"She's with my boss . . . my ex-boss now, Ernesto. He's family, her godfather. He takes that stuff seriously."

"You say you're doing this for Dylan, but what about your daughter?" I say. "She's alive and she needs a father and yet you voluntarily put yourself in this place. You'll probably never be free again. How could you do that to her?"

"Her name is Emily," he repeats. "And she's your *sister*. You can denounce me all you want, can deny Dylan, because what does it matter, but Emily has nothing to do with this. She's your blood relative. And she can't stay with Ernesto forever."

"Why not?" I ask.

"He's a good guy, but he's having some problems at home, so she can't stay there permanently. I want you to make sure she's okay, Parker.

She's a good kid, but all teenagers struggle, and now she's got this to deal with. There's no other family."

"Why can't your brother, Jerry, watch over her?" I ask.

"Jerry's from the past. I don't even know if he's alive."

"I'm from the past, too," I say. "More accurately, the never-was."

"Well, now you're very much my present."

The only person I've ever had to take care of was my mother, and that was when I was a child. When Lovely and I were together, I protected her, but she's a person who looks after herself. Mostly, I've been alone, satisfied with drinking good coffee and reading good biographies and trying interesting cases.

"I didn't sign up for this," I say.

"We don't sign up for a lot of things," Lovely says. "They sign us up." She knows. She took responsibility for the ten-year-old son she'd given up at birth.

As usual, when things get difficult, I default to the law. "Give me a name, Ian. A place to start so Emily won't be an orphan."

He looks at me with a combination of disappointment and distaste, then says, "Talk to a man named Moses Dworsky. He works in Van Nuys as a private investigator. He was a lawyer once. He represented Rachel O'Brien. He blamed me for the bombing, but I trust him."

Lovely and I exchange glances. We've both heard of Moses Dworsky. I thought the man was dead.

CHAPTER FIVE

The next morning, a Saturday, I meet Lovely at The Barrista, dodging the news reporters who've gathered at the front entrance. She grumbles that she's missing her son Brighton's soccer game but in the next sentence tells me how excited she is to work on this case.

The capture of Ian Holzner is already big news, even bigger because I'm on the case. The tabloids and celebrity websites have a bizarre interest in Little Parky Gerald. The usually even-tempered Romulo, who's working the register, frowns when I walk in and won't look up at me—his silent indictment for my allowing my legal career to interfere with the shop's business. It isn't the first time that it's happened. As a lawyer, I've tried some newsworthy cases. People close to me have died because of them.

I hurriedly brew myself a double espresso and make Lovely one of those cloying chocolaty mochas with extra whipped cream. Together, we escape out the back entrance and get into my Lexus. After a forty-minute drive through Beverly Glen into the San Fernando Valley, we arrive at a seedy strip mall in Reseda.

Moses Dworsky's office is located on the second floor, over a half-price sushi restaurant and a dry cleaner. We squeeze into a creaky elevator, which seems to take forever to ascend. The doors open onto a dank, mildewed alcove that bears the sign *Moses B. Dworsky Private Investigations*. Business must be better than I thought, because Dworsky has the whole floor, though his office is furnished in cheap pine that's been stained dark.

I tried to set up an appointment but couldn't reach anyone, so this is a cold call. Fortunately, the door is unlocked. There's no receptionist at the front desk, which is bare except for an old-fashioned telephone that I'm surprised has buttons rather than a rotary dial. In response to my loud "Hello," a voice bellows, "Please make yourself comfortable in the waiting room. I shall only be a moment!"

Thirty seconds later, a hulking man in his midseventies shuffles out of one of the offices. By the time he'd turned twenty-seven, Moses Dworsky had already become one of the leading activist lawyers of the 1960s, known for his stentorian voice, jarring physical appearance, courtroom theatrics, and confrontational press conferences that often violated judicial gag orders. He was once six-foot-five, but age and hunched shoulders make him look a few inches shorter. He has wispy white, shoulder-length hair that he hasn't bothered to tie in a ponytail. His huge ears stick out like tail fins on a '59 Cadillac, and, combined with his enormous nose, give him an elephantoid aspect. His bushy, white eyebrows shoot upward, like weeds sprouting through a crack in the sidewalk. By objective standards he's an ugly man, but in his heyday he was quite the womanizer. There's something uniquely attractive about a homely man who exudes power and confidence. Friends and foes alike called him "Militant Moe." Only foes called him the "Eloquent Elephant." He glances at me and cements his eyes on Lovely, establishing that he still likes women and that I can still feel jealousy.

In this era of business casual, I'm wearing slacks and a blue shirt, and Lovely is dressed in a rose-print frock. However, Dworsky is wearing a business suit and tie. He peers at us with droopy eyes through a pair of bifocals precariously perched on his nose. In the 1970s and '80s, he was destined for that rare fame reserved for brilliant trial lawyers who shape their careers by cultivating unconventionality, but he had a fatal flaw—he was a true believer. In 1993, he allegedly relayed a message from his inmate-client to a militant group planning to bomb a military base. The message reaffirmed his client's views that Islamic jihadists were justified in carrying out attacks on American soil because of the United States' military presence in the Middle East. The Justice Department charged him with obstruction of justice and conspiracy to provide material support to terrorists. In response, Dworsky insisted that he was merely exercising his and his client's rights of free speech. He avoided prison only because a federal appellate court overturned his conviction, holding that the search of his law office had been illegal under the Fourth Amendment. That didn't stop the California State Bar from stripping him of his license on the grounds that his conduct constituted moral turpitude. At first, Dworsky was denied a private investigator's license, but he miraculously convinced a judge to overrule the state licensing board. He's been working as a PI ever since.

"I'm Parker Stern," I say. "And this is Lovely Diamond. We represent—"

"I am not familiar with those monikers, sir." His pontificating tone and rabbinical cadence is apparent even in this short sentence. He apparently loves hundred-dollar words and avoids contractions in normal speech. He's one of those rare lawyers who must've come out of the womb wailing behind a lectern. Lovely's boss, Lou Frantz, is another.

"Ms. Diamond and I represent Ian Holzner. She's with the Louis Frantz law firm."

He regards her with one eye open and one closed. "You work for Lou Frantz?"

"Yeah. I'm an associate in the trial department."

"Louis Frantz is a low-class prostitute without the cheap eau de toilette," he says. "Frantz never held a firm belief that could not be changed with the payment of a five-figure retainer. Although I would wager it is six figures in this era of inflation." He waves his hand dismissively. "Bah!"

Dworsky is the only person I've heard utter the word "bah" who isn't a pre-1960s movie actor.

"What's this about Ian Holzner?" he says.

"He's been in federal custody since yesterday," I say.

"I did not hear. I do not follow the news." He raises an arm and thoughtfully strokes his hair, or more accurately, his liver-spotted scalp. After a long silence, he says, "Did Holzner pull a Kathy Power or a Kathleen Soliah?"

"Excuse me?" I say.

"Mr. Dworsky is talking about Katherine Anne Power and Kathleen Ann Soliah," Lovely says. "Power's group robbed a bank in nineteen seventy. A police officer was killed. She avoided arrest, was a fugitive living in Oregon, but she turned herself in twenty-three years later because she was depressed. Soliah was a member of the Symbionese Liberation Army and was allegedly involved in a bank robbery where a mother of four was killed. Soliah lived as Sarah Jane Olsen, a nondescript Minnesota housewife, until her mug shot appeared on TV and she was captured. Holzner's mug shot appeared on the same show, but no one ever recognized him." How like Lovely Diamond to be prepared and have the right answer. She was a remarkable law student and is a brilliant lawyer.

"Holzner turned himself in," Lovely adds.

Dworsky engages in another round of scalp scratching. "Fascinating. I never thought Ian Holzner would become a Kathy Power." He takes a halting half step forward and extends his hand. His grip is feeble, that of an extremely strong man who's afraid of hurting someone.

He leads us into a spacious office. The window is open, so the room reeks of exhaust from the freeway and putrid fish parts from the sushi restaurant's dumpster. I expected to see photographs of Dworsky with his famous clients and framed press clippings recounting his greatest trials, but the only items on the wall are his private investigator's license and a water-damaged poster of a Georgia O'Keefe petunia. He ushers us over to his desk. Lovely and I sit in client chairs so worn and uncomfortable that they seem as if they were rescued from the dumpster in the parking lot. He slowly lowers himself into his chair, wincing when he's halfway down, blinks his eyes twice, and gives me a sad-pachyderm look. "Contrary to what I implied, I do know why Holzner directed you to me. But I'm not sure that you're going to like what I'm going to tell you."

"Does that mean you won't help us?" I ask.

His earlobes wobble in rhythm to his headshake, and he lowers his head to glower. "When did the law schools begin teaching classes in how to interrupt? In my day, one of the skills of an effective lawyer was the ability to listen. But anyone who went to law school after nineteen eighty loves to hear himself talk. Or have television and video games and computers effectively ablated your generation's prefrontal cortexes? If you want my explanation, please do not interrupt me!"

I glance at Lovely, who puffs out her cheeks, doing a poor job of stifling a laugh.

"My apologies, Mr. Dworsky," I say.

"I accept your apology," he says. "You may call me Moses." And if you closed your eyes and heard only his voice, you'd truly believe that you were hearing the voice of God's first prophet.

"Here's Holzner's apparent misconception in referring me to you. He evidently believes that I remain sympathetic to his cause, or at least to the revolutionary ends we both fought for during the late sixties and early seventies. Otherwise, he would not have sent you to me. But you should know that I do not believe in those goals any longer, have not for quite a long time. The movement in which I believed, in which I invested my soul and my heart, was predicated upon a Fabian socialist theory that there should be equal rights for all, that unbridled capitalism is evil, that a government elected to serve the people had no right to use young men as cannon fodder to fight an unjust, senseless war. I wanted to preserve the American system of government, not tear it down. In sharp contrast, Ian Holzner was a terrorist, no better than the terrorists who followed him. Regrettably, I unwittingly played a role in encouraging such acts by advocating for individuals whom I believed to be dedicated to ensuring human rights and justice for all. As it transpired, many of these people were villainous, mere terror mongers. And though I did nothing criminal despite what you might have read, my naïveté in believing in these people cost me my legal career, the greatest love of my life. What brought me to my senses was one seminal event, namely the coordinated attacks on this country that occurred on September eleventh in the Year of Our Lord two thousand and one. It was then I realized that this country is under siege and must be preserved against blind radicalism, Islamic or otherwise. To make a long story short, I do not agree with what Ian Holzner did, and I am no longer in sympathy with the political left. Indeed, full disclosure requires that I tell you that since 9/11, I have voted Republican, though heaven knows I do not agree with many of their ideals." His forehead is damp from the effort of explaining. He removes a cloth handkerchief from his pocket and wipes his brow. "As far as I am concerned, Holzner is, in the vernacular, a flaming asshole. He used his charisma to prey on innocent young women so he could get them to do his bidding. That is what he did to Rachel O'Brien." He folds his arms across his chest in a Poo-Bah pose.

"So you argued in her defense," I say. "I take it that means you won't help us?"

"That depends."

"On what?"

"On whether you retain me."

"I don't understand."

"You will need a private investigator. That is what I am. Two hundred and fifty dollars per hour. Inexpensive, especially because you will also have the benefit of my considerable legal skills. And you will gain access to the files from the O'Brien case. The nonprivileged portions, I might add."

I'm not sure if my eyes have widened or my jaw has gone slack or both, but Dworsky says, "Oh, don't look so surprised. I might not agree with Holzner, but one has to make a living, especially in this economy. And to set your mind at ease, I am an advocate. You know as well as I that we often work harder for our culpable clients than we do for the innocent ones. It is human nature to try to justify our poor choices with increased effort."

"Let me be clear," I say. "You've kept the files after all these years?"

"I do not throw anything away," he says. "*Everything* is safely archived. And if you retain me, you will get much easier access to the Rachel O'Brien files. A subpoena would only generate an assertion of the attorney-client privilege that would keep you tied up in court on the collateral issue for weeks."

I glance at Lovely, who's nodding. She's smart but also inexperienced. Sure, Dworsky can give us access to old documents that only he might still have. But the man is a stranger. Worse, he committed a criminal act against the United States and dislikes the client. He's untrustworthy and a PR nightmare, in other words.

"We'll hire you on one condition," Lovely says.

"We need to talk," I say to her.

She flutters her hand in the air as though I'm a wisp of secondhand smoke. "You have a lot of office space, Mr. Dworsky."

"It's Moses. Please."

"Okay, Moses. Parker and I need an office. How about you provide us the office space rent-free and we hire you at your normal hourly rate?"

I nearly bolt from my chair. "Lovely, we can't impose on Moses."

She doesn't turn to look at me. "I'm not going to spend my days cooped up in The Barrista Coffee House pretending it's a real law office."

"I don't mind working out of the Frantz offices," I say. "You must have space for one more attorney."

"I tried, but Lou says no way. He doesn't want the Holzner case in the office. He thinks it'll be a distraction."

"That is so typical of the man," Dworsky says. "He craves the publicity but eschews the headache."

"This isn't Century City, but it's a real office," Lovely says. "Plus, we need those documents. We owe it to our client to get them. Do we have a deal, Moses?"

Dworsky is leaning back in his chair, enjoying this. I know what his answer will be, if only because he's clearly a man who favors the underdog.

"We do have a binding deal, Ms. Diamond."

I start to object but think better of it. Despite my reservations about Dworsky, he can help us with the case. And Lovely is right when she says we can't work out of The Barrista. This is a capital murder case, and we need as many amenities as possible.

"I guess it's fine with me," I say, but the words tumble to the floor when Moses and Lovely look at each other and roll their eyes in tandem.

We agree to speak further, say good-bye to Dworsky, and leave. The ride down Dworsky's elevator is more harrowing than the ride up. The rattle of the hoist mechanism is louder; the car's shaking is more violent. The journey seems interminable.

When the door opens, I notice that across the parking lot, Mariko Heim, the woman from the Sanctified Assembly who knocked on my condo door the day my mother and Holzner showed up, is leaning against her blue Mercedes, its engine running. She's wearing sunglasses. When she sees us, she nods her head slightly and frowns. I walk toward her, but before I can reach her, she quickly gets into the back seat of the Mercedes, and the driver speeds away.

CHAPTER SIX

The following Monday, Lovely and I take the elevator up, open the door to Dworsky's suite, and stop short when we see an older woman sitting at the reception desk. She takes a sip of tea from an "I Love the Weekend" mug from which she hasn't bothered to remove the Lipton tea bag. Then she starts typing on a computer keyboard with the look of someone who doesn't quite know how the gizmo works. Her short, curly, gray hair gives her an androgynous look, as does her wrinkle-scored skin. She's wearing a drab gray shirt. With her longish nose, thin face, and short hair, she resembles a pigeon. She's probably not much older than my own mother, but because this woman hasn't had extensive cosmetic surgery, she and Harriet appear to be from different generations.

"Hi Lovely, hi Parker, good morning," she says as though we've worked in this office for years. "I'm Eleanor Dworsky, the brains behind Moses." She winks like an over-the-hill film-noir bimbo and gestures toward the far corner of the waiting room. "Meet my only progeny, Brandon Soloway. The product of my first marriage."

I hadn't noticed the young man sitting hunched over in a chair. He's got dark hair cropped close to the scalp, two days' worth of dark stubble, and broad shoulders.

"Hey," he mumbles, not meeting my eyes.

"Brandon is twenty-six years old, which is very young, and the product of a broken home," Eleanor says. "You, Parker, are a famous lawyer and former actor. You, Lovely, are a slightly famous lawyer and a former . . . well, let's say you're a slightly famous lawyer, though knowing Brandon, he's much more interested in your former career as, shall we say, a performer. It's understandable that he's intimidated." She frowns at him, her mouth no more than an inverted line that resembles one of her wrinkles. "Brandon, be polite, act like the grown man you aren't, and look these people in the eye."

"Jesus," he says, making eye contact for no more than half a second. "I'm out of here, Mom." He springs to his feet and stomps out of the office.

Why did I think Militant Moe wouldn't have a secretary, much less a wife and stepson? Eleanor seems as if she was born with that slight smirk. It suits her the way dimples suit some people. She raises a knobby shoulder, a gesture that signals a mixture of disgust and resignation. "I love him dearly, but he's an asshole."

"Who *are* these people?" Lovely whispers through clenched teeth.

Eleanor reaches over the credenza and extends a hand. When I take it, she squeezes hard.

"I've followed your cases on the news," she says. "You're a big-time lawyer, my friend. We're strictly small-time in this office. Oh, Moses was a big-time lawyer once, but that was before I met him. I've been his secretary for eleven years and his wife for eight. And how are you today, Lovely?"

Lovely nods, her lips pressed tight in the lock position. She doesn't suffer fools, and she doesn't usually brush off insults.

"Aren't these interesting times?" Eleanor says.

"Is there something wrong?" Lovely asks.

"Is Moses ready to speak with us?" I say, taking a step down the hall. Lovely doesn't budge.

"You're a very perceptive girl, Lovely. What's wrong is that I don't like your client. I remember the Playa Delta bombing vividly. I abhor what Holzner did."

"He's innocent," Lovely says.

"*Presumed* innocent," Eleanor says. "It's not the same thing. But as Moses says, anyone is entitled to a defense. I suppose."

"Is Moses available, Eleanor?" I repeat.

She raises her hand, sticks out a thumb, and makes a hitchhiking motion to our left. "Enjoy yourselves, kids. And don't ask me for information. The answer will always be, 'How the hell would I know?'"

We go inside and find Dworsky in his office, dressed in a suit with his coat on, as if he's about to plead a case in court. He motions for us to sit.

"How may I help you?" Dworsky asks.

"We'd like to hear about the other members of the Holzner-O'Brien Gang," I say.

"At your service. Where shall we start?"

"Let's start with your former client. Holzner said she lied at her trial about his involvement in the bombing."

"Rachel did not lie. Truth be told, she was meticulous about not implicating him directly, though I wanted her to. She simply told the truth about his penchant for violence and his ability to make the bomb. It was I who blamed Holzner in valid defense of my client. I must say my strategy saved her life." His entire body, even his large ears and nose, seem to expand with pride at his accomplishment. "But now we are on to a different case and a different strategy."

I can sense Lovely's discomfort, which is interesting because she was the one who wanted Dworsky on the case.

"Tell us about O'Brien," I say.

"The sad tale of a brilliant young woman led astray by an older man with whom she thought she was in love. It was very typical of the radical movement that women would turn to violence because of a man's influence. She met Holzner at Berkeley. He was already an established leader in the movement. She fell under his spell and embraced violence at his behest and counsel. Eventually, Holzner began to have so little regard for the sanctity of human life that Rachel had second thoughts. Ultimately, several months before the Playa Delta bombing, she recanted her avowed support of terrorism and refused to participate. But because she had been involved in the planning, she went to prison anyway. I saved her from being unjustly convicted of first-degree murder, fortunately." He folds his hands in front of him.

"That's it?" Lovely says.

"Yes, essentially that is it, Ms. Diamond. These things are usually not complicated."

"Do you know where she's living now?"

"I lost track of her after she was released on parole. She moved back to the Bay Area where her family lived, but they wanted nothing to do with her. In the early nineties, I tried to look her up. I was between marriages, and Rachel was always an attractive woman, though not in the classical sense, so my motives were personal. I was quite something in my day. Eleanor, the love of my life, has tamed me. But I could not locate O'Brien, even with my formidable investigatory skills, which I had even as a practicing attorney."

"What can you tell us about her background?" I ask.

"Nothing you cannot get from the *Wikipedia* entry. She was the school valedictorian, the offspring of upper-class liberal parents against whom she rebelled by becoming radical. A common story. She was an excellent witness at trial. Of course, I prepared her."

"And based on her testimony, you believe Ian Holzner bombed the Playa Delta VA?" Lovely asks.

"That is what I believed then," he says. "Since I am currently working for Holzner's defense team, it is not what I believe now."

"Tell us about Charles Sedgwick," Lovely says.

"They called him 'Chicken Charlie,'" Dworsky says. "He was a philosophy major enamored of leftist politics, an activist who seriously believed in the need for violent revolution. But he was a thinker, not a doer. He evidently would become physically ill in the presence of the explosives. There is a story—I do not know if it is apocryphal—that he lost bladder control when he was supposed to plant a bomb at the Treasury Building in Washington, DC. I will say this for him—he was the one person who stayed loyal until the end. He would not participate in the trial and was convicted of first-degree murder because of the bombing deaths. The only one. And he had very little to do with it, except some amorphous planning. The man is still in prison, consistently denied parole because he is unrepentant and persists in his refusal to cooperate. A tragedy. Had I represented him, I think I could have gotten him off with time served."

"I take it you don't think he assembled or planted the bomb at Playa Vista?" I ask.

"He was incapable of it. He had neither the courage nor the know-how. Which did not stop the FBI and Justice Department from destroying the man's life. A scapegoat for what they believed Holzner did. Egg on their faces for letting Holzner escape."

"Will Sedgwick talk to us?" Lovely asks.

"I have not seen the man in many years. He refused to assist in Rachel O'Brien's defense. Whether he has changed since then is anyone's guess."

"That leaves Belinda Hayes," Lovely says. Hayes pled guilty to conspiracy and served five years in prison because she'd acquired some of the bomb parts.

Dworsky crinkles his nose as if he's smelled something more rank than putrid fish. "She was an atavistic, nihilistic psychopath, sexually aggressive in a way I found abhorrent."

"Do you think Hayes could've planted the bomb?" I ask.

"Oh, she would have liked to. The woman craved blood. But she was intellectually ill equipped to plan the operation, to make the bomb, or even to place it in the restroom. Belinda Hayes might not have been able to find the restroom."

Lovely and I glance at each other. When I taught her law-school class I'd often repeat my mentor Harmon Cherry's observation that some of the smartest people use stupidity as a weapon.

Dworsky lists the names of a dozen other people who flitted in and out of the Holzner-O'Brien collective but says that none of them were credible suspects. Most people shrank from the use of violence once they understood that Holzner was serious about human targets.

"Holzner must have had enemies," Lovely says.

"Jealousies and rivalries abounded," Dworsky says. "I have a recollection that he got into a fistfight with a man named Craig Adamson over something. A testosterone-fueled battle over power rather than about something more exalted. Adamson is now reconstructed, an evangelical right-winger. No one ever suspected him of involvement in Playa Delta, I might add. Alas, all roads lead to Ian Holzner. You have a difficult task ahead of you, my friends."

The meeting lasts another ten minutes, mostly with Dworsky telling us how much he'll be able to help our case. Despite the professions of loyalty to Holzner, Dworsky can't mask his belief that our client destroyed O'Brien's life.

When we leave, Lovely narrows her gray eyes in consternation and says, "You're keeping him on because you want to keep a potential enemy close, right?"

I nod.

"Good call."

CHAPTER SEVEN

We spend the next days researching Rachel O'Brien's 1976 trial, scouring the Internet news archives and even scrolling through archaic microfiche at the downtown library. During the nine-week trial, the government called twenty-three eyewitnesses to testify to the horror and carnage, a ploy to enflame the jurors' passions. The judge was a young man named Carlton F. Gibson, a recent appointee. Because Gibson handled the O'Brien case, he's drawn *US v. Holzner*. He's now in his mideighties.

The trial lasted so long because Moses Dworsky put all of the witnesses, victims and innocent bystanders alike, through grueling, often cruel cross-examination. He questioned their memories, attacked their political views, accused them of lying for the publicity, and even dismissed the severity of their injuries. He filed obstructionist legal motions, engaged in bombastic oral arguments, and held press conferences that violated the judge's gag order and so got him thrown in jail for contempt. He tried to wear the jurors down, to rub them the wrong way so they would become callused to the evidence. Most importantly, he laid the blame on Ian Holzner.

Belinda Hayes dropped a dime on Holzner, or so said the media. She was a principal in the Holzner-O'Brien Gang. She'd been kicked out of the Weather Underground as insubordinate, used heroin, and worked as prostitute to finance the revolution. At the time of the O'Brien trial, she was already serving her five-year prison sentence for conspiracy. She testified that Holzner carried out all the important phases of the Playa Delta attack.

Contrary to what most lawyers would've done, Dworsky called O'Brien to the stand. Admitted terrorists usually don't make good witnesses, but she came across as a naïve young girl who'd fallen under the emotional and sexual thrall of the mesmeric Holzner—exactly as Dworsky described her to me a few days ago. When the jury found O'Brien guilty of conspiracy, even reporters who early in the case had believed in her guilt were surprised that she wasn't acquitted of all charges.

Was my father truly so wrapped up in childish war games that he couldn't tell the difference between murder and revolution?

Now, Lovely and I sit in the "conference room" across from Dworsky's corner office. The windowless space has the feel of a utility closet. The table is covered with storage boxes, each bearing the label *US v. O'Brien*.

Lovely removes the lid from one of the boxes so gingerly you'd think the cardboard was sizzling. "I hate document reviews."

"I do, too, but it has to be done. Let's find the trial transcripts."

We spend hours reviewing documents. Lovely and I have been moving in different directions for so long that it's nice to share a common goal. The files contain voluminous and bombastic motions to exclude evidence and witnesses; attempts to disqualify Judge Gibson based on bias; accusations that the FBI agents engaged in police brutality; reams of prosecution documents quoting the homicidal rhetoric of the Holzner-O'Brien Gang; and scores of press clippings alternatively praising Dworsky's trial abilities and denigrating him for obstructing justice. But no trial transcripts.

At around eleven o'clock, Eleanor Dworsky walks into the room carrying two cups of coffee and a box bearing the words *Etiwanda Donuts*. "I know it's not what you're used to, Parker, with that upscale coffeehouse of yours. But this is the best we can do in this lower-class neighborhood of ours."

I thank her and take a sip of coffee, burning my tongue. Why do these junk-food shops make their coffee so hot? They burn the beans and ruin the taste. I open up the box and notice that the assortment of doughnuts has already made a grease stain in the cardboard bottom.

"You can have mine, Parker," Lovely says.

These doughnuts are so laden with fat that I can't disagree with her decision to refrain, which doesn't stop me from grabbing a blueberry-buttermilk bar and taking a huge bite. It tastes heavy and overly sweet—perfect, in other words.

As Eleanor is about to leave, I quickly swallow and ask her, "We've been through these boxes and can't find trial transcripts. Any idea why?"

"Moses anticipated that question. He told me to tell you he never ordered them. He was on a shoestring budget and was confident he'd avoid the first-degree murder rap. After that happened, he agreed to waive O'Brien's right to appeal in exchange for a reduced prison sentence. He says you should ask the US Attorney or contact the court reporter about the transcripts."

"We already tried that," Lovely says. "The US Attorneys says they don't have it. The court reporter has disappeared. We also looked for the transcripts in the federal court archives. They gave us some story about a flood in the warehouse back in the early eighties. We need to talk to Moses about this. When's he coming back?"

"How the hell would I know?" Eleanor says and walks out.

CHAPTER EIGHT

When I was a kid, Southern California was rarely humid, but lately every August seems to have a monsoon feel. I exit the dank parking garage beneath the Los Angeles Mall and have to shield my eyes from the afternoon sun. The Xanax–Valium cocktail I've been prescribed has left me half anesthetized, as if I'm a video-game player watching a Parker Stern avatar cross the street. I'm also feeling numb because inevitable defeat instills resignation, not fear. And defeat is inevitable today. I'm about to walk into the federal courthouse and make a fool of myself by asking the judge to release Ian Holzner on bail and put an admitted bomber, a suspected murderer, and a four-decade fugitive back on the streets.

I pass the TV-news satellite trucks parked outside the courthouse. Lately, the news reports and Internet blogs have been calling Holzner the progenitor of Oklahoma City bomber Timothy McVeigh and the Boston Marathon terrorists. A dozen reporters are waiting near the courthouse entrance, and when they spy me, they hurry down the concrete stairs and stick microphones in my face. No comment. I don't like the media, and, anyway, what's there to say?

I take the elevator to the second floor and walk down the corridor to the courtroom of the Honorable Carlton F. Gibson. Lovely Diamond is waiting outside.

"Finally," she says. "I thought I was going to have to handle the hearing myself." She's upset with me and has been for several days. She wants me to go see Emily Lansing, my half sister. I just haven't had the time, or so I tell Lovely and myself.

"Is this still about Emily?"

"It's about your tardiness."

"What's your problem? I'm ten minutes early."

"That's not early for court. Ninety minutes is early. Ten minutes is late."

What stings about her statement is that she's quoting me when I was her law-school professor.

"The US Attorney needs to talk to you before the hearing starts," she says.

"About what?"

"She wouldn't tell me. She said she'll only talk to you or Lou. She's a real bitch, actually."

"Did Frantz talk to her?"

"He's here but says it's your show."

That's a surprise. Lou Frantz craves the spotlight more than any other lawyer I know. I was sure he'd try to horn in on my case.

Lovely turns abruptly and marches into the courtroom. I follow and find the gallery packed with news reporters, curious spectators, and courtroom regulars who flit from trial to trial craving the excitement they see on *Law & Order* but rarely find in a real courthouse. The disheveled, basset-eyed orator Louis Frantz, my nemesis and now advisor, is sitting in the third row with his arms crossed and an irritated look on his razor-sharp face. Mariko Heim and her Assembly enforcers have commandeered four seats in the back row. Why are they here? When I pass her, she glances in my direction and then dismisses me with a severe turn of the head.

Marilee Reddick, the United States Attorney, pops up out of her chair and blocks our way before we can check in the with the court clerk. Reddick and I were law-school classmates. Her most distinctive feature is her silver-sand gray hair, cut pixie style. She still weighs no more than a hundred and five pounds. There are a few more wrinkles at the corners of her eyes and a softer chin, but she has the same determined black eyes, the same grin that can be disarming or devastating depending on her objective.

"What is this bullshit, Parker?" she says in a whisper so precise that despite the packed courtroom, I'm sure only I can hear her. Reddick hasn't changed in another way—she spews out more profanity than anyone I've ever met.

"I don't know what you're talking about," I say.

"What about *you*?" she says, pointing an accusing finger at Lovely. "Because this is bullshit."

I hear Lovely breathing heavily beside me. She sometimes has a temper.

Fortunately, Reddick realizes it and takes a conciliatory step backward. "It's your funeral, Parker," she says.

"I still don't know what you're talking about."

"So you claim." She leans in close and says, "On another matter, I was wondering whether your client would be interested in pleading guilty in exchange for a life sentence rather than the death penalty. He deserves to die, but a plea would save the taxpayers the cost of a trial."

"Let's check in, Lovely," I say. I don't know what Reddick has in mind, but I'm not going to reward her gamesmanship.

Lovely glares at Reddick but soon turns and follows me. Lawyers are supposed to present two business cards, one for the clerk and the second for the court reporter. Lovely presents hers, but I don't carry any. Until a few days ago, my only office address was The Barrista Coffee House in West Hollywood. So I begin filling out a yellow Post-it with my information. As I'm writing, the courtroom goes quiet so suddenly that the drop in decibel level actually hurts my ears.

I look up to see three marshals in blue blazers escorting Ian Holzner into the courtroom. There's a collective whoosh of air and a secondary gasp from those in the gallery who are slow to comprehend. Holzner is handcuffed and in leg irons, and he's dressed in his orange jail jumpsuit. I sent over a suit and tie for him to wear. His head is down, and he's shuffling as if in pain, like a movie extra playing a jailbird in a thirties gangster film. He bears no resemblance to the acrobat who only a week ago vaulted over my balcony wall and somehow landed unhurt a story below. The sight of my father in chains slices through the anesthetizing fog that's been keeping my fear at bay. My legs quiver and nearly buckle.

Pride is a much-maligned emotion, but it serves a purpose, because now my pride won't let me succumb to stage fright.

I walk over to Reddick. "What's this about?"

She looks like she's about to swear at me again, but then her face relaxes. "Jesus, you really didn't know. Talk to your client. That's his wardrobe choice. Chains and all. We'd hoped that you could get him to dress properly. As I said, it's your funeral. Or more accurately, your client's." She turns her back on me and sits down.

Courtrooms are bastions of tradition. Criminal defendants have to respect that. Which means that the skinhead gang member with a Mohawk must come to court looking like an investment banker, that the promiscuous party girl has to dress for church. I wanted Ian Holzner to dress as if he were attending his daughter Emily's wedding.

I take a seat at the table farthest from the jury box but in the jurors' line of sight. The defendant has the right to face his peers, though there will be no jury today. Lovely leaves an empty chair between us. The marshals shepherd Holzner over and direct him to sit between Lovely and me. When one of the marshals bends over and makes what's nothing more than a halfhearted attempt to remove the handcuffs, Holzner pulls away violently.

"Why are you doing this?" I whisper to Holzner. "Other than sabotaging your standing with the judge and the public?"

"I'm honoring my son Dylan's memory," he says. "I'm a political prisoner who's exposing a country that would send him to his death for the oil companies and financial conglomerates." He raises his arms and gently touches my shoulder with his bound hands. "And know this, Parker. It's just the beginning."

CHAPTER NINE

There was a time when I delighted in the clerk's solemn announcement that court was in session, in the metallic click of the lock on the chambers door, in the judge's ascent to the bench. Ever since the glossophobia struck, the intercom buzz makes my muscles tense; the door's opening is sniper fire aimed directly at the center of my chest; the judge's entrance transforms me into a callow law student first-chairing the trial of the century. I never know whether to feel cowardly for experiencing the stage fright or brave for fighting it.

When the clerk calls, "All rise," everyone in the courtroom stands— everyone but Ian Holzner, who remains seated at the table with his head down. It's the ultimate act of disrespect, but it also distracts me from the fear.

In federal court, a magistrate judge usually conducts routine bail hearings. But our case has been assigned to District Judge Carlton F. Gibson, and he's made the exceedingly rare decision to conduct the bail hearing himself. Ever since he was appointed to the bench over forty years ago, he's relished handling high-profile cases. The walls of his chamber are covered with photographs of him and celebrities who've appeared in his courtroom—actors, singers, reality-TV stars, a software magnate, and a couple of crooked politicians.

He was an all-conference lineman at a small college in El Paso, Texas, just across the border from Juarez, and he often talks about his stellar football career while court is in session. He fancies himself bilingual in Spanish and English. Once, when he got tired of an attorney raising repeated hearsay objections, he left the bench, got down in a three-point stance, and challenged the attorney (a former college-football player himself) to block him. The poor lawyer refused, of course, and ended up losing the case. His client appealed the ruling, arguing that Gibson's antics showed judicial bias. The appellate court held that the actions might have been peculiar but didn't indicate bias. Judges give their brethren a lot of leeway.

"United States versus Holzner," the judge says, reading from notes and blinking his puffy eyes on every other word. He rubs the top of his head, which is bald except for a ring of feathery white hair. "Counsel, have you ever appeared in this courtroom before?"

"I have, Your Honor," Reddick says.

"Of course you have, Marilee. You're the US Attorney. I know that. I was speaking to defense counsel, Mr. Parker."

"Parker Stern for the defense," I say, making it sound like I'm announcing my appearance rather than correcting him. "It's been a while, Your Honor, but when I was with Macklin & Cherry, I appeared before you on a case for Lake Knolls." Knolls is a former actor who was elected to Congress and then got into some trouble a few years ago because of his secret relationship with the Sanctified Assembly. There's a photograph of him and Gibson hanging in the judge's chambers.

Judge Gibson scrutinizes me as if I've said something offensive, half stands, and peers down at me. His bulbous nose twitches scavengerlike, and for a moment I think he's going to climb over the bench and challenge *me* to a tackling drill, and while I'm decades younger, I don't know that I'd come out on top. But then he sits back down, nods, and smiles knowingly.

"I know you, Parker Stern. You were that kid actor who went underground."

I'm not sure whether his reference to going underground is inadvertent or a dig at Ian Holzner.

"Let's proceed," he says. "This is a bail hearing. Let's hear from the government. *Pronto*, Ms. Reddick."

Reddick goes to the lectern, juts out her chin, forcefully pulls down the hem of her black jacket, and puffs out her chest, a series of maneuvers that makes her resemble a gender-confused bantam rooster. "The government opposes bail, Your Honor." Her alto voice is so smooth and deferent that it seems impossible that only minutes ago she was hurling invectives at me. "Holzner's been a fugitive from justice for decades, so he's clearly a flight risk. He's a master of flight. His crimes are some of the most heinous in American history. He slaughtered innocent people believing he could ignite a revolution to overthrow the United States government. He's not entitled to bail." Her lips curl in a slight victory smirk, an expression she used in law school when she'd put something over on someone.

The judge squints one eye as if he's looking down a gun sight. "Do you find something funny about this, counsel?"

Smirks and sneers are implements in an attorney's courtroom tool chest. So Reddick didn't do anything differently from what most lawyers do every day. Judge Gibson doesn't like her. Or maybe they're friends and he wants to prove he's not biased. The reason doesn't matter. A legal proceeding is just a set of probabilities sometimes thwarted by the whims of gods you say you don't believe in but really do. So I'm hopeful that the judge's reaction to Reddick is a small indication I can defy the odds and win bail for Ian Holzner. I don't necessarily believe Holzner should be free, but it's my job to free him. Besides, I like to win.

Reddick tugs at the hem of her jacket again, gives a slight shake of the head, and lowers her jaw almost imperceptibly. It's a small sign of submission. But she's facile, able to regroup so quickly that I'm probably the only one in the courtroom who noticed the glitch in her presentation—other than Judge Gibson, I hope.

"I completely agree that there isn't anything humorous about this case," she says. "Ian Holzner is a retrovirus. His crime was an early symptom of a disease that's infected this country, namely terrorism. He was a coward, targeting not the military or the police, but civilians working in clerical jobs at a facility intended to assist military veterans and their families. He launched the attack in the city where he grew up, a small town having nothing to do with the government or the Vietnam War effort. He's cheated justice far too long. The government seeks detention without bond under sections 3142(e) and 3142(f)(1) of the Criminal Code because the defendant is both a danger to the community and a flight risk." She shakes her head slowly, well-timed courtroom theatrics. "No, Your Honor, this is no joke. A virus like Ian Holzner is no joke."

"*Muy bien*, Ms. Reddick," the judge says. "Let's hear from the defense."

I stand and will my legs not to buckle. When I get to the lectern, I interlace my fingers and squeeze tightly so that if I have hand tremors, people are less likely to notice. "Your Honor, the United States Attorney said nothing about the defendant as a human being, and the beauty of our criminal-justice system is that the Constitution orders us to treat all people accused of a crime as human beings. By calling him a virus, she denied his humanity. So let's talk about who Martin Lansing, the human being, really is. Mr. Lansing is a hardworking man who—"

Reddick hops out of her chair. "Your Honor, I object to Mr. Stern's use of that name. The real Martin Lansing was a baby who died in infancy. It's offensive for Ian Holzner to continue to use that innocent child's name, and I'm not going to sit idly by and let counsel use the name to try to deflect attention away from his client's crimes."

"The defendant has been known as Martin Lansing for forty years," I say. "So by using that name I'm only—"

"I'm Ian Holzner, not Martin Lansing," Holzner shouts. When I turn and look at him, he's standing up.

"Mr. Holzner," the judge says. "I instruct you not to speak again unless you're given permission to do so. You're represented by counsel, and you will speak through them. Do you understand that?"

Holzner doesn't respond, just stands there with his head bowed.

"My client does understand that, and certainly won't interrupt again," I say.

The judge looks at me with justified skepticism but nods for me to continue. I wait a moment, and from the clanking of chains realize that Holzner has sat back down.

"As the Court well knows, in this day and age, bail is the rule rather than the exception," I say. "And yes, Mr. Holzner was a fugitive, but he's lived in the same location for over twenty-five years, raised a family, held a stable job as a mechanic, and has been a productive member of the community. The crimes alleged in this case occurred forty years ago, and in those four decades, he hasn't gotten so much as a parking ticket. Mr. Holzner's son gave his life in the service of his country. There's no merit to the government's argument that a sixty-five-year-old man who's lived an exemplary life and who's raised a son to be a Marine officer is a threat to the community. I say that fully cognizant of his behavior today, which is a result of grief over his son Dylan's death and nothing else. The alleged crime, certainly, is serious, but the evidence is weak, the product of illegal activities by a clandestine organ of the FBI. And he's got a teenage daughter whom he loves and takes care of. He's her only surviving parent."

"Suppose that's true, counsel," the judge says. "Your client has been a fugitive from justice all this time. Doesn't that automatically make him a flight risk? Why should I release him? *Por qué?*"

"The best evidence that he's not a flight risk is that he turned himself in and so voluntarily subjected himself to the judicial process. He'd still be free if he hadn't done that." I glance at Holzner, and for the first time since the hearing began, he's looking up not at the judge, but at the frieze above the bench, a painting of the Hellenic deity Themis, who symbolizes divine law. I learned long ago that what happens in a courtroom is anything but divine, that every court case arises out of a confluence of human frailties.

"What about that, Ms. Reddick?" the judge says.

"It doesn't really matter," she says. "The FBI already suspected that the man who pretended to be Martin Lansing was Ian Holzner. There were irregularities in connection with the military's attempt to figure out who got Dylan Lansing's death benefits."

The judge taps his pen on the desk, using it as a makeshift gavel. He scans the gallery, turning his head slowly like an actor in a silent-movie melodrama. "Ladies and gentlemen, I cannot believe my ears. Did the United States Attorney for this district really just represent to this court that it doesn't matter that the defendant turned himself in?"

"Exactly," Reddick says.

I give her a lot of credit for not backing down.

The judge flips his pen into the air and catches it just before it hits the desk. "I was a lineman, but I had the hands of a tight end," he announces. "Ms. Reddick, isn't someone who turns himself in the opposite of a flight risk?"

The question makes the courtroom go from quiet to silent. I glance at Reddick. Her cheeks are ruddy. She looks as if she's on the verge of telling the judge to go fuck himself—one of her favorite phrases in school. I can only imagine the teamster's profanity that she'd like to unleash on me right now. She stands, tugs her coat hem, and sidles over to the podium, but I won't give ground, so she has to stand to the side.

I glance over at Holzner, who's still staring forward. He's abandoned some of the *oppressed prisoner* act, because he's sitting up straighter and his eyes are clear and engaged. While he's willing to be shackled during a short court hearing, he desperately wants out of jail. Otherwise, the moment I got up to speak he would've objected to my attempt to get him released on bond.

"At the risk of repeating myself," Reddick says, "it doesn't make a d . . . darned bit of difference that the defendant surrendered now. He had forty years to surrender and face his accusers. Who could be a greater threat to the community than someone who killed four people in a cowardly bombing? He hasn't changed his views—look at his disrespectful behavior. He's already fled justice once. He'll do it again. He's an unreconstructed terrorist."

Judge Gibson tosses his pen so high that he fumbles it on the way down. It rolls off his desk onto the floor. One of his law clerks, a young brunette, immediately brings him a replacement. Her efficiency makes me think that this isn't the first time the judge has thrown his pen overboard.

"Ms. Reddick, were you using profanity in my courtroom?" the judge asks.

"I believe I used the word *darn*, Your Honor. Like what you do with your socks?"

"No, no, no, no, no, counsel. I meant *before* the hearing started.

When you were talking to Mr. Parker, or Stern, or whatever he calls himself."

Reddick reflexively spreads her arms and gives a childish *Who, me?* shrug but then realizes what the judge is referring to. Federal courtrooms are miked so the law clerks can stay in the judge's chambers and listen to the attorneys argue the cases. Gibson obviously had the microphone on before the hearing began, so he probably overheard not only Reddick's profanity but also our entire conversation. It's highly inappropriate for a presiding judge to listen in on off-the-record conversations between attorneys.

"I was having a private conversation with defense counsel before the proceedings began," she says. "And a few inappropriate words might have slipped out. As I'm sure you know, sometimes in the heat of battle, the language gets a bit salty."

"You will not defile my courtroom with such language, *comprendes?*" the judge says.

"Very well, Your Honor," Reddick says, using language that sounds polite but that really conveys displeasure. "But to return to the argument at hand—"

"*Un momento*, Ms. Reddick," Judge Gibson says. He begins writing on a legal pad. After a minute—it seems much longer, because time always moves more slowly when you're waiting for an authority figure to decide your fate—he starts speaking without looking up. For a split second I think he's talking to himself.

"Here's my ruling. The government hasn't shown that the defendant is either a danger to the community or a flight risk." Nothing bolsters a weak case better than a crazy judge who's irrationally on your side.

Reddick stands so forcefully that her chair teeters backward and barely rights itself with a defiant clatter. "I request a continuance so the government can brief this issue in more detail."

"Denied. Please don't interrupt me again, counsel. You might want Holzner to be Holzner, apparently the defendant himself wants to be Holzner, but this is two thousand fourteen, and Martin Lansing is here in court. And I don't think Martin Lansing is dangerous or a flight risk."

"Your Honor—"

"Not another word, counsel," the judge says. "*Nada.*"

The thunder of recognition quickly comes after the lightning bolt that is the judge's ruling. Silence gives way to the clicks of keypads, and the creaks of folding chairs, and the shocked whispers, muted sounds that nevertheless agglomerate into a din that the clerk stifles with a shout of, "Order."

Holzner looks at Lovely in astonishment. She takes one of his shackled hands in hers.

"Here are the release conditions," the judge says. "And for the record, I want to make it clear up front that I'm not letting the defendant go free to roam the streets. I am not *loco en la cabeza.*"

I doubt anyone in the courtroom believes Gibson's disclaimer of insanity. I certainly don't.

"The defendant will be confined to an acceptable secure residence with a family member or close friend who is deemed acceptable by this court. He'll be subject to electronic monitoring. I'll set bond in the amount of six million dollars. Plus constant surveillance of said residence by the US Marshal's office, defendant to defray the cost." Judge Gibson rocks back in his chair and beams at the gallery with self-satisfaction. "Yes, that's my ruling. *Sí.*"

With the judge's words, the pall of righteous indignation enshrouding Marilee Reddick lifts like LA fog on a March afternoon. She knows that Holzner can't even afford the cost of twenty-four-hour surveillance, much less a six-million-dollar bond. And there's the problem of relatives. None have come forward, and if Holzner knows where any of them are, he hasn't told me. Ernesto, his former boss, denounced him to the conservative Orange County newspapers. He doesn't seem to have any other friends. I guess that when you're a fugitive from justice, you can't let people get too close.

I start to object to the judge's conditions, but before I can utter a sound, he shakes his finger at me. "Don't go there, Mr. Gerald. My order stands. But I would like you to come back to chambers when we adjourn so we can get a photograph together."

I glance over at Holzner, who's gazing at me with brown eyes I now recognize as a paternal version of my own—intense, stubborn, righteous. Those eyes radiate an almost-serene fatalism, as if he's finally aware that this hearing is the beginning of an inevitable end game in which he'll die by lethal injection. I've never been a fatalist. I learned as a child actor that no matter how scripted a scene is, no matter how constraining the rules, much of life is improvisation. Words often form of their own volition, seemingly unrelated to cognition. Maybe it's because Holzner is my father. Maybe it's simply because this crazy judge is a star struck, and I don't like star fuckers. But without thinking I blurt out, "I'll post bond for Mr. Lansing, pay the surveillance cost, and let him serve his confinement at my residence."

Behind me, Lovely gasps, seemingly triggering a rising wave of murmurs that finally breaks at the judge's sharp glance.

Gibson reclines in his chair, looks at the ceiling, shuts his eyes, and taps his pen on the bench. When he returns to an upright position, he says, "I don't think that's going to work, counsel. The ethical rules clearly prohibit an attorney from paying his client's financial obligations. That includes bail. So says the California State Bar. In any event, I ordered that the defendant reside with a family member or intimate friend. Less incentive to skip out and leave a loved one holding that bag. You're a lawyer, not a loved one, Mr. Stern."

A second chance to stick to the script, and a second time departing from it: "No problem, Your Honor. Nothing in the ethical rules prevents a lawyer who's also a relative from posting the defendant's bail. The defendant, Ian Holzner, happens to be my father."

CHAPTER TEN

While Lovely accompanies Holzner to the detention center for processing, I stay at the courthouse and arrange to post the six-million-dollar bond. I'm good for the amount. I saved enough from my earnings as a child actor and don't need to work. But if Holzner jumps bail, I will have to practice law to make a living. All the while, the media follow me down the airless corridors shouting questions, nipping at my heels like stray dogs not sure whether they want a hunting prize or a handout. When I finish the paperwork, I take refuge in Judge Gibson's courtroom, one of the few places where I can more or less avoid the media. The courtroom deputy is kind enough shoo them out so they don't harass me for too long. A couple of reporters grumble about the First Amendment, but I'm clearly not going to answer their questions, and they know better than to piss off a court clerk who can make their lives difficult by subtly delaying their access to court rulings. To a reporter, time is worth more than factual accuracy.

At about three in the afternoon, the door opens, and in walks a portly older man with a scraggly salt-and-pepper beard covering multiple chins. Despite the summer heat, he's wearing a black windbreaker bearing the San Francisco Giants logo and a red-and-black flannel work shirt. His old-man baggy jeans are too short, revealing scuffed tan moccasins and white crew socks. He carries a Giants cap in his left hand. His twiny, gray hair barely covers a high forehead. He looks around the courtroom like a lost child. When his eyes alight on me, he limps forward, favoring his right leg. I doubt he's media, but he might be a regular courtroom watcher. As he approaches, the clerk, who's sitting at his desk pushing paper, glances up without concern.

"Mr. Stern?" the man says in a timorous voice. He takes a deep, resolute breath. "I looked for you after the hearing, but you rushed out and looked so busy, so I asked a nice guy from the *Times*, and he said I could find you here. Anyway, my name's Jerry Holzner, Mr. Stern. I'm Ian's brother." He has a speech impediment that affects his pronunciation of the letter *R*, so that "Holzner" comes out "Holznew," "Stern" is "Stewn," and "brother" is "bwothew." Perhaps he's hearing impaired. He looks nothing like Ian. But he wouldn't, because, according to the *Wikipedia* article I read, Ian was adopted. Then the next epiphany—this man is my uncle.

"Nice thing you did for Ian," he says. "I would of, but I could never afford it. I'm just a school custodian, you know. Was. Retired, living on the disability and the pension. I live in Foster City. Not far from San Francisco." He raises his cap and points to the Giants logo. "Anyway, Ian was a good brother. A good boy. He wanted to stop the war." He looks at his feet like a sad child trying to justify his best friend's bad behavior. "Hope I'm not bothering you, sir."

Despite what I revealed during the hearing, he doesn't acknowledge that he and I are related. Is he just overly deferent or a bit slow? As Ian's attorney, there's so much I should ask him. What does he know about the Playa Delta bombing? Can he help me locate any of Ian's former fellow travelers? Did the FBI really hang him by his heels off a balcony to make him rat out his brother? But I ask the only thing a long-lost child could. "Jerry, I'm your nephew. Ian's son. Did you ever see me when I was a baby?" My adult ears detect a plaintive, childlike cast to my voice, a simple yearning that was absent when I asked Ian and Harriet about my childhood. How could it have been otherwise? The interrogation of my parents was imbued with resentment.

Jerry smiles. His teeth are surprisingly straight and white. It seems important. Maybe it proves that not everything about this man is broken, that he has residual strength to help me fight this formless battle on behalf of Ian.

"Oh yeah, yeah," he says, patting my shoulder. "You're the baby. I only heard about you from my mother. She didn't like the girl. Hated her, I think so."

"The girl?"

"The baby's mother."

"Harriet?"

"After the cops rousted me I freaked out, you know? I was afraid of everything, shell-shocked the shrinks said. I had horrible nightmares. I was in the loony bin for a while. All I know is after the thing that happened at the VA, my parents—my pops—wouldn't talk about Ian, didn't want to have anything to do with him. Or his baby son." He looks down at his hat. "Not your fault. But it sounds like you did good. I mean, you were a famous kid actor. Hell, you're famous now. Who would've thought?" He frowns. "I guess Ian is famous again, and that's not so great."

Time to play lawyer again. "You came all the way down from the Bay Area for this hearing, Jerry?"

"Yap. As soon as I read about Ian. I wondered where he was all these years. Missed him. He's my little brother, but he was like my big brother. Smarter, braver, nicer than me. He protected me from bullies. I thought I'd never see him again. I thought he was dead or something."

"Look, I'm going to defend him in this case, and I need your help."

"You're his attorney," he says. *Yew his attoonee.*

"Because the events—the bombing, I mean—took place forty years ago, you might be able to help me piece together what happened."

He nods. "The war. Nam. I served, you know. I think that's why Ian done what he done."

My cell phone buzzes. It's a text from Lovely: "Client free but big problems courthouse steps NOW!!!"

As I gather up my things, I say to Jerry, "How'd you like to say hello to your brother?"

"Yes, I sure would, Parker."

"Let's go." I head out of the room at a near sprint but slow down when I realize that Jerry can't move very well.

"You have to go fast, so go fast," he says. "I'll catch up with you. Where will Ian be?"

"Courthouse entrance. Two flights down." I actually do start sprinting, balancing my briefcase and hoping that I don't trip while running down the escalators. I wish I'd inherited Ian Holzner's gymnastic abilities.

When I get to the automatic double doors, the problem is obvious—Holzner, now dressed in the clothes that I wanted him to wear to court, is surrounded by a media throng. "... and frankly, I'd be bullshitting you if I told you otherwise," he says in his resonant sixties-rabble-rouser voice. "No way am I remorseful for what happened in the seventies. The bombs we set off in the seventies were the clarion call of the masses, the chimes of freedom protesting a capitalist system that lined the pockets of the rich at the expense of working people and the poor. It's no different today. The American government mires itself in foreign wars, keeps widening the gaping crevasse between rich and poor, rewards the multinational corporation for its exploitation of children, develops the latest technology not to solve the nation's ills but to invade the privacy of its citizens. In the words of Malcolm X, 'There's no such thing as a nonviolent revolution.' So I make no apologies for taking a stand. To tell you the truth—"

Just then, Jerry Holzner limps out of the courthouse doors. There's a concussive jolt, shouts, shrieks, and moans, and only when daggers of glass shoot out from a courthouse window does my father stop talking.

CHAPTER ELEVEN

I'm on the ground, on top of Lovely, shielding her body from debris or another explosion or follow-up sniper fire. There are screams and shouts. Lovely groans and tries to get up.

"Stay down!" I shout.

She relaxes in my arms. I rise up slightly and look around. I feel oddly detached. People are slowly getting to their feet, taking anatomical inventory. A woman I recognize as an online legal blogger has a bloody gash on her forehead, though fortunately she's sitting up. A few others are bleeding but alive. Thankfully, I don't see anyone who looks seriously injured. If that's true, the bomber either made a mistake or didn't want to kill anyone.

I feel a hand on my back. "Parker, Lovely. Are you kids all right?"

I look up to see Ian Holzner, his brow furrowed in concern.

"Lovely, are you okay?" I say. I hold my breath, waiting for an answer that seems to take forever.

She looks up at me and nods, then wraps her arms around me, and what should feel like a surprise seems perfectly natural, though we've been apart for so long. One of her stated reasons for leaving me was that I attract danger, and she has a child to protect. At this moment we're close again, but what will this horror mean to her when she has time to reflect on it?

"Oh my god, Parker," she whimpers.

Holzner grasps my hand, and with his gymnast's power, lifts me to my feet and then helps Lovely up. She gapes at him, her eyes bright with anger and fear. "Oh my god, who would do something like this?"

He doesn't answer, just stares at us and then drops his eyes.

"Do you think this accomplishes anything?" she says. "I don't believe you'd . . . how could anyone but an insane person do something like this?"

"I had nothing to do with this," he says.

I look past him and scan the area. Gawkers are assembling on the sidewalk, though not too close. Several windows have been shattered. But the damage looks minimal. Was this a warning or did the bomber screw up? Sirens blare from all directions. LAPD headquarters and several hospitals are only a short distance away.

"Where's your brother?" I ask.

Holzner shakes his head, confused.

"Jerry. He was at the door when the explosion hit."

"Jerry was here? He couldn't have been here."

Before I can reply, there's an angry shout from a young man who's standing at the bottom of the stairs. He points at Holzner, and he and three other men and two women start up the stairs with martial efficiency, their desire to do violence to my father palpable. What's truly frightening about mobs is not how unruly they are but how organized. The two US Marshals who were flanking Holzner while he was giving his press conference appear out of nowhere, each taking one of his arms. They escort us into the courthouse and down a flight of stairs to a secret tunnel that leads to the federal building next door. At least, the tunnel was a secret from me—just like so many things in life.

Holzner skims the printout of the e-mail and tosses it back to FBI Agent Jason Neville. I pick up the paper and read it for a third time:

Subject: Communiqué #1
To: Dishonorable Chief Judge of the Fascist Court of America
From: JB

This afternoon, at 3:23 p.m., we blew up the federal courthouse in downtown Los Angeles. The American government is *our enemy, acting through their leaders, some are named Bush, others Clinton, and others Obama. The names are different but the crimes are the same.*

We demand the immediate dismissal of charges against Ian Holzner, the release from political prison of Charles Sedgwick, the dismantling of the Gestapo NSA, the immediate withdrawal of all U.S. Military troops from Afghanistan and the Persian Gulf, and the imprisonment of the capitalist billionaires who control this country and who commit racist genocide on a daily basis, who enslave women and the poor on a daily basis.

The government's vulnerability has been exposed since 9/11, and we and the oppressed people of the world will continue to exploit it until our demands are met. We are numerous. Free Ian!

"I don't know anything about this piece of shit," Holzner says.

"Don't say another word," I say.

Neville twists his lips in a disbelieving smirk. "So it's just a coincidence that the bomb went off while you were spouting off to the reporters? It's just a coincidence that the e-mail calls for your release? How convenient." The bomb was apparently left outside in a gym bag. It was both too close to the building and too far from the crowd to result in carnage, luckily.

Holzner counter-smirks. "Do you think I'd be stupid enough to—?"

"Shut up *now*, goddamn it!" My words echo off the interrogation-room walls, though the room is acoustically designed to tamp down the noise. Lovely actually covers her ears, and Holzner flinches. His cheeks redden the way mine supposedly do when I'm about to become enraged—or, so says my mother.

"I demand my client's immediate release," I say.

"He just orchestrated the bombing of a federal facility," Neville says.

"Given that he's been in your jail for the last few days, that's impossible. And you sure as hell don't have any evidence supporting your unfounded allegation. You have no right to keep him here."

But they do try to keep him here. Marilee Reddick's underling shows up and gives notice that the government is going in *ex parte* to ask Judge Gibson to revoke bail. I leave Lovely with Holzner and return to the courthouse, where I argue for two hours in chambers that there's no evidence that Holzner had anything to do with this crime, that on the contrary, he was continuously in federal custody or surrounded by marshals, that he had no opportunity to communicate with anyone when he was in jail. Reddick responds that the plan could've been in the works for years, to be carried out if and when Holzner was caught. She keeps repeating that the JB communiqué calls for Holzner's exoneration. She reminds the judge that he has discretion whether to grant bail and argues that he should exercise that discretion to protect the public from Holzner. She claims that his impromptu press conference was a pretext for gathering a crowd so his accomplice could inflict damage.

Fortunately, Carlton Gibson is a stubborn man. He lets his order granting supervised bail stand.

After the hearing, I ask Reddick if she has any information on who planted the bomb or on who JB is.

"Yeah, your client planted the bomb, Stern. Preliminary forensics says it's the same kind of bomb that blew up the Playa Delta VA. A Holzner bomb. Your client is JB, whatever that's supposed to mean. Why don't you ask him." She walks away, the middle finger of her left hand raised in the air until she gets on the elevator.

It gives me little solace that in the almost forty years since Playa Delta, terrorist bomb making has come a long way.

At six-thirty that evening, I'm driving in my Lexus with my father, who's been fitted with an electronic ankle bracelet. This is the first time we've been alone together. Well, we're not actually alone. There are US Marshals' vehicles both directly in front of and directly behind us—a motorcade for a terrorist.

The Friday-evening rush-hour traffic is a snarled train of frustrated

LA drivers, all of whom must be fearful and angry that the city has become the target of a terrorist attack. I pray that no one looks in the window and recognizes Holzner. The marshals avoid the freeways, where they would have less control, and lead us down Venice Boulevard through the gritty, rundown neighborhood just west of downtown. We pass the check-cashing stores and health-hazard cantinas and dingy bodegas, the signage in both English and Spanish; and a mile or two down, the authentic Korean dress shops, credit dentists, and acupuncturists, the signs in English and Korean. Gang graffiti scores the walls. The throng on the sidewalks comprises mostly poor workers: day laborers on their way back from landscaping and rough-carpentry and moving jobs; housekeepers coming home from the tony Westside; home-health workers waiting for the bus so they can start the swing shift taking care of infirm octogenarians; homeless men and women alternately talking to those elusive voices in the air and seeking a handout. Precisely the kind of people Holzner once fantasized about leading in armed uprising against the government. Few, if any, seem interested in rebellion at the moment—Holzner's brand of revolution or any other kind. This mostly admirable group of people, waging a peaceful war against poverty and hardscrabble existence, silently prove how much of a fool my father was. Is he still?

We don't speak for the twenty-five minutes it takes to get to La Brea, not even a third of the way to my place. It's almost as if we're in a contest to see who can stay silent the longest. I feel as if I rescued a stray dog from the pound and only now realize that he might bite me or piss on my rug when I get him home.

Finally he says, "What happened to my brother?"

"I looked around for him, but he was gone. He probably took shelter in the building and got out of LA as quickly as he could. That's what I would've done. But I have to ask. He seemed a bit slow."

"Everyone thought that. It's not that simple. The war started his decline, and the FBI finished it when they tortured him. I hope Jerry did go home. He has no business getting involved in my problems." He shifts slightly in his seat. "You were good in court. Well spoken."

I glance over in a reflexive response to the remark. He's facing the window, but his head is tilted back and his eyes are shut tight.

"I'll say this," he says. "You're far more attuned to other people than I was. I thought I could persuade without listening. That was my downfall."

"Downfall how?"

"You listened, Parker. You sensed what the judge wanted to hear."

"Answer my question. How was your failure to listen to other people your downfall?"

His eyes are still closed as if in sleep. I half wonder whether I'm speaking with a somniloquist in the midst of a dream.

"You performed a miracle and got me out of that cage they call a humane jail, all because you have an innate ability to read people."

We drive another five minutes in silence.

"Who do you think bombed the courthouse?" I ask.

"It wasn't me."

"I didn't ask you that. I want to know who you think is responsible. Because I'm pretty sure you know who JB is."

"What makes you think that?"

"Call it my innate ability to read people."

Keeping his head forward, he shifts only his eyes to look at me, then crosses his arms and slides down the seat in a reclining position. In less than a minute, he falls asleep for real, not awakening until I pull into the underground garage of my condo. Outside of my building are a half dozen US Marshals whose job it is to ensure that the Playa Delta Bomber doesn't lam out again.

CHAPTER TWELVE

On this overcast Saturday morning, the day after the courthouse bombing, I pull up to Ernesto's Automotive, Inc., which offers *Collision Repair, Free Estimate*. I get out of the car and walk into the waiting room. It's immaculate, with an almost-spotless off-white linoleum floor, burgundy and black-metal armchairs, a couple of bar stools by the window, and an IKEA dark-wood coffee table with a glass top. There are two ficus plants. On one wall are the shop's certificates of merit from the Better Business Bureau, the Fullerton Chamber of Commerce, and various automotive trade organizations. Underneath a big-screen TV in the corner is a table with coffee service, with real cream and raw sugar provided. None of it can mask the acrid smell of metallic paint and automotive grease coming from the garage.

An attractive teenage girl is sitting behind a counter, typing on a computer keyboard. When she sees me, she stands, although she's so short her head seems to be almost at the same level as when she was sitting down. She's dressed in a light-blue chambray pullover, a tie-dyed pink, white, and red miniskirt, and white Birkenstocks. Her long, straight hair is California surfer-girl blond, and her face is heart-shaped with a refined chin. She gives me the rote yet genuine smile of a shy person forced into a sales position. The smile vanishes when she realizes who I am.

"Omigod, freaky, you're my . . . you're him," she says in a voice that has the timbre of a wonderful woodwind. She checks her wristwatch and looks over her shoulder nervously. "We don't have much time. Ernesto will be back any minute."

"Yes, Emily, I'm your half brother." I say the words out of obligation. Maybe I'm callous, but what connection do I have to her? I'm forty and this person—this *stranger*—is seventeen, the age of a daughter, not a sister. For the first time in my life, I truly feel ancient.

She covers her mouth with a dainty hand. "Omigod, you were in the bombing at the courthouse. Is my dad okay?"

"He's fine."

"When can I see him?" Even her whisper sounds melodious. She nervously twists a strand of hair between the thumb and index finger of her right hand. "Omigod, you look so much like Dylan."

I've seen an official photo of Dylan in his Marine Dress Blue Alpha uniform, his cap pulled down over his brow and his lips pressed hard in a military frown—more like a study of a warrior in granite than a portrait of a human being. "I don't see much of a resemblance," I say.

She turns, leans over to open a drawer, and hands me a photograph. In this picture, he's standing next to the arching trunk of a potted palm, rocky cliffs and the ocean in the background, evoking Laguna Beach or La Jolla. Here, he's a blond version of me, or how I looked in my mid-twenties just out of law school. The same determined eyes (though his were blue and mine are brown), oval face, longish straight nose, and narrow smile I see in photos of myself. It's proof not only that I had a biological connection to Dylan but also that Ian Holzner is really my father. The pressure builds behind my eyes, unexpected tears for the loss of someone I never knew existed. I hold the picture up to my face as if I'm myopic, trying to hide my eyes so Emily won't notice that I'm struggling to compose myself.

"See?" she says.

"Yeah. I see it."

She sighs softly. "When can I see my father? He told Ernesto he didn't want me at the jail, didn't want me to see him like that. But now he's living with you."

"Ian is under house arrest. I'm not sure he's allowed to have visitors."

"I don't know any Ian. My father is Marty Lansing. A kind, peaceful man." She points toward the reception area. "Let's go sit over there."

"How are you doing, Emily?"

She shrugs and gives an exaggerated tilt of the head, a movement I associate only with teenage girls. "Good, I guess. Ernesto is so pissed at my dad. They were such good friends." Another shrug. "Is he okay?"

"He's fine."

"He didn't do it, you know? It's all lies. He's a sweet man, never hit us, never even yelled at me or Dylan." She puffs her lips and lets her shoulders go limp. "I miss Mama and Dylan. I miss my family." I expect tears, but she's composed. Maybe she's all cried out. I would be. She glances over her shoulder and whispers, "I mean, he didn't do it, did he? It doesn't make sense."

"That's why I'm here," I say. "I want you to tell me about Ian . . . Marty. So I can defend him."

"Oh, so you're here as a lawyer, not as a brother." How can someone with such a sweet voice suddenly sound so glacial?

I don't know much about teenagers. Nothing, really. But they're not exactly children.

"This is all new to me, Emily. I grew up without a father. I didn't have a clue about you and Dylan. The best way I can be a good son is to be a good lawyer. So help me understand Marty Lansing."

As she's deciding, she fiddles with her hair again. "I'm going to tell you about Dylan first," she says. "Because that's the way you understand my dad. Dylan was his favorite."

"I'm sure that's not so."

"Oh, it is. But I don't really care. Dylan was my favorite, too. He was a jock who got decent grades when he should've gotten straight As, but all he cared about was girls, playing lacrosse, and having fun. He was also the sweetest, kindest person I knew. But I got the good grades." She says it without a hint of arrogance. I fight the sexist assumption that her fluty voice and diminutive size are inconsistent with scholastic achievement.

"What about Dylan's politics?"

"He wasn't political. I was interested in stuff like that. Dylan didn't care about politics, my mom didn't care, and my dad especially didn't." She cranes her neck forward, like a student trying to decipher an obscure mathematical formula scrawled on a blackboard. "When Mama died, Dylan got so angry. He kept it inside, but you could feel it. Then he read Ayn Rand's *Atlas Shrugged* and got the idea that he was special. I hated that awful book, didn't want to read past the third page, but my American Lit teacher required it. This is Orange County, a lot of libertarians, you know. One of the only times Dylan and I argued was over that book. I've never been able to figure out why it had such a huge effect on him." She checks her watch again. "I really shouldn't be doing this. Are we almost done?"

"Why shouldn't you be doing this?"

"It's just that Ernesto is totally pissed at my dad."

"Tell me as much as you can."

She fills in the details of the Lansing's family's life, describing an existence so mundane it's hard to believe that Holzner's role in it was counterfeit.

"Was there anything unusual about your father?" I ask.

She stiffens. "What do you mean?"

"I have to ask these questions so I can learn the truth. It's the only way I can help him."

"No, my dad is totally boring. Boring in a normal way. The only thing was the community theater. He started acting, and he was really good. Better than that, and I'm not just saying that because he's my father. People started saying he could've been a professional. But after he got a write-up in the local free newspaper, he stopped acting. He said the publicity bothered him, that he didn't deserve it. I thought he was just being humble, but now I think it's because he was afraid." She lets out a combination grunt/hum, one of those noises that would sound annoying from anyone other than an attractive young woman. "You were an actor, too, Parker. I guess it runs in the family, huh? I'm no good at it, though. I get so nervous. All those people watching is freaky."

I guess stage fright runs in the family, too.

"But anyway, after my mom died, my dad started yoga and meditation. After Dylan was killed in the war, he'd meditate for hours. I couldn't cheer him up." She gives a resigned palms-up shrug. "There's one thing I wanted to tell you, though. There was this weird guy who came by the body shop a couple of days after my father turned himself in. Kind of a big guy. My dad's age, maybe older. Wearing an old baseball cap that made him look like a big, overgrown kid. And he had this speech impediment, couldn't say his *R*s. It was mean, but Ernesto said he sounded like Elmer Fudd from those old Bugs Bunny cartoons."

"Jerry Holzner," I say. "Ian's brother. Our uncle."

"He's our uncle? Seriously? He didn't say that, he wouldn't even give a name. He just kept saying he had a message for Ian from Charlie."

"Charles Sedgwick?"

"He just said *Charlie*. He asked me to get a message to Ian. He said it was a warning."

"What message?"

"I don't know. Before I could ask, Ernesto threw him out of the shop."

"Just like I'm going to throw you out." The man speaks with a pronounced Hispanic accent, but his words are clear, precise. Gray-haired, squat-faced, and work-muscular, he's wearing a greasy mechanic's jumpsuit. The name *Ernesto* is embroidered over his heart. His cheeks are already flushed, and I don't think it's because of his work.

Emily jumps out of her seat. "Ernesto, this is Parker Stern, my father's—"

"I know who this man is," he says. "I read the newspapers. Lansing or Holzner or whatever that fraud calls himself betrayed me, betrayed you, Emily. He abandoned you."

"That's bullshit!" Emily shrieks. Her jaw is clenched in rage, and she's glowering. The change in demeanor is jarring but also typical of a teenager, or so I surmise. I don't know for sure, because at fifteen years old I became an emancipated minor and, like Ian Holzner, was determined to hurl myself into obscurity. Which means that I wasn't an ordinary teenager and that I had no true teenage friends, so I don't really know what behavior is typical.

"That's disrespectful, Emily," Ernesto says. "That's why you should have nothing to do with him. He disrespects authority."

I take a step toward the guy. "That's a harsh thing to say to a man's daughter. And it's not true. Ian . . . Marty wants to clear his name so he can live a life outside the shadows. He's doing that for you, Emily. No more hiding."

There are tears in her eyes.

"What do you know about it?" Ernesto says. "You're a stranger. I've known her since she was born. A second daughter to me. You know nothing. Lansing, or whatever his name is, pretended to be my best friend. He was like a brother, except he turned out to be Cain. I let him into this business that I built. I spent more time with him than I did with my family, and he used me, betrayed me. Worse, betrayed his country and killed innocent people. I am not going to help a liar and traitor and a murderer. He abandoned you, Emily. You're my responsibility now. Your mother wanted me to be your godfather."

She's pulling at her hair again; the nervous habit seems to calm her. "Mr. Stern is just asking me questions. Just like any lawyer would. He's been very polite."

"I'd actually like to ask *you* some questions, Ernesto," I say.

"It's Mr. Alfaro. Get out of my shop."

"I'm only trying to get to the truth, Mr. Alfaro."

Though he's across the room, he looks as if he's about to spit at me. "Do not use the word *truth* when referring to that bastard. I didn't escape Castro's Cuba to help some Communist terrorist escape justice. And I'm not going to help his lawyer. I don't care if you are his son." He takes a half step forward.

"Emily, the man who showed up and said he had a message from Charlie," I say. "Did he say anything else?"

As she shakes her head, Ernesto takes another step forward. "You're trespassing, sir. You have ten seconds to leave."

"God damn it, Ernesto," Emily shouts. "This man is my brother."

"And Martin is innocent until proven guilty," I say.

"I will not help a terrorist," he says. "And your brother is dead, Emily. This person is a stranger and a representative of a murderer." He clenches and unclenches his fists. "Get out!"

I thank Emily and am about to leave when she throws her arms around my waist and buries her head in my chest. I pat her back awkwardly, a clumsy attempt to comfort her. I think she perceives my uneasiness, because she pulls away and says, "Tell my dad I love him."

On the drive home I replay this meeting over and over. Emily's loyalty and love for our father makes me want to defend him with fervor. Family is more than genetics, I tell myself. So why has my genetic connection to Emily Lansing so affected me?

Then I think of how our father's best friend and longtime employer, Ernesto Alfaro, hates him for being the murderous turncoat. What will a jury of strangers think of my client?

CHAPTER THIRTEEN

I arrive at the office at nine o'clock the following Monday. Eleanor Dworsky is already ensconced at the reception desk, leafing through the slim, post-Internet version of the *Los Angeles Times*. She's wearing a drab man's dress shirt again. This time it's light blue rather than gray.

She holds up the front page and points to an article on last week's bail hearing and courthouse bombing. "Explosive developments in court the other day," she says.

"Not funny, Mom. People were hurt." The words come from Brandon Soloway, who's again sitting in the corner chair and tapping something into a smart phone.

"Lighten up, Brandon." She offers me the newspaper. "An article about your hearing and your amazing victory. Keep the paper as a souvenir."

"Thank you, but no." I don't believe in keepsakes. They interfere with the natural evolution of memories.

She gives a suit-yourself shrug and tosses the paper in the blue recyclable bin. "So you're living with the Playa Delta Bomber now."

Harmon Cherry would say that while people who exercise diplomacy usually get farther in life, in the end we most admire those who say what they think. Harmon wasn't always right. At this moment, I'm having a hard time admiring Eleanor Dworsky.

"Don't call him that," I say. "He's our client. Which means he's innocent."

"Yeah, right. But what's it like to live with him? I'm guessing you don't call him *Dad*."

Even if I wanted to answer Eleanor's question, there isn't much to tell. After Holzner and I got inside my condo Friday night, the first thing he did was ask again about his brother, Jerry. I went to the Internet and searched for a Jerry Holzner in Foster City, California. No information. Same with a search of San Francisco, Oakland, Marin, San Mateo, and the whole Bay Area. No listing for Jerold Holzner or Jerome Holzner, either. The two Gerald Holzners I located were less than forty years old. During my search, Ian stood behind me and watched the computer screen. When I exhausted all the possibilities, he asked where he should sleep. I showed him to the second bedroom. He closed the door, and I didn't see him the rest of the evening. On Saturday and Sunday mornings, I heard him chanting. He didn't come out of his room except to use the bathroom or get something to eat. He's a vegan, apparently, because he's eaten only fruit and vegetables and ignored even the Greek yogurt. It's fine if he wants to make his stay with me a self-imposed solitary confinement, so long as he eventually takes the time to cooperate in his own defense.

Eleanor sticks out a thumb like a hitchhiker in a thirties screwball comedy and pumps her arm back. "Lovely and Moses are in the conference room. He's got some info for you."

"About what?"

"You'll have to ask him. I'd never dare step on Moses Dworsky's lines."

I go back to the conference room. Moses is telling some kind of war story about his courtroom prowess, and Lovely is smiling. When they see me, they fall silent, as if I'm a schoolteacher who's walked in on an unruly class. Or maybe Moses was talking about me. It doesn't matter. If you're anything other than a boring person, there's always someone talking about you behind your back.

"Terrible about the bombing," Dworsky says. "I am so pleased that you and Lovely are in good physical health. How are you doing? Psychologically, I mean."

"I'm fine," I say.

"On the merits, I want to commend you on a marvelous job in the courtroom," he says. "Kudos. Carlton Gibson is a tough coconut to crack. Holzner getting out on bail was a most astonishing result. The only other lawyer who might have managed it is yours truly." There's something disingenuous in his tone, a kind of damnation by fulsome praise. He's implying that I got lucky.

"I didn't see you in court," I say. "You should've been there."

"Incorrect. Carlton F. Gibson has despised me since the Rachel O'Brien trial. Did you not read it in the file? He did not appreciate my tactics, though they were brilliant, if I may be so bold as to blow my own horn. But the last straw was when Gibson accused me of mooning him. He has never forgotten it."

"Did you moon him?" Lovely asks.

"Let me just say that I found it essential to bend over to retrieve a document out of my briefcase at an inopportune moment, as far as Gibson was concerned. My briefcase happened to be directly behind me, and when I turned and bent down, my posterior region happened to come into the judge's line of sight. I will add that I was fully clothed and my shirt was tucked in, so there was no question of indecent exposure. I did not deserve incarceration. So held the Chief Judge of the Ninth Circuit Court of Appeals only an hour later. In any event, if I had been in court today and Gibson had recognized me, it would have caused problems for you and your client."

"You should've been there," I insist. "We hired you for this case and it's part of your job."

He shakes his head, making his huge lobes wobble.

"Eleanor said you had some information for me," I say.

"Indeed. I have located a number of individuals in Playa Delta who might provide some necessary background on Ian Holzner. Believe it or not, they have not left that small town. It will be a good place to start—the scene of the crime, the hometown of the accused. Two birds with a single stone." He slides a piece of paper over. "Here are names and addresses and phone numbers—work, home, and cellular. Along with detailed summaries of their backgrounds. Catch them unawares lest they not want to speak with the attorney for the Playa Delta Bomber. Only you, not Lovely. Bad strategy to inundate them with lawyers. Now, go with God."

I glance at Lovely, who gives an affirming nod.

Dworsky stands and slowly unfolds his massive body. "No need to apologize for accusing me of shirking my duty. Although it was precipitous and unjust. Moses Dworsky does not shirk his duty." He turns and walks out of the conference room.

"How did it go with your sister?" Lovely asks.

"Emily is my *half* sister," I say curtly. That's an attorney's rote reaction—parse the language, debate the merits, shift the focus from reality to rhetoric. It's a great way to avoid dealing with real life.

Lovely, a lawyer herself, is about to argue back, but I hold up my hand.

"My sister is a sweet kid," I say. "Her world has been shattered, and she's trying to fit some of the pieces back together. She can't do it. At best, all she can try to do is ignore the broken pieces. Whatever, it makes me want to win—not for Ian, but for her."

Lovely reaches over and caresses my cheek.

CHAPTER FOURTEEN

Playa Delta, California, has its own municipal government and police force and school system, but it's surrounded on all sides by the city of Los Angeles—a small town engulfed by a megalopolis. According to Lovely's research, the town had a population of about twenty-four thousand in 1975 and has a population of about twenty-four thousand today. One movie studio or another has headquartered there since the twenties. I did four of my own movies there. What's changed is that forty years ago, the city was mostly lower-middle and working class, a landlocked bedroom community of greater Los Angeles. Today, it's become trendy, home to ritzy private schools and upscale restaurants.

The first place that Moses Dworsky has sent me is Playa Delta's one public high school. Despite the city's resurgence, the campus seems a bit ramshackle. Much of the school grounds have been paved over and used for bungalow-style buildings. There's a separate building with a modernist circular design, a brick and glass façade, and flying buttresses. The auditorium was probably a semiprecious architectural jewel once, but now there are cracks in the brick and graffiti on the walls. A sign identifies the structure as the Carl Sandburg Auditorium, though I doubt Sandburg ever set foot in Playa Delta, California.

I park my Lexus in the visitors' parking lot, pass through security, and find my way to the administrative offices. A few nervous students sit with heads bowed, obviously waiting to meet their school's chief disciplinarian. I approach a young man working at reception, identify myself, and ask to see Carol Diaz, the school principal. When he asks if I have an appointment, I lean close and say, "No, but tell her my name is Parker Stern. I represent a man named Ian Holzner."

The kid obviously knows Holzner's name, might even recognize me now, because he falls back in his chair, and his elliptical eyes morph into circles of surprise. Rather than speaking into an intercom or sending a computer message, he stands and jogs down the corridor. Not long after, he returns, accompanied by a tall, broad-shouldered woman with short-cropped gray hair and green, narrowly set eyes that give her a predator's aspect.

"How dare you intrude on the school day," Diaz says. "How dare you intrude at all. Please leave, or I'll call security."

"I understand that you and Ian Holzner were childhood friends," I say. "That you and he led a protest senior year that shut your high school down for three days. Supposedly you and he . . ." I say the words loudly enough for some of her students to hear and don't finish the sentence so as to give Diaz a choice. Maybe no one would've cared about the principal's old friendship with an alleged terrorist before Holzner turned himself in, but now everyone will care. Moses Dworsky is thorough, I've discovered. How did he manage to unearth this information about her?

"Okay, okay," she says, holding up her hands without relaxing her scowl. "Come back to my office. But I only have ten minutes."

"I just have a couple of questions."

"Lawyers never just have a couple of questions."

"You're probably right. So look at me as Holzner's son, and not as his attorney if that makes it easier to talk to me."

She smiles slightly, proof that I've disarmed her a jot. She ushers me into her surprisingly spacious corner office. One window faces a flower garden; the other overlooks the main quad, allowing her to keep watch over her dominion.

"Ian Holzner *was* my friend as a kid," she says, naïvely believing that she can preempt my questioning by talking first. People often try that. All it does is make the lawyer think of more questions. "And yes, we led a strike against the war, and yes, someone threw a trash can through the principal's window." She gestures to the main quad. "Broke this very one. It was a long time ago. June nineteen sixty-seven. No one in administration mentioned it when I was hired as a teacher back in seventy-seven. It doesn't matter anymore, because I'm retiring when the school year is over."

But I can see from her tired, resigned expression that it *does* matter to her that people might discover that she and the Playa Delta Bomber committed an act of vandalism, no matter how juvenile. She's been a teacher at this school for almost as long as I've been alive, and the principal for two decades.

"Anyway, it was the last week of school and just before graduation," she says. "And a couple of weeks before LA police attacked protesters at the Century Plaza Hotel, where President Johnson was staying. Ian was at that rally, too. The moment he broke that window, I stopped being his friend."

"You had nothing to do with it?" It's not a question designed to get in her good graces, but sometimes you just can't help asking the follow-up.

"I tried to stop him." She hesitates and tilts her head to the side, a soft, maternal expression on her face. Or at least I think it's maternal, since Harriet Stern never looked at me like that. "You look like him, you know. Or how he used to look. You're a little taller."

"He's much leaner than I am."

"He wasn't skinny then, not in high school. He was built like you, because of the gymnastics."

"You mentioned antiwar activities in high school. I thought he became radicalized in college. Before that he was the straight arrow, the engineer/athlete."

"Yeah, the high-school counselors did a good job of keeping that myth alive. Ian was the school's golden boy. He was a great athlete, a top scholar, and a leader all rolled into a handsome boy. The school administration wasn't going to let him blow his chance for a scholarship and Olympic fame. They not only wanted him to succeed; they wanted to use him as a living commercial for Playa Delta High. Ian going to the Olympics would've put the school on the map, given it recognition that only Beverly Hills High, and maybe Culver High, had in the area. Scholastic politics weren't as bad as they are now, where schools measure their worth entirely by where their graduates go to college or how prominent their alumni become. But Ian was the star of stars, so even back then, he was a commodity for good old Playa High."

"What changed him?"

She simultaneously smiles and shakes her head, as if I'm a dense pupil who hasn't done his homework. "The Vietnam War suddenly changed him. It changed all of us."

"The war didn't change everyone."

"Let me finish. How old are you?"

"The big four-oh last birthday."

"You couldn't possibly understand. It was over before you were born. Everyone's assumptions changed forever—about the government, about the country, about their role models, about their parents, about morality. The Vietnam War changed the world for your generation and the one after it."

"As I started to say, the war didn't radicalize every teenager. Ian Holzner was in the small minority."

"That's true. But it was personal with Ian. He became rabidly antiwar when Jerry got drafted and was sent to Da Nang."

"What do you know about Holzner's college days?"

"Ian's or Jerry's? Because Jerry only went to community college for a semester."

"Ian's."

"Absolutely nothing. I told you, after high school we were no longer friends. I didn't go to Berkeley because I didn't have the grades. I went to Cal State Northridge. I saw Ian only once after high school, when he came back for summer break after freshman year. I was working at the Foster's Freeze. It was an ice cream chain, now long gone. And he came by for a burger and a chocolate malt. That's what he'd always ordered when he was a kid. That was probably the only thing that hadn't changed about him. I took a break, but we weren't talking for two minutes before he started spouting that insane radical rhetoric. It was the summer of sixty-eight, the worst time in the country, the Martin Luther King and Bobby Kennedy assassinations, the resulting riots, the Chicago cops' attack on protestors at the Democratic Convention. Ian was enraged at the world. Ranting, raving. It was scary, actually, because he screamed at me for being too passive. I cut my break short, said good-bye, and never saw him again. Except on the news, of course. Then and now."

"What was he like as a kid?"

She sits back in contemplation and nods again. For a moment I feel as if I've been called to the principal's office. "You're asking as his son, not his attorney?"

"Assume I am."

She arches her left eyebrow, a singular feat of muscle control because that brow goes quite high and the other doesn't move a bit. "You are all lawyer, aren't you? Okay, I'll *assume* you're asking as Ian's son." She shakes her head. "The news said he had another son who died in Afghanistan. Sad. And it's ironic that Ian ended up living an ordinary, sedate life. Anyway, I lived two doors down on Ridgeway Road. We went to kindergarten together, rode our bikes, played ball in the street. His father was a kind man, but rarely said a word. An ex-acrobat who worked for the post office. Died too young of prostate cancer. Very tolerant of his children's foibles. But Ian was his mother's favorite, with his intelligence and athleticism. The opposite from what usually happens, because Jerry was their biological kid and Ian was adopted. I once heard their mother say that there must have been a mix-up, that Ian must've been the one who sprung from her loins—she used those words—and that Jerry was just dropped on the doorstep by mistake, so what could they do but take him in? Cruel. Probably one of the reasons Jerry was such a hood. A 'ho-dad,' we called him back in the day. An obsolete word from an obsolete era. But in a Southern California city so close to the ocean, the tough guys were ho-dads, the popular kids surfers, and the rest of us just nonentities."

"I ran into Jerry in court yesterday," I say. "He lives up in the Bay Area. He told me that Ian protected him."

"The way I remember it, people needed protection from Jerry. He was four years older, so I don't know how Ian could've done that."

"Maybe Jerry was referring to what happened after he came back from the war?"

"Could be. Like so many of them, Jerry wasn't the same. *Shell-shocked*, they called it back then. *Post-traumatic stress disorder* these days. Kind of a cliché now, but it wasn't back then. Anyway, when I was a kid I was afraid of Jerry. Not only was he a thug, but he seemed creepy. Nothing I could put my finger on, but as a female . . ." She folds her arms over her chest and shivers as if she were still that young girl.

"I was wondering who else Ian hung out with."

I run through a list of names that I got from Dworsky, but she assures me that all of them, three of whom are dead, broke off with Holzner by sophomore year of college. None were very political. They were mostly Ian's science friends or fellow jocks who all led unremark-able lives as far as Diaz knows.

She does have information on one person, a girl named Alicia Bowers.

"She was this little girl who lived down the block," Diaz says. "Five, six years younger than Ian and me, a shy, unremarkable little kid who by the time she was twelve had a crush on Ian and followed him around like a puppy dog. Just because he was friendly toward her, I think. Ian prob-ably kept her from being bullied. Most of the kids her age teased her mer-cilessly and some did worse. There was only the father, a World War Two vet who was shell-shocked himself, and on welfare. People said he was a drunk, but I think maybe he was schizophrenic and no one realized it. Or maybe it was physical, maybe he actually suffered a head wound. They say people aren't as nice these days, that the culture has lost the ability to be kind, but today people are far more forgiving of a person like Pete Bowers than they were back then. Anyway, Pete and Alicia lived in a seedy motel at the end of our block. Their neighbors were Sam's Liquor Store and Helen's Toy Palace. The dad would ride this old one-speed bike without fenders around the neighborhood, babbling and waving at pedestrians. Alicia seemed like the classic wallflower who survived by shrinking from the heat. I left the neighborhood, but my father said that she'd walk to high school every day and wave at him when she passed our house without looking up. She never got into trouble, as far as I know. But then I heard years later from a guy who also lived on Ridgeway Road that he saw her at an antiwar rally on the UCLA campus where Holzner was speaking. She was up on the platform with him, cheering, raising her fist in the Black Power salute, shouting for peace and revolution, dancing around like she was tripping on LSD. He said he tried to talk with her, but she left with Ian and his people before he could get there. I can't believe I still remember that. Maybe it's because I'm a teacher, and kids surprise me all the time. But it was so strange."

"When was that?"

"It would've been nineteen seventy-two, seventy-three. Alicia was still a teenager. But she's the only person I know from Playa Delta who supposedly had contact with him after he became an icon of the radical left. If it's true." She raises an index finger, gets out of her chair, and goes to a cabinet across the room, where she leafs through some files and comes up with a document.

"The nineteen seventy-three yearbook," she says. "Alicia Bowers's senior year." She flips the pages, stops, purses her lips, and hands me the book. There is no picture of Bowers, only her name and a silhouette and the words *Had better things to do*.

"It was worth a shot," she says.

"An earlier yearbook?"

"This is the earliest I have. Inherited them. I think they tossed a lot of old ones out in the eighties. Nostalgia wasn't what it is now."

"I thought that's what year books were all about."

"For the students, not for people who need file space. Everything was in hard copy back then."

"Do you have any idea where Bowers is?"

"None."

I ask a few more questions, but when it's clear that I've exhausted her knowledge, I thank her and get up to leave.

"Do you think you can get him off?" she asks.

"Do you think he deserves to get off?"

She swivels her chair and, with her back to me, gazes out the window, the same one my father broke so many years ago.

CHAPTER FIFTEEN

After I leave the high school, I cold-call Barney Kinsella, another current Playa Delta resident who appears on Moses Dworsky's list of potential witnesses. Kinsella is a retired electrical engineer whose beer-bottle bifocals are his most distinctive characteristic. He met Holzner when they were in elementary school and was in the science club with Holzner from the eighth to the eleventh grades. He tells me that Holzner was brilliant and generally a nice guy, especially for a popular, athletic teenager. While most people in Ian's position shunned nerds like Kinsella, Ian almost flaunted their friendship. But after their junior year, Ian became "political," stopped participating in extracurricular science activities, and treated anyone not vehemently opposed to the Vietnam War with undisguised contempt. Kinsella finishes with a disturbing story. When Holzner was twelve, he somehow got ahold of nitric and sulfuric acid, combined them with cotton balls to make gun cotton, all with the intention of blowing up Kinsella's tabby cat, Marmalade. Kinsella claims to have shooed the cat away before the explosive went off.

So now I'm the spawn of a psychopath.

After finishing with Kinsella, I drive half a mile south into an area of the city known as Playa Crest, low-lying foothills where the city's wealthier families live. At the top is Santa Theresa Manor, which Dworsky's notes describe as "a skilled nursing facility for the care of elders." I pull up to the complex of Mediterranean-style buildings made of stucco walls and adobe-tile roofs. Jacaranda and palm trees shade the parking lot. The west-facing second-story rooms provide an unobstructed view of the ocean. I hope beauty and tranquility truly do comfort the old and infirm.

I'm here to see Gladdie Giddens, a victim of the explosion at the Playa Delta Veterans Administration and one of the key witnesses implicating Holzner as the perpetrator. I can't bring myself to open the car door. I didn't go to law school to cold-call octogenarian bombing victims and try to shake their testimony. I finally force myself to get out of the car and walk over to the main office.

A floral fragrance predominates, but there's a suggestion of disinfectant and institutional processed food in the air. No matter how nice these eldercare facilities seem, you can never quite escape that smell. I introduce myself to the woman at the front desk—Sister Mary Eunice, she tells me. She looks to be about my age. I thought nuns under fifty no longer wore habits, but I guess I'm wrong. The ash-blond hair visible under her wimple is parted in the middle. She's wearing tortoiseshell glasses that magnify her green eyes.

When I tell her why I'm here, she knits her eyebrows so tightly that the cloth on her headpiece quivers. She shrugs in a kind of disdainful resignation. I expect her to ask me to leave, but she invites me to have a seat and walks down a hall. While I wait, I read a glossy brochure that makes the grounds look both brighter and drearier than they really are. The facility is run by the Carmelite Sisters of the Sacred Heart, who provide temporary and long-term nursing care. I've never been one for religious institutions—not after my mother forced me into the clutches of her church when I was a kid—but at least this is what religion is supposed to do. The Sanctified Assembly runs some nursing homes as well, but they're propaganda centers as much as care facilities. The Assembly promises that through cleansing of the nuclei of the cells through devotion to the what it calls the Celestial Fount, seniors and the infirm will be cured of congestive heart failure, emphysema, Alzheimer's, and scores of other afflictions of old age. The false promises attract converts, earn contributions, and turn a huge profit by gouging the families of the residents.

Five minutes later, Sister Mary Eunice returns and says, "She won't see you. She wants you to know that she told everything to the FBI and testified at the trial of Rachel O'Brien."

"That's one reason why I want to speak with her. The transcript of the O'Brien trial has been lost. So I don't really have her version."

"Gladdie Giddens is very frail physically. More importantly, she does not want to help Ian Holzner."

"I just want to hear her story."

Although I didn't think she would, she goes back to Giddens's room. When she comes back, a young woman in a white nurse's uniform and an old woman in a walker are following her. Gladdie Giddens is hunched over into a tight, tired C. She couldn't be more than four feet ten. Her hair, the strands like fraying threads, is colored a dowdy brown. I'm never certain whether elderly women make themselves look older or younger by dying their hair. Giddens is moving with surprising speed, though she seems to be almost dragging her left leg. She has a section of a newspaper under her arm. I stand, but before reaching me, Giddens and the nurse turn left and go inside a room. Sister Mary Eunice beckons me over with a not-so-kind wave of her arm.

When I reach her, she says, "She'll tell you her story. But she won't answer any questions. So don't try to ask any, don't do anything to upset her. As I said, she's eighty-eight years old and fragile."

Inside the small conference room, I find Giddens sitting at the head of the table. The chair's synthetic cushions and curved hardwood arms seem to have consumed her. Her skin is more droopy than wrinkled, and though her eyelids are hooded and thin with age, the brown eyes themselves are pellucid and resolute. I didn't think the nuns would leave this ancient woman alone with someone they consider a predatory lawyer, but when the nurse and Sister Mary Eunice suddenly walk out, Giddens doesn't flinch. Rather, it's I who experience a quiver of anxiety.

"So you're that boy's attorney," Giddens says in a voice so soft that I have to strain to hear. Despite her lack of strength, the timbre of her voice is almost youthful—no old-lady cackle. Like so many her age who immigrated to Los Angeles, she has a light southwestern twang. She holds up the newspaper. "They have a picture of you in here. You've lived quite a life for a young man."

"Not so young."

She doesn't come close to smiling.

"Ms. Giddens, I'm sorry to disturb you, but I'd just like to ask you a few—"

"Please let me say my piece, sir. Why, I've been waiting forty years to say my piece to Ian Holzner, and I will do that if the good Lord blesses me and I survive long enough to testify at his trial and see him in court. But right now, since I can't get at him, you're the next best thing. That's why I'm willing to tell you my story, but no more. I told it all before, but you say the transcript is lost, so . . . If that's not okay with you, I'll call Sister Margaret Mary to take me back."

"Of course it's ok. I'll appreciate hearing anything you can tell me."

She takes two shallow, labored breaths. "I don't want to talk about the bombing. Not now. My friends died and my leg was shattered forever. But I blame myself because I could've stopped it. Earlier that morning, I was visiting the ladies' room. I passed by a young man coming from the opposite direction. Dressed in a T-shirt, cap, and military camouflage pants. The hat was pulled down real low. Told him that he had the wrong floor, that this was the second floor, he was probably looking for the third. He didn't belong there. He must have just planted the bomb. I should've called security, the FBI, somebody. It was him, Ian Holzner. I recognized his picture in the paper when I woke up in the hospital. He was one of the prime suspects, face all over the papers. I should've recognized him right away. He and my son, Mark, were in the same grade in school. He even visited my house a few times when the boys were teenagers."

This scrap of information is more detail than Lovely and I have found in the arrest records and the indictment. I'd very much like to interrogate her gently and ask why she didn't recognize Holzner until she saw his picture in the newspaper while she was hospitalized, probe into whether her injury affected her perceptions, determine whether the FBI improperly influenced her to identify Holzner by showing her his photo in the paper. I'm sure Moses Dworsky didn't do that at O'Brien's trial—he wanted to lay the blame on Holzner, so he was aligned with the prosecution on that issue. Sure, I can ask these questions on cross-examination if she's a witness at Holzner's trial, but that won't get me what I want, which is to shake her resolve now, to make her doubt her own memory. Socrates formulated an entire body of philosophy by asking questions. That's probably why Gladdie Giddens won't let me ask her anything—questions are weapons. Still, there's one thing maybe she'll answer.

"I know you said you wouldn't answer questions, but I was wondering if I could have the address and phone number of your son."

"No, sir, you cannot," she says, and when her bird-bony shoulders droop, she looks even more frail and diminutive. "Mark passed last year. The lung cancer. A smoker, and he could never give it up. You know the sad part? He was a doctor. An internist. Couldn't kick the habit, much as he tried." Her head begins to shake slightly, a rhythmic, palsied movement rather than a voluntary action. "My son was sixty-eight years old, an old man. But not so old in this day and age, and a young man—no, a child to his mother. Please excuse me, young man. I'm tired, and I've said my piece."

I get up to leave, but before I do, I ask, "Was it your son, Mark, who was in Ian's class at school?"

"Yes, like I just said not thirty seconds ago."

"Then I don't understand something, ma'am. Ian Holzner is sixty-five. That's four years younger than Mark, so how could they be in the same grade? Are you sure your son's friend wasn't Ian's older brother, Jerry? Mark and Jerry would've been about the same age."

Her eyes narrow in momentary confusion, and the constant shaking of her head gets worse, but then she *voluntarily* shakes it. "I told you no questions."

"Ms. Giddens, it's very important that we get to the truth."

"I will not answer questions." If she were younger, the words would've come out in a shout, but her lungs and vocal cords are much too old to accomplish anything other than a feeble whoosh of air. "You'll only try to confuse me with them, as you're doing now. I know what I saw. I know who planted that bomb. Please call the sisters. I'm very weary." The palsied movement of her head has become irregular, a combination nod and shake.

I'm not going to push this fragile old woman any further. She is, after all, a victim. I go to the door, call the nuns in, and thank Giddens for talking to me. As I'm about to leave, she holds up the newspaper. "Let me ask you a question. It says in here that you're Ian Holzner's son. Ezekiel 18:19–20 says, 'The son shall not suffer for the iniquity of the father.' I do hope for your sake that's true."

CHAPTER SIXTEEN

I get in my car and drive southwest toward my condo in Marina del Rey, past two miles of strip malls and apartment houses and then through the undeveloped wetlands, the last in Los Angeles County. Western ragweed, sedges, plantain, and saltbush grow in a brackish swamp bordering the irrigation canal people still call a creek. In a flash, the square stucco-and-wood apartment houses reappear, and then the area becomes commercial—warehouses, machine shops, paint stores, taco stands, and a pastry shop with a huge rolled-steel and gunite doughnut on the roof. I drive into my neighborhood, with the contrived maritime and Polynesian street names—Bali, Mindanao, Fiji, Panay, Palawan—more reminiscent of those old Bob Hope/Bing Crosby Road pictures my mother used to love than of the South Seas. No matter how high the housing prices, Marina Del Rey remains not the thriving, upscale beach resort that the city parents intended but a flimsy Hollywood replica of a marina. As I drive down Admiralty Way back to my home, to the place where my "father" resides, I wonder if my own existence has been nothing but a replica of a life. As a child, I was an actor. As an adult, I chose a profession that requires me to take on a role depending on which side is the first to shell out a retainer. Today, in the next town over, I finally dug up a fossil-trace of my family history. I wish I could rebury that fact under the loam of time.

As I pull into my underground garage, I wave to the US Marshals guarding the condominium complex. Their shifts must seem like eternal damnation—what could be more hellish than sitting in a parked car and watching to make sure a sixty-five-year-old man wearing an electronic ankle bracelet doesn't make a run for it? Or maybe it's more than that. Maybe, after the courthouse bombing, they want to make sure no one tries to spring Holzner or tries to harm him.

There are two more marshals in the courtyard. I wonder whether they need permission from the homeowners association to stay here, whether technically they're trespassing, until one of them approaches and says, "Your neighbors aren't happy with you, counselor. They say they didn't pay a million dollars to live in the same building as a terrorist. It could get a little tense for you. Our office has stationed us here to defuse the situation."

I guess I'm the one who should've asked the association's permission before I told Judge Gibson that Holzner could serve his house arrest in my condo.

I start toward the stairs, but he says, "Tell your visitor she better show some courtesy to a federal law officer. We're just trying to keep everybody safe here." He abruptly turns away and raises a hand to his ear. Someone's talking into his earphone.

I take the stairs two at a time and open the door to my unit. Holzner is sitting on the love seat in my living room. He's wearing one of my T-shirts and a pair of my blue jeans. He's reclining, and his legs are crossed as if he's a guest on an afternoon TV talk show. In the wicker chair opposite him is my mother.

"Harriet, why would you mess with a cop?" I ask.

She stands and looks at me, her lips sculpted into a good-natured smile. Her hair is up in a careless bun. There's a playful aura about her that I thought was a victim of the Sanctified Assembly's sterile righteousness. "That man was rude to me. He asked me for identification. Government oppression, invasion of privacy, pure and simple."

"Do you even carry identification?"

"Sit down and tell us how your day went," she says. "You spoke with some witnesses."

"Why would you ever reveal that?" I ask Holzner. "What I do for your case is confidential."

"I have nothing to hide from Harriet," he says. "But speaking of hiding, I had no idea you suffered from stage fright."

"You told him that?" I say.

My mother blushes ever so slightly.

"I wheedled it out of her," he says. "As good as you were in court yesterday, you seemed a little . . . let's call it *affectless*. I worried it was drugs. It turns out it *was* drugs, though I guess you really need them."

"You had no right, Harriet."

"I had every right as your mother to tell your father about your affliction. As his attorney, you had an ethical duty to inform him. If you'd only try to cleanse yourself in the celestial waters, what you call stage fright, but what is actually a manifestation of cellular impurities of your limbic system, would soon . . ."

She stops talking when I shake my head, because I'm sure she expects me to call her on her Assembly-speak, and I almost do, almost respond that I'll pass on the religious cant and just stock up on Smartwater and tofu. Not this time. Maybe at long last I'm weary of the whole debate.

"You saw Carol Diaz," Holzner says. "How is she?" There's a slight vocal crack, a subtle show of restraint.

"She's retiring at the end of this year."

"She's an old lady, just like I'm an old man," he says.

"Who's Carol Diaz?" Harriet asks.

"My best friend as a kid."

"They grew up on the same street together," I say. "She's currently the principal of Playa Delta High School."

"A nice person who's shouldn't have been dragged into my problems," Holzner says. "Why did you bother her?"

"Moses Dworsky suggested it. He also found Barney Kinsella."

"Kinsella was an asshole."

"And I talked to Gladdie Giddens. She told me that you grew up with her son."

He shows no emotion at all, only utters a flat, "I didn't know him very well. He was Jerry's age."

"She claims to have seen you at the VA the morning of the bombing."

"Old news. FBI misconduct in showing her my photo. They suggested to her that I did it."

Not a bad defense posture to take. Of course, he's had a long time to craft his own legal arguments.

"So Diaz told me you broke a school window with a trash can," I say. "Did it stop the war?"

"Oh, Parky," Harriet says. "This sarcasm won't—"

"It absolutely stopped the war," he says. "That and thousands of other small but significant acts of rebellion against an oppressive government. The school window was a great start."

"Diaz also said that she was afraid of your brother, Jerry. That he was a hoodlum and a creep around girls."

"My mother wasn't kind to him," he says. "Jerry had some limitations. He had to be tough. No, that's not right—he had to *act* tough. He never hurt anyone, just tried to survive."

"Barney Kinsella says you loved explosives. That you made a bomb from gun cotton. I didn't even know what that was until I looked it up on *Wikipedia*."

He laughs. "Powerful stuff. Better than fireworks. It doesn't really explode, it creates a flash fire."

"You think it was funny? Kinsella says you used the stuff to try to kill his cat."

He recalls the moment without an iota of hesitation. "Barney has it backwards. He hated the cat, it hissed at him, scratched him, and still his mother made him feed it. He said he wanted the cat dead. I thought he was joking. The cat wasn't in any danger, anyway. She was smarter than Barney. The experiment—and that's what it was—didn't hurt anything. These days they teach you to make the stuff on YouTube."

"Both Diaz and Kinsella said you berated them about their position on the Vietnam War."

"Barney was a fascist and Carol a liberal. And yeah, I screamed at them. That's who I was. I thought I could get people to do the right thing by shouting at them."

"Or bombing them."

I expect Harriet to chide me again, but she doesn't. She just primps her hair, sucks in her lower lip, and looks at us as if she's a front-row mourner at a funeral.

"Tell me about Alicia Bowers," I say.

"A little kid who lived down the block," he says. "Crazy father who was a POW in World War Two. He showed me what war could do to the common man."

"She had a crush on you. Years later, someone saw her on the podium with you during one of your protest rallies at UCLA."

"She had a crush on me because I threatened to kick some kids' asses when they were teasing her," he says. "As for the rally, who remembers? A lot of people wanted to be around me. I was a celebrity. You know what that's like, Parker. But Alicia wasn't involved in the movement, as far as I know. Anything else?"

I shake my head.

He gets up, tenderly places his hand over Harriet's, and then goes down the hall and disappears into his bedroom.

Harriet stands, walks over to me, and puts her arm around me. I fight the urge to recoil, not in disgust but in shock, because I can't recall the last time she touched me with affection.

"He's a good man," she says.

"That's what you've always said about Bradley Kelly despite his crimes against nature."

"Leave that alone for once," she says. "Anyway, this is different. Your father might've made mistakes, but he isn't a bad man."

I'm about to argue with her until I notice the tears in her eyes. Another shock—Quiana Gottschalk, divine prophet of the Sanctified Assembly, doesn't cry.

What is it about Ian Holzner that makes her behave like someone else? She's never acted like this with any man, not even Kelly, who was more of a partner in a perverse business venture than a paramour. Could Holzner really be the love of her life? Before Holzner showed up, I didn't believe my mother could truly love anyone.

CHAPTER SEVENTEEN

Our best defense is that, if Holzner didn't bomb the Playa Delta VA, Rachel O'Brien did. So where the hell is she? Is she even alive? If so, has she gone far away, or is she near and just concealed by that most effective of camouflages, ordinariness?

Moses Dworsky told us he lost touch with her in 1983, after she won parole and moved back to the Bay Area. Her family disowned her, so they're of no help. Reddick claims the FBI can't find O'Brien, either. I believe her, because O'Brien would be the US Attorney's key witness. Lovely's theory is that O'Brien went into the witness-protection program, maybe to hide from the mysterious bomber JB. It's speculation, but I never discount what Lovely has to say.

Holzner continues to live like a monk, taking meals in his room and meditating for hours. The already-gaunt man is becoming emaciated, his face taking on a bony, angular, almost Lincolnesque quality. And yet he does hundreds of push-ups and sit-ups per day. At sixty-five, he's in far better shape than I am. The only thing he's asked me for is a chinning bar that he can mount in the doorway.

I've stopped asking him about O'Brien or the other members of his collective. I'm tired of the stock answer *I don't know what happened*, sick of his misplaced honor among criminals, disgusted by his conviction that there's nobility in shielding murderers.

Or maybe he won't name anyone else because he's guilty.

—⁓—

Although it's October, the Santa Ana winds have heated the coast to a temperature that bears no relationship to the concept of autumn.

The days are oppressive, but the nights are balmy, such that Lovely Diamond and I can share dinner on the balcony of my condo. Her blond hair falls insouciantly down to her shoulders, and she's dressed in a Juicy Couture cerulean tracksuit. On an ordinary day, her clothing would've kept her warm in the cool sea breeze, but on this night, the winds sweep in hot from the desert, so her cheeks are rosy, like they were when we'd make love. She seems indifferent to the candlelight, neither buying into the romance nor retreating from the implications. My cooking skills might be rudimentary, but hers are nonexistent. I've made penne arrabbiata with grilled chicken strips, which I serve with an aged Amarone that a grateful client gave me five years ago.

The last thing I want to talk about is the Holzner case, but that's all she wants to talk about.

"We should do to O'Brien what she did to him—blame her *in absentia*. She's not going to show up as a witness, so we can say what we want about her."

"What if she testifies in rebuttal?"

"I worked for the US Attorney's office. Reddick wouldn't be foolish enough to hold O'Brien back."

"You only worked there for a little over a year, and that was for Reddick's predecessor."

"I talked to Lou about it."

"I don't care what Frantz thinks."

"You should. Speaking of which, you're supposed to be consulting with him."

"Whatever."

"Lou agrees that Marilee Reddick wouldn't hold O'Brien for rebuttal. What if we decided to rest without putting on a defense case? She'd have nothing to rebut and no chance of getting her star witness before the jury. Besides, if Holzner didn't do it, O'Brien must have, with the help of Hayes and Sedgwick. We've got to blame all of them."

"You won't do that," Holzner says from the shadows in a tone so soft and threatening that I suspend my forkful of pasta in midair, inches from my mouth. Lovely flinches so violently that some of her wine spills on her top.

"Damn it," she says. "I just bought this outfit."

I look into the dark living room. He's a silhouette in warrior's pose—legs spread and slightly bent, arms curved and held away from his body, hands balled up in fists, as if he's about to assault us.

"Why don't you come outside where we can see you," I say.

He joins us, as expressionless as an ancient Greek statue whose face has been eroded by time. Only when he sees Lovely using a napkin and Pellegrino water to try and remove the red stain from her top does his expression change from blank to embarrassed.

"I didn't mean to startle you," he says.

"It's okay." Her impatient tone makes it clear that it's not okay. Still dabbing at her top, she turns toward him. "So tell me, Ian. Why shouldn't we blame Rachel O'Brien for the bombing?"

The wind gusts, dog-howling between the buildings.

"Because she couldn't build it," he says. "Neither could any of the others. So no one will believe that defense."

"O'Brien was smart," I say. "So was Sedgwick. It wasn't that hard to cobble together a bomb."

"Not the way I built them. Rachel was a sociology major. Charlie studied philosophy, and Brenda Hayes could hardly write her name."

"Did you build the bomb, Ian?" Lovely asks.

"Of course not."

"Then who did?" I ask.

He stands up. "You will *not* argue that one of the others built the bomb."

"One of them must have planted the bomb," I say.

"Feel free to argue that," he says and then turns and walks back into the living room.

"The problem is we can't prove it," I call after him. "Gladdie Giddens will testify she saw *you* at the scene."

Lovely uses a napkin to take another swipe at the stain on her shirt, then dabs at her mouth. I turn toward the sea and gaze at the illuminated decks of the mega-yachts anchored at the berths, at the lighted masts of the sailboats and skiffs riding the strong adiabatic winds and skittering toward the jetty like overwound toys in a child's bathtub.

"Talk to him," she says. "He's your father."

"No, he's our client."

"He wants you to treat him more like a father than a client. You should. It'll help the case. And it's a second chance for both of you."

"It's never going to happen."

"I also dumped my child, and I got him back. It was the best thing that ever happened to me."

"Brighton was ten years old. I'm not."

"Do you think your father is innocent?"

"I have no idea. It's not a question that a criminal-defense lawyer should ask."

"It's a question a son should ask," she says. "And for the record, I think he's innocent."

"Based on what?"

She reaches over and covers my hand with hers. "Believe your father is innocent, Parker. If not for him, then for you. And for Emily."

I won't do it for him or for me. I might do it for Emily.

CHAPTER EIGHTEEN

Belinda Hayes was, during her days in the Holzner-O'Brien Gang, an imperial fuck-up and a profligate. The one time she tried to plant an explosive device to cause property damage to a bank in Venice Beach, California, she buried the bomb so deep that the blast only kicked up some sand. She worked as a stripper and a prostitute. Although she used her earnings to help finance radical causes, her brazen drug abuse and promiscuity drew unwelcome attention to the collective. Unlike her comrades, she didn't try to escape when the police identified the Holzner-O'Brien Gang as the perpetrators of the Playa Delta bombing. Instead, she remained paralyzed in her filthy apartment, where the FBI found her cowering under a Murphy bed.

When I ask Moses Dworsky to join me at my meeting with Hayes later that afternoon, he says, "I would rather not be in her presence. You know that she and I were not fond of each other."

"That was a long time ago."

He wrinkles his long nose in distaste. "It would not be a productive session. I skewered her on cross-examination. If I attend, she will not be forthcoming. In fact, she would be utterly hostile."

"What do you mean you skewered Hayes? She was your witness."

"She was going to be the prosecution's witness, but they decided not to call her because of her gross mental instability. I decided to call her to the stand at the eleventh hour because I felt I might need a Hail Mary. I actually cross-examined her as an adverse witness because she was so favorably disposed to Holzner. She tended to want to protect him. Or maybe she feared him."

"But you got her to say what you wanted?"

He nods. I'm fascinated by the way his earlobes shimmy with every shake or bob of his head. It's almost as if he subconsciously uses his unfortunate physiognomy to distract and disarm.

"Come to the meeting with me," I say. "Your history with her will help. We can play good cop, bad cop."

"Lovely can accompany you."

"She's got an emergency motion on something else she's working on."

He mumbles something indecipherable and says, "Give Eleanor the address, and I will think about it."

"Don't just think about it. I need you there." I want to see the dynamic between Dworsky and Hayes, to see how she might react to stress on the witness stand. I want to see Militant Moe in action.

Several hours later, at about four in the afternoon, I drive solo to the foothills above Lakeview Terrace in the north quadrant of the San Fernando Valley. Down below is a neighborhood consisting of small wood-and-stucco homes built in the 1950s and of grungy light-industrial and commercial businesses. Up in the hills are shanties, a trailer park, and old, ranch-style homes with stables. Lakeview Terrace is one of the few places in Los Angeles where equestrians with modest resources can afford to stable their horses.

I park at the bottom of a gravel-and-dirt driveway and wait for Moses Dworsky. When he doesn't show up after fifteen minutes, I drive up a steep hill to a one-story box house with copper-wood and white-aluminum-siding walls and a flat composition roof. The landscaping consists of concrete and scrub brush. There's a rusted lawn chair and a sooty Weber barbecue on the front porch. The windows have bars, painted white to match the siding.

I knock on the screen door. Hayes opens it, wearing a tattered blue T-shirt touting the "Kale and Saffron Vegan Restaurant." Her black tights are so threadbare that her skin is visible in places. Her silver-gray hair, which frames a round, surprisingly wrinkle-free face, falls down her back 1960s style. She's undoubtedly added some pounds since her days as an exotic dancer. But she's still shapely, an earth mother whose huge breasts are unencumbered by a bra. Her green eyes greet me as if

I'm the bearer of joyous tidings rather than a corporate suit here to resurrect what should be the darkest period of her life.

"Come on in, sweetie," she says.

When I thank her for agreeing to talk to me, she says, "God is good."

I'm still trying to decipher this non sequitur as I follow her into a living room not much larger than a walk-in closet, into which she's managed to cram a massive burgundy Naugahyde sofa, two almost-matching crimson wingback chairs serving as storage areas for old fashion magazines, and an end table so scored and chipped that the dark-stained surface is speckled white. On the faux-fireplace mantle are a Buddha sculpture, a stained-glass image of a Greek-Orthodox Jesus holding the bible, a menorah, an aluminum Ganesh, and a lighted votive candle that fills the room with the heavy odor of patchouli.

She sits down on the sofa and pats the cushion next to her. It's unprofessionally close, but because of the magazines on the chairs, there's nowhere else to sit.

"So you're Ian's son," she says. "Who's your mother?"

She posed the question so abruptly that I answer, "Harriet Stern." Only after the words come out do I wonder which of us is the expert interrogator.

She rolls her eyes upward, as though the memory of my mother is a spirit trapped in the cottage-cheese ceiling. "Ian fucked a lot of girls, me included. We all fucked each other, all of us. It was all part of the revolution we made. But he loved that evil cunt, Rachel."

I don't know what's more jarring, her vulgarity, her free-associative personal revelations, or her hatred for Rachel O'Brien. Only the last is relevant to why I'm here.

"You didn't like Rachel, but the news reports say you sided with her at her trial, that you testified that she backed out of the conspiracy to bomb the VA."

"Damn straight I did. She was right there in court, not twenty feet away, staring at me with those witch's eyes, laying a curse on me. Ian was long gone, so what did it matter if I dumped on him? Besides, even if I testified against him, he wouldn't have done to me what Rachel would have if I had crossed her. Ian was always spiritual, always forgiving. Not Rachel."

"She was dangerous?"

"She was a . . . What do you call those poisonous snakes?"

"Vipers?"

"No, Ian once called her a Queen Cobra. Fearsome and poisonous."

"You perjured yourself because you were afraid?"

"Sweetie, there's no such thing as perjury in a fascist kangaroo court. Besides, that lawyer of hers, Dworsky the Elephant Man or whatever, beat the shit out of me, got me to say what he wanted me to, because even with Rachel sitting there I hated to accuse Ian. But yeah, I was scared shitless."

"Are you telling me Rachel bombed the VA?"

"She could've done it for sure. I don't know. I don't know. Rachel thought I was a fuck-up. They left me out of the operation." She makes it sound like a painful memory of youth, like not getting asked to the high-school prom.

I have only to ask a general question to get her to launch into a rambling narrative about how the Weather Underground expelled her for promiscuity, but that was okay with her, because the Holzner-O'Brien Gang accepted her and didn't care about what she wore or that she made money for the collective by turning tricks. Even better, the group, in theory, was much more willing to use violence as a means of fomenting revolution. The gang made a pilgrimage to San Francisco to protest the arrest of two members of the Symbionese Liberation Army for killing the Oakland, California, superintendent of schools. On the trip up from Los Angeles, a fellow traveler drove the van while Holzner, O'Brien, Sedgwick, Hayes, and four others dropped acid and had a six-hour orgy in the back. "Everybody fucked everybody—boys and girls, girls and girls, boys and boys. It was great!" She boasts about her most publicized mistake, the abortive bombing attempt on the Venice Beach Community Bank, which was evidently providing the construction financing for a luxury hotel that would've displaced some low-income tenants in a housing project. She dressed up like a Santa Monica house-wife and carried the bomb in a Gucci handbag. "It was like foreplay," she says. "Better." Her only regret was she blew up sand, not the building.

"And then there was Ian," she says, her eyes misty-moist like a moony schoolgirl. "He could hypnotize you with his words, his look, his touch. No one was like him. No one had his passion. He was a fan-tastic fuck. You look like him."

So Belinda Hayes is just another cultist, worshipping at the church of Ian Holzner. He might as well have been an elder in the Church of the Sanctified Assembly.

She places her hand on my knee. "Sure I can't get you something to drink, sweetie? Maybe some white wine?"

I decline again.

"I'll have some." She comes back with a glass in one hand and the bottle in the other, fills the glass to the brim, sets the bottle on the coffee table, and takes a sip. When she sits down, she narrows the dis-tance between us. "Where were we, sweetie?"

I discreetly try to create more space because I don't want to antago-nize her. She's giving me some good information. But I can't manage to move away in these tight quarters.

"You told me about the bank bombing," I say. "Tell me about the other attacks."

"They were covert guerrilla operations," she says indignantly.

"Tell me about the other covert operations."

She goes on to describe other bombings the group committed over the succeeding months. Each time, Holzner insisted that someone call in a warning. There were no injuries. Hayes's account helps one of my defense theories—the Playa Delta bombing didn't fit the gang's pattern.

"Could anyone else in the group besides Holzner have built a bomb?" I ask.

"Not me."

"I mean, the others. Rachel, for example. Or Charles Sedgwick."

"No way when I was there. But I was expelled just before Thanks-giving, so . . ."

"Why?"

She gulps down the wine and fills her glass again. "Rachel didn't like me. I wasn't a very good guerilla soldier, I guess. And I think she was jealous. She didn't love Ian. That bitch couldn't love anyone, but she was jealous of anyone else who wanted him. And I did love him. So did all the women and some of the men. But I gave the best blow jobs. Ian said so. Anyway, when Rachel tells me I'm out of the group, she goes . . ." And here, she sucks in her cheeks and makes herself resemble the O'Brien I've seen in photos, the girl with the thin face, slightly receding chin, wild and fiery eyes. "She goes, 'If you ever truly become committed, perhaps you can find another group, maybe one that you'll love more. Che Guevara said revolutionaries should swim among the masses like fish in the sea. If you're serious, you can do that. But not with us.'" Hayes says this in a rapid-fire cadence and gesticulates wildly, as if O'Brien were a fast-talking carnival huckster. "Anyway, I went to Ian, begged him to let me stay, but he wouldn't. He would've let me stay, I'm sure of it, but that fucking bitch Rachel . . ."

"Their decision probably saved you from spending your life in prison. Or worse."

"You don't get it, do you, sweetie? Ian would say back then that there was tinder in the air, a sense that the world could burst into flames at the smallest spark. I wanted to help set that fire. The Playa Delta bombing proved that the government was vulnerable, a paper tiger. Rachel and Ian didn't do me a favor, they stole my chance to be part of history. The loss has haunted me all my life."

The woman is a psychopath. I force her insanity, her misguided callousness out of my mind. "Tell me about Charles Sedgwick," I say. "You said he couldn't build the bomb, but could he have planted it?"

She laughs and bends forward, her face close to mine. Her hand lands on my knee again. "Poor Charlie should've gotten his PhD and taught philosophy in college. That's all he did, philosophize. He liked to read Marx and Mao and Marcuse, write this revolutionary poetry no one could understand. He tried to do what Rachel and Ian wanted, but the one time he tried to plant a bomb—it was in a restroom at the

Treasury Building in Washington, DC—he literally pissed his pants as he walked up the steps carrying the briefcase. Rachel screamed at him because she paid seventy-five bucks for the suit he was wearing and he soiled it. The collective was always broke. Rachel didn't want to spend the money to have the suit dry-cleaned."

"Why couldn't he have built the bomb? He was a smart guy."

"No fucking way. Charlie was so freaked out after those Weathermen blew themselves up in Greenwich Village that he'd shake when he was in the same room with the explosives. No, Charlie was the Minister of Information, but that's it."

"Tell me about the collective's political ideology."

"Hasn't Ian told you about all that shit?"

He hasn't, but I don't want her to know it. "I'd like to hear it from you."

She takes a sip of wine at the same time she shrugs with the shoulder of the free hand. "I didn't pay much attention to that. Didn't really understand it. I just wanted to blow up the whole fucking world."

I ask her about other, less prominent members of the collective, people who seemed to flit in and out of the organization but haven't been implicated in the bombing. She says that they were mostly hangers-on who disappeared once Holzner and O'Brien branded them bourgeois or sell-outs or weaklings for not buying into the group's violent tactics.

"Did you ever meet Ian's brother, Jerry?"

She ponders this for a moment. "Yeah. I met him. It was right before they kicked me out. I don't remember for sure, but I think I fucked Jerry. Yeah, I did. When Ian found out about it he got really pissed at me." Her face droops in an epiphanous frown. "Do you think that's why Ian let Rachel exile me from the collective?"

You'd think the question couldn't be anything but rhetorical, but she's waiting with an expectant look.

"I wouldn't know about that," I say.

She almost lunges forward and grabs my arm. She smells of Chardonnay and cheap freesia-scented perfume. "Will you ask Ian if that's why he didn't overrule Rachel? He could've overruled her, you know."

I half nod, a noncommittal gesture that I'm sure she'll take as assent.

My next question comes from instinct, not intellect. "Do you remember anyone named Alicia Bowers?"

Another lifting of her eyes, another appeal to the Lords of the Dappled Ceiling. "That doesn't ring a bell."

"She supposedly had a crush on Ian. Much younger."

She laughs. "That could describe a hundred girls. All of whom Ian probably fucked."

I ask her to tell me about the plan to bomb the Playa Delta VA. She assumed it was going to be like all the other bombings, that they'd call in a warning and that they'd destroy some property. But then Sedgwick, of all people, suggested that they might want to escalate their revolutionary activities, and O'Brien jumped on it. Of course, Belinda thought it was great to kill the fascist pigs. Holzner seemed to be on board with it.

"Did you ever hear Holzner object to targeting humans at Playa Delta?"

She starts to shake her head, but then says, "One week, two weeks, three weeks before they kicked me out, I don't know, I was really strung out at the time, I heard Ian and Rachel arguing in the bedroom. I thought it was about sex or something. Rachel liked it rough and Ian was a gentle type. But then he yelled 'I won't do it, I know people who work there.' That's it. I don't know for sure if they were talking about Playa Delta, but . . .'"

I only need to prove reasonable doubt to win acquittal. Belinda Hayes might have given me that. She's a crass, unstable woman—a typical witness in a criminal case.

"Would you be willing to testify to what you just said? To help Ian?"

She closes her eyes and takes a deep breath. "What about what I said at the last trial? Couldn't they arrest me for perjury?"

"You don't have to worry about perjury. Tell the truth, which was that you were afraid of O'Brien. She was intimidating, a violent person."

"Yeah, but what if she comes back?"

"We've been looking for her, and so has the US Attorney. They want her more than we do. Not even the US government can find her. Rachel O'Brien has disappeared off the face of the earth. Besides, she's in her sixties, and this is two thousand fourteen. What could she possibly do to you? Please, Belinda. Ian's future depends on it."

"Sure, sweetie," she finally says. "I shouldn't have dumped on Ian at Rachel's trial. I was disloyal and a coward. Charlie was loyal."

"And he's the only one who got a life sentence."

"He did the right thing. 'Revolutionary purity,' he called it. I guess Charlie was braver than I gave him credit for." She laughs. "I'm probably the first person ever to call Charlie brave."

I tell her what she should expect as the trial date approaches and thank her for her time. Then I get up to leave.

"Are we done so soon, sweetie?" She slides a bit closer and rests her hand on my thigh. With the other, she brushes her hair away from the back of her neck and tosses her head, a coquettish gesture that might've worked when she was younger but not anymore.

I slowly begin to stand, trying not to offend my newfound star witness.

"I can make you feel good," she says, standing with me and pressing her body against mine. "Just ask your father. He'll definitely remember." When my body tenses in protest, she says, "Hey, sweetie, indulge me. I always wanted to do a father and a son."

I'm about to pull away when a knock on the door saves me from the need to reject her.

"Moses Dworsky here," the voice says in a megaphonic bellow. "Apologies for my late arrival."

I know he doesn't want to be here, but I didn't figure he'd use passive aggression to avoid it. The man makes his own rules, but at the moment I'm grateful for his tardiness.

Hayes puts two hands on my chest and shoves me away in disgust. "What the hell is this? You brought Rachel's lawyer to my home?"

"He's a private investigator now. Working for me. For Ian."

She shakes her head in disbelief and stomps over to the door, her huge breasts swaying aggressively under her T-shirt. I follow. She flings the door open and cowers as if a huge, menacing giant has just parked himself on her doorstep.

Which describes Dworsky at the moment. He's looming over her on the other side of the screen with arms crossed, and his frown makes it seem as if his nose will touch his chin. Forty feet away is Eleanor Dworsky, leaning against an old Ford Taurus. When she sees me, she waves and calls out, "Hey, Parker, make it snappy. I want to get Moses home. We have guests coming over."

"Get the hell out," Hayes says, pushing me so hard and so unexpectedly that I almost trip and fall into the screen. "I told you, I have nothing to say to you."

"Belinda, I'm sorry, I should've mentioned that Moses is working for me."

"Did you ask her about JB?" Moses asks.

I didn't. How could I have forgotten that? "Belinda, have you ever heard of someone who uses the initials *JB*?"

"Get out, motherfucker!" she screeches like a profane fairy-tale crone.

I mumble a thank you and an "I'll be in touch," to which she replies, "No you won't," and slams the door.

Dworsky looks down at me and shrugs his already-hunched shoulders. "I warned you. She does not like me. You should have brought Lovely if you needed backup. Now, what, may I ask, did I miss?"

I recount my conversation with Hayes, how she could shed reasonable doubt about Ian's guilt. He nods. Finally, Eleanor, who all this time has been leaning against the car, calls out, "Move it, Moishe. We need to get home."

He spreads his arms, palms raised as if in benediction. "My dear wife is the only one allowed to call me *Moishe* since my mother passed away. It is the Yiddish version of Moses, you know. But I leave you with these words: you did well with that recalcitrant, unstable woman. The trick will be to convince her that I am not her enemy." He gives a quarter bow, lumbers to the Ford, and gets into the passenger seat. Eleanor, who's already climbed behind the wheel and started the engine, gives me a cursory wave and drives away, kicking up dust from the road as if she were a hot-rod racer jumping the starting lights.

I take a look back at the house and see Belinda Hayes peering out at me from between the drapes. When she sees me looking, she pulls them together hard. Seconds later, the lock on the front door clicks shut with a final rebuke.

CHAPTER NINETEEN

I walk into The Barrista the next morning, greet the staff, and freeze. Mariko Heim is sitting at a back table, drinking coffee—*my* back table. She appears to be alone, but the place is crowded, and I'm sure her enforcers are scattered incognito at neighboring tables. Someone in Heim's position doesn't travel without muscle. She's wearing her brown sunglasses with the opaque lenses. When a barista passes, she surprises me by ordering a second cup of coffee. It's a venial sin for a true believer like her to consume caffeine.

I walk over to her. "Please leave my store, Ms. Heim."

"Sit down, Mr. Stern," she says, and as an afterthought forces out the word, "Please."

"That won't happen."

"I don't know if I'm supposed to be afraid of the First Apostate or in awe of him."

My body folds down into the seat across from her. As a young teenager, I defied Bradley Kelly, the Sanctified Assembly's founder, and was branded a heretic, the Assembly's *First Apostate*. Except that afterward, the Assembly denied my existence as part of the cover-up of the abuse that I and many other children had suffered. I can't believe Heim has breached the titanium curtain of secrecy surrounding the First Apostate.

"What do you want?" I ask.

"You're surprised I know you're the First Apostate? If that's the case, I'm sure you'll be surprised that I want to talk to you about Ascending Sodality."

If her reference to the First Apostate made my legs shake, her reference to Ascending Sodality leaves me dumbstruck. I don't like to think about the vile practice that, to this day, could land many of the original Sanctified Assembly founders in jail, possibly including my own mother.

"Oh, don't be so surprised," Heim says. "Most successful institutions have dirty secrets. Just like a human being, the Church of the Sanctified Assembly is a living organism susceptible to cellular contamination. The key to an organization's long-term survival is curing itself of disease. As a member of a new generation of Assembly devotees, I feel it's my duty to help cleanse the Assembly of contamination. That involves purging the organization of those who engaged in depraved practices."

"If that were true, your divine prophet would be your first target."

"Whoever or whatever the flesh-and-blood man was, his soul has transcended the human being. His spirit is pure. It matters not what the Prophet or the Divine Son or the Bearer of God's Law did in life. It's what He means in death. That's what redemption is all about."

"So you think the rotten fruit can germinate a pristine seedling? How progressive of you." Romulo brings me an espresso. I thank him, but I don't take my eyes off Heim, who through her dark lenses is looking . . . somewhere.

"We can assist each other," Heim says. "Information for information."

"What information can I possibly give you?"

"I want to know the names of everyone who was involved in the practice of Ascending Sodality. And I want to know whether Harriet Stern practiced it."

How disrespectful. She didn't refer to Harriet as *Quiana.* "You want me to implicate my own mother in criminal activity?"

"It's no secret that you and she don't see eye to eye, shall we say. Have I understated it well enough?"

Heim doesn't give a damn about cleansing her Assembly. She wants to depose my mother.

"I also want to know about Harriet Stern's relationship with Ian Holzner," she says. "The unsullied Assembly elders have a right to know why Stern is consorting with a murderer."

"My client isn't guilty, and my mother has nothing to do with him," I say, a lawyer's knee-jerk attempt to state his position for the record, odd because I don't owe this woman an explanation about anything. "But if I've got it right, you want me to provide information about both my mother and my father, as if I'm a brainwashed child in some totalitarian state giving up his parents for the greater good. Out of curiosity, what would I get out of doing something like that?"

"Just to be clear, I'm not interested in Holzner, but only your mother's relationship with him."

"She has no relationship with him. Hasn't for forty years." I don't expect her to believe it, but I have to say the words nevertheless.

"As for what you can get out of it, I know you're looking for witnesses. Well, one in particular—Rachel O'Brien."

"How could you possibly help me find O'Brien?"

"The Assembly has the ability to locate people even the government can't find. Or doesn't want to find." As she speaks, she keeps her head down, as if I'm some kind of ghastly creature she can't bear to look at.

"You've got it all wrong. The best thing that can happen to my case is for Rachel O'Brien *not* to show up at the trial."

"True. But you need to know whether she's going to appear as a surprise witness. That way, you can prepare for that possibility."

"I'll take my chances. I've been told I'm a good cross-examiner, and I'll use those skills if O'Brien does pop up. Meanwhile, let her stay missing."

She touches the coffee cup to her lips without sipping and says, "We might be able to influence whether she shows up or not."

"Unlike you and your cult, I don't intimidate witnesses."

She jerks her head up to look at me for the first time, and although I can't see her eyes, the suddenness of the action proves she's rattled. "I wasn't implying that we would intimidate anyone."

"Sure you weren't." I stand and walk toward the entrance. She's virtually succeeded in chasing me out of my own store.

"Stern!" she calls after me, and as I walk away I notice a couple of men at a table near the entrance about get up from their chairs, but they stay seated, and I don't have to look behind me to know that Heim commanded them to back off—for now.

CHAPTER TWENTY

At five-thirty in the morning on January 8, 1976, a little more than three weeks after the Playa Delta bombing, four agents working in the clandestine COINTELPRO unit burst into Jerry Holzner's motel apartment, rousted him out of bed, and demanded that he tell them where his brother, Ian, was. When Jerry said he didn't know, the agents interrogated him for two hours, at the end of which they accused him of conspiring to bomb the Playa Delta VA. When he stuck by his story, they slapped his face, twisted his arm, broke two fingers, and pummeled his torso with closed fists. When that didn't work, they dragged him out of his bedroom, lifted him up, and dangled him by ankles from the balcony of his third-story apartment. Only then did Jerry give up the address of the West LA apartment where the Holzner-O'Brien Gang was living. Whereupon the federal agents got a warrant citing third-party-witness Jerry's "cooperation." They searched the gang's apartment, where they found bomb-making equipment similar to that used at the Playa Delta VA, along with a hand-drawn map of the Veterans Administration.

Ian's fingerprints were found on the bomb parts. When I ask him why, he tells me that he touched all the explosives—he was the bomb maker, after all—and that the material the FBI found in the apartment obviously wasn't used for the Playa Delta killings, which had occurred several weeks earlier. He claims he didn't know about the map, which, he says, judging by the handwriting, must've been prepared by Charles Sedgwick. Sedgwick refused to cooperate in his own defense and so said nothing about the map or anything else. According to newspaper reports, Rachel O'Brien testified at her trial that Holzner drew the map. Belinda Hayes testified that she didn't know who drew it, but Holzner had drawn many of the maps of targets.

Three weeks ago, Lovely Diamond drafted a motion to suppress the fingerprint evidence, the map, and any adverse testimony from Hayes. In opposition, the US Attorney admits that COINTELPRO tortured Jerry Holzner but argues that it makes no difference to the admissibility of the evidence because while the rogue agents might've violated *Jerry* Holzner's constitutional rights, they didn't violate *Ian's* rights. This is because the feds had a valid warrant to search Ian's place. So even though the evidence is the "fruit of the poisonous tree," as the case law describes it, Ian can't complain because his rights weren't impaired. Except that Lovely has crafted a legal argument that just might appeal to a maverick judge like Carlton Gibson.

The night before the hearing, I'm sitting at the desk in my bedroom, mapping out my presentation to the judge on Lovely's motion to suppress. Three hard knocks on the wall startle me. Holzner barges in and sits on the edge of my bed. His hands are folded in his lap, and his eyes are docile with paternal concern. I swivel in my chair to face him.

Before he appeared in my life, I would've traded my legal career and my actor's residuals to have my father living in my home, to get to know him, to delineate my family history, to confirm that in the grand river of humanity I'm something more than an existential droplet randomly spewed into the atmosphere. Now that he's here, I don't want to ask about him or my grandparents or my extended family. It would feel like a lawyer's interrogation rather than a son's curiosity. Most of the time, we behave like aloof post-college roommates who have nothing in common.

"So there's really no way I can come down to court tomorrow morning?" he asks.

"We went over it. It's a legal argument, so your presence isn't required."

"I can help you."

"Help me like you did last time by showing your disrespect for the judge, your contempt for the entire judicial process? Help me by refusing to take off your shackles so you look like the murderous terrorist everyone thinks you are?"

"Do you believe that?"

"I'm your lawyer. I'm paid *not* to think about your guilt or innocence. Except I'm not being paid."

"I get it. You're a man of principle. Good for you. I mean I can help you with your fear."

"How can you possibly help my stage fright?"

"Let's just say a father's presence can have a calming effect on a child."

"I'm forty years old, not a child. You tried to turn the hearing into a circus. That's hardly calming. I managed to get through it because I took prescription drugs, not because you were there." And because Lovely was there, and I didn't want to let her down.

"Maybe so. But how about listening to me right now?"

"I'd rather you tell me how to find Rachel O'Brien and your brother, Jerry."

"I know fear, Parker. I lived with it every day for almost forty years. Afraid I'd run into someone who recognized me from the old days, afraid that the person in the next restaurant booth was FBI, afraid that Jenny and Dylan and Emily would discover who I really was. Fear consumed me. No, that's wrong, it desiccated my soul from the inside out, so I thought I was alive when, in truth, Ian Holzner died the moment he went on the run. As for Marty Lansing, he never existed—not in this shell of a body. Reddick was right. Stealing a dead infant's identity was shameful. So much of what I've done has been shameful."

I wonder if that includes murder.

"How can you help me, Ian?" By this, I mean, *How can I help you?*

"By teaching you how to embrace the fear."

"You learned to overcome the fear when you became a fugitive?"

"I learned to embrace it when I decided to build bombs. You have to realize that fear keeps you sharp."

"A little bit of fear keeps you sharp. A lot paralyzes you."

"Listen to me. When you walk into the courtroom, behave like an emergency-room doctor performing triage. Focus on eliminating the real threat, whatever that might be. Single-mindedness makes you forget the trivial. When I was assembling explosive devices, I couldn't worry about the cops bursting in or an FBI rat infiltrating the group. I had to make sure I didn't cross a wire and blow myself up."

"What's that got to do with my glossophobia?"

"Don't be so centered on self. Rely on—"

"Narcissism runs in the family."

"I didn't mean—"

"You and Harriet are the most—"

"Rely on Moses Dworsky. He—"

"Dworsky postures, second-guesses, and works only when he feels like it. I only tolerate it because I need his office space."

"Then Lovely Diamond. She's in love with you."

"You might be right, but she won't have me."

He reaches his hand out as if to place it on my shoulder, but he must see my muscles tense, because he hesitates and gives two fatherly pats to the air. "What I'm trying to say is that if you have the love of others, you're less afraid. That's how I got through it, mostly—Jenny and Dylan and Emily. It's a double gift. Your loved ones make you feel protected, and you don't want to let them down, so you fight for them despite the fear."

"I'll take your advice to heart. Truly. But now I have to get back to work."

"I know that I sound naïve," he says, standing up. "White-bread, Orange County conservative. But I learned after so many years in hiding that the simplest, most sentimental ideas can be the best." The man sounds like an omniscient father in one of those old-fashioned TV sitcoms. After the polemics and the radical tracts and the bombs, the change in attitude is almost bizarre. Which causes me to feel that he's insincere, that he's engaging in some sort of diversionary tactic. To divert me from what?

"Focus, friends, and love, Parker. They're what'll defeat your fear."

—꘎—

On a cool, dry morning in November—the kind of day that during the twentieth century drew millions from the inclement parts of America to Southern California—I'm going to ask Carlton Gibson to exclude key evidence against Ian Holzner. Since JB's bombing of the courthouse, security has tightened. The line of attorneys and spectators trying to get inside extends down the exterior steps and onto the sidewalk. I arrive quite early, but with this crowd I might be late for the hearing. I wend my way to the front and ask the marshal in charge whether I can jump the line. He refuses my request. He knows who I am and undoubtedly blames me for this mess. Once I reach the magnetometer twenty minutes later, the marshals order me to remove my shoes and belt. After I pass through the metal detector, they insist on patting me down.

Lovely greets me in the second-floor foyer, and we take the escalators to the courtroom. Before we go inside, she says, "Do you need me to go over the relevant cases with you once more?"

"Nope."

"I could argue the case if you aren't up to it. You know, if you're feeling shaky?"

"The meds are working fine, thank you." The truth is, I didn't take the antianxiety medication this morning. It's not that I'm taking Holzner's advice about overcoming fear—I simply forgot.

"The meds make you logy," Lovely says. "I prepared an oral argument just in case."

My sharp look of incredulity quiets her.

We walk down the corridor to a courtroom that's filled with media reps and curious onlookers, just as it was for the bail hearing several months ago. Mariko Heim has showed up again, her enforcers flanking her. Lou Frantz is sitting in the last row on my side of the courtroom. I haven't consulted him about the case at all. I let Lovely do that. He nods and smiles slightly without showing his teeth. Sitting next to him is his old nemesis, Moses Dworsky, whom I asked to come. Like so many over-the-hill enemies do, they're chatting amiably. I was hoping Jerry Holzner would show up again, but he hasn't. Was there ever an Uncle Jerry, or did I make him up?

Marilee Reddick and her gaggle of Assistant US Attorneys walk into the courtroom and pass by without acknowledging me. I'm certain Reddick would love to aim some choice invectives at me for wasting her afternoon, but Judge Gibson's microphone must be deterring her. I approach her and say, "Any leads on the JB bomber, Marilee?"

"Same answer as before. Ian Holzner and whoever is working with him."

"It's relevant to my defense in this case. You have an obligation to disclose it."

"Take it up with the judge." She turns away and pretends to talk with one of her assistants.

Suddenly, the judge, dressed in his robes, walks out of chambers and clambers into his chair. Even the courtroom personnel are surprised. The clerk cries out a tardy, "All rise!" and the spectators half stand and sit down because Gibson already has. Reddick and I remain standing.

"*Buenos días*, ladies and gents," the judge says. "United States versus Holzner. Motion to suppress evidence. I'll hear from Mr. Parky . . . Mr. Parker Stern." The joke is getting old.

I go to the lectern, and the room rotates on its wobbly axis. The fear scorches my cheeks from the inside. I inhale, but the room won't stop shaking. I steal a quick glance at Lovely. Her face shows no emotion. She's undoubtedly worried that any show of concern will cause me to panic. She reaches for her black binder, where she has notes for her proposed oral argument. I'm actually about to ask her to take over when I realize why Holzner's methods won't work for the kind of fear I have. He was afraid of capture, afraid of prison, afraid of humiliation, afraid of losing his family. Those fears were real, and so when he tried to control them by focusing on something else, he knew what he was running from. My fears are about nothing—they just exist. It's impossible to hide from a feeling that has no boundary. Paradoxically, this epiphany of hopelessness calms me down enough so I can speak.

"Your Honor, Parker Stern and Lovely Diamond appearing for the defendant, Ian Holzner. This is a motion to suppress a hand-drawn diagram of the Playa Delta Veterans Administration and certain finger-print evidence of equipment traditionally used to make explosives. To admit the evidence would offend due process of law under the Fifth Amendment to the Constitution. It's quite simple: agents working for the government of the United States, the greatest democracy ever known to humankind, dangled an innocent man over a third-floor balcony railing to force him to provide information about his brother. The word *appalling* doesn't describe the horror of the government's crime."

"What the government did back then was a major no-no," the judge says. "But it was Jerry's rights that were violated, not Ian's. Isn't Ian out of luck under the case law?"

Lovely starts shuffling papers, a sign that she's agitated, though the judge asked an obvious question.

"Your Honor," I say, "that's ordinarily true about motions to sup-press, where the police have conducted an illegal search of someone's property, which doesn't involve a deliberate threat to a person's life and limb. This case is different. The test for a violation of due process is whether the government engaged in conduct that was shocking, out-rageous, and intolerable. What COINTELPRO did to Jerry Holzner fits all three requirements. It was heinous coercion of a witness, typical of the actions of a totalitarian state—Stalinist Russia, Nazi Germany. That it happened on American soil is sickening. There's never been a reported judicial opinion where the government was able to rely on physical coercion of a third party to obtain evidence against a defen-dant. To put it bluntly, the government shouldn't be acquiring evidence by torturing an American citizen who's done nothing wrong."

I glance at Lovely, who's nodding approvingly. I'm doing a decent job of putting her sophisticated thoughts into simple words. As strong as she thinks the argument might be, however, most courts and legal scholars have rejected her theory. The conservative Supreme Court has consistently favored the police, even when they violate a third party's constitutional rights. So I have to drive the argument home.

"How rogue can a government agent go and still get away with it?" I say. "What if those criminals had decided to drop Jerry Holzner from that ledge and kill him after he disclosed the information just so they could cover up their activities? Would it comport with principles of due process to allow the government to use the evidence against his surviving brother? Of course not. Evidence that is the fruit of murder and torture is not constitutionally admissible against anyone, and to allow it in this case would forever taint this court and besmirch the criminal-justice system."

"Didn't Jerry Holzner bring a civil suit?" the judge asks. "Wasn't that his remedy? Why let Ian, a criminal—an alleged criminal—get a windfall?"

"We haven't been able to locate Jerry Holzner to get the entire story. The public files have long ago been lost or destroyed. But contemporaneous news articles reported that in 1977 Jerry Holzner settled his claim for two thousand dollars. Even back then, that amount was a pittance. Hardly compensation for being tortured the way he was. It's pretty clear Jerry's lawyers didn't think he could stand up to the Federal Bureau of Investigation, which at the time accused Jerry of aiding and abetting Ian Holzner, which was a blatant lie to cover up the government's crimes. Plus, how attractive would Jerry have been as a plaintiff against the revered FBI of J. Edgar Hoover? Jerry's brother was a wanted terrorist. No jury of the time would've had sympathy for him. No jury would've awarded damages against the FBI. And damages couldn't begin to deter and punish the government for its behavior. An award of millions wouldn't have made the government flinch. The civil remedy simply isn't enough to vindicate due process. The *only* remedy consistent with the Constitution is to exclude this evidence here and now."

Gibson has closed his eyes, and his nodding has continued throughout my presentation. I fear his head movements are not an expression of approval, but a sign that I've lulled him to sleep.

But then he says, "How do you respond to that, Ms. Reddick?"

Reddick hops out of her chair and sidles over to the lectern. "I respond with the Supreme Court's opinion in *United States v. Payner*. The IRS set up a Bahamian banker. He was in Miami, transacting illegal business with some Americans. They arranged a date with a woman.

Except, she wasn't a woman—well, she was—but she was also an IRS plant. When the Bahamian was on the date, IRS agents broke into his hotel room, seized his brief case, got a locksmith to make a key, opened the case, and copied four hundred incriminating documents. What's relevant is that they didn't use the illegally seized documents against the Bahamian banker whose rights were violated, Your Honor, but against an American criminal named Jack Payner, who was convicted of falsifying his income-tax returns. Payner made the same due-process argument as Mr. Stern has made here, but the Supreme Court rejected it in a footnote. End of story, end of the defendant's motion." For emphasis she pounds on the lectern, but her fist catches the microphone and amplifies the noise into a sound that resembles a gunshot. The courtroom deputy starts, the marshals hop up, spectators gasp, a male voice lets out an elongated, "Whoa," and Lovely Diamond springs up out of her chair, whether intending fight or flight I'm not sure.

Judge Gibson and I are among the few people who don't react. I saw Marilee Reddick bump the microphone with her hand, so I knew it wasn't a bomb. Old Judge Gibson is probably crazy-fearless in the same way I'm crazy-scared.

"Calm down, people," he says. "False alarm. There will be no acts of terror in the courtroom of Carlton Gibson." He rubs his bald head as if it's a white-fringed crystal ball, foretelling a future of peace and harmony in his courtroom. Then he picks up his pen and points it at me. "So how do you respond to the US Attorney's argument about the Payner case? Isn't that *finito* for your motion, counsel?"

The nervous energy still buzzing in the air from the microphone mishap has a calming effect on me, maybe because for once I'm not the most frightened person in the room.

"Let's start with the *Payner* decision. Setting a crook up on a fake date is hardly the same as dangling an innocent man from a three-story-high balcony. But let's put the legalities aside for a moment, Your Honor, and talk about what really happened. You can only do justice when you focus on what really happened. During World War Two, the Italian partisans who captured Benito Mussolini hung him from meat hooks. That's essentially what the FBI did to Jerry Holzner. There are two differences: first, Mussolini was an evil fascist dictator, whereas Jerry Holzner was an innocent citizen; second, Mussolini was a corpse when they hung him by his heels, whereas Jerry Holzner was very much alive, such that he could experience the torture that our government inflicted on him. We don't allow such things in America, especially from people sworn to uphold the law. It's nothing short of outrageous for the US Attorney to come into court today and ask you to sanction such horrifying behavior. The evidence *must* be excluded under due process of law." I sit down. Like I always do after I finish an oral presentation, I feel unburdened, my stage fright washed away like a penitent's sins.

But I'm not finished. Judge Gibson asks, "Mr. Stern, give me the name of a case that says that such a defense survives the Supreme Court's decision in *Payner*."

He's looking for a legal basis for ruling in our favor. Keeping the map and fingerprint evidence out could mean freedom for Ian Holzner. I leaf through our legal brief, looking for some cases decided by a court in Philadelphia. While the judge waits for me, he uses his pen to tap out a rhythm on his legal pad. Five seconds later, he abruptly stands, points the pen toward the back of the room, and hollers, "You there! I will not countenance that! You're disrupting these proceedings. Stand up!"

At first I think that he's speaking to Lou Frantz. Then Moses Dworsky points his own thumb at his chest in the classic *Who, me?* gesture.

"Yes, you, sir. Stand up, I say!"

"I beg the Court's pardon, but I do not believe I have done anything to cause offense," Dworsky says.

"I know you," the judge says. His face turns a bluish-red, almost as if someone is strangling him—true lividity is part of a classic Carlton Gibson explosion. "You're the Elephant Man. Didn't I tell you years ago never to set foot in my courtroom again? Didn't I, sir?"

"My moniker was the *Eloquent Elephant*," Dworsky says, in a soft, deferential voice that still projects throughout the room. "I shrink neither from that appellation nor from my physical appearance. With respect, Your Honor, you had no right to bar me from a public courtroom. The idea offends all concepts of a transparent system of justice."

Although as Holzner's lawyer I wish Dworsky had never uttered the words, as an officer of the court I know that he's absolutely right about the law. Gibson's attempt to bar him does offend justice.

"*Amigos*, this is Moses Dworsky," the judge says. "A corrupt, radical lawyer who was disbarred for treason. Should've been imprisoned. Sir, what business do you have in my courtroom?"

Dworsky folds his hands in front of him deferentially. "I am now a private investigator, retained by attorney Parker Stern to assist him in the defense of Ian Holzner, wrongly accused by an unjust system. So my presence in the courtroom is not intended to annoy Your Honor, but rather to assist the defense team."

Judge Gibson looks at me, his rheumy eyes now round as obsolete half-dollar coins. "That man works for you?"

"Your Honor, he works for me in the capacity of—"

The judge uses his fists to lift himself out of his chair. "The defendant's motion to suppress evidence is denied. We're adjourned." He angrily tosses his pen on the desk, and when it rolls to the floor and his law clerk goes to retrieve it, he barks, "Leave it!" and exits the courtroom.

Lovely reaches over and clamps my forearm with her fingers. She doesn't have to say it—we were winning, and Dworsky derailed it. What did he do to anger Gibson so?

CHAPTER
TWENTY-ONE

Turning my back on a smirking Marilee Reddick, I sprint up the aisle in pursuit of Moses Dworsky, who's already skulked out of the courtroom. I get outside just in time to see him disappear into the men's room down the hall. As I wait, Lovely Diamond comes out of the courtroom.

"What a clusterfuck," she says. "Where the hell is he?"

"Restroom."

We wait another minute, then three, then five.

"Are you sure he's in there?" she asks.

"I saw him go through the door. And there's no other exit."

"Go get him."

"I'm not going to follow him into the bathroom."

"If you don't, I will, Parker."

She's in her battle stance—shoulders back, eyes shiny and hard as glazed ceramic. I start walking toward the restroom, but before I get there, Dworsky emerges. Lovely might as well be pointing a handgun at him, because when he sees her he raises his hands.

"Apologies," he says. "I am a man in his seventies who still has his prostate gland, which creates certain complications better left unarticulated."

"What did you do to upset the judge?" Lovely asks. "The timing was so bad it's almost as if you intended to . . ." That her voice trails off only intensifies the power of the accusation.

Dworsky's ears turn scarlet. The hair on the rims seems to prickle with electricity. "Miss Diamond, are you seriously implying that I sabotaged your hearing?"

"Did you?"

"Stern, are you going to stand by and let her make these unfounded and scurrilous accusations against me?"

While Lovely has been interrogating him, I've tried to determine whether I can read something in his expression or body language that would indicate that what happened was anything other than an unfortunate accident. I can't. His righteous indignation, his red-tinged ears, tell me nothing. I've never been much for trying to assess a person's truthfulness by observing his behavior. As a kid, I worked with too many good actors to believe that body language conveys anything about reality.

"Calm down, Lovely," I say. "We can't be sure that Gibson was going to rule in our favor."

"He absolutely would have."

"Where does this leave our relationship, Parker?" Dworsky says.

"Status quo," I say. "Unless you want to end it."

"Absolutely not. When I undertake a task, I finish it." He pauses, and when Moses Dworsky pauses, you can almost see the less-used punctuation marks—a colon or a dash—floating over his head like a comic-book caption. He raises an index finger. "Apropos of doing the job, I have arranged for you to have a meeting with Charles Sedgwick at the California State Prison at Santa Bernardina, his locus of incarceration."

"He refused to talk to me," I say. "What's changed?"

"He discovered that I was involved in the case. Believe it or not, Parker, I give you credibility. In my day I was really something. You are to meet him on Tuesday, November twenty-fifth, eight days hence. Is there anything else I can help you with? If not I must get back to the office."

"We'll see you back there," I say.

He turns and walks toward the escalator, swinging his arms like a happy-go-lucky bridge troll.

Almost immediately, Lou Frantz exits the courtroom and approaches us. I bristle whenever the man gets close.

"You have no idea why the judge got mad at him, do you?" he says.

"He appeared in the courtroom after the judge told him not to," Lovely says. "A gazillion years ago."

"Not even close," he says.

"Then why don't you tell us, Lou," I say.

"He was scratching his nose with his middle finger but then stopped scratching and left the finger against his nose. It kind of looked like he was flipping the judge the bird. Perhaps it was just an unfortunate coincidence, but I don't know."

"Right when the judge was going to rule?" Lovely asks.

"Come on, Lovely," I say. "You don't seriously think Dworsky intentionally sabotaged our argument by picking his nose?"

"Scratching," Frantz says.

"It was unlucky timing," I say. "And anyway, who would've thought the judge would notice?"

"I don't believe in coincidences," Lovely says. "Judge Gibson's irrational. All Moses had to do was catch his eye and give him the finger, and *kaboom*. I'm getting out of this hellhole. It reeks of injustice in here." She turns and marches down the hall, like a retreating soldier trying to maintain her dignity until the next battle.

CHAPTER TWENTY-TWO

The Santa Bernardina State Penitentiary is a maximum-security prison in Northern California, an hour's flight plus a forty-five-minute drive from Los Angeles. By the time I park the car and pass through the rigorous security check, I'm exhausted.

Charles Sedgwick is serving his life sentence for the Playa Delta murders even though he neither built nor planted the bomb but only carried out reconnaissance. During his trial, he refused to cooperate in his own defense, instead turning his back on the judge, chanting political slogans while court was in session, putting his feet on the table, and making obscene gestures at the judge and prosecution witnesses. Finally, the judge had enough of Sedgwick's outbursts and bound and gagged him just as Judge Julius Hoffman did to Bobby Seale in the trial of the Chicago Eight.

When I enter the noncontact visiting room, Sedgwick is waiting for me behind the Plexiglas-and-light-hardwood partition. On the upper wall a sign reads, *KEEP HANDS IN PLAIN VIEW AT ALL TIMES.* Although there are a dozen booths, I'm the only visitor in the room. Most of the inmates are in prison gangs, and according to the associate warden, an unaffiliated old radical like Charles Sedgwick is a target of violence. So he's housed in the PHU—the protective housing unit.

Sedgwick looks surprisingly fit for a man of sixty-six who's spent half of his life in prison. The photos from the sixties show him with a beard, but now he's clean-shaven, his face lined with the inevitable wrinkles. His gray hair is thick, and his cobalt-blue eyes have a manic intensity.

We simultaneously lift the intercom receivers. Before I can greet, him he says, "You're an attorney. When I first got in here, this was hell. But I was able to survive by acting as a jailhouse lawyer. No formal legal education, but my graduate work in philosophy was enough. When the street gangs and White Power groups took over the prison in the eighties, they had their own people, and even if they didn't, they weren't going to have anything to do with someone like me, a gay man, unaffiliated, politically on the far left. Since then, it's been worse than hell. You'd think they'd leave me alone at my age. But I hold on, keep a-keepin' on, because a change is gonna come."

If I'm not mistaken, he's quoting Sam Cooke, a 1960s soul singer.

"You think I'm crazy," he says. "And how can I blame you? Realize that I have no one to talk to most of the day, much less an intelligent man like yourself, so when I get this opportunity it's like a chocoholic in a candy store. I just talk. What I want to say is that the revolution is coming. It's closer than you think. It's being fueled on the streets and in the prisons, and finally we'll finish what we started back then."

He seems stuck more deeply in the Vietnam War era than Ian Holzner or even Belinda Hayes. The good news is that he wants to talk. Harmon Cherry would say that if a witness wants to talk, jump to the punch line.

"Who built the bomb that exploded at the Playa Delta Veterans Administration? Who planted it?"

"I've read enough law to know that's a compound question, counselor. But there's one answer. Our collective accomplished both."

"Your *collective* meaning the Holzner-O'Brien Gang?"

He laughs—no, snorts—so loudly that I have to hold the phone away from my ear. "Of course not. That's what everyone believed, and back then wasn't the right time to disabuse them of that notion. I studied Japanese political and business theory in college and learned to take the long view. Americans can't do that, especially now. Our *true* collective took the long view. We ignited a fire back then, and now we're fanning the long-burning flames."

I've had it with these geriatric propagandists. But you should never get angry at a professional recalcitrant witness. "Maybe you could explain something to me," I say. "You claim that you know what's going on in this country. In your day, nonviolent movements and the rule of law accomplished social change—the civil-rights movement, *Roe v. Wade*, feminism, the mainstream peace protests. Today, the right wing calls mainstream democrats Marxists. A woman's right to choose is in more jeopardy than it's been in decades. The gap between rich and poor is greater than ever."

"Exactly! The Playa Delta bombing, the activities of the Weather Underground, the actions of the SLA galvanized the reactionary forces in this country. The Christian right, the Tea Party, the Oklahoma City bombing, 9/11—all the result of our military actions. The capitalist regime had to become more violent, society had to become more polarized to crumble. With our acts of rebellion, which you mistakenly call violence, we set that in motion."

"Who's we?"

"*We* are the radical abolitionists who met violence with violence before the Civil War. *We* are the St. Petersburg Soviet of Workers' Delegates before the Russian revolution of nineteen-oh-five. *We* are Cuba's Twenty-Sixth of July Movement in the early fifties."

"Besides you, who are the members of your group?"

He affects a fright-film evil-genius grin. "You don't expect me to name names, do you, Parker? It's okay if I call you *Parker*, right? I haven't ratted out my comrades for almost forty years, so why would I do so when we're at the razor-sharp cusp of revolution?"

"Moses Dworsky said you'd talk to me. I assumed you had something to say. Or was having me fly four hundred miles and drive another sixty to visit you your idea of a joke?"

"I do have something to say. The revolution is coming, and all the traitors and the counterrevolutionaries will be called to account."

"What's that supposed to mean?"

"Ian will know."

"I can't just—"

"Ian will know."

"Is that the message you sent through Jerry Holzner?"

Another malevolent smile.

"Jerry has disappeared." Sometimes overstatement is an effective tactic.

He lets go of the receiver, which falls on the table with a loud clatter. He sits with eyes closed for a long time. For the first time during the interview, if it can be called that, he's abandoned his antiquated revolutionary persona. He now looks like what I suspect he is—a frightened, broken-down old man. He finally picks up the receiver and says, "Disappeared how?"

"He's been gone since the bombing of the LA federal courthouse. Not only have my people been looking for him, but so has the US Attorney. No trace."

"Is there evidence of foul play?"

"With all your revolutionary blather, you've been threatened, haven't you, Charlie? It's okay for me to call you *Charlie*, right?"

"Jerry's a good guy. Of all the people from back then, he was the only one who visited me. Not even my family has visited me."

"How did you even know him? I didn't think he was part of your gang."

"Holzner-O'Brien was a creation of the FBI and the press. People came in and out, secret alliances. But not Jerry. Jerry was a friend. A man broken by Vietnam and the FBI."

"From what I hear, you weren't really a violent man, Charlie. You were afraid to make a bomb, afraid to plant one. Sometimes fear lets us follow our moral compass when outside forces are trying to lead us astray. So, I don't think you're really part of this. I think you're feeding me all this crap because you're afraid of someone. Who?"

"Why don't you ask your father?"

"Belinda Hayes says he's innocent. She says Rachel O'Brien was the one who wanted to bomb the Playa Delta VA."

"Belinda was in love with Ian. Rachel banished her. You can't believe anything that woman says. She's a traitor."

"Who's threatening you, Charlie?"

"I'm the one who's the threat." He glances up at the ceiling, obviously remembering at long last that an inmate has no rights and that the security cameras and recording devices might be preserving his every word. "Well, not me. I wouldn't threaten anyone. I'm talking about the revolutionary movement, something bigger than myself. Even if I don't have the strength or the freedom to carry out the necessary acts personally, I serve. The Playa Delta bombing was the catalyst, and our movement continues."

It would be helpful to my cause if the prison authorities would use his violent rhetoric to pressure him to talk, to threaten to take him out of the PHU and put him back into the general population if he doesn't tell what he knows. But they're not going to do anything to help the Playa Delta Bomber.

I spend the next ten minutes asking questions about the group, but Sedgwick has steeled himself again and refuses to answer. Mercifully, the prison guard comes in and announces that my time is up. Without thanking Sedgwick, I start to hang up the receiver.

"Wait, Parker!"

I place the receiver against my ear.

"You won't forget to tell Ian what I said?"

"Yeah, counterrevolutionaries and Judgment Day. I'm sure he'll love to know you're thinking about him."

"He'll understand. Ian was a beautiful man once. Physically and spiritually. People change. I've spent my life in here trying not to change, but . . . Anyway, Ian was a beautiful man."

"And yet, you want me to convey a threat against him."

"*Threat* is your word not mine."

Before I hang up, I faintly hear the words, "You look like Ian, you know."

CHAPTER TWENTY-THREE

When I return late that nights, I find Holzner on the balcony, staring out at the ocean. The marine layer has rolled in, and though Marina Del Rey is less than a mile away, the thick fog has obscured the normally bright lights, so he's looking into a black gauze. I call his name, but he doesn't answer. When I reach out and touch his arm, he doesn't flinch, doesn't react at all. It takes several moments for him to turn and face me on his terms. I shiver, less from the chilly November night than from the look in his eyes. His gaze seems to be turned inward with a pensive ferocity—not in an introspective way that excludes the external, but in a way that beckons—a hypnotic, smoldering fire that hasn't yet burst into flames. Was this the look that so many decades ago allowed him to convince all too many young minds to answer his call to violence? Then again, maybe his eyes are only reflecting the outdoor solar lanterns from the neighboring condo.

I tell him about my meeting with Sedgwick and convey the threat about counterrevolutionaries and Judgment Day. He claims not to know what Sedgwick is talking about, insists there couldn't possibly be any new collective.

"Charlie has gone crazy in stir," he says. "Very sad."

I suspect Holzner knows more about Sedgwick's message than he's admitting. These people all seem to aggrandize themselves by keeping secrets at the expense of their own liberty.

"I think you're all crazy," I say, and immediately regret it, because by now I should be treating Holzner with the respect a client deserves.

"You're probably right, Parker. But it's the crazy people who get things accomplished, for good or ill."

"If you hadn't gone insane and set off bombs, hadn't been forced to suppress the truth about who you were, you wouldn't have lost everything."

"Have you found the truth about who you are?"

"Sure. I'm Parky Gerald, the kid with a fugitive-terrorist dad and a mythical-goddess mom."

He rarely smiles, almost never laughs—what's he got to laugh about?—but he laughs now. He goes inside the condo, and I follow. It's one of the few times I crave contact with him. I expect that he'll continue on to his bedroom, but he sits down in the wicker chair. I go to the couch. It's nearly midnight. Is it the fatigue that's made me receptive to him?

"Three weeks and one day until the trial starts," he says. "And after it ends, I'll be out of your hair. Out of everyone's. In prison like Charlie Sedgwick until they strap me to the gurney. Charlie really didn't do much harm, and they all know it. He should've been out years ago, like Belinda and Rachel. He's serving a life sentence for being pig-headed."

"Hayes admires him for standing on principle. Not you?"

"Sometimes you only accomplish things by abandoning principle. In any case, since the day I turned myself in, my conviction was a foregone conclusion."

"Not if I can just get Hayes to say what she told me before Moses Dworsky showed up."

"She won't return your phone calls. On the off chance she changes her mind, no one will believe her anyway. She condemned me in Rachel's trial, so everyone will know she's a liar."

"If she's well prepared, I might convince a jury that O'Brien intimidated her. She's certainly afraid of Dworsky."

"The truth is that Belinda Hayes was always a liar. So were we all. The difference was we did it for the cause whereas for Belinda it was pathological."

"Do you still trust Moses Dworsky?" It's a question I should've asked weeks ago. That I didn't shows that my abilities as a lawyer have suffered by virtue of being this man's son.

"Implicitly."

"Even though the day I met him he told me he thinks you're guilty?"

"Because of that kind of candor."

"And despite his belief that you manipulated women sexually in the name of revolution?"

"He's right. Sexual freedom was a revolutionary imperative, and I was a male in my twenties. The revolution didn't suppress testosterone levels, it raised them."

"Belinda Hayes turned on us because of Dworsky."

"And he explicitly told you to take Lovely to the meeting, but you insisted he attend. That one's on you. As for antagonizing the judge during the motion to suppress hearing, that's your black mark against Moses, isn't it?"

I nod.

"You told me yourself it was quite a long shot that the judge would look up at that very moment, and even less probable that he'd recognize Moses and react the way he did."

"This Sedgwick debacle today—"

"Moses got you the interview. It's not his fault you couldn't take advantage. So that's also on you. Maybe it's your loyalty I should be questioning."

That he's joking doesn't stop my cheeks from stinging with embarrassment. "If you want to win the trial, how about sharing what you really know about the Playa Delta bombing? We both know that you haven't done that—not even close."

"It's late," he says, rising to his feet. He takes three steps to the bedroom before turning around. "Sorry it turned out this way. I would've liked to have gotten to know you. I always considered Dylan to be my second chance to do the right thing. That was a selfish thought. There was only one chance with you, and I blew it."

It's one of the few things we agree on.

CHAPTER
TWENTY-FOUR

I spend Thanksgiving with Lovely Diamond, her son, Brighton, and her father, Ed. The kid admires me because not long ago I handled a libel lawsuit on behalf of the creator of his favorite video game. Ed, who's retired from his seemingly contradictory occupations of certified public accountant and director of tasteful, hardcore-pornographic motion pictures, delights in needling me about my career as a child actor and my current representation of, as Ed calls him, *a fucking nut-job murderer, and I don't give a shit that he is your father.* For once, Lovely doesn't talk about the case. Maybe it's because she reveres tradition, and her late mother wouldn't let the family discuss serious topics on Thanksgiving. I have a wonderful time mostly because it's relaxed.

When I get back home that night, I tense up as soon as I begin to climb the stairs to my condo unit. I perfunctorily offered to spend the evening with Holzner, but he knew I didn't want that, and I got the impression that he didn't want to spend Thanksgiving with me. His family was Jenny and Dylan and Emily, and I can't replace them. I can't even really be his newfound son because as his lawyer I'm always analyzing him, assessing his credibility, probing for truth. It was better for both of us that I wasn't there tonight. So why do I suddenly feel guilty about leaving him alone?

When I put the key in the lock and open the door, I realize that he wasn't alone at all. He's standing in the living room, frowning. Across from him is Emily Lansing, a teenager's know-it-all grin on her face.

"Hello, brother," she says when she sees me. "Happy Thanksgiving. I've come to live with you and my dad."

"It's not happening," Holzner says. "You're staying with Ernesto."

"I'm not going back to that asshole's house. He's a right-wing fascist. He and Theresa are talking so much shit about you all the time in front of me that—"

"Clean up your language, young lady," he says like some sitcom-fuddy-duddy dad who doesn't understand the younger generation. He glances at me and shakes his head, and for the first time I can see his paternal side, his eyes weary with exasperation and concern. He hugs himself more tightly, as if he has to keep his arms and hands in check because he doesn't know what they'll do if they're freed.

"He doesn't want me anyway," she says. "I'm only still there because of Theresa."

"What do you mean?"

"I kind of lost my temper with him."

"How lost your temper?"

"I might've thrown a plate of chicken and black beans against the wall."

He makes a full three-hundred-and-sixty-degree turn, apparently trying to control his own temper. "Jesus, Emily."

"He was talking crap about you. I was sick of it."

Holzner looks at me as if I could possibly help him with this. I don't have an inkling.

"What about school?" he says.

"I'll enroll here, or you can homeschool me. You have nothing to do until the trial. After that you'll homeschool me the rest of the year."

"Emily, after the trial . . ."

"You'll homeschool me some more," she insists.

"You can't stay here," I say. "There's no room, but more importantly—"

"I checked it out already, and I can sleep in your study or whatever," she says. "Cool place by the way. I wish I would've known you before. I love the beach, and you're so close to it."

"But more importantly, you can't stay because this is basically your father's jail cell."

"That isn't true, either. It's your house, and you're my brother, and he's my father, and no court will say that I can't stay here." She walks over to Holzner. "Come on, Dad. Ernesto Alfaro is a jerk. All the Alfaros are jerks."

"Dina's your friend."

"*Was* my friend. She's just like her father. Do you know that Ernesto keeps calling you a murderer? I'm not staying there. I'll run away."

"You're being ridiculous, Em."

"Yes, I will. I only have to be a runaway for three months until I turn eighteen and can do whatever I want. It'll be easy to be a runaway for three months. You managed to do it for forty years, right?"

I can't tell if her stance is feigned or real. "You can stay if you don't get in the way," I say, surprising myself. But why not? It's Thanksgiving, I've had a lot of wine to drink, and I've just spent the evening with a happy family.

She runs over and throws her arms around me. "Thank you, thank you, thank you, Parker!"

I give her an awkward, belated hug in reply. Only when she draws away do I see the new tattoo on her forearm: The words *Free Ian*, emblazoned over a clenched fist.

When Emily notices me looking at the tattoo, her cheeks turn rosy, but she holds up her arm proudly. "I got it because of what Ernesto and the others were saying about our father. And I'm not sorry."

Holzner shakes his head, conveying that contrary to what I first believed, Emily Lansing hasn't held it together at all: that he's failed her as a father, just as he failed me; that she doesn't belong here, but she has no place else to go; and that he can no longer protect her. Yes, a parent's shake of the head can convey all that.

CHAPTER
TWENTY-FIVE

The following Monday, I walk into the office to find Eleanor Dworsky chatting with her son, Brandon. She gives me a big wave, but he looks away.

"Brandon is a machinist," Eleanor says. "Unusual in this day and age. Someone who's actually a member of the dying proletariat class, as Moses calls it. Unemployed, unfortunately. That's more typical. So he had to move in with his mother and stepfather. We live in a small two-bedroom condominium that's almost too small for Moses alone. He's a large man. Brandon wants the job he wants, won't take anything beneath his skill level. Unfortunately, that job doesn't seem to exist. Don't you think he should look for something else, at least temporarily, so he can move back out?"

He walks over to the reception chair and slouches.

"Not my business, Eleanor," I say.

Eleanor dons her reading glasses—she always appears birdlike, but these glasses make her look like a hen. She riffles through a stack of Post-It notes and reads from one: "Lovely is in the back and anxious to see you."

"You needed a written reminder to tell me that?"

"I'm a record keeper and a note taker. It's the way I keep Moses organized. Oh my heavens, you should've seen him before I came to work with him."

"Is he in?"

"Down at the Hall of Records on an icky child-custody case." She hands me the Post-It. "So you won't forget to talk to Lovely."

I start toward Lovely's makeshift office, but Eleanor calls me back.

"Moses wanted me to ask you how the meeting with Charles Sedgwick went," she says. "It's been almost a week. I almost forgot to ask you because I didn't write it down."

"Nothing to tell. It was a total waste of time. Sedgwick won't talk."

"What a shame. After you traveled all that way."

I go to Lovely's office. She's at her desk, sipping coffee from a disposable cup and devouring one of those Etiwanda donuts that Eleanor is always buying.

"What's up?" I say.

Though I spoke quietly, she shrieks, "Damn it, Parker, don't scare a girl like that." She slides the pink pastry box toward me.

"Why are you eating those?"

"Because they taste good?" She leaves the "duh" unspoken.

"Eleanor said you wanted to talk to me."

"Oh, yeah, yeah." She wriggles her finger at me so I'll close the door. When it's shut, she says, "Belinda Hayes. She wants to meet with you."

"Where did you see Belinda Hayes?"

"This morning at The Barrista, at about seven a.m. She was looking for you, skulking around, all nervous. I recognized her, and when I approached her she tried to leave, but when I told her who I was she relaxed."

"What did she want?"

"She said there was a misunderstanding, that she'll only talk to you or Ian."

"She's not going to talk to Ian."

"She made me promise I wouldn't tell a soul other than you. She said you should just go up to her house, she's almost always there. Don't call her. She's worried that her phones are bugged and that her e-mails are being hacked by the NSA."

I try to tamp down my excitement at the thought that Hayes has changed her mind about testifying for us.

"I'll go out there right now," I say.

"I'm going with you. You blew it last time."

"Let's go," I say. "Just let me take the lead in the interview."

She picks up the doughnut box and follows me to the reception area. As I pass, Eleanor holds up a pad of Post-It notes and says, "Any messages before you leave?"

CHAPTER
TWENTY-SIX

I exit the 210 Freeway and drive through the shabby flatland and up the canyon road to Belinda Hayes's house. I park the car, and Lovely gets out and hurries onto the porch. She knocks on the door, and when Hayes doesn't answer, she starts pounding on it.

"If she's home you're going to scare her to death," I say.

She goes to a window and tries to peek through the bars. "There's nobody in the living room. Or, not that I can see."

"Calm down, Lovely."

"I can't calm down. The coffee and the sugar from all those dough-nuts made me hyper."

"Sugar doesn't really do that."

"It does when I'm about to get my period. Just let me do this." She goes to the side of the house and looks in both windows. "Clothes and crap on the floor, and the bed's unmade. This place is a shambles. These windows are so filthy dirty. It's like she's erected an ecumenical religious shrine in a pigsty. This is our key witness?"

"She lives better than most witnesses in these criminal cases. At least her address isn't a cell-block number."

"Not anymore." She goes to the back fence, which is made of termite-ridden redwood. She tries to open the gate, but it's locked. When she rattles it, there's a growl and a deep bark, and a dog of uncer-tain breed, but undoubtedly part pit bull, batters a loose wooden fence slat with his snout and barks ferociously. I didn't notice him when I last visited. Hayes has obviously gotten him for protection.

"Jesus," Lovely shrieks, running back to me so quickly that for a moment I think she's going to jump into my arms.

"You've never been afraid of dogs."

"I'm afraid of those kind. They should be illegal."

"He's just doing his job, and you're annoying him."

She walks over to my Lexus, retrieves the pastry box from the front seat, takes out a doughnut, and leans against the car while she devours it.

I look up at the sky, blue except for some translucent white cirrus clouds fanned out like harrowing specters from some psychedelic cartoon. In the low foothills of the North Valley, the sun heats by compression, and the morning is becoming warm—a typical December day in Los Angeles.

The dog won't stop barking.

I spend the next twenty minutes trying to get my smart phone to work, but there's no cellular connection this far up in the foothills. I read an e-mail I received earlier from an ex-client, asking for some advice about a dispute with his insurance carrier. At the moment, insurance law seems a lot more appealing than biding my time on a dusty hill, waiting to meet with a sociopath on whose testimony my entire case depends.

"Let's get out of here, Parker," Lovely says after another twenty minutes. "It's hot. And that dog is driving me crazy."

"We're here. Give her five more minutes."

She takes the box of doughnuts from the hood, opens the lid, and offers me what's left—about a third of a greasy apple fritter. When I decline, she says, "Who would've thought? You're eating healthier than I am." She reaches in and picks up the fritter, but puts it down again when Hayes's white van pulls into the driveway.

"Finally," Lovely says.

Hayes gets out of the van and shields her eyes from the sun—oddly with the hand in which she's carrying her keys. She looks in our direction, takes three steps toward us, and vomits, the gross bile spewing out like rank water from a broken sewer line. Only when I process that Hayes has crumpled to the ground like bent cardboard and only when I recognize the metallic rat-a-tat of gunfire do I realize that she didn't vomit, but rather has been shot in the head, and that what I took for half-digested gazpacho and kale salad was blood and brain matter and skull shards splattering onto her driveway.

The gunfire continues, its location uncertain because of the echo off the canyon walls. Bullets shatter the driver's side windows in my Lexus, which means we can't even think about trying to get into my car and driving away. As I reconnoiter the terrain, I'm brave and analytical. Then I feel a violent tug at my belt and hear Lovely Diamond say, "Get down, Parker! Under the car!" She's already taken cover, and I fall to the ground and try to fit myself next to her. My body is so heavy, my breathing is so labored, that I feel as if I've been transported to an alien planet with ten times earth's gravitational pull.

We lie pressed to the ground, eye to eye but strangely unconnected. Perhaps we're instinctively focusing only on individual survival. I try to shake off the stupor so I can get on with the process of reasoning. Holzner's advice about overcoming fear suddenly makes sense—think only about your immediate priority, which for me is staying completely covered by the car chassis.

I reach into my pocket, grope for my cell phone, and punch in 9-1-1. No ring, no response. I check the screen. No cellular connection in this god-forsaken place. From the way the bullets are hitting my car, I guess that the sniper is somewhere on a hill overlooking the front of Hayes's property. Or so it appears until gunfire starts coming from the opposite direction.

"Why are they trying to kill *us*, Parker? We can't identify them."

"They don't know that. And anyway, they're not sure of what Hayes told us."

"Unless she's the collateral damage and we're the targets."

The firing is so rapid and ceaseless that the area sounds like a battle zone—or what I imagine a battle zone sounds like. Although the nearest neighbors are at least a quarter of a mile away, they must hear the shooting. At least, I hope so. I think of my half brother, Dylan, who fought and died in a real war. How could he have had the courage to volunteer?

"Why don't they just come down and finish us?" Lovely says, as much to herself as to me.

She's prescient, because as soon as she finishes uttering those words, the sound of gunfire seems closer.

"They're making their way down to us," I say and begin crawling out from under the car.

"Jesus, what are you doing?"

"I'm going to use the phone in the house. I need her house keys."

"That's insane. You'll never be able to get them without being shot."

"If they're coming for us, we have to do something." I manage to squeeze out from under the car, and only then do I realize how the gravel and rock have bruised and scratched my face and body. Mimicking actors in soldier films, I use my elbows to scoot across to where Hayes is lying, keeping low and close to my car and hoping the house is high enough to block a shot from the sniper to my right. When I reach the exposed gap between my Lexus and the van, I pause. I'm breathing hard, sucking in valley dust. I refuse to look at Hayes until it's absolutely necessary, but her prone body never escapes my peripheral field.

Two crows swoop down and alight near the corpse. When I bang my fist against the fender of the Lexus to scare them away, Lovely screams, curses at me, and implores me to get back under the car. One of the crows flies off, but the other gives me an indifferent look and takes a tentative peck at Hayes's head. I turn away and force myself to sprint from behind the Lexus to the van, and that sudden movement frightens the hideous bird.

I command myself to focus only on getting the house key.

On hands and knees, I duck-walk over to Hayes. She's lying on her left side. The top half of her face is an unrecognizable mishmash of macerated flesh and bone. Her mouth is frozen in a subrictal frown more reminiscent of those crows than a human being. She's still holding her keys. It takes no effort to open her fingers and take them. The *death grip* metaphor is a myth, at least for Belinda Hayes.

Three bullets clang off Hayes's vehicle.

"Stay put, Parker!" Lovely shouts from under the car.

I keep low, take a deep breath, and prepare to dash across the driveway to the front door. Then I hear sirens. Thank God for those neighbors, whoever they are.

The shooting stops abruptly. Behind me, where the shot that killed Belinda Hayes came from, there's a growl of an engine, possibly a motorcycle, but I'm not sure, and I'm not going to stand up to find out. Whatever that vehicle is, it flees the scene with Doppler aggression. Moments later, above Hayes's house where the second sniper was located, a blue Mercedes-Benz speeds down the hill on a street or fire road I didn't know existed. I catch a quick glimpse of the driver before the window is rolled up. Though I can't be sure, she looks like the Sanctified Assembly's head Celestial Warrior, Mariko Heim.

CHAPTER TWENTY-SEVEN

After ninety-seven minutes of interrogation, the cops finally let Lovely and me drive out of that horrible gravel graveyard in a rental car that Lovely's firm arranged for us, a newer-model Lexus (she insisted on that make). The cops impound my bullet-ridden car as evidence. She and I don't speak for a long time. When I glance over, I see that she's crying.

"It was ghastly," I say. "But we'll be okay. We *are* okay."

She tries to speak but can't through the tears. She's so distraught that I pull the car over to the curb, cut the engine, reach over and take her hand.

"I'm sorry, Parker," she whispers.

"For what?"

"I'm so sorry."

"I don't understand. You have nothing to be—"

She draws away and leans back against the door. When she composes herself, she says, "How could I have told you to go?"

"You have a son to worry about. And you were right. My life is unpredictable. And I'm certainly not father material."

"I was so stupid. I almost lost you. We almost lost each other." She looks at me with plaintive eyes, revealing a rare vulnerability.

I start the engine and drive until I see a building called the El Rincon Inn, a white structure with an adobe-tile roof and red doors and trim.

"It's not the Ritz," I say. "It's not even a Radisson."

"It doesn't matter. I've missed you so much."

I finally cut the engine, get out of the car, and open the passenger door for her. She extends her hand as if we were royalty just arrived at a lavish ball. With arms around each other, we walk into a lobby. Whatever the desk clerk thinks of our tattered and bloodied professional clothing, she asks no questions.

We find the room, and help each other forget the horror of the day, remind each other that we should never have been apart.

—⚛—

The Los Angeles Police Department received this message five hours after the murder of Belinda Hayes:

Subject: Communiqué #2
To: Chief Pig of the LAPD
From: JB

Judgment Day has dawned. The turncoat Belinda Hayes sold out the revolution. Her body lies moldering in the trash heap of betrayal.

We demand the immediate dismissal of charges against Ian Holzner, the release from political prison of Charles Sedgwick, the dismantling of the Gestapo NSA, the immediate withdrawal of all U.S. Military troops from Afghanistan and the Persian Gulf region, and the imprisonment of the capitalist billionaires that control this country.

We and the oppressed people of the world will continue to exploit the vulnerabilities of Imperialist America until our demands are met. We are numerous. Free Ian!

~JB

The homicide detectives assigned to the investigation insist that Holzner is JB, that he somehow masterminded the killing from my apartment—never mind that he's under house arrest or that he has no cell phone or access to my laptop, which I've password-protected and carry everywhere. Never mind that I don't have a landline. Never mind that the killers tried to murder me, his own son.

As for Mariko Heim, I think she showed up at The Barrista so she could determine whether I'll reveal the Assembly's dark secrets. She's not interested in exposing them, as she claimed, but in hiding them. She probably concluded that I pose an ongoing risk. I know things and won't hesitate to reveal them if ever the time is right. As for my identification of her, the cops say she has an alibi—what that is, they won't reveal. The Sanctified Assembly must be covering for her. They also maintain that if Lovely and I were the targets, we would've been dead long before Hayes arrived home. Maybe so. Or maybe Heim and her people weren't in position in time to do that.

Now, two days after the shooting, my mother and I sit in my living room, arguing with each other. As soon as we raise our voices, Ian and Lovely escape to the balcony. He leans against the wall, his usual gymnast's posture replaced by slumped shoulders, a bowed spine, and stiff legs. He hasn't been working out for the past couple of weeks—no multiple sets of push-ups, pull-ups, and squats. Men his age lose muscle tone quickly—another milestone to look forward to if I live as long as he has, which after the shooting at Hayes's house is highly debatable. Lovely, wearing black slacks and a vanilla wool turtleneck, follows him outside and assumes an identical posture. They both stare silently out at the ocean, the morning sun shimmering off the surface like burnished chrome. Emily Lansing has been remanded to the care of the deputy US Marshal downstairs.

Why are my mother and I arguing? I want the revered Quiana to put pressure on the Assembly elders to stop protecting Heim, but she won't do it.

"You just have to snap your fingers," I say.

"For the tenth time, it doesn't work that way anymore. It's not nineteen ninety, Parker. There's a new generation of devotees who—"

"But you're the Assembly's patron saint."

"Stop the sarcasm. It's disrespectful; I'm still your mother. And after all these years it's gotten tiresome. You're forty years old."

"It's not sarcasm, it's the truth. Bradley Kelly became a god, and you've been canonized, on your way to sainthood. Which gives you the power to force Heim to come clean. I don't get why you're afraid of her."

"I don't even know how Heim was able to . . ." She actually throws her hand to her lips as if to clamp her mouth shut.

"How she was able to what, Mother?"

"I can't. It's forbidden to discuss Assembly business with a nonbeliever."

"So you'll just let them get away with trying to murder me, is that it, St. Quiana?"

"Parker, please stop!" She covers her face with clawed fingers. She's suddenly so overwrought I fear she'll rake her eyes with her fingernails. Holzner rushes inside and puts an arm around her. She buries her head in his chest and begins to cry.

"Let's assume you're right about this sainthood business," he says to me. "That's why the Catholic Church only confers sainthood on the dead. It's too fucking hard for the living." All the while, my mother's shoulders are heaving, her face still glued to him. For the first time in years, I'm in the presence of the mother who raised me, vulnerable and sad.

Lovely comes inside, and my mother immediately straightens her spine and places her hands in her lap like a royal at a state function, an act all the more ludicrous because her cheeks are shiny with tears.

"Here's how I see it," Lovely announces. "Parker, you really don't know what you saw. Maybe you saw Heim, maybe you didn't. The car was a hundred yards away, speeding from the scene, and your gut was ripped with fear and your brain muddled with adrenaline shock. That's certainly how I was feeling. Not to mention the sight of Belinda Hayes with her brains lying on the driveway and you had to pry her keys out of her hand. No way you could get a positive ID on the driver. And like the cops say, we were sitting ducks long before Hayes arrived." She turns to Harriet and points a finger at her. "You got Parker into this, you got me into this, and now you won't help us get to the bottom of it. The Assembly's celestial attributes—*fortitude, rectitude, beatitude*, right? You're not showing any of those. How come?"

"You're impertinent," Harriet says, but her haughtiness is belied by the slight catch in her throat.

Lovely places her left hand on a hip and bends her opposite leg like an impatient mother.

Harriet glances at me and then folds in on herself. "I can't do it."

"Can't do what?" Lovely says.

"I can't control Heim. She became a devotee and somehow rose with the speed of a comet. I don't know how she managed it in what, three or four years? Except for the fact she's ruthless." She looks at me sadly. "I'm not the woman I used to be, Parker. The Assembly values youth—Brad and I wanted it that way, because we were young, truly believed that if you drank of the Celestial Waters you'd never age. Bradley died, so he never aged. But me . . ." She places her hand on Ian's shoulder. "Ian returned to my life, reminded me of youth, but it's all just a memory. Parker, you're forty years old. How can I have a child who's forty years old?"

Parents always seem old to a child, so their aging process is meaningless until the child himself begins truly to age. That's happening to me, which is why I can finally recognize how time has taken its toll on Harriet Stern.

"How did he find you?" I ask. "You're not the easiest person to locate."

"Not that difficult if you know where to look." This isn't an explanation, it's a rebuke. I start to follow up, but she crosses her arms tightly, like a complicated high-security lock tumbling closed. Pursuing this question will get nowhere. But I wonder—did they somehow keep in touch over so many years despite the risks to both of them?

"Heim is out to get you, Mother," I say. "You know that, don't you?"

Her hands are still in her lap, no longer folded but knotted tightly. "I've known that for some time. I have no idea whom to trust anymore. What is she after? My position?"

"She came to The Barrista and asked me about Ascending Sodality."

She gasps and covers her mouth with her hand. "How would she know about that?"

"There are a lot of children of the original founders who are now adults," I say. "Someone was bound to talk. You either repress sexual abuse or you think about it every day of your life. I'm surprised no one has gone to the cops. Maybe she wants to use it to expose you, or maybe she's after me because she thinks I'm finally going to tell what I know."

"Do you even know what we're talking about?" Lovely asks Holzner.

"I don't pry into others' secrets," he says. "I'm a lot of things, but I'm not a hypocrite."

"Were you part of that?" Lovely asks my mother.

"Never! I was the one who stopped it."

When Lovely looks at me for confirmation, I nod, because it's literally true. Not that my mother stands on high moral ground. She claims she didn't know, but I don't think that's possible.

"I have to tell you this, Parker," my mother says. "I don't know if Mariko Heim was one of the people shooting at you. But she's quite capable of it. A big reason she's risen in the hierarchy is that she's promised to rid the Assembly of its enemies. You, my son, remain high on that list."

There's a knock at the door. When Lovely answers it, Emily walks inside and whines, "Aren't you guys done yet? It's freezing out there, and that marshal guy won't even tell me who he thinks tried to kill Parker and Lovely."

CHAPTER
TWENTY-EIGHT

It's less than two weeks before trial, and the government has added a new witness to its list, a man named Ilan Goldsmith. They identify him as an FBI informant with knowledge of Ian Holzner's role in the bombing of the Playa Delta VA. Holzner doesn't recognize the name and neither does Moses Dworsky. After a day of digging, Dworsky comes up with the pseudonym Goldsmith used in the 1960s and '70s—Secretary Cracknamara.

"Cracknamara was a knockoff of the more famous General Hersheybar, who was himself a parody of General Hershey, at the time the odious head of the Selective Service, sending innocents to fight in a useless war," Dworsky says. "Cracknamara would dress up like former Secretary of Defense Robert McNamara and engage in performance art at antiwar rallies. He was amusing, I will concede, but he also appeared to be emotionally disturbed, though harmless enough. I thought he was schizophrenic, to be quite candid. And all this time he was an FBI informant. A *rat*, in the vernacular. Quite brilliant, really. I am sure no one suspected. Evidently our client was snookered."

Unfortunately, Dworsky hasn't been able to find Goldsmith, and we can't determine what Goldsmith will actually say at trial because the US Attorney has been vague. I'd complain to Judge Gibson about Marilee Reddick's ambush tactics, but he hasn't been favorably disposed to our side since the day Dworsky scratched his nose in court.

Emily's presence in my home makes it hard to talk to my client. She doesn't go to school—Holzner is indeed studying with her during the day. But she sometimes goes out at night, where, she won't say. I know nothing about parenting, but if she were my daughter, I'd want to know where she's going, almost eighteen or not. Tonight, though, her absence is convenient, because I can ask Holzner about Ilan Goldsmith. When I tell him that *Secretary Cracknamara* is on the government's witness list, he turns ashen.

"Jesus," I say. "What?"

After several false starts, he says, "It was three, four months before the Playa Delta bombing. We were deep underground by then. Belinda Hayes showed up at our apartment one night with the secretary in tow. Cracknamara was no fool, he only played one. He was resourceful, dedicated to the cause, or so I thought. And he was a source of two things we needed—dynamite and drugs."

"An FBI informant provided you with explosives?"

"Evidently."

"What did you tell him?"

"See, that's the problem. This time, he was supplying us with drugs. We all took LSD. Me, Belinda, Rachel, Cracknamara—everyone except Charlie Sedgwick, who was afraid. I'd had so many beautiful trips, but this one was ugly. I remember dropping the acid, and as soon as I came on to the drug, I went to the bathroom and looked at myself in the mirror. My face, my entire body resembled a Jackson Pollock painting, all spattered with dots and dribs and streaks. It was beautiful, until the streaks began to wriggle and slither and became maggots that were eating my flesh, consuming my eyes, crawling up my nose, devouring my lips." He closes his eyes and shudders. "Even all these years later my stomach churns when I think about it. Whenever I dropped acid, I'd write myself a note beforehand just in case, reminding myself that it wasn't real, that it would end soon enough. This was the first time I resorted to the note. But when I read it, the letters were poisonous snakes and scorpions that tried to bite my face. Everything went a fiery red, and I thought I was blind, thought I'd gone insane—I was insane. Charlie got me through it, believe it or not, by starting one of his discussions on political theory. But during it ... well, I might've said that the Weathermen had copped out when they stopped targeting human beings after the Greenwich Village townhouse explosion. It was all talk, a way to fight off the disgusting insects that were gnawing at my flesh, to silence the hideous guitar-amp feedback squealing through my brain. If Charlie hadn't started talking politics, I would've jumped out the window. Debating Marx and Mao and Marcuse was normal for us. He was trying to give me *normal*."

"What did the others say?"

"Who knows? It's been forty years."

"But you remember the incident."

"The bad trip. The debates were always the same. Charlie would've said it was wrong to harm civilians, though cops and military personnel were fair game. I might have said something about a VA being an appropriate target. Belinda would've agreed with me because she got off on the thought of violence. Ironic that all these years later, she died violently."

"Was O'Brien there?"

"Rachel wouldn't have said anything. She was cautious around people who weren't in the collective, like I should've been. Cracknamara might've been a fellow traveler, but he was an outsider. We talked through the night and into the morning and then stopped, and I remember my head resting in Charlie's lap when finally I came down. So I don't really know exactly what I said."

"You've consistently maintained you didn't have anything to do with Playa Delta. If that's true, how is it possible that he's going to implicate you in the attack? Is he going to lie, like you said Hayes and O'Brien did? It's hard to believe that they're all liars."

He gapes at me, and now I'm the one who feels that insects are probing at my flesh, because I finally understand. "You *might* have mentioned targeting a Veterans Administration building because that's what you were planning to do," I say. "*You* were planning it."

He exhales audibly and rubs his eyes with his thumbs, almost gouging them. His hands flop hard into his lap. "I called it off, Parker. We all agreed."

"You've been lying to me all this time."

"Not about the important part. I had nothing to do with it. I don't know how it happened."

"Why did you call it off?"

"Because I realized it was murder, not revolution."

"That's not what you'd believed for years. What changed your mind so abruptly?"

"Maybe your birth had something to do with it."

"Why don't I buy that?"

He shrugs, then stands up and stretches his arms toward the ceiling. "Wish I had a cigarette."

"I didn't know you smoked."

"I don't. Not in forty years."

"Why didn't you tell me this before so we could've prepared for it?"

"I never suspected Cracknamara was FBI, and I certainly never thought that he'd come forward and implicate himself."

"I'm your lawyer. I need to know all the facts."

"No matter what you think of me, you're my son. You've been in my mind for all these years. A father doesn't want to disappoint his son."

"Who the hell cares what was in your mind? Your imagination had nothing to do with my reality. What's real is you were doing these awful, violent things until I was, what, a year, a year-and-a-half old? While I was learning to walk and talk, you were playing guerrilla soldier."

Despite my harsh words, I know he cared about me. There's the photo taken in the forest when I fell and scraped my knee. At least at that moment, he was my father. More than that, when the photo was taken, he would've been on the lam for six months. Long gone, one would think. Yet he apparently risked his freedom to see my mother and me. Harriet took a huge chance, too. She was harboring a fugitive and could've been charged as an accessory to murder.

Who shot that photo? I haven't bothered to ask my parents. I'm sure they won't tell me.

CHAPTER TWENTY-NINE

Wednesday, December 17, 2014: to the day the thirty-ninth anniversary of the Playa Delta bombing, and the first day of trial in *United States v. Holzner*. Judge Gibson's morbid scheduling joke. As a defense lawyer, I would ordinarily welcome a trial at Christmas time, because jurisprudential folklore has it that jurors are more likely to show mercy during the holiday season. Not in this case. Their tendency will be to give a gift to the bereft families of the Playa Delta dead.

Ian Holzner insists on wearing prison garb and shackles again, and this time Marilee Reddick doesn't object. Why would she? JB's courthouse bombing and the murder of Belinda Hayes have changed everything. The media has speculated that Holzner is an unreconstructed terrorist who orchestrated the acts of violence while under house arrest. It's just fine with Reddick if Holzner looks like a jailbird and a mass murderer. And that's just what he looks like, dressed in those clothes. Never mind that earlier this year he became eligible for Medicare.

What I do know is that despite his bravado, Holzner is frightened. When the marshals arrived at my condo unit this morning to transport him to the courthouse, he was trembling. He calmed down only when Emily came into the room. It's not that surprising, really. He spent a lifetime running from this day. Is that why he insists on coming to court in shackles and jail garb? Not to make some political statement, but to fend off the fear? I'd find something ignoble in his attempt to play detached warrior except for one thing: I, too, am a man who's scared and trying not to show it.

Reddick and I stand before Judge Carlton Gibson, who's just called our case. Before we attorneys can state our appearances, the judge begins admonishing Holzner, who once again refused to rise when Gibson entered the room.

"That's your freebie, Mr. Holzner," the judge says. "You *will* stand when the prospective jurors are brought to the courtroom. Once we impanel a jury, you *will* stand when they enter and leave the courtroom. If you don't, you'll be ejected, and you'll observe the proceedings in a tiny room we have for recalcitrant witnesses. I call it the *poco* room. Some describe it as a cell. I hope you're not claustrophobic. *Comprendes?*" Without waiting for a response, he gestures toward the marshal. "Bring them in, *ándale!*"

It takes twenty-five minutes before the marshal comes back with the jury pool. The prospective jurors file in, seated both in the jury box and in the first three rows of the gallery, which have been kept empty for them. There are about fifty people in the pool, some with their eyes on Holzner, but just as many staring at me, as if I'm the one who's on trial. Maybe that's a good thing—I've got a better chance of winning the jury's sympathy than he does.

"This is a murder case," Judge Gibson says to the jury. "It'll last some weeks, into January, so kiss your Christmas good-bye. Don't give me any phony excuses. You have a civic duty as American citizens to serve, and you'll do so unless I say so." His voice crackles with irascibility. The vast majority of judges treat prospective jurors with patience and compassion. The court process is unfamiliar and intimidating, exponentially more so when the trial involves a notorious defendant charged with murder. Gibson is the only judge I've ever seen who's shown hostility to prospective jurors.

"Whoever believes he or she can't serve on the jury, raise a hand," he says.

No response at first, but then a few hands timidly go up. The judge twists his mouth in disdain and calls on each. A young woman owns a flower shop and almost tearfully says her business will suffer if she's absent for more than a week; a well-dressed blond says she's a working actress and has an audition at Paramount next week; an elderly woman says she's hearing impaired and can't serve effectively; an even older man says he's caring for his wife, who suffers from Alzheimer's disease.

The only person Gibson excuses from jury duty is the actress.

"I'm going to ask each of you some questions, and you better answer truthfully," he says. "It's your obligation." If we were in state court, the lawyers would get a chance to ask the questions—*voir dire*, it's called—but here in federal court it's the judge's show. Both sides have suggested questions in writing, but the judge is free to ignore them.

The clerk calls fifteen names. Those who were chosen take seats up front. After asking some basic background questions—age, marital status, occupation, level of education, relationship to the parties or lawyers—the judge says, "Those of you who've heard about this case, or what's called the Playa Delta bombing, raise your hands."

The only one who doesn't raise his hand is a young man with long, oily brown hair, an acne-scored complexion, and an indelible smirk. He says his name is Joey. He's twenty-eight years old, an animator for an Internet company that creates online commercials.

"How could you possibly not know about this case, sir?" the judge snarls. "It's all over the news." It occurs to me that Judge Gibson hasn't peppered his language with Spanish words in the presence of the jury pool. I suspect half the man's eccentricities are contrived. I worry about the other half, however. I also worry that those people who are ultimately selected as jurors will so despise Carlton Gibson that they'll take their wrath out on Ian Holzner.

"I don't follow the serious news," Joey says. "No gossip or talk radio, either. Bad Karma."

The judge conducts a scathing cross-examination, asking whether Joey knows who the president is (*of course he does, but he didn't vote, all politicians are the same*); whether he's heard of 9/11 (*horrific, he was in the ninth grade, and his school in Salinas, California, was closed for a week*); and whether he's aware that there were wars in Iraq and Afghanistan (*that's why I don't listen to the news, all that stuff is such a downer*). He avers three times over that he could weigh the evidence objectively and apply the law (*that's what it's all about, Judge, right?*).

"I like this guy," Lovely whispers.

"Not me," I say. I don't believe he hasn't heard about this case. I think he's trying to look unsullied so he can wheedle his way onto the jury. People who do that have an agenda, and Joey's might be to convict a terrorist and sell his story to the tabloids.

Judge Gibson lets Joey remain in the box and moves on, asking the others what they know about the case. He excuses several jurors for cause. One persistent woman says she'll hold it against Holzner if he doesn't take the witness stand, even though that's his right. Two others say they already know that Holzner is guilty. One guy proclaims that Holzner is a worse terrorist than Osama bin Laden.

After exhausting the subjects of Playa Delta and Ian Holzner, the judge says, "How many of you know that defense counsel Parker Stern used to be Parky Gerald?" Almost everyone raises a hand, including Joey.

After four hours of voir dire, the judge's scalp is blotched and beaded with sweat, and he's continually rubbing his eyes.

Because this is a death-penalty case, each side has twenty peremptory challenges—the right to get rid of a prospective juror without cause. Marilee Reddick uses her challenges to excuse a college history professor who ran for office on the left-wing Peace & Freedom Party ticket, numerous others who oppose the death penalty, and four people who appear to be of Middle Eastern descent. Lovely reminds me that it's illegal to excuse prospective jurors solely based on their ethnic background. But I don't object, because I'm not beyond a bit of stereotyping myself. I worry that jurors who might be the victims of government profiling will want to convict Holzner as a way of affirming their loyalty to America.

We use our peremptory challenges to excuse an arrogant woman with a law degree who gave up her practice to raise her children but boasts about rising to leadership positions in five different school organizations. I ding seven people whom Judge Gibson should've excluded because of hardship, but didn't—not because I feel sorry for them but because they're more likely to want to convict quickly so they can get back to their normal lives. I excuse a scowling retired police officer who never once stopped glaring at our side of the table. I eliminate a number of others who say they're active in their church or whose looks I simply don't like. Jury selection brings out the worst in lawyers, forces them to evaluate people based on gross stereotypes. It's a dark business that's essential to justice.

I have one peremptory challenge left, and I intend to use it on Joey the animator when I hear the clinking of chains. I lean back so Holzner can whisper in my ear. I'm not pleased that the prospective jurors will believe he has control, but it would be worse to ignore him in front of the jury.

"You'll be stuck with whoever they put in that box next," Holzner says. "We could do worse."

"I don't think so."

"He's a crap shoot, I know," he says. "But this whole trial is a crap shoot. Worse. Let's go with him. I feel it's right."

Harmon Cherry once advised me that when I'm in a court of law the only instinct that matters is my own, but I stand and say, "The defense accepts the jury as now constituted."

So we have a jury. There's a grad student who's pursuing a PhD in comparative literature at UCLA; a retired mechanical engineer who enlisted in the naval reserve to avoid being drafted and sent to Vietnam but who ended up being stationed at the Da Nang air base; a recent college graduate and former fraternity president who's interning at a stock brokerage house; a woman in her late thirties who heads up a law-firm marketing department; a middle-aged man who works as a checker at Costco; the flower-shop owner and the elderly man whose wife has dementia, both of whom wanted off the jury but both of whom seem fair-minded; a voice-over artist who serves as a volunteer cantor at his synagogue; a showroom designer for an upscale furniture store; a house-wife from the San Fernando Valley; a driver for Federal Express; and Joey the animator. There are five women and seven men, three Hispanics, two Jews, two African Americans, and one person of Persian descent. A jury of Ian Holzner's peers? Decidedly not. The only way Holzner could get a true jury of his peers would be if all the newly sworn jurors had misspent their formative years bombing government buildings.

The judge asks the jurors to stand and raise their right hands, and the clerk has them swear that they'll "true deliverance make" between the United States and Ian Holzner and "a true verdict render." Judge Gibson, all warmth and smiles now, welcomes the jurors to his courtroom. As he's instructing the jury not to discuss the case among themselves or with third parties, there's a clanking of chains, and I experience maybe a dozen tachycardial heartbeats when I sense Holzner standing behind me. Lovely draws in an audible breath. When I glance back, it seems as if he's about to speak, but instead he respectfully clasps his hand in front of him and waits for the jury to stand, and then we all rise and watch as the jurors file out.

Judge Gibson nods. "Counsel, be ready to give your opening statements after the lunch break." He pushes himself out of his chair and dodders off the bench and into chambers.

All morning, I've avoided looking at the gallery—Holzner's advice to focus on the task. So far, along with the drugs, it's staved off the stage fright. But now habit takes over, and I turn and watch the spectators file out. There's no Moses Dworsky. He announced he wasn't showing up before I had to tell him not to. There's Lou Frantz, my advisor who hasn't advised at all. The last person to file out is Mariko Heim, who before she leaves the courtroom looks over her shoulder, scowls at me, dons her sunglasses while still looking my way, and only then walks out the door.

One person who doesn't file out is Emily Lansing. She stays in her seat in the front row, and thankfully her *Free Ian* tattoo is covered by a conservative cotton dress shirt that makes her look like a future candidate for an MBA.

CHAPTER THIRTY

Marilee Reddick hasn't sat down since Judge Gibson recalled the jury, and when the judge nods at her, she brushes back her short gray hair, pulls at the hem of her black woolen jacket, and brushes imaginary lint off her black skirt. If it looks like she's dressed for a funeral it's because she is. She goes to the lectern. I spoke last so, she has to lower the microphone to lip level. Like the best advocates, she doesn't use notes.

"Ladies and gentlemen, December seventeenth, nineteen seventy-five, was a beautiful day in Playa Delta, California. At least, it started out that way. The temperature was seventy degrees. The sun was shining, the sparrows and blackbirds were singing. There were some puffy white clouds in the sky. One of those wonderful Southern California winter days when you can go outside in short sleeves. A day very much like today. That morning, Elaine Smith kissed her husband Jack good-bye—it was his day off from the car dealership—and escorted her eight-year-old, Julia, and six-year-old, Talia, onto the school bus. It was Elaine's thirtieth birthday, and later that night they planned to go out to dinner. Perelli's Restaurant, a real treat, because they didn't eat out much, couldn't afford it, especially not a fancy steakhouse. Afterward, they were going to stop at the lot on Ballona Boulevard and buy their Christmas tree. Before they left for the bus, little Talia, as small children often are, was fussy. She said she didn't want to go to school, begged Elaine to skip work so the family could celebrate her birthday early. How do we know this? Because Jack remembers this, and so does Julia and so does Talia despite her young age at the time. They remember it to this day because it was the last morning of Elaine Smith's short life."

"Elaine worked at the Playa Delta branch of the Veterans Admin-

183

istration, the federal agency that takes care of those who have served in our country's military. At three twenty-nine in the afternoon, just after Elaine and her coworkers gathered in a conference room for a combined staff meeting/birthday celebration, a massive explosion sent shockwaves throughout Playa City. People in homes six blocks away felt the blast. At first, they thought it was an earthquake. But it was a lethal bomb that killed Elaine Smith, along with Russell Breen, a devoted husband and father and Little League umpire who loved children; and Floyd Corwin, a grandfather and World War Two veteran; and Lucille Gomez, a forty-two-year-old single mother of three children under the age of fifteen. The only reason these people died was because of hatred. Ian Holzner, an avowed antigovernment radical, hated the United States government so much that he took innocent lives to further his perverse objective, which was to foment revolution that would bring down the American government.

"What did Holzner do after he perpetrated this cowardly, heinous crime, ladies and gentlemen? He ran like a coward. And he lived as a normal citizen for forty years, enjoying the benefits of freedom that the Constitution of the United States guarantees, while the families of the Playa Delta dead grieved, while those families knew that justice hadn't been served."

Opening statements are supposed to foreshadow what the evidence at trial will show. But good openings tell a story, and Reddick is telling a marvelous one. I could object to her comment about justice not being served—it's argument, not evidence—but that would only underscore how powerful her words have been so far.

She talks about Holzner's stable background and nurturing and devoted parents who, despite limited income, gave him not only everything he needed but also everything he wanted. He had a nice home in Playa Delta's top-flight school district; Little League and gymnastics to develop his athletic skills; piano and guitar lessons; even magician's lessons when he showed an interest and aptitude for *prestidigitation*— that's actually the word Reddick uses. He excelled at all academic subjects, but particularly science. "That's how he learned at a young age to blow things up," she says.

She knows more about my father than I do.

Keeping her left hand in contact with the lectern so she can technically abide by the rule that a lawyer can't leave the podium, she walks toward the jury and almost blocks my view. "As a high-school senior Ian Holzner developed an abiding hatred of the United States government. His excuse was that his older brother, Jerry, was drafted into the army, served in Vietnam, and came back with post-traumatic stress disorder. Unfortunately, many Vietnam vets returned that way, but their families didn't turn to violence." She recounts Holzner's transformation from potential Olympic gymnast to antiwar demonstrator to radical bomber. "The defendant went to the University of California, Berkeley, on a scholarship. It was there he began building his radical network. There's an irony in that, ladies and gentleman. UC Berkeley was then, as it is today, a public institution. So the defendant developed his dangerous radical theories and his terrorist tactics while enjoying the largesse of the very government he despised."

She goes on to describe the genesis of the Holzner-O'Brien Gang, lists the many bombings the gang took credit for, and reads from some of their most inflammatory communiqués: *The pigs are our enemies, but we will find their soft, fat underbellies; we will combat American genocide with guns and bombs and rocks and bottles and feet and hands— if we must, with our lives; America's genocide won't end until its streets are bathed in blood; with an eye for an eye, a tooth for a tooth, a life for a life, we shall avenge the state-sponsored murders of innocents and revolutionary heroes if it takes fifty years.* And then the most damning: *Our bombs will reduce our bourgeois-diseased hometowns to rubble.*

"Playa Delta, California, was Ian Holzner's hometown," Reddick says. "On December seventeenth, nineteen seventy-five, he essentially reduced his hometown to rubble. The bomb exploded in a second-floor lavatory. It was built to kill and maim the maximum number of humans. It was timed to explode during working hours when a crowd of people would be in the building. The amount of explosives exceeded that in any other bomb that went off during the volatile nineteen sixties. The bomb, constructed out of pipe, was packed with ball bearings inside and three-and-a-half-inch carpenter nails taped to the outside. Nails and ball-bearings aren't necessary to inflict property damage. Their only purpose was to kill and maim human beings. The forensic evidence will show that the only person capable of building a sophisticated bomb like that was Ian Holzner. The *only* person."

Over the next two hours, Reddick provides a litany of evidence against Holzner. No one else could have built the bomb. Gladdie Giddens saw him on the scene. His fingerprints were found on bomb parts seized at the gang's apartment. Ilan Goldsmith heard him boast about the forthcoming operation. Holzner's flight to avoid prosecution shows a guilty mind.

"You'll hear testimony about how Holzner compared himself to communist guerrilla fighters, to international revolutionaries spreading the gospel of Karl Marx, even to the patriots who fought against the British for American independence," she says. "But Holzner wasn't a soldier. A soldier doesn't target mothers and wives and older men and civilians. Ian Holzner is a terrorist, plain and simple." Violating the rule that she has to stay at the lectern, she maneuvers herself next to me and to the side of Holzner and points an accusing finger at the back of his head. "Members of the jury, the evidence will show that *this* man planned the crime that took so many lives, that *this* man assembled the bomb that killed and injured so many, that *this* man planted the bomb that caused such horrible death and destruction. The evidence will show that *this* man is guilty of multiple murders." Each time she says the words *this man*, she jabs her tiny index finger at him. Using the silence that seems to hold the courtroom in a bear hug, she stands and looks at the jury, undoubtedly making eye contact with each one. Finally, she concludes by saying, "When all the evidence is in, we will have proved beyond a reasonable doubt that the defendant, Ian Holzner, is guilty of murder in the first degree." She sits down.

I fear that the judge will call a recess that will permanently etch Reddick's words in the minds of the jurors, but to his credit he says, "Counsel for the defendant."

I stand and expect the glossophobia to level me, but it doesn't, and

I realize it's because suddenly, with all my being, I don't want my father to be a terrorist, and if he is a terrorist, I don't want him to die by lethal injection. Whoever he is, whatever he's done, I don't want to lose him again.

CHAPTER
THIRTY-ONE

I move behind Holzner and rest my hands on his shoulders. He recoils but then relaxes. I'm not surprised by his response. Though we've lived in the same place for many months, this is the first time we've touched.

"This is my client, Martin Lansing. For the past forty years, he's lived an exemplary life, working as a mechanic in an auto-repair business. He's obeyed the law and raised a family. Marty has made a parent's ultimate sacrifice—his son was killed in Afghanistan while serving in the United States Marines." I almost said his *only* son.

Reddick jumps out of her chair. "Objection. Irrelevant and argumentative and violates a court order."

She's right. Earlier in the proceedings, the judge ruled that we couldn't mention Dylan Lansing's death. A ruling *in limine* lawyers call it. I had no intention of flouting the order until I stood up to speak.

"Get up here now, counsel!" Judge Gibson says. He could hold me in contempt. So be it.

Reddick and I, along with the court reporter, approach the bench. The courtroom deputy presses a button on a control panel, and white noise is transmitted over the speaker system so the jurors and spectators can't hear what we're saying. When I get close, the judge glowers at me and wipes his bald head with his palm.

"If this wasn't a murder trial I'd hold you in contempt in front of the jury," he says. "But like your client, you get one gimme. Get back to the lectern and do your job right."

I start to retreat, but Reddick says, "Your Honor, I'd request that you instruct the jury that Mr. Stern has violated a court order."

"Go back to your table now, Ms. Reddick," the judge says. "I've got it covered."

The judge instructs the jury that Dylan Lansing's military service is irrelevant to the trial and should be disregarded. Of course, the jurors can't do that, not really. The question is whether the fact of Dylan's death will humanize Ian Holzner.

When Reddick is settled in her chair, I say, "Members of the jury, four months ago, Martin Lansing walked into the office of the Federal Bureau of Investigation, identified himself as Ian Holzner, and surrendered himself to law-enforcement authorities. He did this because he believed that, after all these years, he could get a fair trial in an American court of law, that a jury of his peers would judge his case fairly and justly. That's not how a guilty man behaves. Ian Holzner—Martin Lansing—is *not* guilty of the crimes alleged against him, and the prosecution will be unable to prove otherwise beyond a reasonable doubt."

As Reddick did, I move as close to the jury as I can without losing contact with the lectern. I try to look each one in the eye, but the designer from the furniture store and Joey the animator look away, an ominous sign.

In a candid moment, a severely bipolar former colleague of mine once told me that the transition between sanity and mania is seamless, that though some part of her rational intellect realizes what's happening, it's precisely that rational part that seems to be The Other, incongruous with her psychological makeup. It's the crazy that seems perfectly natural, she says. That's not true for me. I know that what I'm about to do is completely insane.

"Members of the jury, the evidence will show you why Ian Holzner, a young man of extraordinary gifts and good fortune, would in the era of the nineteen sixties give up everything to fight injustice. And injustice is exactly what he was fighting. The Vietnam War might be a historical footnote to our generation, but when Ian Holzner was a young man it was systematic government-sanctioned slaughter of this country's youth. Over fifty thousand young Americans died for nothing, and that's what he wanted to stop. Ian's own brother, Jerry Holzner, served in Vietnam and was never the same when he came back. The president of the United States sent American troops into Laos and Cambodia in clear violation of the law. It was the act of a dictator, not the leader of a democracy. National Guardsmen fired without provocation on Ohio college students and killed four. The police met nonviolent protest not with the rule of law, but with violence. The FBI created something called COINTELPRO—a so-called counterintelligence program—a covert, illegal operation that trampled on the rights of American citizens, including..."

Marilee Reddick half stands to object, probably because she thinks I'm about to tell the jury that COINTELPRO tortured Jerry Holzner. Not yet.

"Including the defendant, Ian Holzner. When a government acts illegally and violently, it loses its legitimacy, and some citizens will turn to violent resistance. Just like the American revolutionaries did in response to British oppression at the dawn of this country's creation." I look at no one but the jury, but I can sense Lovely Diamond's shock, Marilee Reddick's outrage, Judge Gibson's disdain, the media's bewilderment at my comparing the Playa Delta Bomber to an American patriot.

"And so, Ian Holzner protested against the government's illegitimate activities by building bombs. No one denies that. He used them, not to kill or maim, but to commit acts of vandalism—blowing up statues and toilets in federal buildings and powerful corporations. These were acts reminiscent of the Boston Tea Party, when early-American radicals dumped British tea into Boston Harbor to protest oppressive taxation. Did you know that the patriot and later US President John Adams called that particular act *majestic and sublime*? Vandalism in the cause of liberty forms the foundation of this country."

"One thing Ian Holzner did *not* do, ladies and gentlemen—he did *not* build the bomb that exploded at the Playa Delta Veterans Administration, and he did *not* plant that bomb. And let's be clear—I'm not just talking about reasonable doubt. Although it's not our burden, we intend to prove Ian Holzner's innocence."

I sit down, having flouted all the rules of opening statements. The government has the burden of proving Holzner's guilt beyond a reasonable doubt, but I've just shifted that burden, promising to establish his innocence. I've set myself up for failure. Neither did I attack the prosecution's evidence as I'd intended. Nothing about Gladdie Giddens's fading memory, the lack of DNA evidence, the government's failure to list the surviving members of the Holzner-O'Brien collective as witnesses. Worse, I've placed my own credibility at risk by lauding Holzner's radical activity, a position I know to be untenable. I don't care. I had to get the jury's attention. If they're listening, there's still a chance; it's when a jury ignores you that you've lost. Just before I finished speaking, the designer from the furniture store and Joey the animator looked me in the eye. They were listening.

After court, Lovely and I go back to the office to debrief Moses Dworsky. When Eleanor overhears me describe my opening statement, she says, "I don't care if you're making it up to save your client, it's disgusting." Lovely lets slip that Lou Frantz texted her and says that he believes Holzner's best defense is now ineffective assistance of counsel. But Dworsky nods somberly and says, "Very astute of you, Parker. There was no other choice than to shake up the trial, and the best way to do that is become a contrarian. I made a career out of being a contrarian. Strangely, it invests the lawyer with a peculiar type of credibility. If nothing else, the jury has become aware that you have testicles."

I get back home that night to find that the sliding door to my balcony is open. Holzner is standing outside, looking toward the ocean, his elbows leaning on the redwood barrier. Emily is standing next to him, hugging herself for warmth. The air is heavy with salt, and it's so foggy that the dew prickles my cheeks.

When I join them, he says, "So you made me out in court to be a modern-day Samuel Adams, when the truth is I was promulgating the principles of Marx, Lenin, Trotsky, and Mao. The jury will never believe you."

"Moses Dworsky thinks it's a wise strategy."

"What do you think, Parker?" Holzner asks.

"I think that I'll only be able to formulate a wise strategy when you finally come clean about what you really know about the Playa Delta bombing."

As one, they turn their backs on me and resume their father-daughter study of the Pacific coast at night.

CHAPTER
THIRTY-TWO

Unlike me, Marilee Reddick must've gotten to bed early. Her dark eyes gleam with energy, and the ambient light gives her unique silvery hair a radiant sheen. Yesterday was a good day for her.

It was *not* a good day for me. I spent so much time preparing for this upcoming court session that I didn't get into bed until three in the morning, didn't fall asleep until an hour after that. My eyes are bleary, and I keep clenching my jaw from the morning's caffeine overdose. I didn't take my antianxiety meds for fear that I'd pass out on my feet. I'll be okay, because I'm asking questions, which are the verbal darts and arrows a lawyer uses to attack the witness. It's not scary when you hold the weapons.

Judge Gibson takes the bench and instructs Reddick to call her first witness.

"The United States calls Dr. Earl Yellin." Another advantage that Reddick has—she can legitimately call herself *The United States*.

A short, slender man with short, white hair gets up from a seat in the second row of the gallery and makes his way to the witness stand. His relaxed gait signals that he's been in a courtroom before—many times. He looks to be in his early to midseventies. He's wearing a dark-brown suit, yellow-and-tan silk tie, and gold-plated wire-rim glasses with bifocal lenses.

"What do you do for a living?" Reddick asks.

"Until my retirement five years ago in two thousand and nine, I was a forensic examiner in TEDAC. That's the Terrorist Explosives Unit of the Federal Bureau of Investigation."

Reddick asks Yellin to summarize his background. He testifies that he graduated from the University of Michigan in 1961 with a bachelor's degree in physics and received his doctorate in mechanical engineering from USC in 1964. After a year in academia, he joined the FBI's Los Angeles office as a forensic examiner specializing in firearms, but later transferred to the Explosives Unit, where he examined evidence associated with bombings. He conducted examinations of improvised explosive devices and their respective remains. He's testified in court approximately five hundred times. In the course of his career, he was promoted to Senior Analyst and was involved in starting TEDAC, which focuses on terrorist attacks.

"You're aware of the bombing of the Playa Delta Veterans Administration that occurred on December seventeenth, nineteen seventy-five, are you not?" Reddick asks.

"I was the physical scientist in charge of forensic analysis of the bomb scene."

"And what did you conclude?"

"It's all in my report, which I finished in February of nineteen seventy-six. The bomb maker who assembled the bomb that exploded at Playa Delta constructed it out of a twelve-inch section of common steel water pipe, which was packed with dynamite."

"Was there anything distinctive about that?"

"Not in and of itself. But evidence at the scene traced the dynamite back to a road-construction company in Temecula, California, inland from San Diego. The company had been burglarized and several boxes of dynamite stolen."

"What, if anything, is the significance of the dynamite's source?"

"The Holzner-O'Brien Gang had taken credit for a number of bombings on the West Coast. The dynamite used in those attacks was traced to the same source in Temecula. No other radical group of the era used dynamite from that source."

"What else did you learn?"

"The bomb was detonated with a blasting cap fashioned out of a spent gun cartridge, mercury fulminate, potassium-chlorate powder, gunpowder, and sulfur." He launches into a narrative using technical terms that probably no one can understand. But arcane scientific jargon impresses a jury.

"Was there anything significant about the detonator?"

"Yes and no. The detonator was characteristic of the Holzner-O'Brien Gang's bombs, but also of other groups' bombs. In fact, that kind of detonator is used to this day." Yellin is an effective witness, building credibility by conceding an insignificant point.

"Was there anything else distinctive about the Playa Delta bomb, in your opinion?"

"Whoever constructed the bomb custom-built a time-delay, special-purpose electrical circuit, which included safety devices and indicators. This would ensure the safety of the bomb maker and shows a high level of expertise in engineering. It was again characteristic of devices used in bombings for which the Holzner-O'Brien Gang took credit."

"So the bomb maker was protecting himself while he was intending to kill others?" Reddick asks.

"Objection," I say. "Argumentative."

"Overruled," the judge says. "The man's an expert."

"Dr. Yellin, in your professional opinion, did you conclude that the bomb that exploded at the Playa Delta Veterans Administration was intended to take human lives?" Reddick asks.

"Absolutely."

"On what did you base that opinion?"

"The device was wrapped in tape embedded with nails and ball bearings. A bomb maker doesn't use nails and ball bearings to damage property. You don't need them to destroy property because the concussive force of the blast will do the trick. The sole purpose of packing a bomb with nails and ball bearings is to kill and injure people. The IED at the Playa Delta VA was what we call an antipersonnel device—an instrument of mass murder."

Reddick pretends to thumb through her examination notes, but she's really letting the jurors digest the information. "Last question, Dr. Yellin. You undertook your investigation in nineteen seventy-six. Are you simply basing your testimony on reading what you wrote in your report so many years ago?"

"I have a vivid memory of those events. I didn't even have to look at the report. The attack on Playa Delta was one of the most destructive terrorist acts of the nineteen sixties and seventies. It was callous, because it targeted civilians and perhaps former military personnel who were in need. The deaths were tragic, and the injuries from the nails and ball bearings and shrapnel were horrific. The construction of the IED was highly sophisticated. When I arrived at the crime scene, the injured and two of the dead were still there. It was the first time in my career that I'd seen the actual victims. You never forget anything like that. Never. Of course, since then the world has gone to hell in a hand basket." He shrugs in resignation, underscoring the evil that humans can do. The evil that he implies Ian Holzner did.

"Do you have an opinion as to which individual constructed the bomb that exploded on December seventeenth, nineteen seventy-five, at the Playa Delta Veterans Administration?" Reddick asks.

"Yes. Ian Holzner."

"Why?"

"The only group that made that type of bomb was the Holzner-O'Brien Gang, and the only person in that group capable of constructing such a sophisticated bomb was Ian Holzner. He was the only one with the engineering background required to do it."

"Your witness, counselor," Reddick says to me.

Before standing up, I tilt my head toward Lovely, hoping she knows something I don't.

She covers her face with a legal pad so the jury can't read her lips and whispers, "That guy killed us."

When you don't have facts in your favor, a cross-examination has to become performance art, meaningful in form no matter how lacking in substance.

"There were a lot of groups who used explosives in the early nineteen seventies, were there not, Dr. Yellin?" I ask.

"Yes, there were."

"The Weathermen, Black December, the Jewish Defense League all used bombs in terrorist attacks."

"They did, but they never—"

"You've answered the question, Dr. Yellin. Just eleven days after the Playa Delta bombing, there was an explosion at La Guardia airport in New York that killed eleven people and seriously injured seventy-four others?"

"That's correct."

"To this day, that crime remains unsolved?"

"Yes, but we think it was a Croatian terrorist group that was behind it."

"There was also speculation at the time that some other terrorist group bombed La Guardia?"

"Correct."

"Not the Holzner-O'Brien Gang, though."

"They were a West Coast group."

"No one took credit for the Playa Delta bombing, did they?"

"True, but three key members of the Holzner-O'Brien Gang served prison terms for their role in the bombing."

There are actually guffaws from some spectators, which cease when Judge Gibson slaps his hand on the desk.

"My question to you, sir, was whether anyone took credit for the Playa Delta bombing," I say.

"No."

"And that was not typical of the Holzner-O'Brien group, was it?"

"No. They liked to brag about their crimes."

"But not taking credit was what happened at the La Guardia bombing a week-and-a-half later?"

"I guess you could say that."

"Eleven days was more than enough time for someone to drive across country from LA to New York, if they kept driving?"

"I suppose so. Traffic isn't in my area of expertise."

A few more titters.

"And you're aware, Dr. Yellin, that sometimes radicals of the nine-teen sixties and seventies moved in and out of collectives, changed allegiances, would work together on discrete operations?" Though I'm pointing a finger at him, Yellin doesn't react. There's no change in expression, no shift in body position. I've rarely seen anyone so comfortable on the witness stand.

"That *truly* isn't within my area of expertise," he says.

"So you don't know one way or another if the people who bombed La Guardia were also involved in the Playa Delta bombing?"

"There's no evidence of that, and all the evidence points to Holzner-O'Brien."

"But you don't know for certain?"

"The only evidence that we developed was that the bomb bore the earmarks of Ian Holzner's bombs."

As I make absolutely no progress substantively—actually, as I lose ground—I speak in an accusatory tone, shake my head in disbelief, turn my back on the witness, pretend to check my notes, and now raise my voice.

"Wasn't that your job, Dr. Yellin?"

"What was, sir?"

"To follow *all* leads even if they contradict the one that you want to push?"

He crosses his legs and bends forward, the first tiny fissure in his solid demeanor. "Yes, sir. Which we did."

"Isn't it the job of law enforcement to *exclude* suspects in pursuit of the truth?"

Reddick stands and objects that I've interrupted Yellin's answer.

"Overruled," Judge Gibson says. "The witness is a professional. And you'll have a chance to question him on redirect, Ms. Reddick."

"And you didn't exclude the possibility that the people who bombed La Guardia Airport in New York also had involvement in the Playa Delta bombing, did you?" I say.

"I don't know how I could've done that."

"And you don't know whether the perpetrator of the La Guardia bombing had the ability to make a bomb like the one that exploded at the Playa Delta VA, do you?"

"I do not know that."

Word games. Cosmetics. I'm getting him to agree with me about facts that don't really mean anything, hoping the jury believes the questions to be meaningful.

"DNA evidence can be preserved after an explosion of the type that occurred at Playa Delta, can't it, Dr. Yellin?"

"That's correct. There's no such thing as vaporization, even with a powerful explosion like that."

"And sometimes hair and blood and clothing can survive an explosion of the type that occurred at Playa Delta?"

"Yes. It's common with a pipe bomb that such material can get caught in the threads of the pipe."

"And you didn't find such material at the Playa Delta crime scene?"

"We did not."

"So there was no DNA or hair or blood left at the scene that would put Ian Holzner at the scene?"

"Correct."

"Fingerprints can also be preserved despite an explosion?"

"That's also true. As I said, no such thing as vaporization here."

"And you didn't find Ian Holzner's fingerprints at the scene?"

"Not Ian Holzner's."

I feel Lovely tense behind me, but I'm with her. We're hoping that Yellin is being evasive, that his answer is what we lawyers call a *negative pregnant*—a partial denial that actually admits a fact. Or maybe he's just being precise. Either way, it's time to go fishing.

"You said you didn't find *Ian Holzner's* fingerprints at the scene," I ask. "What about someone else's fingerprints?"

He inhales and closes his eyes briefly, aware of his error. I wonder if he would've made the mistake if he were five years younger, if he were still working for the Bureau.

"We did find a set of partial fingerprints."

"On remnants from the bomb parts?"

"No on . . . there was a silver earring left at the scene. It was pretty much intact. We were able to get a print." He's trying to maintain his composure, but he knows that he slipped up. I'm trying to keep my composure, too. The US Attorney never disclosed this evidence to us, even though she was constitutionally obligated to do so.

"Did you ever identify the person who left the fingerprint?" A lawyer should rarely ask a question on cross that he doesn't know the answer to, but now there's no risk, because I know that it wasn't Holzner.

"We were never able to identify the fingerprint."

"Could you tell the gender from the fingerprint analysis?"

He chuckles. "You can't even do that today, though there are new techniques that claim you can."

"Was it a woman's earring? Not the type that a man might wear?"

"Probably so, because it was long and diamond shaped. But it's not totally clear."

"In nineteen seventy-five, dangly earrings for males weren't exactly a fashion trend, were they?"

Lifting only her backside off the chair—a mocking recognition of the rule that a lawyer must stand when making an objection—Reddick says, "This is getting ridiculous, Your Honor. The witness isn't an expert on fashion or popular culture."

"That's not a legally correct objection, Ms. Reddick," the judge says. "But it's an accurate one. Get this over with, Mr. Stern."

"Do you know where the earring is now?" I ask.

"It's been misplaced over the years. The FBI doesn't lose things, but sometimes it takes a while to find them."

"Dr. Yellin, in nineteen seventy-five, did all federal employees have to be fingerprinted?"

"Yes. By an executive order issued by the president in the nineteen fifties."

"And in the course of your investigation did you check to see if the fingerprint on the earring belonged to any of the employees of the Playa Delta VA?"

"We couldn't match the fingerprint to anyone who worked at the Veterans Administration."

"And would you agree that few visitors had business on the second floor of the Playa Delta Veterans Administration in December of nineteen seventy five?"

"That's correct. The second-floor offices were strictly for government personnel."

I nod sagely. It's always nice to put my childhood acting lessons to some use. "I have no further questions."

Lovely tugs at my sleeve, and again we're thinking the same thing. I ask to approach the bench, and the judge nods.

"Your Honor, I move for a mistrial under *Brady v. Maryland*," I say. "The government withheld exculpatory evidence from us, namely the earring."

"It's not exculpatory," Reddick says. "It could've been dropped by anyone, weeks earlier."

"The explosion took place in the men's restroom," I say. "Why would there be a woman's earring in there?"

"The witness said it wasn't clear whether it was a woman's or not."

"Oh, come on, a long, dangly earring in nineteen seventy-five was worn by a man?"

"It could've been dropped by a cleaning person or just a woman who couldn't wait for the women's room to become free."

"Okay, okay," the judge says. "The motion is denied without prejudice to renewing it at the end of the case."

I might not have succeeded in getting the case dismissed, but what I do have is a straw man—or straw woman—whom I can use as a springboard to create reasonable doubt. It's far more than I had before Earl Yellin took the witness stand. Sometimes gifts are bestowed by the most unlikely of benefactors.

But my happiness is short-lived, because Marilee Reddick says, "The United States calls Gladdie Giddens."

CHAPTER
THIRTY-THREE

Those of us in the courtroom suffer in agonizing silence as a hunched-over Gladdie Giddens shuffles forward to the witness stand, leaning on a walker and sliding her damaged leg as best she can. Her struggle to climb the single riser to the stand is epic, made all the more poignant when she refuses the proffered assistance of her caretaker, a US Marshal, two AUSAs, and Marilee Reddick herself. She's so small, her head barely clears the wooden bar. She's put on lipstick, and her threadlike brown hair has been styled, but the attempts at glamor only make her look like a decrepit lawn gnome. If the jurors don't hate me now, they will when I'm through questioning her: she's the one eyewitness who can place Ian Holzner at the scene of the crime, and I have to decimate her on cross.

The clerk asks her name.

"Gladys Giddens," she says in that surprisingly youthful voice. "But all my life I've been known as Gladdie."

"Good morning, Ms. Giddens," Reddick says.

"Good morning, ma'am."

"If you need anything or get tired, you'll tell me?"

"Yes, ma'am."

"Please tell me what happened on December seventeenth, nineteen seventy-five."

"I worked at the Playa Delta VA. We helped disabled veterans. Not just from Vietnam, but any veteran, going all the way back to World War One. My title was administrative officer. A fancy name for an office manager. I was really the department den mother, responsible for making sure everything ran smoothly. It was December seventeenth, nineteen seventy-five, Elaine Smith's thirtieth birthday. Elaine was a vocational counselor. The night before, I baked a carrot cake for her. I was known for my carrot cake, but I haven't made one since that awful day."

"What happened that day?" Reddick asks.

"Why, we were going to have the birthday cake after the three-thirty staff meeting. One of my chores was to round up the meeting attendees so we wouldn't start late. Heavens, that was a tough job. So at about three fifteen, I began herding people into the conference room. I went first to Elaine's desk. She hugged me and thanked me for arranging her birthday celebration. She picked up some papers and went off to the meeting. I went over to Russell Breen's desk. Russ was another one of the counselors, a sweet man but always tardy. So I reminded him that our meeting was about to begin. Then I stopped by Lucille Gomez's desk. She wasn't there, so she must have already gone into the conference room. Floyd Corwin had to finish some notes for the meeting, but his typewriter had run out of ribbon. Floyd was hope-less with the machine. So I helped him change the ribbon." Sometimes digressions like this can make an old person seem senescent, and so not credible. Not so with Giddens. One of the female jurors already looks to be on the verge of tears.

"After that, did you ever see Elaine Smith alive again?"

"No ma'am."

"Did you ever see Russell Breen alive again?"

"No, I did not."

"Did you ever see Floyd Corwin or Lucille Gomez alive again?"

"No, I did not." She uses her sleeve to wipe her eyes, stiffens her spine, and says, "I will not cry. I swore to myself that I would not do that."

"What happened next, Ms. Giddens?"

"I finished my rounds and started over to the conference room. Then I realized I forgot Elaine's cake. So I hurried over to my office and fetched it. Just as I reached for the conference door handle, I felt the explosion. I think my life was spared because someone had already closed that door. I never heard a thing, just felt the blast. Why, we live in California after all, and the shaking reminded me of the Long Beach Quake that happened when I was a little girl, so I thought it was an earthquake. I was knocked to the ground. People were screaming and running. I tried to get up, but couldn't. I reached down to touch my right leg—I don't know why, because I wasn't in pain yet—and it was covered with blood. Then I saw. There were nails like the kind you hammer into wood protruding from the flesh above my knee. My slacks were shredded to bits." She inhales and sighs, the breath so shallow that it sounds like she's panting. "That's when I knew it wasn't an earthquake. I knew it was a bomb. There was debris everywhere. Reams of paper had flown off the desks. Typewriters were all over the floor, and furniture was in splinters. I must've blacked out. I woke up in the in the hospital a day later. They tell me I passed out from loss of blood, that I almost died. My leg got infected. Eight surgeries. It's a wonder they didn't amputate." She folds her arthritic, mottled hands on the side bar and looks at the ceiling.

Reddick lets the jury absorb the testimony and asks, "Earlier in the day, was there an unusual incident?"

"Yes. Earlier that morning I was walking over to use the ladies' room. I passed by a young man coming from the opposite direction." As she did when I met her at her care facility, she describes what the man was wearing—a T-shirt, military camouflage pants, and a pulled-down cap. "At first I told him he was on the wrong floor, that he should be on the third floor because that's where the veterans go. He looked so familiar, so I thought he was one of the regulars. After, I realized who he really was."

"And is that man in the courtroom today, Ms. Giddens?"

"Yes ma'am." She points to Holzner. "That's him. He's older of course, but he still looks the same. I'll never forget that face. Never forget that day. I know him because he was a friend of my son, Mark. They grew up together."

"I have no further questions," Reddick says.

I need to be gentle—otherwise I'll lose the jury forever. I need to be firm—otherwise I'll lose the case. I stand behind the lectern and try to seem composed, though I'm fighting off the queasiness and flop sweats that come with stage fright. Thank God my mother forced me to act in live theater when I was a kid.

"Ms. Giddens—"

"It's *Mrs.* Giddens," she says. She didn't have the same response when Marilee Reddick called her *Ms.*

"Pardon me. Mrs. Giddens. You testified that you walked by a man you believed to be my client and stopped to talk to him?"

"That's right. To tell him that he was on the wrong floor."

"You were within what, five, six feet of him?"

"That's about right."

"You didn't say, 'Hello, Ian, how are you?'"

"No, because even if he looked familiar at that time, I couldn't quite place the face. Like I said before, I thought he was one of the vets. He had his hat pulled down. And it was a long time after the boys had been in high school together, you know."

"You only identified Ian Holzner after you awoke in the hospital after the bombing, isn't that right?"

"Yes, sir. But as I said, he looked familiar that morning."

"And in the hospital you were suffering from serious injuries, including a severe concussion?"

"Yes, Holzner's bomb almost killed me."

"And while you were in the hospital you learned that four of your friends had died and many more had been injured?"

"Yes. Horrible, horrible. The worst time of my life. And to think it was almost Christmas."

"And you were angry?"

"Of course, sir. Angry, but not hateful."

"You wanted justice to be done?"

"The law's and the Lord's, yes sir."

"You wanted the police to catch the person responsible for all that terror, didn't you?"

"Yes. What person in their right mind wouldn't?"

"And then the police showed you a photograph of Ian Holzner, and it was only then that you identified him as the person you saw on the second floor of the Veterans Administration?"

"Oh no, sir. As I recall it, I told the police it was Holzner, and they brought me a picture to confirm it."

Now I get it—this old woman is an audacious liar. My problem is that she's a liar the jury loves. I'll have to do what lawyers hate to do on cross—ask questions I don't know the answer to. And Giddens's answers can do a lot of harm.

"You testified in the trial of a woman named Rachel O'Brien, didn't you?"

"Yes sir. That was your client's partner in crime."

"In that trial, didn't you testify that you only recognized Holzner after you were shown his photograph?" I read that in a newspaper story. I wish I had the actual transcripts.

"I don't recall it that way," she says. "But I do remember that I was the one who remembered Holzner and asked the police for a picture, because I was ninety-nine percent sure it was him, and I wanted to be one hundred percent sure. Which I am."

"You said Ian Holzner and your son Mark were friends. But wasn't it Jerry Holzner, Ian's older brother, who was Mark's friend?"

"Yes, Mark and Jerry were the same age, but Jerry was always bringing his little brother, Ian, around, I knew exactly who he was." Again, this isn't what she told me when I met with her. Age hasn't affected this woman's powers of prevarication.

Fortunately, we're prepared for this lie—with the help of Ian's childhood friend, Carol Diaz. On cue, Lovely hands me a photograph. What I'm about to do could rescue our case or doom it, just like those assistant district attorneys doomed their case when they had OJ Simpson try on the ill-fitting glove.

Lovely projects the photo onto the courtroom monitors so the judge and jury can see. The clerk marks the hard copy and hands it to Giddens, who holds it in a withered hand and squints at it. It's a picture of a twelve-year-old boy with short brown hair, cut straight and parted on the side. For the first time today, Giddens looks befuddled. There's a perceptible rustling as those in the gallery who were reading their iPads and iPhones refocus their attention on the witness. Several jurors sit straighter in their seats.

Giddens looks up at me in anticipation of my next question. I'm certain Marilee Reddick showed her pictures of the adult Jerry and Ian and made sure she could tell them apart. But the boy in this picture looks like neither of those adult men.

"Is this picture one of the Holzner brothers?" I thought of simply asking which brother it is, but that would give her a fifty-percent chance of guessing right. By asking this question, she has two chances to be wrong. Of course, if she truly recognizes who's in the photo or guesses right, this case is lost.

"Objection," Reddick says. "There's no foundation for what this picture is."

"This is impeachment on a critical point," I say. "A man's freedom is at stake. We could interrupt Mrs. Giddens's testimony and sequester her out in the hall, and I could call a witness to authenticate the photo. It seems like a waste of time to interrupt Mrs. Giddens's testimony to do that, though, when we can do it later."

"I agree," the judge says. "You can prove it up later, Mr. Stern. The objection is overruled." One advantage in having Gibson as the judge is that he's not much younger than Gladdie Giddens and so is perhaps less likely to see her as grandmotherly—as I did, until she started telling the brazen lies.

"I'll repeat the question," I say. "Is this one of the Holzner brothers?"

"Yes, I believe it is," Giddens says without hesitation. The odds of shaking her testimony have just gone way down.

"Is it Ian or Jerry?"

Her forehead knitted in thought, she stares at the photo a long time and tries to guess the right answer—not the truthful answer, but the one that will help condemn Ian Holzner.

"I don't know from this picture," she says. "Those brothers looked so much alike. Back then I knew Jerry was younger—"

"Did you say *Jerry* was the younger one, Mrs. Giddens?"

Her eyes glaze over with a kind of geriatric indignation. "Excuse me sir. I meant to say Ian was the younger one. Jerry was my son Mark's friend, Ian the little brother."

"You just told us the brothers looked very much alike," I say, abandoning my deferential tone and replacing it with incredulity. "If that's true, how do you know it wasn't Jerry you saw at the Playa Delta VA on the day of the bombing?"

Behind me I hear the tinkling of Holzner's shackles, a sign of unease, because I'm implying his brother Jerry planted the bomb, and he doesn't want that. Who cares? My only job—my sworn ethical obligation—is to defend Ian any way I can, even if he won't do the same for himself.

Giddens crosses her arms. "No sir. I know who I saw that morning. It was Ian Holzner."

"Even though the brothers looked so much alike?"

"Even though."

I nod to Lovely, who hands me the second photograph that Carol Diaz gave her. It's a picture taken the same year, but of a ruddy faced, stocky, round-shouldered kid of sixteen with a blond flattop haircut. His smile is sad and innocent. The clerk hands the photo to Giddens, and Lovely projects it on the monitors.

When Giddens sees the photograph, her hand starts trembling.

"You recognize this photograph, don't you, Mrs. Giddens," I say. She nods.

"You'll have to answer audibly," I say.

"Yes. I recognize it."

"This is Jerry Holzner, your son Mark's friend, isn't it?"

"Yes," she replies in a raspy whisper.

"He doesn't look anything like the young Ian Holzner, does he?"

"No sir. Not so much as I remember."

"And you remember now that Ian was adopted into the Holzner family?"

"I do remember that now."

"You didn't remember the picture of the younger brother, Ian?"

Her failure to reply is the best answer I can get.

"You were a bit confused about the Holzner brothers, weren't you?"

She tries to speak but only lets out a phlegmy wheeze. I let that stand as her last answer and pass the witness.

On redirect, Reddick gets Giddens to testify that because the brothers looked so different it *must* have been Ian whom she saw at the crime scene. The testimony falls flat. A factual misstatement during testimony is like a dropped stitch that causes the entire fabric of a story to unravel.

Judge Gibson calls the lunch recess, and the jurors file out. Before the marshals take Holzner back to the holding area, he whispers to me, "Don't lay this on Jerry." No paternal pat on the back for a job well done in discrediting a witness who threatened to put him on death row.

Lovely and I intend to repair to the attorneys' lounge, where I can force-feed myself some energy bars and pore over my cross-examination notes for this afternoon's witnesses. We exit the courtroom, but before we can turn toward the lounge, there are shouts and a shriek. The reporters have encircled someone and are shouting unintelligible questions. When I understand what's going on, I sprint over and throw a body-block through the crowd that former gridiron star Carlton Gibson would be proud of. Amidst the predatory reporters is a cowering Emily Lansing, her body turned half to the side, her arms pressed together against her chest and shoulders, her fists clenched, her knees bent—a standing fetal position. These pillars of journalism don't break rhythm:

"Hey, Stern, did you know that your client's daughter was expelled for physically attacking another student and vandalizing his car?"

"Does violence run in the family, Parker?"

—◊—

Lovely knows this building. She finds us a conference room two floors up, where the media and public don't go.

"Ben Harwood deserved it," Emily says.

"What did you do to him?" Lovely asks. I'll let her handle this. I know nothing about teenagers.

"I punched him in the face and broke his nose. Then I keyed his new Prius. It was worth it. Harwood is a spoiled rich kid, a fascist asshole."

"Why did he deserve a broken nose?" Lovely asks.

Emily starts twisting her hair.

"Stop playing with your hair and act like the grown-up you think you are," Lovely says sharply.

Emily flinches like a reeling drunk slapped on the cheek for her own good. "It was only six weeks after Dylan died. I was telling some friends how I thought the damn government had wasted his life and the lives of others for no reason. I mean, what's Afghanistan even for? The oil companies? Harwood started arguing with me, and it got ugly. When he told me that I was being a traitor to Dylan's memory, I hit him."

"And then you keyed his new car?"

"A few hours later, after school. Maybe I shouldn't have done that. I guess I was still mad."

"What did the school do to you?"

"I got suspended for a week. I still aced my classes. And . . . and the Harwoods threatened to sue my parents and me, but when everyone realized what Ben said about my dead brother, they backed off. And that's it."

"You're sure?" Lovely asks.

"Absolutely."

"Is there anything else we need to know about you?"

Emily gives a contrite half shrug. "I have a temper sometimes. I'm not the only person who does. But that was the only time I was suspended." Then the realization. "Omigod, is this going to hurt my dad's case?"

"It's irrelevant to him or what happened in nineteen seventy-five," I say.

"Nothing's irrelevant," Lovely says.

"What do I do?" Emily says. "I could tell the reporters—"

"No!" Lovely and I shout in unison.

"Here's what you'll do," Lovely says. "You'll go back in the court-room and sit in the first row and support your father and keep your mouth shut. And think about whether there are going to be any more surprises like this."

"Yes, ma'am," Emily says.

"I'm going to walk you back and then Parker and I are going to work on this afternoon's testimony."

"I'll walk her," I say.

"No you won't," Lovely says. "You're liable to punch one of these media people, and as much as I like trying cases, I'm not about to handle this one alone. And I know you don't want Lou to take over."

—ɷ—

After lunch, Reddick calls three other survivors of the bombing, who describe the events leading up to the explosion consistently with Giddens's testimony. I don't bother cross-examining them, because they shed no light on the identity of the bomber. The testimony of the day's last witness, the pathologist who performed the autopsies on the Playa Delta dead, is both gruesome and tedious—minute detail about missing extremities, faces shredded beyond recognition, identification only through dental records.

When the pathologist finishes, the judge adjourns for the evening. As Lovely and I are packing up, Marilee Reddick walks up, hands me the agreed-upon notice of the witnesses she intends to call tomorrow, and says, "We're going to hang your son-of-bitch client." She's either forgotten about the courtroom microphones or no longer cares. Only after she walks away do I look at the paper. It has only one name on it. Ilan Goldsmith. When I show it to Lovely, she sighs. Marilee Reddick intends to call Secretary Cracknamara to the witness stand to testify that Ian Holzner bragged about his plans to bomb the Playa Delta VA.

CHAPTER
THIRTY-FOUR

I don't want to go back to my condo. Holzner and Emily will distract me. Lovely has gone back to her own law office. Dworsky's place is too far away in rush-hour traffic. So I decide to work at The Barrista. When sitting at my back table, I feel an odd serenity amidst the café's tumult. I miss my friend Deanna, and though I'm not spiritual enough to believe that her essence is present in the shop, memories of her abound, and that's pretty close to immortality.

I spend hours crafting a cross-examination that will chip away at the credibility of the prosecution's second star witness, Ilan Goldsmith. You'd think it would be easy. He was a radical, a clown, a terrorist, a snitch. But most informants in criminal cases have a sordid past. If they didn't, they'd have nothing to tell.

Just before closing time, as I take a sip of my fourth—or is it fifth?—cup of coffee of the evening, a sallow-faced, gray-haired man approaches my table. Probably in his seventies, he resembles a world-weary Satan—hair shaped like small horns growing out of the top of his earlobes, a straight-angled Vandyke beard, and eyes burdened by heavy, dark half circles. He's dressed in a herringbone sport coat, white turtleneck sweater, and pleated brown slacks. The flesh hanging over his belt is more flab than fat. He sits down across from me, takes out a deck of playing cards, and begins shuffling expertly, making him look like the devil rehearsing a Vegas lounge act.

When he notices me staring at his hands, he says, "Faro shuffle. It relaxes me. At the moment, I need to relax." He talks fast, like someone hawking products on a basic-cable infomercial.

I look up from my laptop.

"My name is Ilan Goldsmith," he says.

I close the cover of my computer. The key witness for the government, a man we couldn't locate, has come to me on the eve of his testimony. Why?

He looks at me with his penetrating eyes, all the while shuffling those cards, the riffling rhythmic, hypnotic. I wait for him to begin. It's a lawyer's nature to interrogate, but sometimes questions just get in the way. At last, he cuts the cards three times and puts them in his coat pocket. "Ian Holzner was quite a magician, you know."

"Meaning?"

"First thing: tell him I'm sorry. I didn't want to rat him out. Never thought I'd have to. By way of explanation, not excuse, the FBI caught me on tape talking to Charlie Sedgwick about selling dynamite to the Holzner-O'Brien Collective. In exchange for immunity, I agreed to testify against those charged with the Playa Delta incident. I thought I'd never have to, but then Holzner turned himself in. Why would he do that?"

"What do you mean caught you on tape?"

"Just tell Ian I'm sorry."

"Mr. Goldsmith—"

"Second thing: maybe there's no apology necessary because I'm not going to testify at trial."

"I thought tomorrow you were—"

"No."

"You don't care about blowing your immunity?"

"I certainly do, and I don't want to serve prison time, but I care more about my life. Even at my advanced age, continued existence on this planet is very important to me. I'm in reasonably good health and not a religious man."

"Who's threatening your life, Mr. Goldsmith?"

He retrieves his cards again, fans them out on the table face down, and dominoes them back and forth. He begins another incessant round of shuffling. "The group is known as the Harpers Ferry Liberation

Front. They're responsible for the Playa Delta bombing, the bombing of the federal courthouse, and in all likelihood the murder of Belinda Hayes."

I don't quite believe him. He's obviously an expert at the sleight of hand. But I'm listening. "Who are they?"

"Rumor was that Rachel O'Brien and Ian Holzner started the organization."

"Sedgwick? Hayes?"

"Of course not Hayes. She didn't measure up. I don't know about Sedgwick. Maybe out of loyalty. The HFLF was formed for efficient acts of terror. Rumor has it."

"And how do you know this?"

He stacks the cards again and looks at me as if I'm a naïve child. "The recent communiqués are signed by JB. The initials of John Brown, the abolitionist who tried to start a slave insurrection at Harpers Ferry, Virginia, just before the Civil War. He was hanged for treason. Forty years ago the group was a dream of a few, a horror to most, a joke to still others. It percolated through the underground back in seventy-six that the Harpers Ferry Liberation Front bombed Playa Delta."

"How do you know O'Brien and Holzner—?"

"Rachel was obsessed with John Brown."

"What about Holzner?"

"He did whatever she wanted."

Not according to Moses Dworsky, who characterized Holzner as Svengali gone Maoist, seducing innocent girls and radicalizing them so they'd carry out his violent goals.

"And what makes you think this is the same group?" I ask.

"Well, the JB—"

"Forty years later? Pardon me, but you're all senior citizens."

"Rumor also has it they've recruited a younger generation."

"Rumor among who? Your movement died just about when Ian Holzner ran away."

He laughs—cackles in a high pitch, really, like a fairy-tale crone. "You don't really think all of us turned coffee-klatsch progressive like

Ayers and Dohrn, teaching school and idealizing the bad old days? Just because Islamic militants and right-wing extremists have seized the spotlight doesn't mean the radical left has died. That's what *deep underground* means. Dormant, waiting. Until now, it seems. As for how I know this? There's still a robust communications system."

"Why come to see me with this?" I ask. "Why aren't you sharing this with the US Attorney."

"You were an actor as a child."

I nod.

"I, too, was an actor. I don't know if anyone told you, Holzner or Dworsky—performance art, caricaturing that evil man Robert McNamara. Before he became secretary of defense, he'd been head of Ford Motor Company, you know. Kennedy appointed a numbers-crunching car salesman as secretary of defense, and Johnson kept him there."

"What did you want to say, Mr. Goldsmith?"

"Six hours ago, I got a phone call from someone warning me that if I testified against Holzner I'd be brought to judgment like the traitor Belinda Hayes. Blocked caller ID, of course. No idea how he got my phone number. I didn't recognize the voice. He said his name was Owen Brown. If you know your Civil War history—"

"I don't."

"I didn't either. I had to check the Internet. Owen Brown was John Brown's son. He escaped capture at Harpers Ferry and lived a fairly long life. But I got the message."

"Which is?"

He leans in close. There's an odor on his breath, maybe coming out of his pores, a garlicky-tobacco smell, though for some reason I don't think he's a smoker. "You're making me say it? Certainly. The caller warned that if I testify against Ian Holzner, I'm a dead man."

"Are you saying Holzner—?"

He looks over his shoulder like a stalked animal sensing danger, then pockets his cards, holds up his hands as if I'm pointing a gun at him, and stands up. His thin lips are turned down in a stiff grimace. He looks back at the front door, which Romulo is in the process of locking.

"Is there a back exit?" he asks.

"Mr. Goldsmith, if you'll just—"

"A back exit, please."

I point him toward the back door, which is totally conspicuous. He apparently could only hold his emotions in check for so long, and now he's about to panic. He hurries away with the rickety gait of an old man whose body will no longer let him run.

Not thirty seconds later, someone pounds loudly on the front entrance. From the frantic hammering, it's clear that it's not just someone in need of a late-night caffeine fix. Romulo goes to the door, says something I can't hear, and shakes his head. There's shouting from whoever's outside and more pounding. Two baristas start forward, but Romulo hollers, "Get back and call the cops!" With quivering hands, he reaches for the keys and unlocks the door, which opens slowly. He backs away with his hands in the air, mimicking Goldsmith's gesture of just moments ago.

Mariko Heim slides inside, wearing her sunglasses, though it's after eleven o'clock. She's carrying a gun, black. I know it to be a Glock 22 Gen 3 because that's what killed my boss Harmon Cherry a few years ago. I don't know why I looked up the gun on the Internet back then, but I had to see what the weapon looked like. I wish I hadn't. I get up and approach her.

"What are you doing here?" I say. "The cops are on their way. You're a Celestial Warrior. They don't leave messes, and now you have a mess." My insides have turned gelatinous, but I can't show weakness in front of her. I can only appeal to the tenets and tactics of her church.

"Where is he?" she says to me.

"Who?"

She shakes her head almost imperceptibly, and while I can't see her eyes, I'm sure she's rolling them—either that, or deciding whether to start shooting.

"Where is he?" she says again, waving the pistol in the air for emphasis. "Is he still here or did he go out the back?"

"The cops are on their way, lady," Romulo says.

Again that tiny shake of the head, now combined with an off-kilter gritting of her teeth. She takes a step forward and I flinch, but she hurries past, stops to look in the storeroom, glances back at me with a threatening shake of the head, and goes out the exit through which Goldsmith fled into the alley.

Esther, the female barista who's been cowering in the corner, breaks down in sobs.

"Jesus, man, what the fuck was that?" Romulo says, breathless.

"That was the Harpers Ferry Liberation Front," I murmur.

CHAPTER
THIRTY-FIVE

Ninety minutes before this morning's trial session is to start, Marilee Reddick and I sit in twin government-issue chairs across from Judge Gibson, glaring at each other. I arrived at the courthouse at 7:00 a.m., immediately went to her office, and told her about last night's encounter with Goldsmith—including his statement that a group called the Harpers Ferry Liberation Front was responsible for both the Playa Delta VA bombing and the recent federal courthouse bombing. I left out Cracknamara's implication that Ian Holzner is a founder and current member of the HFLF. I have no obligation to walk into the US Attorney's office and hand her the rope to hang my client with. I also told her about the sudden appearance of Mariko Heim of the Church of the Sanctified Assembly. Reddick says she'll ask the FBI or the LAPD to check my story out, but she's clearly not interested. The Sanctified Assembly's involvement in this bizarre promenade of horrors doesn't fit the government's prepackaged theory of the case.

Now, as we face a bleary-eyed Judge Gibson, Reddick is blaming me for Goldsmith's disappearance.

"Counsel for the defense should be sanctioned," she says. "Goldsmith is in contempt, and as an officer of the court, Mr. Stern was obligated to do everything in his power to get the witness to honor the subpoena. I believe you should instruct the jury that Mr. Stern encouraged a prosecution witness to flee."

"That's absurd," I say. "I specifically told Goldsmith to talk the US Attorney. He wasn't buying it. He fears for his life, truly believes this Harpers Ferry group wants to kill him. The FBI should be investigating Mariko Heim and the Sanctified Assembly's role in all this. Did I mention that Heim was one of the people who killed Belinda Hayes and was trying to kill me? Ms. Reddick is so fixated on Ian Holzner that she forecloses every other possibility. It's unbecoming of someone in her position."

"Give me a break, Parker," Reddick says with a dismissive flap of the hand.

Gibson—in shirtsleeves and a bow tie and sans robe—says, "I'm a judge, not a law-enforcement officer, Mr. Stern. I care about this trial, not about getting the FBI to play cops and robbers with the Church of the Assembly, or whatever it's called. As for you, Ms. Reddick, there will be no sanctions and no adverse instruction to the jury. I don't know what you expected Mr. Stern to do. He couldn't very well horse-collar tackle the man. Well, he could have, but he had no obligation to do it."

Reddick is about to jump out of her chair, but when Gibson crosses his arms in final judgment, she sits back. "Very well, Your Honor. We'll proceed with other witnesses."

I didn't think she'd be ready with another witness, thought she'd ask for the day off. I'm completely unprepared. "Your Honor, I didn't get notice of anyone other than Goldsmith," I say. "I'd request a continuance—"

"No continuance, counsel," the judge barks. "You're not going to take advantage of a witness skipping out on a valid subpoena, especially when he did so right from under your *nariz*."

"I need a name so I can prepare," I say.

"Get out of my chambers, Stern. You, too, Reddick. I have court business to attend to. You're not the only fish in the sea. *¡fuera de aquí!*" He picks up a pen and starts scribbling on a legal pad.

When we're in the empty courtroom, Reddick heads for the exit ahead of me but turns before she opens the door and silently mouths, "You're an asshole." As soon as she leaves, Lovely comes into the courtroom, this time followed by a long-striding Lou Frantz, lean and spry for a man in his early seventies. As always, his tie is loose and his shirttails are half out of his slacks, as if this were the end, not the start, of a long day.

"We need to talk," he says.

"About what?" I address the question to Lovely, and she shakes her head in an apologetic denial.

"Not here," he says. Of course not—the place is bugged.

We go to the attorneys' lounge, where he commandeers a conference room, literally ordering two young lawyers to wait outside while we talk. They obviously recognize the great Louis Frantz.

"Lovely told me what happened with Cracknamara," he says. "I don't blame you, Stern. But Lovely was already shot at, and she tells me that Goldsmith believes Ian Holzner threatened him. Witness intimidation is a crime, and I'm not going to be part of that, nor is Lovely."

"I don't know how many times I have to repeat myself," Lovely says. "There isn't a shred of evidence that Ian was involved." Not many young associates would use that tone to an omnipotent boss like Lou Frantz.

"So you say," Frantz replies. "But I want to know what Parker thinks. I want to know if Holzner is still perverting the law, still attacking the justice system. He certainly seems to be with his radical statements and erratic, disrespectful behavior in court." He has trouble keeping his cannonball voice quiet, and now it's loud enough to be heard on the other side of the thin walls.

"I don't think Holzner had anything to do with Goldsmith skipping out," I say.

"Then who did?"

"Mariko Heim and the Sanctified Assembly," I say. "She was chasing him last night. And Ian Holzner has been under house arrest in my condo unit for months. I don't have a landline, and my computer is password protected and always in my possession when I'm not there."

He regards me with a look of incredulity. "Lovely and I are going to move to withdraw."

"No, we are not, Louie," Lovely says.

I don't know what makes me more jealous—that they're bickering like an old married couple, that she can so easily control him, or that she called him *Louie*. I would wager the future Screen Actors Guild residuals from all my movies that no one else at his law firm calls him that. That she can talk to him that way is also one of the reasons I love and admire her. That's what jealousy is, I guess—the fear that the loved one will treat other people in a way you want them only to treat you.

"Are we good, *Louie*?" I ask.

"We're not good, *Parky*, we're not good at all."

"Because it's all academic," I say. "Carlton Gibson wouldn't let you withdraw in the middle of trial and you know it. It would result in a mistrial."

He harrumphs once and crosses his arms. This is one of the premier trial lawyers in America, perhaps the most arrogant, and with good reason—he dominates courtrooms, chooses his clients, helps decide who becomes elected officials. He even has a law-school building named after him. He's not accustomed to being a backbencher.

"Whom do you think Reddick intends to call to the stand?" I ask. "I can think of only a couple of potential witnesses."

"Oh my god," Lovely says. "She's going to call Rachel O'Brien."

CHAPTER THIRTY-SIX

Reddick walks to the lectern and says, "The United States calls Craig Adamson."

Moses Dworsky told us about Adamson the first day Lovely and I went to his office. At a conclave of fools (that's how Dworsky describes it) somewhere up in Northern California, Adamson called Rachel O'Brien a vile name. Soon after, Holzner and his cohort retaliated with a brutal beating. Adamson was on the prosecution's witness list, so we've had time to prepare in case they actually called him.

Adamson swaggers toward the witness stand. Wearing a charcoal suit and red paisley tie, he's a pasty, flabby man with short, thinning gray hair. In the pictures of him taken forty years earlier, he was seventy-five pounds heavier, a bellicose Jerry Garcia—huge belly, shoulder-length hair, and a dark, curly beard so thick you couldn't see his neck. When Adamson passes the defense table, Holzner glances up at him solemnly, but Adamson doesn't return the look.

After swearing to tell the truth with disingenuous fervor, he proclaims that he's a writer and a professor of political science at Mather University in Tacoma, Washington. He has the whisky-tinged voice of a honky-tonk singer.

"Were you involved in the antiwar movement of the nineteen sixties and seventies?" Reddick asks.

"I was one of its chief architects. First the civil-rights movement then the peace movement." His chest involuntarily swells with pride. Good. He's arrogant, which means he's vulnerable.

When Reddick asks him to elaborate, he says he was a civil-rights worker and later joined the antiwar group the Students for a Democratic Society in protest of the Vietnam War. By 1968, he'd become a Marxist and formed the New Progressive Left Party, which went underground in 1969. He admits his group committed its share of bombings but claims he always opposed violence against human beings. He faces no risk of prosecution—the statute of limitations on these crimes has run long ago.

"Have your beliefs changed since then?" Reddick asks, widening her eyes as if she hasn't asked him that twenty times during witness prep.

"I saw the light and found God in the late seventies. Thanks in part to Ian Holzner and what he did to me. I'm a spiritual conservative. I've spent my life atoning for the horrible mistakes I made in my youth. My life's mission is to educate Americans about the evils of godless liberalism and leftist polemics and atheism."

"So you obviously know the defendant, Ian Holzner." Marilee Reddick is a good choreographer of the slow dance that is direct examination.

"Sad to say, I do . . . did. I first heard of him in the late sixties. He was a leader of the antiwar movement. Everyone knew of him. He was one of the best orators around, a natural born leader. A waste of talent."

Lovely stands. "Object and move to strike the last comment. Irrelevant."

There are murmurs in the gallery, and several jurors smile. Lovely hasn't handled a witness until now. Adamson belongs to her.

"Sustained," the judge says, and he's smiling, too. Lovely has that effect on people.

Marilee Reddick presses her lips together, clearly not pleased that Lovely has for the moment taken the jury's attention away from her witness. "When was the last time you saw Ian Holzner before today?"

"March fourth, nineteen seventy-five."

"The same year as the Playa Delta bombing?"

"At a gathering of underground collectives in San Raphael, California. In a warehouse in an industrial area. We weren't supposed to be there, but we bribed a security guard with marijuana. We wanted to coordinate the activities of the radical underground groups. Everyone was working against each other, fumbling around. I was there to plead with the crazies to back off the violence. The crazies wanted to injure and kill human beings."

"Did the crazies include Ian Holzner?"

I nudge Lovely to object, but she shakes her head. She's all-in on her strategy.

"He and his girlfriend, Rachel O'Brien, and their whole loony gang."

"Tell me what Ian Holzner said at the San Raphael meeting."

"He and O'Brien were nutcases, ranting about all-out guerilla warfare against the US government. Talking about how Fidel Castro started in Cuba with a small band of insurgents and how we freedom fighters in America could do it, too. Holzner thought *he* was the American Fidel. Everyone was afraid of him. Not only was he incredibly physically strong for a small guy—all that gymnastics, I guess—but he also had some Black Power types supporting him. I wasn't afraid of him, though. So I got up and told him I thought he was talking murder, not revolution. Then O'Brien got up, called me a traitor, a fascist, when the truth was that that girl hadn't been through anything. I got my head beaten in fighting for civil rights, and Holzner and O'Brien were preaching to me about revolution? I told her she was full of it, a little girl playing soldier. Then they and their supporters started shouting at me, swearing, making threats. I remember that they both pointed at me. Anyway, the room went crazy, and after a few minutes when things calmed down I went out into the alley to smoke a cigarette."

"What happened next?"

"I was alone out there in the alley, just puffing away at the cancer stick. Stupid. To smoke, but especially to be out there alone. So then Holzner, O'Brien, and a bunch of their thugs jumped me, one guy started strangling me with this choke hold, and Holzner started hitting me in the ribs with his fists, and I tried to call for help, but I couldn't breathe with that guy's arm around my neck, and Holzner backed away and let O'Brien kick me for a while, like kids taking turns playing with their favorite toy, and I . . ." Breathless, he inhales twice. His forehead has a perspiratory sheen.

Lovely still doesn't object, though the testimony is now improper narrative and doesn't have anything to do with the Playa Delta bombing.

"What happened next?" Reddick asks.

"That O'Brien woman—she stepped back, looked at Holzner, and said, 'The face, Ian.' Just as cold as ice. And I'm struggling, but one guy still has the arm-bar hold around my neck, and two others are holding my arms, and Holzner starts punching my face, and I'm gagging on the taste of my own blood, thought I would drown in it. I lost my front teeth, top and bottom. Finally they let me go and I fell to the ground. Then Rachel—she was wearing these heavy work boots or hiking boots or something—began to kick me some more. She kicked me in the torso. Then she kicked me in the groin."

"What did Holzner do?"

"He leaned over and whispered in my ear, 'Next time I'll kill you.'"

"Anything else?" Reddick asks.

He folds his hands in his lap and glances up at the ceiling. "I lost consciousness."

"Did you suffer any permanent damage from the attack?"

"Yeah, like I said, I lost my front teeth. The damage to my jaw has caused all kinds of problems, because it wasn't set properly. It's arthritic. I suffer from TMJ. I have problems chewing. My knee was injured in the attack, and about twelve years ago I needed surgery. I still get excruciating migraine headaches, bouts of vertigo where I want to vomit."

I don't have to look at the faces of the judge or the jury or to turn toward the gallery to know that Adamson's testimony has sickened them. It's sickened me.

Reddick glares at me in disgust, as if I was the one who attacked Adamson. "No further questions."

Lovely springs up and hurries to the lectern. Good—it shows that she's not worried about Adamson's testimony, that she can't wait to get at him. She's had a lot of time to do her research, and more importantly, for once Holzner stepped up to help us with this witness.

"At this San Raphael meeting, you started the shouting match with Rachel O'Brien, didn't you?" she asks.

"Yeah. She wanted to kill people."

"You called her—and I apologize to everyone in the courtroom for this—a *dumb cunt*?"

"I don't recall using that word, but, yes, I was upset at her and Holzner for preaching premeditated murder."

"After you called her that name, you got out of your chair and walked up to her?"

"If you say so."

"You got in her face?"

He doesn't answer.

"She was what, five-feet-one and a hundred pounds?"

"I didn't have a yard stick or a scale with me, but yeah, she was small."

"And at the time, you weighed about three hundred pounds, didn't you?"

"Yeah, luckily I lost the weight. A lot easier than cutting out cigarettes." He mugs at the jurors and waits for laughter that doesn't come.

"Were you trying to physically intimidate Rachel O'Brien?"

"Of course not."

"You wouldn't try to physically intimidate a woman?"

"Of course not."

"Do you know the name Ramon Weisser?"

Adamson hesitates, probably calculating the likelihood that he can get away with lying. "I remember him."

"In Chicago in nineteen sixty-nine at the national convention of the Students for a Democratic Society, you and other supporters of the radical group the Weathermen beat Ramon Weisser senseless because he disagreed with your political position."

"Objection," Reddick says. "Irrelevant." Reddick is correct on the law, but we're hoping the judge gives us some leeway. It's a capital murder case, after all.

"It goes to the reasonableness of Mr. Holzner's actions," Lovely says. "Whether he was protecting himself." She places her hands on her hips and cocks a hip coquettishly. *If you've got it, use it to win*, she's told me before. *If sexism works to your client's advantage, fine.*

"Overruled," Judge Gibson says.

"You beat Ramon Weisser senseless, didn't you Mr. Adamson?" Lovely asks.

"I don't recall the extent of Mr. Weisser's injuries."

"Broken leg? Fractured ribs? A collapsed lung?"

"I don't remember."

"Well, you beat the crap out of him, didn't you, sir?"

"Objection," Reddick says. "And the language is highly inappropriate."

I want to laugh at toilet-mouth Marilee Reddick's show of moral indignation.

"Withdrawn," Lovely says. "You beat up Ramon Weisser for his political views, didn't you?"

Adamson tries to speak, but nothing comes out.

"Did you or did you not physically attack and severely injure Ramon Weisser in nineteen sixty-nine?"

"I've spent my adult life trying to atone for behavior like that."

"Behavior like that? So it was a pattern?"

He sits straighter in an almost-prissy way. "I didn't say that, counsel."

"Do you know the name Louis Rubinstein?"

"I recall that name."

"You physically attacked him as well? Detroit, nineteen seventy?"

"We had a physical altercation, yes."

"That physical altercation resulting in Mr. Rubinstein suffering a broken collarbone and a ruptured spleen, correct?"

"I don't know."

"Your group—what do you call it?"

"*Did* call it, not *do*. The NPLP."

"The NPLP publicized these beatings, correct?"

"I wouldn't say we publicized them."

"You let it be known that you carried them out."

"I think we—"

"You wanted your political opponents to know about your willingness to use violence, is that fair to say?"

"At the time. I was in the clutches of the Devil Marxism."

Lovely walks over and whispers in my ear, as if consulting me. What she says is, "I've got this motherfucker."

I nod slowly, as if affirming some piece of complex trial strategy.

She returns to the podium and says, "Mr. Adamson, do you know the name Beverlyn Wallace?"

The blood drains from his face. "I don't see the relevance—"

"It's Ms. Reddick's job to make objections, and yours to answer questions," Lovely says. "Answer my question, sir. Did you know a woman named Beverlyn Wallace?"

"Yes."

"She was your girlfriend in early nineteen seventy?"

"Yes."

"Your *old lady*, as you referred to her back then."

He furrows his brow, clearly not sure where Lovely is going or what evidence she has. And that makes him afraid to evade the question. "It was a slang term we all used."

"Objection," Reddick says. "This testimony is so far removed from the issues in this case, which is whether the defendant bombed the—"

"They opened this whole propensity to violence issue up on direct," Lovely says. "We're just countering it to show the full context."

"Overruled," the judge says. "You made your bed, Ms. Reddick. Lie still in it."

"Ms. Wallace was also an official in the NPLP?" Lovely says.

"Assistant Secretary-General."

"In the summer of nineteen seventy, Beverlyn Wallace ended her relationship with you, am I right?"

"We mutually agreed to end it."

"You and she broke up because she got pregnant, and you insisted that she have an abortion, but she wouldn't do it?"

No response—he knows what's coming.

"Is there something you don't understand about the question?" Lovely asks.

"As I said before, I've spent my life trying to make amends for who I was back then."

"Let's explore who you were back then. When Beverlyn Wallace broke up with you, she dropped out of your organization because she didn't want to raise a child while advocating violence?"

"Something like that. It was a long time ago."

"You don't recall?"

"It was a long time ago."

"And in response, you and two of your fellow NPLP members broke into Beverlyn Wallace's apartment and beat her up, correct?"

"Still irrelevant," Reddick says.

"Still overruled," the judge says.

"I refuse to answer . . . on . . . on Fifth Amendment grounds."

"Oh come on, Mr. Adamson," Lovely says. "The statute of limitations ran long ago."

"That is objectionable, Ms. Diamond," the judge says. "And needless. You were doing fine staying on the straight and narrow."

Eyes don't really flash their own light, but all the light in the room seems to coalesce in Lovely's gray irises and laser back at the witness. Her outrage isn't feigned.

"As a result of the brutal beating you inflicted on her, Beverlyn Wallace had a miscarriage, is that correct?"

"I refuse to answer that on Fifth Amendment grounds."

"And when she miscarried, she was five-and-a-half months pregnant."

He shuts his eyes, but doesn't answer.

"Pleading the Fifth again, sir?"

Reddick half stands but thinks better of it.

"Any chance Ian Holzner attacked you because he was proactively defending Rachel O'Brien based on your history of brutally beating women?"

"That's enough, Ms. Diamond," the judge says. "Any other areas with this witness?"

"No, Your Honor."

"Then sit down, counsel," the judge says. "Does the US Attorney have any redirect?"

Reddick shakes her head. It's not that Adamson destroyed her case—who beat up whom in 1975 has little to do with whether Ian Holzner killed four people. But by trying to underscore Holzner's violent nature, Reddick got greedy, and as a result, Lovely's cross-examination has thrown her credibility and judgment in question. Just like most things in life, trials are as much about perception as truth.

Adamson starts to leave the witness stand, but the judge says, "Stay where you are, sir. The jury is excused."

Judge Gibson waits for the jury to leave and then waggles his index finger at Adamson. "Before you go, I want to say that you are a *pot*, sir. A scorched, sooty pot! And you've come into my courtroom and called the kettle black. Unbecoming. Get out of my sight this minute."

Adamson stands down and walks toward the exit. As he passes, Holzner looks at him with venomous eyes. This time, Adamson returns the stare, and as soon as he catches Holzner's eye, his hands begin to tremble, and a knee buckles. Even after all these years, he's afraid of Ian Holzner—not just afraid, terrified.

CHAPTER
THIRTY-SEVEN

It's only lunchtime, and Reddick has already finished with Adamson, which means she either has another witness for the afternoon or she'll rest her case and force me to begin mine. We wait for the gallery to file out. Frantz winks at Lovely and gives her a thumbs up. Lovely and I head for the attorneys lounge, ignoring the reporters lingering behind.

"Wait." She takes my arm, and we make a turn down the hall and go through a door marked *Restricted*. She leads me into a back corridor and up some stairs, to Holzner's holding cell. I didn't know the route existed. The marshal on duty lets us into what's supposed to be a cell but is more like a conference room. A still-shackled Holzner is eating a half-peeled banana, the chains on his cuffs clinking with each bite. He stands when he sees us and flashes a rare smile.

"Nice job, Lovely," he says. "Adamson was always this—"

She raises her arms and almost flails them in disgust. "I just came up to tell you that you make me sick. And don't talk about your mis-spent youth. Some things are unforgivable."

Holzner clamps his jaw shut.

"I'll meet you in the attorneys lounge, Parker," she says. "But first I have to go to the ladies room to scrub the filth off." She turns and storms out the door, which has one of those slow-closing hinges that thwarts her three tries at slamming it. On another occasion, I'd laugh, but there's nothing funny about this.

"Do you agree with her that what I did so long ago is unforgivable?" Holzner asks.

"That depends on what you did. I still don't know."

—ɯ—

When Reddick calls her next witness, an elderly man in the first row gets up and walks to the stand with the hobbling gait of a washed-up linebacker in need of dual hip replacements. His small, round head is perched on a brawny body. His name is Elias Roudebusch.

After the clerk swears him in, Reddick asks, "What is your occupation?"

"I'm a former Special Agent for the FBI. Retired."

"Did you play any role in the investigation of the December seventeenth, nineteen seventy-five, bombing of the Veterans Administration at Playa Delta, California?"

"Along with my partner Ralph Hilton, I was the agent in charge of the investigation." The man's voice is so rough, it sounds like he's swallowed a wood rasp.

"Please summarize for the jury your educational and job background."

The best witnesses prove the cliché that you shouldn't judge books by their covers. Pleasant surprises win instant credibility. So it is with Elias Roudebusch. He graduated from Ohio State with a BA in sociology, enlisted in the army, served two tours of duty in Vietnam, and enrolled in Georgetown Law School, where he served as an editor of the law review and finished in the top ten percent of his class. After practicing criminal law at a large Washington, DC, firm, he joined the FBI. By 1975, he was a ranking agent in the Los Angeles office.

He was on the witness list, and we're well prepared for him. What more can he do but recapitulate what the jury has already heard from the other witnesses? He yet again quotes the Holzner-O'Brien Gang's radical rhetoric, describes the crime scene, and confirms that Holzner was the only person who could assemble the type of bomb that exploded at the Playa Delta VA. He tries to rehabilitate Gladdie Giddens by insisting that she unequivocally identified Ian Holzner as the perpetrator. He speculates that the silver earring found at the scene belonged to one of Holzner's many women. We can deal with all this testimony.

But then Reddick asks, "Agent Roudebusch, did you ever hear a tape recording of the defendant in nineteen seventy-five?"

"Yes. Many, as a matter of fact."

"In any of those tapes was Ian Holzner discussing the Playa Delta bombing?"

There's a click-clack of laptop keyboards and murmurs of surprise from the gallery. The jurors stay impassive: the magic of our legal system is that it causes ordinary citizens to osmotically internalize the essential principle that justice is stoic.

"Objection, Your Honor, best-evidence rule, undue surprise," I say, trying to sound unconcerned but doing a piss-poor job of it. The quaver in my voice and the trembling in my limbs aren't caused by stage fright. That seems to have lifted in this trial, probably because I'm battling for my father's life. I'm frightened because it sounds like Elias Roudebusch might ensure that Ian Holzner will die by lethal injection.

"Overruled," the judge says.

"May we approach, Your Honor?" I ask.

"Hurry it up, counsel."

We go to the bench and huddle around the court reporter.

"Your Honor, the government provided no recording or any transcript of it. The tapes themselves are the best evidence of what's on them. If they ever existed."

"Oh, they existed," Reddick says.

"If not the tapes, then transcripts made at the time. For Ms. Reddick to spring this on me now without a word of—"

"There's no undue surprise because we only learned about them last night while preparing Agent Roudebusch. The best-evidence rule doesn't apply because the original recording has been lost and so have the transcripts. The agent's testimony is the best evidence of what's on those tapes. Rule of Evidence 1004." It's a good argument, all the more galling because though Reddick was a good student, she struggled in our evidence class. I helped her through it.

"The objection is overruled," the judge says. "The tape is missing, so he can testify to what was in it, to the best of his recollection."

"Your Honor, that's crazy. Because the government commits neg-ligence or worse and loses the tape, this witness will be permitted to testify all these years later about its contents?"

"That's my ruling, counsel. Go back to your table."

"Your Honor, may I be heard further?"

"I've ruled, Mr. Stern. I'll let the 'crazy' comment go this time."

"Your Honor, we were in your chambers this morning, and the least Ms. Reddick could've done was disclose to me that she intended to have this witness testify that—"

"Step back, Mr. Stern, or we'll have a problem. No, *you'll* have a problem."

Once we're back in place, Reddick says, "We were talking about tape recordings. In any of those tapes was Ian Holzner discussing the Playa Delta bombing?"

"Yes, he was," Roudebusch says.

"Before telling us what you heard on the tape, how did you learn about the recording?"

"Pursuant to a valid warrant, we'd obtained the right to wiretap the telephone line of one Charles Sedgwick, a member of the Holzner-O'Brien collective. We consistently tape-recorded conversations that occurred via that telephone. The tape in question was recorded on the morning of December seventeenth, nineteen seventy-five, about six or seven hours before the Playa Delta bomb exploded."

"What happened to the original tape?"

"I don't know for sure. Somehow over the forty years it was lost. I understand the agency has searched high and low for it. As best as we've discerned, the original and copies were transported to the federal courthouse during the trial of Rachel O'Brien. Someone working in the clerk's office probably destroyed the tape after trial when no one came to pick up the evidence. It was a screw-up. I wish we could find it."

"Who were the participants in the call?"

"I believed the caller was Rachel O'Brien. On the other end of the line was a man we believed to be Charles Sedgwick."

"My original question to you related to Ian Holzner and his par-
ticipation in a conversation about the bombing."

"Yes. There was a man's voice in the background. My recollection
of the tape is that Mr. Sedgwick called him *Ian*."

"What was said on the tape?"

"The woman caller—whom I believed to be O'Brien—was very
emotional. She said something about a bomb in a restroom. She seemed
to be upset by the fact."

"What else did you hear?"

"Sedgwick sounded like he was trying to keep the woman calm. He
seemed surprised over what the woman who I believed to be O'Brien
was saying. Sedgwick apparently covered the phone with his hand
and said something about the bomb to the man I believed to be Ian
Holzner. There were some raised voices, and then Sedgwick said, 'Ian
will handle it.' Then one of the parties hung up, we don't know which."

"That's bullshit!" Holzner shouts. He stands and points his cuffed
arms at Roudebusch. "It's a lie, and you know it." Then a three-quarter
turn until he finds his daughter in the front row of the gallery. "Emily,
it's a lie. It never happened. I didn't do this. I didn't do what they say."

Emily nods, the rims of her eyes sparkling with tears.

"Sit down, Mr. Holzner!" the judge says.

Holzner points to Roudebusch again. "You're a lying fascist pig!"

"Marshals, sit the defendant down now, and if he won't be quiet,
drag him out of here."

"I object to that," I say. "My client has a right to be present in court
to confront witnesses like this man."

"Your objections are irritating me, counsel," the judge says.

"I'm sorry about that, Your Honor, but I'm going to make them for
the record anyway."

The jurors look like guests at a dinner party where the host and
hostess have started quarrelling with each other. One of the marshals
takes a tentative step toward Holzner—he, too, wants this just to go
away—but Holzner continues standing and glowering at Roudebusch.
My father is committing suicide by jury trial.

Emily stands and says in her fluty voice, "Sit down, Dad. Please."

He shakes his head slowly and says, "Dylan would've wanted me to—"

"He wouldn't have wanted any of this. So please sit."

He nods like a dazed man who claims he knows what day it is when he doesn't. Then he almost falls into his chair. As he should have, he addressed his plea to Emily, his daughter. I'm not truly his son. But as his lawyer, I now believe that he's innocent. Guilty men don't behave the way he just did.

None of which will help undo the damage he's done by losing control and calling an esteemed FBI agent names. No matter that I believe his behavior proves his innocence—the jury will only notice the slur and the rage and the lack of respect for the judicial system. They would've expected him to make his case on the witness stand.

Holzner looks left and then right as if he's just become aware that he and Emily aren't alone in the room. Acting strictly as his attorney, I go close to him and place my hand on his shoulder, then lean over and whisper, "You've just hurt yourself a lot more than Roudebusch did. I had this covered. The next time you want to destroy yourself at least wait until I've finished my cross-examination. Now, relax and be quiet."

When the room settles, Reddick says with a flourish, "Thank you, Agent Roudebusch. No further questions."

Lovely whispers that we should ask for a recess, but I don't need it. I want to get at this guy as quickly as possible. I haven't felt like this since before the stage fright hit me five years ago. I almost lunge at the lectern.

"You said you 'believed' that the female voice on the tape was Rachel O'Brien, Agent Roudebusch?" I ask.

"That's right."

"You'd heard O'Brien's voice before?"

"Many times."

"But you're not certain that it was O'Brien's voice?"

"No, sir."

"Why is that?"

He shrugs. "Technical difficulties. The tape was badly garbled."

This is one of those times on cross-examination where you have to push your luck. "And attempts at enhancing it didn't make it better?"

"That's correct. Enhancement technology in the nineteen seventies wasn't what it is now."

"So the FBI wasn't even sure that it was Rachel O'Brien calling?"

"That's right. We believe the caller was using a pay phone on a busy street." He looks at the jury. "For those of you too young to remember a pay phone, it was a telephone in a glass booth that you put coins in to make a call. Usually a very grimy glass booth."

Like a safety valve on a pressure cooker, the laughter releases much of the pent-up tension in the room. That's too bad—I wanted to keep the room on edge.

"But it sounded like O'Brien to me," he adds.

"Were you sure it was Charles Sedgwick who answered?"

"Yes, it was clear enough from the timbre of his voice, though it was sometimes unclear what he was saying."

"You say you concluded that the second man on the tape was Ian Holzner because Charles Sedgwick said something about 'Ian taking care of it'?"

"That's not my testimony. Sedgwick made that statement, but I concluded that it was Holzner because Sedgwick seemed to call the other man *Ian*."

"You just said *seemed to*."

"Yes, sir."

"You're not a hundred percent sure."

"No."

"Was there static on the tape?"

"Yes, sir."

"Hissing sounds?"

"As I recall."

"And you said traffic noise?"

"Yes sir."

"And not only was the tape garbled, and there was traffic noise, but you said that Sedgwick apparently covered the phone with his hand when talking to this second man?"

"That's correct."

"But despite the garbled tape and the muffled receiver and the traffic noise, you still believe the second man in the room was Ian Holzner?"

He crosses his arms and sits back in his chair to convey finality. "Yes, I do."

I'm about to pass the witness when Lovely hands me a note, suggesting a question I don't know the answer to, that ultimate risk on cross. Holzner's core meltdown forces me to take the risk.

"Was this tape recording used in Rachel O'Brien's trial?"

"Not that I recall."

"You don't recall or the recording wasn't used."

"It wasn't used."

"Why not?"

"Objection," Reddick says. "It calls for the witness to speculate about the reasons the attorneys—"

"Overruled," the judge says.

"Do you know why the recording wasn't used at the O'Brien trial, Agent Roudebusch?" I ask.

"Yes. Ralph Hilton and I had a disagreement about who was speaking on the tape."

"Which was?"

"He didn't think the other man was Ian Holzner. And . . ."

"And what, sir?"

"He didn't believe the woman caller was Rachel O'Brien."

"You and he agreed on Charles Sedgwick?"

"Yes, counselor. We agreed on that."

"Do you know if Ralph Hilton is still alive?"

"Yes, sir. Ralph Hilton is retired and living in the Portland area with his daughter."

"Oregon or Maine?"

"Oregon. His daughter and son-in-law own a vineyard."

"Ralph Hilton isn't on the government's witness list, is he?"

"It's my understanding that he's not."

"I have no further questions," I say.

Roudebusch climbs down from the stand and leaves the court-room. Once the jury is excused, I say, "The defense has a motion, Your Honor."

"The motion is granted," the judge says. "How many days do you need, Mr. Stern? And keep your seat, Ms. Reddick."

"Given the travel, three days, Your Honor."

"Okay, Mr. Stern. You have three days to interview Ralph Hilton and Charles Sedgwick. For good cause shown, the motion to continue the trial is granted. Marshal, notify the jurors that they get a few days off."

CHAPTER THIRTY-EIGHT

After rising in the ranks of the FBI and being promoted to headquarters in Washington, DC, former FBI Agent Ralph Hilton retired in the late 1980s and then publicly condemned a number of FBI practices that supposedly had been discontinued in the 1960s, including "black-bag operations"—breaking into and entering onto private property without a warrant, declared unconstitutional by the Supreme Court in 1972. Hilton claimed that the practice had continued under the Reagan administration, an allegation that was never proven. For years after, he served as a private consultant and taught classes on government and criminal justice at Pomona College, east of Los Angeles. He currently resides in Portland, Oregon.

It's December, rainy season—the locals say it's always rainy season—and while it's hardly pouring, there's a steady drizzle that has the streets slick. Fortunately, Hilton doesn't live far from the airport. I drive up a hill to Portland Northeast, an evolving neighborhood where the working class is being pushed out by an urban-professional gentry—rising stars at Intel and Nike—who are renovating the stately Cape Cod-style homes. The rain picks up, and worse, the intersections in Hilton's neighborhood don't have stop signs, so I have to move at a crawl.

Hilton lives in a small, two-bedroom A-frame that must have been built in the 1920s. He answers the door, and when he sees me, he grunts. It's not a cold call—he agreed to meet with me—but he repeats exactly what he told me on the phone. "I can't help you. I don't want to help you. Your client is guilty."

In his seventies, he's a tall, elegant man with ashen hair, an ashen complexion, and an ashen disposition. When I reiterate that I'd like to speak with him, he invites me in and offers me tea. The house is immaculate. Books and magazines are neatly organized in a large bookcase that occupies an entire wall. There are family pictures on the mantle—Hilton with a wife, daughter, and son at various ages, and then in later years, Hilton with a daughter, grandchildren, and no wife. There are also official documents—diplomas from the University of Arizona and Vanderbilt Law School and a picture of Hilton shaking hands with President Lyndon B. Johnson.

He goes to the kitchen and minutes later returns with two mugs of tea. As soon as I take my first sip, he says, "Stay and drink as long as you want. But let's keep the conversation short. It's true Elie Roudebusch and I disagree about whose voices were on that tape. I don't think O'Brien or Holzner were part of that conversation. But that doesn't help you. Because whoever was on that tape wanted to *prevent* the bombing, as I interpreted it. They were frightened, not brazen, not calculated. I think Holzner and O'Brien did exactly what they were charged with, and these fellow travelers got scared but couldn't prevent it."

"What about Charles Sedgwick?"

"Oh, Chicken Charlie was definitely on that tape. That's one of the injustices of this whole sorry saga. In my opinion Sedgwick wanted to prevent the bombing and is the only one who spent his life in prison. Whether Holzner has the lethal poison injected into his veins or not, he's escaped justice. I'm sorry to say that, because I know he's more than a client, though he obviously wasn't father of the year."

"But he is my father," I say almost without volition. "And he was a terrific father to his other children."

"And you want to save his life. I can understand that. Apologies for my bluntness, which some call callousness. It's who I am."

"If you're so vehement, why hasn't the US Attorney called you as a witness?"

He straightens his long legs and crosses them at the ankle, wincing from what's probably an arthritic knee or hip. "I don't like what the

Bureau did back then. I hated what happened to Jerry Holzner. It's a black mark on this country that should be prominently featured in history books but that's been buried in the slag of time and deceit. I don't like practices that continue to this day. I don't agree with Elias about what's on that tape—he was a good, honest cop, by the way, just mellower than I am—and that would make for conflict. I've always thought O'Brien might've been the moving force behind the group. Holzner was more charismatic, a good front man, but I heard a lot of those tapes. O'Brien was soulless, if you ask me. Holzner was conflicted. His megalomania came from ego, a young person's reaction to adoring followers. O'Brien's megalomania was sociopathic."

I ask for some examples.

"Holzner had a love for his family, especially his father and brother. Jerry was older in years but acted more like the younger brother, always trying to emulate Ian. But Ian kept him away."

"Could Jerry have—?"

"Been involved in the bombing? Who knows? As I said, he wanted to be like his brother."

"You said O'Brien was different?"

"No soul. She cut her family off at the knees. She'd mock their liberalism, their upper-middle-class values. On one recording, she calmly proclaimed that she'd kill her parents herself if it would advance the cause of the revolution. It wasn't hyperbole, in my opinion. Which, along with the different speech patterns, is why I do not believe the woman on the tape is O'Brien. That woman was scared. Rachel O'Brien didn't know fear."

"And yet she wasn't convicted of the Playa Delta murders."

"She was a wonderful actress and had that son of a bitch Moses Dworsky as a lawyer. He was as brilliant as he was despicable."

"Dworsky was just doing his job."

"He was not just doing his job. He's a true believer and that's dangerous in an attorney."

"Is it? I think passion—"

"Are you a true believer, Mr. Stern? I'm not talking about the facts of a particular case. Do you believe in something so strongly that it colors every move you make in a courtroom in every case?"

Though I don't say it to Hilton, my answer is no. The most effective lawyers are anything but true believers. You have to be malleable to take a side that you disagree with, have to let go of firmly held beliefs, even have to make odious arguments, all based on the premise that a democratic system of justice requires it. You can't be the kind of true believer that Ralph Hilton is describing.

"Do you know that he's my private investigator?"

"Of course. I'm following this trial closely, hoping justice will finally prevail. I don't know how you got under the covers with that man."

"He's changed his political views after 9/11. He voted Republican."

He lifts his teacup with one hand and gives a scoffing wave with the other. "There's an adage about leopards and spots, Mr. Stern. I'd advise you to look it up. But never mind all that. Since Dworsky is working for you, why don't you have a copy of the tape recording in question?"

For a moment I mistake the confusion in his voice and his slightly slack jaw for nascent senility until I see the intense clarity in his eyes. He's a man who enjoys games and secrets.

"Why would Dworsky have a copy of that recording, Mr. Hilton?"

"He was given a copy of the tape for the O'Brien trial."

Upon learning this information, I thank him and end the interview. As soon as he shuts the door behind me, I take out my cell phone and punch in Moses Dworsky's number. It's raining hard now. I open my umbrella and make a dash for my rental car, a fire-engine-red Mazda 6 that shines through the gloom, but my clothes are wet before I get inside. The call rolls over to Dworsky's voice mail after one ring, meaning that the phone is off. Still, after I leave a message for him to call me right away, I retry his number twice more and then send him a text, though he's such a Luddite that I doubt he even knows about text messaging.

I try the office and reach Eleanor Dworsky. "What do you mean, where is he? He's away on business for you."

"What business?"

"How the hell would I know? You would know, not me." She promises to have Moses call me if she hears from him and hangs up before I can say, "Thank you."

Then I call Lovely Diamond. Her phone, too, immediately rolls over to voice mail. Again, I leave multiple messages.

I sit at the curb in the rental car. The rain pounds on the metallic roof, the sound like corn kernels popping in a microwave. I can't fathom Moses Dworsky's objective. He's helped our case by locating background witnesses, setting up the meeting with Charles Sedgwick, and providing an office and staff (if you can call Eleanor *staff*). And yet, intentionally or not, he cost us the chance to win the motion to exclude evidence because the FBI tortured Jerry Holzner, and he's possibly withheld relevant and potentially useful information. Is Dworsky's goal to look cooperative while sabotaging us? Ian keeps insisting that even after forty years, even after helping O'Brien avoid a murder conviction by blaming Holzner, Dworsky is fair-minded. Either my father is a fool or he knows something about Dworsky that I don't.

I check my text messages one last time and look for new e-mails just in case. I'm about to start the engine when my phone rings. I'm hoping it's Moses, but it's Lovely.

"Do you know where Moses Dworsky is?" I ask. "Hilton said Moses knows about that recording and once had a copy in his possession."

"Parker—"

"Eleanor says he's doing something for me, but I don't know what he's talking about. Do you—"

"Parker, just listen!" she shouts.

I listen.

She takes two heavy breaths and says, "Dworsky went to visit Charles Sedgwick in prison. Did you tell him to go see Sedgwick?"

"Of course not. But it's not a bad idea. He's the only one whom Sedgwick might talk to."

"Omigod, Parker, he posed as Sedgwick's attorney, got in the same room with him, and stabbed him to death."

"How would he get a knife past prison security?" It's not the logical first question, but sometimes shock makes you jump five steps ahead.

"It was a prison shiv that he must've gotten inside. The whole thing had to be planned in advance. He convinced the prison officials that he was Sedgwick's lawyer. He showed them his old bar card from ninety-one, and they just let him meet with Sedgwick alone."

So Moses Dworsky just murdered the only identifiable person who could testify to what was on that recording and who could maybe, just maybe, exonerate Ian Holzner, which means that Dworsky's objective has been to sabotage our case, and Holzner was a fool for trusting him. But there's another, more troubling explanation. What if Sedgwick was finally going to verify that Holzner was on that recording, that Holzner truly committed the crime? What if Dworsky killed Sedgwick at Ian Holzner's request in a last-ditch attempt to avoid a conviction?

"Where are they holding him?" I ask. "Has he revealed anything?"

"He's dead, Parker. After he killed Sedgwick, he attacked the prison guard. He was a powerful man. He wrestled the gun away from the first guard, and another guard shot him. It was suicide by cop."

I don't say anything. What's there to say?

"There's more, Parker. Before Moses was shot, he shouted, 'This is for Ian!'"

CHAPTER
THIRTY-NINE

Four hours after Dworsky murdered Sedgwick, Judge Gibson's chambers received this:

Subject: Communiqué #3
To: Judge Carlton Fascist Gibson
From: JB

The brave Charlie Sedgwick and the steadfast Moses Dworsky belong to the ages, martyrs to the cause. Moses knew what had to be done; Charlie understood why it had to be done. Moses and Charlie died by fire, like true revolutionaries.

Free Ian!

~JB

I make the motion for a mistrial on the grounds that the news of Dworsky's crime has gone viral, the publicity destroying whatever evenhandedness the jurors had left.

"This means *nada*, Mr. Stern," the judge says. "*Nada.* The jury has been instructed not to read the newspapers or watch the news on TV or read it on the Internet. That's sufficient. So we're going to move on. Anyway, Dworsky belonged to your side, and I'm not going to let you take advantage of your investigator's crime." He shakes his head. "First Ilan Goldsmith, now this. Bad things happen to witnesses when you're involved, Mr. Stern."

———

For the last day or so, Holzner has mostly stayed in his bedroom. His melancholy stupor borders on catatonia. In an effort to get him to talk, I gather . . . well, I gather the "family"—Emily, Lovely, and my mother. It's all I can do to get him to come out of his bedroom and sit on the living room sofa. We're all seated across from him, but I'm the chief inquisitor.

"Once and for all, did you have anything to do with this?" I ask.

"He wouldn't," Emily says.

"I didn't ask you," I say, and she recoils because it's the first time that I've spoken harshly to her. "Dworsky was your guy from the beginning, Ian, even after Lovely began having doubts about him when he antagonized Judge Gibson in court that day. I want to know if you've orchestrated all this, just like Marilee Reddick and the FBI believe."

He's been sitting with his head down, but now he looks up at me and shakes his head. I realize that before this happened I saw something oddly noble in his enigmatic statements, in his refusal to do anything to save his life, in the undercurrent of radicalism that still seemed to inform his every move. At this moment, he seems shattered, and I feel a combination of sadness and betrayal. Is this the disillusionment children feel when they finally recognize their parents' flaws? Is this horrible murder case the way I experience the arc of father-son relationship, warped and twisted into some perverse joke?

"I'm risking a lot to be here," Harriet says. "I think Heim and her people are following me. I can't keep coming here. So listen to what I have to say."

Here it comes—her inevitable defense of Ian Holzner.

"I want you to tell the truth, Ian," she says. "The whole truth. I'm sick of the whole thing."

He forces himself to stand, and when he rises, Harriet does, too.

He looks at me. "The truth is I was wrong about Moses Dworsky. There's nothing more to it."

"So you brought this man into the case without really knowing who he was?" Lovely says. "You trusted your life to him? Hard to believe. Everyone is going to say you've been working with him for years, planning your comeback. That you're the leader of the Harpers Ferry Liberation Front that Ilan Goldsmith was talking about."

"You want to call me a fool for trusting him?" he says. "You're right. But if you're calling me a liar, you don't know what you're talking about."

"Ian, what are you hiding?" I ask.

He crosses his arms in front of him and shakes his head.

I appeal to my mother.

"Tell Parker the truth," she says.

He tilts his chin up slightly as if he's about to say something but stays mum. He wearily shuffles over and kisses Emily on the cheek, and to my shock kisses Harriet on the lips. As he passes me, he tentatively extends his hand out to pat my arm, but thinks better of it, then walks into the bedroom and shuts the door. The only sounds in the room come from Emily and Harriet, soprano and alto weeping in counterpoint.

In the space of two days, the medical examiner autopsies Dworsky's body and releases the remains to Eleanor, who has him cremated without ceremony—not that anyone would've attended. The surprise is that Dworsky had pancreatic cancer, with a few months to live. He hid it well. I thought the stooped posture and the ashen pallor and the occasional wincing were the results of aging.

The trial resumes on Monday, and during the weekend we're still working out of Dworsky's office.

"This place gives me the creeps," Lovely says. "I know it's a silly thing to say, but there's evil in here."

The statement surprises me, because she doesn't scare easily and because she's an observant Jew who's not big on mysticism. I'm pretty much a nonbeliever—my time embroiled in the Sanctified Assembly has made me treat the spiritual with skepticism—but I reply, "I know what you mean."

We sit, not in our makeshift offices, but in the conference room, neither of us wanting to be alone. After about a half hour, Lovely glances up from her computer and considers me for a while. She leans over, softly kisses me on the lips, and says, "I love you, Parker Stern."

The words lift me through the next dismal hours as I try to craft some defense for Ian Holzner. Then I stand, go to the reception area, thumb through Eleanor Dworsky's old-fashioned Rolodex, and find the number. I dial from the office phone.

Brandon Soloway's "Hello" sounds sullen—he's always sullen—but now he's got a reason. When I identify myself and ask to speak with Eleanor, he says, "She's not talking to anybody. I'll give her your, what do you call them, condolences."

"Yes, please tell her how sorry I am. But I'd also like to ask her if Moses kept other files about the Rachel O'Brien case. Something he didn't share with us."

"My mom just lost her husband and found out he was a psycho murderer and you're worried about your case? You're pathetic, man."

"Brandon, I didn't mean to—"

"My mom blames Holzner for this. She thinks he convinced Moses to kill Sedgwick to shut him up for good. We knew about Moses's cancer, he didn't have long to go, but now his legacy is fucked up forever. Do you know what that's done to my mom?"

"I'm just doing my job."

"That's what all scumbag lawyers say. Well, your job sucks, man. Moses was a lawyer, and he was an asshole. You're an asshole." He hangs up the phone.

So imagine my surprise when, three hours later, the office door opens and Brandon Soloway walks in carrying three old boxes bearing a Bekins logo. He sets them on the table, mumbles, "My mom told me to bring these to you," and walks out.

CHAPTER FORTY

The missing transcripts from Rachel O'Brien's trial are in the boxes. So is the December 17, 1975, tape recording. It's the old reel-to-reel kind that won't work even on the obsolete audio-cassette player that I found in Dworsky's desk. Lovely calls the Frantz Law Office's crack IT woman and takes the tape back to see if they can make sense out of it.

After she leaves, I spend hours skimming the O'Brien trial transcripts. The transcript of Gladdie Giddens's testimony is missing. Too bad. I'd welcome the chance to impeach her at our trial with her prior sworn statement. I do locate Belinda Hayes's testimony, and, just as she told me, Dworsky browbeat her into exonerating O'Brien and implicating Holzner, despite the best efforts of the prosecutor and the judge to rein Moses in.

In the first trial, both Hilton and Roudebusch testified, and both expressed their belief that Holzner was the bomber. The testimony and evidence in these documents implicate Holzner at every turn. In his closing argument, Dworsky said over and over that Ian Holzner and others unknown, but not Rachel O'Brien, bombed the Playa Delta VA. Would this man later commit murder at Holzner's behest?

At eight in the evening, Lovely calls. "Our expert couldn't do much," she says. "You can hear some of what Sedgwick says, but that's it. The bad news is that it does sound like Sedgwick is saying, 'Ian will handle it.'"

"We don't know the context. Anyway, let's get someone other than your IT person to enhance this tape. She might be good, but she's not an expert."

"We contacted someone Lou used in a trial a couple of years ago,

Ezekiel Bauman. Tops in the business. He says it's a third- or fourth-generation version, so there's nothing more that can be done. Bad luck. This whole fucking case feels like bad luck."

"We'll find someone else."

"There's no one better. I looked on the Internet and LexisNexis, and all roads lead to Bauman. I'm sorry, Parker."

"Call your office and have someone bring the tape to Romulo at The Barrista. Right away."

"What do you have in mind?"

"If it works, I'll tell you. Just get Romulo that tape."

After we hang up, I carefully consider whether I should make this next move. There are people who could help me, but they might refuse, might not be in the country much less close enough to LA to examine the tape recording before the trial ends. But there's no choice. While the tape might convict my father, it's the only thing that might save him.

I use my smart phone to e-mail my former client, a reclusive video-game designer and computer genius known to the world only as Poniard. An hour later, I get a reply saying I should be at The Barrista at precisely 12:07 tomorrow morning, which I consider later tonight. My ex-client has an annoying fondness for offbeat drama—perfect for a designer of fantastic, violent video games, but not so comforting to someone like me, who's looking for a reliable ally.

I wait in the darkness at my usual table. There's a comforting eeriness to The Barrista after closing time. The wooden chairs and stools are stacked upside down; the mephitic smell of ammonia from the wet mops contends with the sharp-tangy fragrance of arabica beans. I welcome the clicks of the foundation settling, the moan of the wooden beams yielding to a drop in barometric pressure. I do hope there's no scurrying that could displease the Health Department.

There's a different kind of creak behind me. I turn to find that a man is already inside—no surprise, though I left the door locked.

When I see him, I have to fight back disappointment. He's not the person I hoped would come. He's dressed in a black gaucho hat and matching black shirt, slacks, and cape. He always dresses like a character in a Poniard video game. Last time I saw him, he went by the name of *Banquo Nixon.*

"Who are you this week?" I ask.

He bows and tips his hat with a flourish. "Call me *Zorro Snowden,* the Cyber Fox." He lifts the hem of his cape to reveal a scabbard and a sabre, real no doubt. The man is a cosplayer, not a clown—a kind of performance artist who appears at comic-book and video-game conventions.

"You have something for me, Mr. Stern. At your service."

I hand him the tape. "It's the only one of its kind. I need to know what's on it, as soon as possible. Sooner. I'll owe you."

"We already owe you, señor." He bows.

"Before you go, can you tell me how—?"

He raises a hand. "We cannot speak of these things now. We are being watched. Possibly more than that."

I'd believe the man insane, but I know from past experience that he isn't. Not that way. "Who's watching?"

"A woman parked in a blue Mercedes-Benz. She's wearing sunglasses at midnight. Be careful, Mr. Stern." He flicks the brim of his cap in good-bye and steals out the backdoor. I'm not sure why I gave him the tape. Even if he and his cohort are able to decipher what's on it, they're perfectly capable of releasing the damn thing as part of an online video game in which Ian Holzner is the villainous Big Boss.

I go out the front. Just as Zorro told me, there's a blue Mercedes parked across the street. Melrose Avenue is empty—it always is this late at night—and the neighboring shops have been closed for at least an hour. The residential side street is forty yards away. If Mariko Heim wants me dead, now's her chance, because we're going to settle this no matter what happens. Few things make you braver than the decidedly un-Zen-like state of being fed up. I circle around to the driver's side window and rap on it hard. It takes a long moment for her to roll it down.

"You could get hurt ambushing people like that," she says matter-of-factly. Contrary to what Zorro told me, she's not wearing sunglasses. Both hands are on the wheel. She's looking straight ahead with eyes closed, like a fourteen-year-old on a joyride that's gotten out of hand. There's no one else in the car. I should be relieved by that, but her enforcers' absence is out of the norm, and the abnormal serves as fecund ground for violence.

"You murdered Belinda Hayes and tried to kill Lovely Diamond and me," I say with a sense of conviction I've held for weeks but suddenly don't feel. "Hayes got caught in some Sanctified Assembly fatwa against me that—"

"If I wanted to kill you, you'd already be dead. I don't have any idea why you think I had anything to do with Hayes's murder. You're unimportant to me."

"I saw you driving away from the scene."

"I don't know what you think you saw, but it wasn't me."

"I think this whole bombing campaign was orchestrated by the Sanctified Assembly."

She nods her head in disdain. "There's a saying we Assembly devotees have. 'Things are always as they seem—but they're not the truth.'" Still, she faces straight ahead; still, her eyes are closed.

"You think your prophet came up with those words?"

The only response is a slight pursing of her lips. It's almost one in the morning, and the night has gone cold. The sky is pristine and starry because many of the city lights have dimmed. LA isn't tropical, so the winter air slices through my dress shirt. Or maybe the ice comes from Mariko Heim's hatred of me. "Quiana wrote those words. I saw her type them to put in Kelly's mouth. As poor an actor as he was, her lines were so good they spoke for themselves. That's not to say I've ever understood them."

"Cooperate with me, Stern. Tell me what you know about the Assembly's practice of Ascending Sodality. And your mother's role in it."

It's my turn to play nonresponsive.

"You know what people are saying, Stern? They think you're involved in this murder spree with Holzner. You're his son, he's been living with you, and now the private investigator working for you killed a key witness. Are you a misplaced sixties' radical, Stern, born twenty years too late? Or are you just trying to please Daddy by following in his footsteps? What about your sister, Emily? Is she involved, too?"

I lean over and stick my head inside her window, my face inches from hers. "Leave us alone, Heim. Tell your followers to back off, too. Your treatment of Quiana is apostasy. You're going to be excommunicated from your precious church if you're not careful."

She presses the button and starts the ignition. I barely jerk my head back before she speeds away. If I'd reacted a nanosecond slower, I might've been decapitated.

CHAPTER FORTY-ONE

I get to court earlier than anyone but the courtroom deputy, who lets me inside. I sit at counsel table. Marilee Reddick will no doubt rest her case, and I'll have to get up and defend Ian Holzner. But with what evidence, what arguments, what passion? I want to tell the jurors that he's the father I never knew, that *I* deserve a chance to spend time with him no matter who he is, that he's no longer the kind of man who'd harm another human being. But the only time I'd ever get to share those beliefs would be as a family member testifying during a death-penalty phase. So I start preparing the questions for my own witnesses, an exercise that feels like donning track shoes to begin a death march.

Five minutes later, the door opens, and Lou Frantz and Lovely Diamond walk in. I expect Frantz to take his usual seat in the gallery, but he walks up to counsel table, opens his briefcase, pulls out a file, and plops down in the chair next to me. Lovely sits on his far side.

"No way, Frantz," I say. "This is our case. Go sit in the gallery where you belong."

"It's my case, too, Stern," he replies in his normal voice, which nevertheless projects so loudly that I'm sure the courtroom personnel can hear him without the aid of those invasive microphones. "This is why I was assigned as consulting counsel. A man's life is at stake, and things are going poorly. Exceedingly poorly. I'm not about to sit back and let that continue without intervening."

"It has nothing to do with my—*our* defense strategy."

"Maybe so, but I'm sitting at the table today. If nothing else, it'll wake the jury up."

"What do you think about this?" I ask Lovely.

"I think..." She shuts her eyes tightly as if squeezing what she really wants to say out of her brain. "Let Lou sit at counsel table, Parker. See how it goes."

When you love someone who's left you once, any disagreement can seem like heartless rejection. I check the clock on the wall, will it to rewind backward three days to when Moses Dworsky was still alive, so I can stop him from going north to the prison. I will the clock to turn thirty-nine years back so that I can know the truth about the Playa Delta bombing, about my father, about myself. The second hand taunts me by sweeping ever forward. I go back to preparing my direct examination. If Frantz tries to get up and speak, he'll have to fight me for the lectern.

The courtroom deputy opens the door to let the public inside. The spectators file in like mourners. Mariko Heim isn't among them, fortunately. Emily sits in her usual place behind her father. She was crying all night—I heard her when I came home at two in the morning—but it's not apparent. She has her shoulders back and her chin raised, a diminutive soldier marching into battle.

The marshals bring Holzner in, the shackles and jumpsuit unremarkable after so many days. At nine o'clock sharp, Judge Gibson calls the session to order, and the jurors file in. They haven't been sequestered, but they have been instructed repeatedly not to watch the news, read the newspapers, search the Internet, or talk to anyone about the case. No matter—they undoubtedly know about Dworsky's murder-suicide. None of them will look at me, except for that Joey character, who won't take his eyes off me and actually smiles grimly, like an executioner certain of his righteousness.

As soon as Judge Gibson calls the session to order, Marilee Reddick says, "The government rests."

I move to the lectern, and fortunately Frantz doesn't try to wrestle it away from me. It's not because he isn't prepared to take over—he doesn't need to be, just as a shark doesn't require preparation to bite.

I call our own explosives expert, an ex-FBI forensics expert and current security consultant, who opines that someone other than Ian

Holzner could've built the bomb that exploded at the Playa Delta VA so long as he or she had a scientific background or had learned from someone who did. On cross-examination, Reddick gets her to admit that she can't identify any other American radical group before 1977 that built a bomb precisely the way that Holzner did. We were ready for that, and our witness is facile. On redirect she testifies that a member of Germany's deadly Red Army Faction—also known as the Baader-Meinhof Group—constructed an almost-identical bomb used in a 1972 attack on a US military facility and that several American radicals had contact with the German radical group well before 1975.

When Lovely calls Father Ray Oliphant, a Catholic priest, college professor, and once-upon-a-time antiwar activist of the late 1960s, there's a clank of chains. Holzner must recognize the name. But I don't know for sure, because I've decided not to tell him anything more about our trial strategy. Irrespective of whether he's guilty or innocent, I'm not going to take the risk that someone else ends up dead because of what he knows.

Father Oliphant has the priest's collar but also a mountain-man beard and silver-white hair that reaches his shoulders. He's wearing ratty jeans. He's Lovely's discovery, so she's going to examine him. Unlike the last time she stood up to question a witness, there's no lessening of tension, no infusion of energy. The very air in the room feels hostile. Half the jurors are frowning at her. Like all good trial lawyers, she behaves as if she's in complete control and winning the case by miles.

She starts with Oliphant's background. He's now seventy-three, and like Craig Adamson, was a nonviolent civil-rights activist turned Vietnam War protestor. Unlike Adamson, he didn't turn to violence after the war escalated but instead entered the priesthood. Since then, he's spent his life opposing war and fighting poverty, maintaining that Jesus was the first practitioner of nonviolent protest.

"Did you know the defendant, Ian Holzner?" Lovely asks.

"I heard him speak several times in the early nineteen seventies and met him once in early nineteen seventy-five."

"Under what circumstances?"

"As a Catholic. I was trying to convince the more radicalized faction of the antiwar movement to disavow violence as a way of ending the war. I believed I had credibility, because between nineteen sixty-nine and nineteen seventy-five I'd been arrested twenty-three times for civil disobedience in protest of government and corporate injustice. I'd suffered documented incidents of police brutality. I was able to arrange a meeting with Ian Holzner and Rachel O'Brien through a man named Charles Sedgwick."

There are murmurs throughout the gallery, which is just on the serrated margin between restraint and bedlam. I try to gauge whether the jurors are confused or aware. All I detect from them is a detached weariness of people who've made up their minds long ago and just want it to be over.

"Where were you?" Lovely asks.

"At a party in Del Mar, California, at a private beach house. One of the children of the owners was interested in radical politics. A groupie of sorts. But she gave money. That was one irony of that era. Many well-to-do kids still enjoyed the trappings of wealth even as they railed against the capitalist system."

"Did you discuss with Holzner and O'Brien the use of violence versus nonviolence as a tactic?"

"We got into quite a debate. O'Brien in particular didn't want to hear from me. She quoted Marx that religion is the opiate of the people and added that nonviolence was just the syringe by which the fascist's smack was administered. She said that Gandhi and Martin Luther King sodomized each other. When I replied that what she was saying was bullshit, she got so upset she threatened me."

"Physically?"

"Yes."

"What was Ian Holzner's reaction?"

"He found someone who was smoking a marijuana joint, grabbed it out of the guy's hand, insisted that O'Brien take a few hits, and told her to relax and have fun. Luckily, she walked away, but not before giving Holzner the finger and spitting in my face."

"She literally spit at you?"

"She literally spit in my face."

"What happened next?"

"Holzner found a napkin and wiped O'Brien's saliva off my cheek. He apologized for her behavior. Then we started talking about the movement again, revolutionary tactics, philosophy. He said he disagreed with O'Brien, that he thought nonviolence had its place but only in a civilized society. He said that America had become a police state, no better than Nazi Germany. I tried to convince him that it was exactly the opposite, that if what he was saying were true, we'd both be dead. Then he said something surprising. He said he'd once believed what O'Brien believed, but then he'd gotten some girl pregnant, didn't even know it, and she showed up with the child. It didn't make him angry like he thought it would. It made him feel like a grown-up. Made him think about things."

There's another buzz in the courtroom, a kind of self-praise for putting together the obvious—Oliphant is talking about me. When Lovely told me about Oliphant, she didn't reveal this part of his testimony, just said he was going to dump on Rachel O'Brien and make Holzner look good by comparison. Does she really think the jury is supposed to conclude that my father isn't a murderer because he had a fleeting moment of paternal concern for the infant son he never wanted and later abandoned? And yet, as his son, that's exactly what I conclude, and I find myself fighting off the cynical view that it's just wishful thinking.

Oliphant's testimony raises another question I've asked myself a thousand times: Why did Harriet give birth to me? After I was born, she had at least three abortions that I know of. There's only one answer to that question: She loved Holzner. She never loved those other men. Does that mean she loved me as well?

"Why do you remember your conversation with Ian Holzner after all these years?" Lovely asks.

"Two reasons. The first is that Mr. Holzner was charged with the Playa Delta bombing not so long after, and he became a fugitive from justice. The second is what he said about his child. It was so unusual, because guys like Holzner didn't talk about kids and family and all those trappings of bourgeois living. The guy's own propaganda maintained that the nuclear family was a tool of capitalism to keep the masses down. The dude was changing. I'm a believer in redemption. I think that true revolutionary fervor—not the urge to do violence, but the desire to radically change the world order to help humanity—sets a person on the road to heaven. Ian Holzner's motives were always noble, and his views were changing."

After Lovely says that she has no further questions, Reddick stands and in less than two minutes of cross gets Oliphant to admit that, in the conversation, Holzner had expressly advocated violent protest and that he has no idea whether or not Holzner bombed the Playa Delta VA. Yet, when Oliphant stands down, I realize he's the first witness in days who's made Ian Holzner sound like a human being.

We break for lunch, but instead of eating, Frantz, Diamond, and I meet with Holzner in a conference room. Frantz and Diamond are trying to convince him to testify in his own defense. If this were an ordinary trial, they'd do everything in their power to keep him off the stand. Shackled rabble-rousers in prison garb who flout the system don't make good witnesses. But we're so far behind that they're desperate.

Except Ian won't agree.

"I'm not going to participate in this trial," he says. "It's a kangaroo court without authority."

"You sound like Sedgwick," Lovely says, and not kindly.

When that doesn't work, Frantz puts his hand on Holzner's shoulder and says, "I've been through this many times, Ian. You can turn this around. You're a persuasive man, you didn't do this, and if you can convince the jury that you're innocent—no, if you can just raise reasonable doubt about your guilt—you can survive to fight another day."

Holzner nods, raises an arm—he's not shackled now—and firmly removes Frantz's hand. "Parker's my lawyer, not you. So, get out of my face."

Frantz gets up and stomps out of the room.

"Does that mean I'm not your lawyer, either?" Lovely says.

"You are. At Parker's sufferance. He's the boss with the power to hire and fire."

"I'm sure that Parker thinks you should testify," she says. "Any lawyer would. It's the only way to save your life. Tell him, Parker."

"I think Parker finally understands," Holzner says.

I didn't until that moment, not really. But I do now. "It doesn't matter if I agree or disagree. Ian won't take the stand."

"Why not," she asks.

"Ian isn't going to testify because he knows the truth about the bombing. And he doesn't want to lie under oath."

"Is that what's going on, Ian?" Lovely asks.

His lack of a response confirms that it's true. There isn't any comfort in that, though, because the truth might be that he committed the crime.

CHAPTER FORTY-TWO

As Lovely and I are walking back to the courtroom, Emily Lansing stops me near the elevators and asks to speak with me alone.

Lovely motions toward the stairwell door. "Go in there," she says. "It's one of the most private places in the building. I don't know why, but everyone takes the elevator or escalator."

We go inside the door and stand on the landing. The late Harmon Cherry used to say that the courthouse stairwell was haunted by the ghosts of those whom the law treated unjustly. Will Ian Holzner's spirit dwell here someday?

"Save him, Parker," Emily says. "Save our father."

"I can't lie to you. It's not good."

"If those jurors don't find him innocent, I'll . . ." She pauses. "What can a girl like me do? I think I finally understand why our father did what he did when he wasn't much older than me. He did something about injustice, took a stand. And people followed him."

"He committed senseless acts of violence."

"Maybe the bombings really did help people in the end."

"I don't believe that. And even if that were true, it wouldn't make it right."

She shuts her eyes, trying to compose herself. "I just get so mad sometimes."

"We all do. But there are ways to fight back that don't involve violence."

She looks at me skeptically. "Just save him, Parker. Save us both." She abruptly turns and walks out of the stairwell, leaving me with the spirits of those whom justice abandoned.

I take a moment to focus on the impossible task at hand. I have no more witnesses to call, no more evidence to present. Ian Holzner's life now depends on my ability to do the miraculous—convince the jurors to ignore the evidence and find that the government has failed to prove its case beyond a reasonable doubt. I do the morbid mathematical calculation. If Holzner is sentenced to death, it'll take from ten to fifteen years to exhaust the appeals and the habeas-corpus process. By that time, he'll be seventy-five or eighty years old, and maybe he'll have already died in prison—not exactly on his own terms, but not at the hands of the government.

I walk out of the stairwell and across the elevator bank, and when I round the corner, I feel a hand on my shoulder. At first I think it's Emily, but I turn to see an older woman dressed in a gray business suit and red blouse. Only when she takes a step back do I recognize her as Carol Diaz, Holzner's childhood friend and principal of Playa Delta High School.

"Thanks for coming down to support Ian," I say. "And for the help with those old photos."

"Parker, can we speak privately?"

"Ms. Diaz, I—"

"It's Carol."

"I have to get to the courtroom. The US Attorney will be starting her closing argument."

"You cannot walk into that room without listening to what I have to say. I think I can save Ian's life."

When I enter the courtroom twenty minutes later, a scowling Judge Gibson is on the bench. The jury is in the box. Ian Holzner is in his seat. Lovely Diamond and Lou Frantz are at counsel table with their heads down.

"You're very late, Mr. Stern," the judge says. "Thirty seconds longer, and I was going to force your colleagues to proceed without you. Do you have another witness? Your colleagues don't seem to know."

"Yes, Your Honor," I say. "The defense calls Carol Diaz."

Diaz, who's been standing by the door, walks resolutely down the aisle, her gait almost militaristic.

"Don't do this, Carol," a stunned Holzner says as she passes.

When she doesn't acknowledge him, he bolts out of his chair so suddenly that two of the marshals rush over, but he brushes by them and whispers in my ear, "Don't let her do it, Parker."

"Sit down and be quiet," I say. "It's her choice. You're not calling the shots anymore."

He starts to argue, but I nod to the marshals, who escort him back to his seat. It's a relief that he goes quietly. In light of what's about to happen, I was afraid he'd react violently.

Reddick objects that Diaz wasn't on our witness list, but that objection is overruled when I tell the judge that Diaz approached me for the first time twenty minutes ago.

"Please raise your right hand," the clerk says.

Diaz complies.

"Do you swear to tell the truth, the whole truth, and nothing but the truth, so help you, God?"

"I do."

"You may be seated."

"State your full name for the record," I say.

"Carol Sue Diaz."

Diaz sits with her hands folded in her lap. Many witnesses swivel in their chair at first, a way to stave off nervousness, but she doesn't waver. I'm the one who's jittery, but not from stage fright.

I start with questions about her background, which palliate my anxiety somewhat. That doesn't mean the answers about who she is aren't vital to her testimony—they show how much she has to lose.

"Ms. Diaz, do you know the defendant, Ian Holzner?"

"Yes. We grew up together in Playa Delta, California. I've known Ian since we were in kindergarten."

I lead her through their childhood years and into 1967, their senior year of high school, when Holzner became radicalized.

"What was your relationship with him after he became political?"

"We jointly led a campus protest against the war. June of nineteen sixty-seven was very early for this. About fifty students took over the senior lawn."

"Did the high-school protest turn violent?"

"Yes, for high school. We broke a window in the principal's office."

"Who were *we*?"

"Actually, there wasn't a 'we.' *I* broke the window."

"You and I met several months ago in your office, and you told me that it was Ian Holzner who broke the window, didn't you?"

"That's right. I lied to you. I've been lying about that incident for years. Ian took the blame back then, and I let him even though I was the culprit."

"Do you know why he did that?"

"My parents were really strict, and my father—even when I was a senior in high school, my father would hit me if I did something wrong. My grades weren't as good as Ian's. If I got suspended, I'd get a beating and might not graduate. Ian didn't want that. When he was fourteen, he actually shoved my father away from me. My father took a swing at Ian, but Ian dodged the punch and laughed it off. By sixteen, Ian was so strong from gymnastics and other sports that my father avoided him. Anyway, Ian could afford to get in trouble, even get accused of vandalism. His parents—especially his mother—doted on him. He was a brilliant student and star athlete, maybe going to the Olympics. So I let him take the fall."

"When we met, you also told me that you cut off all contact with Ian Holzner after his freshman year at Berkeley. Was that true?"

"It was both true and not true. I told you I saw Ian only once after that, which was true. I stayed in LA and he went to college up north. But we communicated, first by telephone and then by letters, until he went underground and we had to break off all contact because the FBI and the police were after him."

"When was that?"

"Early nineteen seventy-one."

"What were your views on what Ian was doing? The bombings."

"I . . . I had no problem with them. At the time I thought, if Ian Holzner is doing it, it must be the right thing."

"Why did you think that?"

"Because I respected and loved him—not romantically, but like a brother. He was my protector. I figured that he was protecting the oppressed people just like he'd protected me." She turns toward the jury. "I know it's no excuse, but we were just kids."

Reddick stands up and, in an uncharacteristically whiny voice, says, "Objection. Where's this going?"

"I'm about to get there, Your Honor," I say.

"*Pronto*, Mr. Stern," the judge says.

"Ms. Diaz, where were you on the afternoon of December seventeenth, nineteen seventy-five, at the time the Playa Delta VA was bombed?"

"In my apartment in Playa Delta, California."

"Was anyone else with you?"

"Yes. Ian Holzner."

Judge Gibson's switchblade eyes dare someone to make a sound.

"Anyone else?"

"No. Just Ian and me."

"How long had he been at your place?"

"Three hours, maybe."

"Was there anything unusual about his visit?"

"Absolutely. I hadn't seen him in four, almost five years. He just showed up at my door."

"What did you and he talk about?"

"He said he was done with activism, that things had gotten too crazy with the violence, that he had a son now and didn't want the kid to have a criminal for a father."

"Objection," Reddick says. "Move to strike the witness's testimony as hearsay."

"It's a statement of Mr. Holzner's then-existing state of mind," I say. "His plans. A clear exception to the hearsay rule."

"Overruled," Judge Gibson says. "But Mr. Stern, if I want elucidation from you on the law, I'll ask for it. I've been a federal judge for over forty years and know what I'm doing."

"Tell us more about the conversation, Ms. Diaz," I say.

"I asked who the mother was, but he wouldn't tell me because he didn't want to jeopardize her safety. He thought the FBI would harass her and the kid if they found out that he was the father. He was real vague about what he'd been doing, which was understandable, because he didn't want to get me involved."

"What happened next?"

"He said he was going to get the kid and the girl and move up to Northern California. Mendocino County, where it's green and quiet and peaceful. Change his name and hope that the FBI never found out about him. We just talked, you know. And then the bomb exploded."

"The bomb at the Playa Delta VA?"

"Yes."

"How far away was your apartment from the Playa Delta Veterans Administration?"

"About four blocks. I was a new teacher, so I wanted to be near school, and the VA and the high school weren't that far from each other. When I heard the blast, I thought the country was under attack by the Soviet Union, because it didn't feel like an earthquake. An earthquake had never been that loud."

"Did Mr. Holzner say anything when the bomb exploded?"

"Objection," Reddick says. "Hearsay."

"Mr. Stern, I will hear you on this one. Approach."

"No need to approach, Your Honor. It will come under the excited utterance exception."

"It better, Mr. Stern. Overruled. You may answer the question, Ms. Diaz."

Diaz shakes her head slightly as if still disbelieving what happened back then. "Ian looked out the window. I did, too. We couldn't see anything, but Ian whispered, 'It's impossible.' And it was like he wasn't speaking those words to me, like he was in shock. Then he screamed. I'd never heard Ian scream, not when he fractured his arm doing a back flip as a kid and wouldn't cry in front of us. But now he was sobbing. He kept repeating, 'It's impossible, it's impossible!'"

Silence is like a gas: formless, capable of indefinite expansion, sometimes toxic, sometimes stable, sometimes inert—and sometimes, like the silence in this courtroom, volatile. I say, "No further questions," because I'm not about to furnish the igniting spark, and I hope that Marilee Reddick won't do so. All Reddick has to do to avoid the conflagration is follow the old saw that a lawyer shouldn't ask a *why* question on cross-examination.

It's not to be.

"How convenient that you show up at the last minute and try to rescue your friend," Reddick scoffs. "Why didn't you tell this to the FBI in nineteen seventy-five, when Holzner was charged? Why didn't you come forward during the trials of Charles Sedgwick or Belinda Hayes or Rachel O'Brien? Why, Ms. Diaz, didn't you at least come forward when Holzner turned himself in?" She's so agitated that droplets of saliva spew from her lips as she speaks.

"I didn't because I was afraid," Diaz says.

"Afraid of what?"

"Of being arrested. You see, I was the one who helped Ian escape. I hid him in my apartment, and then I drove him to a women's commune in Scottsdale, Arizona, that sheltered him. I was active in the women's underground railroad until nineteen seventy-seven. I've come forward now because I won't sit by another second and watch Ian sacrifice himself for me. He's an innocent man. I saw his face, I heard him sob. He had no idea that there was a bomb at the VA."

Lovely exhales a "Holy crap." Lou Frantz lets out a noncommittal grunt. I glance back at Holzner, who's resting his head in his shackled hands. When he looks up, he shakes his head at me in reproach. There are tears in his eyes.

Over the din coming from the gallery, Judge Gibson hollers, "*Silencio!* Everyone be quiet! Especially you, Ms. Diaz. Do *not* say another world. Marshals, get the jury out of here *pronto!*"

When the jurors are out of the courtroom, the judge says, "Mr.

Stern, before you called this witness, did you advise her that this testimony could incriminate her as an accessory to murder? That there is no statute of limitations on that?"

"I'll answer that, Judge," Diaz says. "That's exactly what Parker told me. Which he didn't have to, because I consulted a lawyer years ago and knew the risks already. That's exactly why I didn't come forward until now."

"I would advise you to consult a lawyer before we go any further," the judge says.

"I want to finish my testimony," Diaz says. "It's the truth. Ian didn't murder anyone."

Judge Gibson takes off his reading glasses, bows his head, and pinches his nose hard. "Okay, Ms. Diaz. It's your funeral. Marshal, get the jury back in here."

When the jury is seated again, Reddick conducts a scorched-earth cross-examination, forcing Diaz to tell the story of how she let Holzner hide in her apartment for three weeks while she arranged with her contacts to find a place to protect him, and how she drove him to the Arizona desert in her Volkswagen van. Over and over, Diaz is forced to admit that she knew that Holzner was charged with murder, knew that he was a fugitive from justice, knew that helping him escape was a crime. The cross is intended less, it seems, to attack Diaz's testimony than to put her behind bars. Marilee Reddick has always been a vindictive shit.

When Reddick finishes, I tell the judge I have no further questions. He excuses the jury again, and as soon as the jurors are out of the room, a marshal approaches Diaz and informs her that she's under arrest as an accessory to murder. He actually puts her in handcuffs.

"This is bullshit," Holzner calls out. "You government pigs haven't changed a bit since nineteen seventy-five."

The judge says, "Ms. Diaz, this is unfortunate. But you made your own decision. I suggest you get a lawyer."

"I'm Ms. Diaz's attorney," Lou Frantz says in a voice that can probably be heard three floors up. "This is a travesty, a miscarriage of justice. Don't worry, Ms. Diaz, I'll have you out in an hour."

The marshals escort Diaz out of the courtroom to the accompaniment of Louis Frantz's taunting.

"We're in recess," the judge says.

Holzner comes over to me and says, "Why did you do it? I didn't want that. I never wanted that."

Emily Lansing suddenly appears. "It doesn't matter what you want, Dad. Parker's doing want *we* want. He's trying to save your life."

CHAPTER
FORTY-THREE

On this morning, Ian Holzner, surrounded by a phalanx of marshals' vehicles, drives with me to court. The media reporters on the courthouse steps seem almost festive, as if a man's last chance to avoid the death penalty is a spectator sport. Holzner pauses for a moment, but I drag him away before he can launch into another polemic.

Lovely is already in the courtroom, setting up our computers and exhibits. I don't ask where Frantz is, because I don't want to know. This is my show. I sit down at the defense table and remind myself of the basic rules of oral advocacy: speak slowly; tell a story; ignore distractions from the prosecution or the gallery; don't use notes; make eye contact with each juror; and most importantly, believe what you're saying. I let a wave of fear pass over me, don't try to outswim or dive under it. I was no more than ten years old when I came to believe I'd never learn my father's identity, fifteen when I decided I didn't want to know a man who'd abandoned me. The belief had become so engrained that I stopped thinking of the elusive "him." Then he appeared, and now I understand that my resentment and anger were so strong because I'd never truly given up. So as any son should, I'm giving my father the benefit of the doubt. I just hope the jury does, too.

Judge Gibson takes the bench. It's one of those rare occasions when he proves he can master the art of judicial solemnity. "Members of the jury, we are ready to proceed with the last two stages of trial, which are the closing arguments of counsel, after which I'll instruct you in detail with respect to the law that governs in this case. Because the government has the burden of proof, you will hear first from counsel for the government, then from counsel for the defense. After that, counsel for the government has an opportunity for a rebuttal argument. Following all of the arguments, I will instruct you on the law. Please remember that it is important that we give full consideration to the arguments that are made by counsel in the case. And we'll proceed, then, and hear from counsel for the government. Ms. Reddick."

Reddick stands, pulls down the hem of her short blue jacket, and adjusts the lectern so she can speak directly to the jury. "May it please the court, counsel, ladies and gentlemen of the jury. Good morning. On December seventeenth, nineteen seventy-five, people in Playa Delta, California, were working, or watching their children, or doing their Christmas shopping, or celebrating birthdays. But for Ian Holzner, December seventeenth, nineteen seventy-five, was the day when his hatred for the United States of America turned him into a mass murderer. On that day, Ian Holzner carried out his plan to wreak death, destruction, and chaos in Playa Delta, the very city in which he was born and raised. That afternoon, a bomb he built exploded just as he planned, killing four innocent men and women and injuring scores of others. As I discuss the evidence with you, bear three things in mind: Holzner's words; Holzner's deeds; Holzner's unique abilities. By his words, I mean his repeated calls for escalating violence against our government. By his deeds, I mean the pattern of increasingly violent assaults against his perceived enemies. By his abilities, I mean his talent for assembling and planting bombs designed to keep him safe and to kill others." If Reddick was shaken by Diaz's testimony yesterday, she doesn't show it. Her delivery is somehow coldly logical and impassioned at the same time.

I look only at the judge, and Lovely looks only at the jury to gauge reactions. We don't take notes, because nothing that Reddick says is important. We don't look at Reddick, because she's not worthy of our attention. At least, that's the game we play, a game that will last for hours.

Reddick's underlings put up on the courtroom monitors a slideshow setting forth every violent, anti-American statement Holzner made in speeches and underground communiqués—a call for the public execution of the president of the United States; boasts about blowing up public property; ever more vicious pleas for blood in the streets and vengeance against the Establishment for its oppression of the poor and minorities. She recounts Holzner's frequent quotation of Thomas Jefferson: "The tree of liberty must be refreshed from time to time with the blood of patriots and tyrants." She reminds the jury that, nearly twenty years after Holzner spouted these words, Timothy McVeigh had them embossed on the shirt he was wearing when he was arrested for bombing the federal building in Oklahoma City. It's an improper, inflammatory statement, but I'm not about to validate it by standing up and objecting. Reddick has us immobilized in a rhetorical chokehold. Just wait, I repeat like a mantra. But wait to say what? Although I should remain impassive, I can't help glancing over at Emily Lansing. Her hands are clasped so tightly that the tips of her fingers have turned an ugly purple. I'm pretty sure she's trying hard not to twist her hair.

In a jackhammer cadence, Reddick next reminds the jury of Holzner's evil deeds—the many bombs he built and detonated; the brutal beating of Craig Adamson; his delight in provoking violent confrontation with the police; and his successful flight to avoid prosecution.

"Ian Holzner hid for almost forty years because he didn't want to be punished for the evil he'd done," she says. "His running away was the cowardly act of a guilty man."

She breaks from her theme and goes into a two-hour discussion of the evidence against Holzner. In meticulous detail, she summarizes the testimony of Agent Roudebusch and the forensics experts and Gladdie Giddens and even Craig Adamson. She projects on the courtroom monitors the map of the Playa Delta VA found in the gang's apartment and leaves it there for the jury to see. She characterizes Carol Diaz as a liar who wants to save an old childhood friend and argues that even if Diaz is telling the truth, Holzner was pretending to be hysterical to give himself an alibi and find a patsy to help him escape.

To conclude, she turns to what she calls Holzner's *abilities*. "He was a practitioner of the black arts," she says. "He could use his charisma, his good looks, his fame as a star athlete to corrupt the minds of the weak and the vulnerable. He could seduce people and convince them to commit violent acts. Most importantly, he could make sophisticated, destructive bombs. If Ian Holzner didn't make the bomb that exploded in the Playa Delta VA, then who did? There's no answer because no one else could've done it. No one else had the know-how. Of course Ian Holzner is the Playa Delta Bomber." With that, she sits down. But she isn't finished. She'll have a rebuttal, and for an attorney the last word is more valuable than platinum.

"Thank you, Ms. Reddick," the judge says. "We'll hear from the defense. Mr. Stern."

Lovely glances up and gives a nod of encouragement. She can't hide her concern that I'll suffer a bout of glossophobia. When I stand, I do feel the overwhelming lightheadedness, the wobbly limbs, the nausea. But all that miraculously goes away when I walk over and lay my hand on Holzner's shoulder.

"May it please the Court, Ms. Reddick, members of the jury," I say. "Mine is the last voice you'll hear from the defense. The government has the last word because it has the burden of proof. You've heard the evidence. You are the final arbiters of Ian Holzner's fate. You've taken an oath of office that you'll decide this case only on the facts and not based on bias or prejudice or likes or dislikes or speculation. That's a hard thing to do, but it's also essential to justice."

I move away from the podium and look each juror in the eyes. All are stone-faced except for Joey, who's wearing that permanent sneer. Why did I leave him on the panel? But he's there, so I speak directly to him first. "The renowned attorney Clarence Darrow once said that great ideas and new truths come from the men and women who have dared to be rebels. Very often such people are despised. Ian Holzner was a rebel, an outlaw, and because of that you might find his words and actions despicable. I, myself, find what he did back then despicable. But if you follow your oath of office, if you resolve to reach a just verdict, you simply cannot convict him for those actions or based on your feelings about what he did or said. You can only convict if the government has proved beyond a reasonable doubt that he committed the Playa Delta bombing. And members of the jury, the government hasn't come close to meeting its burden." Inadvertently channeling the bombastic Moses Dworsky in his prime, I point my index finger skyward and bellow, "There's almost nothing that you heard in the courtroom that's *free* from doubt."

I give them my own view of the evidence. Gladdie Giddens didn't know which Holzner brother was which and was led by an overzealous FBI agent to identify Ian Holzner as being present at the crime scene. Craig Adamson was out for revenge. FBI agent Roudebusch admitted that his partner, Hilton, disagreed about who was on the missing tape recording. The government didn't call Charles Sedgwick or Rachel O'Brien. Risking criminal prosecution, Carol Diaz testified that the bombing so shocked Holzner that he became hysterical.

I describe Martin Lansing's exemplary life and remind the jurors that he turned himself in—not the actions of a guilty man, especially one with a young daughter. I argue that none of the government's experts could say with certainty that Holzner had made the bomb, which was of the type constructed by a number of other radical cells, including the Baader-Meinhof Group in Germany, and that the prosecution had presented no fingerprint or DNA evidence. I remind the jury that a woman's earring was found at the scene.

"Let's talk about why Ian Holzner fled," I say. "Let's look at what was happening in our country at the time. There were the conspiracy trials of the Chicago Eight and the Seattle Seven, both travesties of justice where the defendants were wrongfully convicted, and both reversed on appeal. There were COINTELPRO's investigations of the Weather Underground, so fraught with illegality that people like Mark Rudd and Bernardine Dohrn and Bill Ayers basically served no time in prison. Ian Holzner fled not because he was guilty, but because he was innocent and couldn't have gotten a fair trial back then. But now, members of the jury, you can give him the fair trial and the just result he deserves."

I move behind Holzner and place my hands on his shoulders again. I want the jury to see that I care about him, to *feel* my concern. "Ladies and gentlemen, you've heard hours of testimony from government witnesses and argument from Ms. Reddick about how Ian Holzner was a radical, how he flouted our country's laws and wanted to overthrow our democracy. An urban guerrilla. A middle-class revolutionary. A spoiled, ungrateful brat. It's all true. In nineteen seventy-five, he had no respect for the law of this land. But now, members of the jury, it's your turn to decide whether you respect the law of the land. If you do, then you'll acquit Ian Holzner, because the prosecution has failed to prove guilt beyond a reasonable doubt. But if, instead, you vote to convict, you'll have flouted our laws and committed an act of radicalism. So, I urge you to follow the law, to do justice, to respect our system of government. It's not an easy thing to do. But if you truly believe in the rule of law, then you can bring back only one verdict—not guilty. Members of the jury, Ian Holzner's life is in your hands."

CHAPTER
FORTY-FOUR

Marilee Reddick is at the lectern before I can sit down. She spends a few minutes scoffing at my argument and the rest of her time talking about Russell Breen and Floyd Corwin and Lucille Gomez and Elaine Smith, the four people who died in the Playa Delta bombing. She reminds the jury of the how precious mundane life is.

"Russell and Floyd and Lucille and Elaine died that day, and there's nothing you can do as a jury to bring them back," she says. "But what you can do is make sure that justice is done in their names. And justice requires that you find Ian Holzner guilty of murder in the first degree." She bows. "It has been an honor, ladies and gentlemen, to represent the United States government and the victims and families of victims of the Playa Delta bombing."

Judge Gibson immediately starts instructing the jury on the law—base your verdict solely on the evidence; don't rely on anything that happened outside the courtroom; a defendant is innocent until proven guilty beyond a reasonable doubt; for a defendant to be convicted of first-degree murder, he must have acted with premeditation and malice aforethought. Then: "The defendant is not on trial for any of his thoughts, beliefs, or statements, which are protected by the First Amendment to the Constitution of the United States. The First Amendment, however, does not prevent the prosecution from offering evidence of a defendant's beliefs in an attempt to prove that he had some motive, knowledge, or intent for committing the crimes alleged in the indictment. Whether you agree or disagree with the defendant's expressed opinions or beliefs is irrelevant. You may no more convict the defendant because you may disagree with his opinions and beliefs than you may acquit him because you may agree with his opinions and beliefs."

I glance at the jury. They're looking in the judge's direction, but I truly don't know if any of them understand the instructions or even care about them.

Gibson takes off his reading glasses and gives the last instruction by memory: "Finally, members of the jury, remember that the question before you can never be, 'Will the government win or lose this case?' Regardless of whether the verdict is guilty or not guilty, the government always wins when justice is done." It's a nice sentiment, but against human nature—Marilee Reddick wants a conviction just as much I want an acquittal, justice be damned.

—⁂—

While Lovely checks in with her office, I go with Holzner when the marshals take him back to his holding cell. Before the marshals take him away, he comes over and embraces me. Now that the audience has left the building, he's allowed his guards to remove the shackles. I hug back, a reaction that feels so natural it's jarring.

"Thank you, Parker," he says. "I'm glad I got to meet you, to know who you really are. You might not want to hear it, but we're very much alike."

I take a step back. "I don't think so, Ian. I don't like evangelical causes that make living human beings their deities. Those are the groups that become deadly. You were a demigod. I'm just a gun for hire working within the system."

"You have the same passion I had. I heard it in your voice."

"It's called advocacy. A form of acting. I do it well."

"No, it's passion, fervor for the ideal. For equality, in my case, for justice in yours. For Harriet, it's spiritual redemption, misguided or not."

"You and Harriet craved power. I'm trying to serve justice. The proverbial cog."

"Then why didn't you suffer a moment's stage fright when you truly started to believe in my innocence? You do believe, you know."

Before I can respond, he nods to the marshals, who take him back to the courthouse holding cell.

As I turn the corner and walk toward the attorneys lounge, I see Lovely sprinting toward me, her pumps clacking on the linoleum floor. When she reaches me, she holds out the phone and says, "It's for you, through my office. He'll only talk to you. Maybe a crank, but I think you should . . ."

I take the phone. "This is Parker Stern."

"Parker, it's Jerry Holzner." *Pahkoo, it's Jehwy Hoznuh.* There's tension in his voice. No, it's more than that—he's just on the controlled side of panic.

How do I play it? Friendly? Detached? I've hinted in open court that the man might be the Playa Delta Bomber. I've wondered whether he really exists. Businesslike and detached is always safest. "What can I do for you, Jerry?"

"I saw . . . I read about what Carol did." *I wed about what Cawol did.* "It's not fair. Not fair for anyone, not for Ian, not for Carol, it's not fair." He pauses for so long I fear I've lost him. "I have to tell you, Parker. It's not fair."

"Tell me what, Jerry?"

"I have to tell you, but I can't tell you on the phone. Ian always says no phones. The FBI is listening. They're always listening. That's what Ian always says." There's deep, labored breathing. "I hate the FBI."

"When did Ian say this, Jerry?"

"He . . . Not on the phone. *Not* on the phone. Where are you, Parker? Why aren't you here?"

"Jerry, I'm at the courthouse. The trial just ended. Where are you?"

"At your office, of course. I called for you, but you're not here. I didn't know when the trial was over."

"What do you mean my office?"

"Your office in the Valley. Dworsky's office."

I've never truly thought of the place as my office, and haven't set foot in the place since the weekend after Dworsky murdered Sedgwick.

"It's *your* office, too, right?" Jerry says. "Why did Moses stab Charlie? It stinks of rotten fish here."

"Is anyone else there?"

"No. The door was open, it's an office, I thought you would be here, I called for you. No one answered. Please, Parker, what should I do? I have to tell you. I don't care if Ian will be mad. I read in the papers about what Carol did."

"Stay where you are, Jerry. I'll be there in forty-five minutes."

A raspy sigh of relief. "'Kay. 'Kay. Good."

CHAPTER FORTY-FIVE

Lovely and I sprint out of the courthouse and toward the lot where the rented Lexus is parked. She's put her shoes in her briefcase and is running in stocking feet. We have to get there before Jerry decides to disappear again. Or the jury could come back with a guilty verdict immediately. If that happens, the US Attorney will characterize anything Jerry has to say as an after-the-fact, self-serving attempt to save his brother.

A few of the media catch sight of us and follow. We must be hurrying after something, right? Fortunately, I'm parked close to the escalator and know an alternate exit that passes under City Hall. When we drive out onto First Street, it looks like we've lost them. In my zeal to get to the Valley, I carelessly swerve into the left lane, almost hitting a Metro bus.

"Jesus," Lovely says. "Let's get there in one piece."

"Sorry."

"Should we be going alone? There's something wrong with that guy."

"He's a little slow. The trauma from what the cops—"

"I don't care what the reason is. He sounds like a nutcase. We should call the cops."

"Which will scare him away permanently. And he's my uncle. Ian's brother."

"You can't be serious. The man's a stranger."

"I'm not calling the police on Jerry. If you don't want to come, you can get out at the next intersection."

Her sigh is accusatory, yet she says, "Just keep driving."

A fine mist starts falling—it's January, after all—and the drizzle snarls the Hollywood Freeway. The forty-five minute drive takes us an hour and ten. Lovely spends the time on the phone with her office, talking to Lou Frantz about other cases, and all the while I grip the steering wheel and pray that she won't tell him where we're going, because he'll certainly insist we call the police, and if we don't, he'll call them himself. Sure, it's the rational thing to do. But I'm not about to lose the chance to get information that will save Ian. Carol Diaz told part of the truth. There's more truth out there somewhere. I also meant what I said—Jerry is my uncle. He clearly still loves Ian, worships him, I suspect, and I'm Ian's son, so I don't believe he'd harm me or my loved ones. It's a kind of trust I've felt with few people: Lovely Diamond; my mentor, Harmon Cherry; Deanna Poulos, my late friend and the founder of The Barrista.

I finally pull up to Dworsky's building and park the car. You'd think the rain would've washed the stench away, but the place now smells of rotting fish laced with creosote. Lovely stumbles on the top step to the entrance, and I barely catch her arm before she falls forward. Her sharp look conveys her unhappiness. There's water on the floor of the rickety elevator. I hope it's condensation and not from a leak that might short out the electrical system.

The elevator makes it to the second floor, and when we step out into reception, we find Jerry Holzner dozing in one of the armchairs, a septuagenarian lump. He's dressed in the same black San Francisco Giants windbreaker and cap that he was wearing when I saw him the day of the courthouse bombing. When I walk over and touch his elbow, he jumps, blinks his eyes twice, springs out of the chair, and removes his cap.

"Oh, thank God you're here, Parker." He nods at Lovely. "I know you, Ms. Diamond. I called your office. I trust you." *I twust you.*

"What do you want to tell us, Jerry?" I ask.

He turns down his lips in a kind of dyspeptic frown. "I'm doing it because of Carol. She was brave. I want to be brave like she is. Even though Ian doesn't want me to tell it."

"I don't want you to tell it, either, Jerry," says a woman's voice, and I look up to see Eleanor Dworsky emerging from the inner suite of offices. "So don't say another word."

Jerry's eyes widen and almost distend like a child with the night terrors. "Waychil?"

It takes me a moment to realize that he's called Eleanor Dworsky *Rachel*. But that's not what frightens me. What terrifies me is that she's holding a very large handgun. Her son, Brandon Soloway, is holding another.

I was wrong when I concluded that Eleanor Dworsky didn't have cosmetic surgery. She's clearly had more than one operation to hide the fact that she's Rachel O'Brien—bone shaved in the nose to make it more beaklike; eye surgery to make them smaller, rounder; dental work that caused her chin to recede. Whatever she did to herself, the objective was to make her homelier, nondescript. That, along with her decision not to interfere with the natural aging process, and she concocted the perfect disguise.

"What, no doughnuts, Eleanor?" Lovely says. Why won't Lovely keep quiet? Maybe it's the fear, or maybe it's some misguided belief that she can prolong our lives by causing them to drop their guard. She's wrong. There's nothing you can do to deter someone like O'Brien.

"Refined sugar and processed wheat are the megacorporations' weapons against the masses," Eleanor says. "You never noticed that I don't touch those things? Keep eating that stuff and it'll kill you, Lovely. Though I'm afraid you won't live long enough for that to happen."

Brandon chortles at that.

"Why did you order Moses to kill Sedgwick?" Lovely asks. "And another question—do you seriously think you're John Brown?"

"I'm disappointed in you, Jerry," Eleanor says. "You always obeyed Ian. Except for now, and look at the mess you've made."

"You are evil, Rachel," he says. "You always were. All the killing, and you let Ian and Charlie and Belinda take the blame. You killed them, didn't you, Charlie and Belinda? After Charlie kept quiet for so long you killed him anyway. It's not fair. You are evil."

"Let's get this over with," Brandon says.

"Not here, Brandon. Think! Maybe Jerry, but if the other two are found dead here, who are they going to look for?"

Brandon's hand starts trembling, and he waves the gun in the air, and for a moment I think he might shoot Eleanor, and then I fear he'll shoot us, but he lowers the weapon.

"You know what sucks?" Eleanor says to me. "Because you showed up here, I think Ian might get off. This time. What do you think, Lovely?"

"If his lawyers disappear or are found dead during trial?" Lovely says. "A no-brainer mistrial."

"But what I'm thinking," Eleanor says, "is that the jury is already deliberating. So says the Internet. The fascists won't want to pay for another trial, won't let the Playa Delta Bomber stay out of prison for another day. And what's left for you lawyers to do? Your boss Frantz can babysit Ian through sentencing. That's good. I've been waiting almost forty years for that son of a bitch to pay for his betrayal, and now it's going to happen, with a bonus—not one, but two sons dead. I only wish I could think of a way to get rid of the daughter so he could see it all go. As Fidel said, 'No thieves, no traitors. This time the revolution is for real.' Ian Holzner is a thief who robbed the masses of his talents, a traitor to the brave revolutionaries who followed him."

Jerry stands to full height. For the first time I realize that he's an imposing man. He holds his arms at his sides in an apelike arc and takes a step toward Eleanor and Brandon. "You are right, Rachel. You can't do it here. Not even to me. Because it is your office. You will be the only suspect."

"Stay back, Jerry," Eleanor says. "You were never a fool."

He keeps advancing, two steps, three steps, and after the fourth, Eleanor calmly shoots him in the gut.

Lovely shrieks.

"I could kill you quickly, Jerry," Eleanor says. "But I want it to hurt."

Jerry emits an animalistic grunt and his knees buckle, yet he keeps approaching like some wondrous gothic monster. When Brandon shoots him in the throat, he gurgles and falls to the floor, then convulses hideously and loses consciousness.

I rush over to Jerry, not even flinching when Brandon raises his

gun and points it at me, but once again Eleanor stops him with a wave
of the hand.

"What do we do?" Brandon asks.

She nods toward Jerry's body. "Pick that up and get it to the van.
I'll move the other two."

"You're insane," Lovely says.

"They said that about Lenin and Trotsky and Mao and Che,"
Eleanor says. "They said that about John Brown."

Brandon holsters his gun, bends over, and lifts Jerry onto his shoulders with surprising ease. Eleanor motions for us to go outside. We all
pile into the elevator. I place myself between Lovely and the others.
Over the creaking cables I listen for any sign that Jerry is alive—a groan,
a shallow breath. Nothing.

The elevator descends, much too quickly this time. The door
opens, and instead of an empty parking lot, there are cars and vans
and a familiar face, and someone pulls Lovely one way and someone
pulls me the other way. I go down, and my cheek is flat to the wet pave-
ment, and there's a shout of "FBI, drop your weapons," but someone—
maybe Brandon, maybe Eleanor, maybe one of the cops, maybe all at
the same time—fires a shot, and Eleanor and Brandon crumple as one,
and Jerry's limp body makes a sickening thud when he tumbles from
Brandon's arms.

When I'm sure it's all over, I scramble to my feet, then go and help
Lovely up.

Walking toward us and holding a badge in the air is Mariko Heim.
"Are you two okay?"

"Fine," Lovely says, though I'm not sure it's true. "You? You're
FBI?"

"It looks that way." Heim says. "Though I don't know for how long.
This mess just cost the Bureau six years of undercover work."

CHAPTER FORTY-SIX

Rachel O'Brien—alias Eleanor Dworsky, among other names—her son Brandon Soloway, and my uncle, Jerry Holzner, are all dead. When I return home that afternoon and tell Ian what happened, he breaks down in tears. I don't know what Jerry wanted to tell me, and Ian won't say, instead withdrawing to his bedroom and leaving Emily and me desperately trying to figure out a way to get him to tell us the truth.

In a media blitz that evening, the Church of the Sanctified Assembly excoriates the United States government for permitting the FBI to infiltrate the inner sanctum of a religious organization. The Assembly's spokesperson calls the government's action a clear violation of the freedom of religion and threatens to bring a lawsuit for violation of the Assembly's civil rights. For once, I agree with the Assembly. The church will never sue, however—Heim was investigating Ascending Sodality, a church-sanctioned practice of child abuse that supposedly ended when I left. Someone my age must have finally come forward. Heim, of course, will reveal nothing, not even that she saved our lives by returning fire at Brandon Soloway on the day he murdered Belinda Hayes and tried to kill Lovely and me. I also realize that when I first met with Hayes, it wasn't Moses who frightened her—it was Eleanor, whom Hayes undoubtedly recognized as Rachel O'Brien.

I thought Jerry was being paranoid when he told me that the FBI had been listening in on his phone calls, but as it turns out, he was right. How else would they have known to come to Dworsky's office?

A search of the Dworsky home reveals an underground bunker, in which the authorities find a weapons arsenal, bomb-making equipment, and a laptop computer containing draft versions of JB's communiqués and something called "The Manifesto of the Harpers Ferry Liberation Front." Not only did Brandon murder Belinda Hayes, but he also assembled the bomb that exploded at the federal courthouse. He left the bomb on the courthouse steps, but too near the building to cause the damage that they'd hoped. His mother must have truly believed he was the screw-up she kept saying he was. And why did Moses Dworsky go along with this? Maybe he was a true believer. Or maybe he loved Rachel O'Brien so much that he was willing to do whatever she asked of him.

The next morning, Lovely and I appear in court and ask Judge Gibson to declare a mistrial, or at least to reopen the evidence phase so we can tell the jury what happened last night. I've actually convinced myself that Marilee Reddick, as an officer of the court and a representative of the United States government, will agree to it.

"We object, Your Honor," Reddick says. "There was nothing found at the Dworsky residence that implicates O'Brien in the Playa Delta bombing. The defendant is on trial for what happened in nineteen seventy-five, not for what's happened during the past year. And who's to say he wasn't the mastermind of the recent crimes."

"That's the most ridiculous thing I've ever heard anyone utter in a courtroom," I say. "O'Brien told me that her goal was to frame Holzner."

"I've read the police report," she says. "That's not what she said at all. She talked about his betrayal, which could mean that he bombed the facility when she didn't want him to."

"Yeah, right," I say. "That's why she's going around murdering people who could exonerate him. Marilee, Ian Holzner is a victim, and by persisting in this prosecution, you're no better than a terrorist. Worse, because you're doing it for self-aggrandizement."

"Fuck you, Parker." She's looks as if she's about to get out of her chair and attack me.

"Calm down, both of you," the judge says.

"I won't calm down, Your Honor," I say. "They killed his brother yesterday, almost killed me twice over. For Marilee to feed you this crap with a straight face is disgusting."

"These fanatics like Holzner will do anything for their cause," she says. "They'll kill their loved ones if they think they need to. Look at what O'Brien had her husband do. A suicide mission. We've had a trial, and we should finish it."

"The truth is finally coming to light," I say. "Carol Diaz, O'Brien as the perpetrator of the recent crimes. This is a death-penalty case, Your Honor. I appeal to your sense of justice. You cannot let this case go forward until the FBI and the police conduct a full investigation into the activities of Rachel O'Brien and Brandon Soloway."

The judge leans back in his chair, looks up at the ceiling, and shuts his eyes. He drums his pen on the desk. "Let's see what the jury comes back with," he says. "If there's a guilty verdict, we can take another look at it."

He's playing it safe, hoping that the jury will acquit so he doesn't have to make the decision himself. I didn't think octogenarian Carlton F. Gibson would care about what the media or the appellate court thinks of him, but I'm wrong—judges always care. I do take comfort in his statement that he'll reconsider if there's a guilty verdict. And with this new evidence, it's highly unlikely that a conviction will survive an appeal. Still, the right-wing media pundits have already decided that the HFLF was merely the present-day name for the Holzner-O'Brien Gang, and that Holzner ordered the execution of his own brother because Jerry was going to implicate him. I don't want just a high probability that the judge will dismiss the case, I want certainty, and I don't have it.

As we leave the courtroom, the marshals are shepherding the jurors in to begin the morning's deliberations. We lawyers stop, assume postures of respect, and let them pass. I spent the entire trial hoping that they heeded the judge's admonition not to watch television or surf the Internet, and now I pray that at least one of them did the exact opposite. It's not an ethical thought, to be sure, but sometimes ethics and justice diverge. My late mentor, Harmon Cherry, told us that such thinking was the gateway drug to corruption. But Harmon never represented his own father in a murder trial.

When the jurors are inside the deliberation room, the air between the US Attorney and us once again ignites with hostility, and we part ways without a word.

"I've got to get back to the office," Lovely says. "Lou has three new cases for me. Including Carol Diaz. Are you going to The Barrista to wait?"

"No, I think I'll stick around in case they come back."

"It's way too soon," she says.

"I'll wait anyway."

She starts to walk away, but turns around, puts her arms around me, gives me a deep, courthouse-inappropriate kiss, turns back, and click-clacks toward the escalator.

The attorneys lounge is empty because this is a Thursday, a slow morning. The clerk has our cell-phone numbers and will call and text if the jury reaches a verdict. I go into a conference room—they're all empty—and start reading a biography of the brilliant civil-trial lawyer Norman Roy Grutman, who represented clients as diverse as the Reverend Jerry Falwell and *Penthouse* magazine, and once represented Penthouse *against* Falwell. I'm a hundred and twenty pages and three hours in when the sliding door opens and a marshal walks in.

"The jury just passed us a note," he says.

Reddick and her cohort are in the courtroom in a matter of minutes. It takes Lou Frantz and Lovely Diamond twenty-five minutes to arrive, and a full hour for the marshals to get Ian Holzner and Emily Lansing to the courtroom. During the wait I can't keep still but don't have enough equilibrium to pace. So I just sit in my chair at counsel table and grind my teeth and bounce my right leg at what must be a hundred and fifty pulses a minute, which is also the speed of my sledge-hammering heart. I continually wipe my sweaty palms with a paper towel, and when that's soaked and torn, on my suit pants.

When Holzner is in his place, the judge brings the jury back. What will follow is the torture of ritual. We stand as the jurors enter the room and sit down when Judge Gibson tells us to. He asks the members of the jury whether they've selected a foreperson. They have, and it's the older man caring for his infirm wife. I try not to speculate about what his selection means, yet can't help hoping that it means the jurors elected someone who was fair. The judge instructs the foreman to hand the note to the marshal who's been attending to them. The marshal brings the form up to the judge's bench, where Gibson fumbles for his glasses before reading the note with a neutral expression that doesn't tip us off to its contents. When he's finished, he beckons the court clerk, who rises out of her chair, retrieves the note, and sits down again. In a practiced flat tone of the bureaucrat, the clerk reads, "We, the jury, are hopelessly deadlocked."

Judge Gibson looks at them in utter disbelief. "You haven't been out long enough to be deadlocked." He flings his pen on the desk, shuffles through a stack of papers, and reads them what's called an *Allen* charge, after an 1896 case called *Allen v. United States*. He asks the jury to go back and deliberate further. He tells them that if they don't reach a verdict, there will be another expensive trial and that they're as competent to decide the case as any future jury. He concludes by instructing them that while they shouldn't give up their honest beliefs, they have a duty to try to reach a verdict. "Now get back in there and do your jobs," he says.

The jurors start to rise, but then grungy Joey raises his hand and starts talking without permission. "It's not going to do any good, Judge. It's eleven to one for conviction. I'm the *one*, and I'm not going to change my mind. I think there's been juror misconduct here. The foreman, Mr. Rudolph, watched the news and talked about how there were these murders of Hayes and Sedgwick and how the media thinks Mr. Holzner is responsible. Your instructions said that we should look only at the evidence, and that's not evidence."

"Is that true, Mr. Rudolph?" the judge asks.

The old man's face has turned almost neon red. "That's not what happened at all. He's making it up because he wants an acquittal."

The judge points a finger at the jury box. "You others. What's the truth?"

No one volunteers. The courtroom sounds like a hornets' nest before an assault on an intruder. I glance at Lovely, who's smiling gleefully. It's not an acquittal, but it's a victory, a chance to start over.

"We're in recess," Judge Gibson says. "Members of the jury, you have gravely disappointed me. You're going to be sequestered in a hotel until I sort this out. Call your relatives and tell them to pack a bag for you. Please leave this courtroom now."

As they file out, Joey looks at us and raises a fist in solidarity. At this moment, I love the guy.

CHAPTER
FORTY-SEVEN

At six o'clock on a chilly, moon-and-lamp-lit LA evening, I arrive back at my condominium. I've spent the day in court. I'd hoped that Judge Gibson would've entered judgment of acquittal immediately, or at least declared a mistrial, but he ordered us to brief the issues while he conducts an investigation into Joey's allegations. He's not convinced that it isn't Joey who's engaged in misconduct, which would mean that an alternate juror, who would probably vote with the majority, would replace our single supporter. We wasted hours wrangling over briefing schedules for a Rule 29 motion seeking a judgment of acquittal or the alternative, a motion for a mistrial.

I pull into my underground garage, and as I get out of the rented Lexus, a large figure emerges from the darkness. I shrink back inside, lock the door, and start the engine. There's a tapping at my window, and I look up to see the man who lately calls himself *Zorro Snowden*. Except he's dressed not in his costume but in khakis and a short-sleeve dress shirt, like a courier for a law-firm messenger service. He's carrying an overstuffed manila folder under his arm, undoubtedly the garbled recording that Brandon Soloway delivered to me. I again ask a question that might never be answered: why did Rachel O'Brien give me that tape? Whatever the reason, what's on the recording will undoubtedly hurt Ian Holzner.

"Were you successful?" I ask.

"Listen and you be the judge. Inside the envelope along with the original recording there is a flash drive. The audio file on it is encrypted. The password is *DonDiego59*. The *D*s are in capital letters."

"I appreciate the help. Please pass it on."

"It wasn't an easy project. Of course, there can be no hint of involvement on our part. We did the science and technology. But we won't be part of the legal proceeding. We know that might cause you grief if you choose to use the tape as evidence, but we cannot become involved."

"So I've always assumed."

"Mr. Stern, it's not pleasant listening. Good-bye, sir." This time when he leaves, there's no bow, no flourish, just a transparent attempt to look restrained as he tries to get the hell out of my parking garage as quickly as possible.

I want to listen to the recording by myself first, so I get out of the car and go around to sit in the passenger seat. I power up my laptop, open the manila folder, and dig past the old audiotape for the flash drive. Once the drive is slotted in the USB port and recognized as an external device, I double-click on the file and enter the password. The audio player launches, and the recording starts. There's silence for the first five, six, seven seconds, and then there's static, followed by the ring of an old-fashioned telephone. Another two rings, and a man answers, and that simple word, "Hello," is intelligible. I'm less excited about learning the truth than resigned to it.

When I hear the muffled voice of a woman say, "Oh my god, Charlie, there's a bomb at the Playa Delta VA!" I immediately pause the recording. Part of me wishes that the voice had stayed muffled forever. Another part realizes that this was inevitable. I take three deep breaths, and with a shaky hand, use the mouse to resume playback.

The trudge up the stairs to my condo unit is painful, taxing to my sore knees and my stiff back and my muddled brain. The burden of the briefcase—no, the burden of what's *in* the briefcase—has my arm trembling.

I open the door to find Ian and Emily in the living room, sitting next to each other and drinking hot tea. Emily is speaking to him quietly, and he's continually shaking his head. Holzner doesn't acknowledge me, just takes a sip of tea and stares at the coffee table. When Emily sees me, she looks up and says, "Parker, please make him listen?"

"Emily, you'll have to excuse us," I say. "I have to talk to Ian alone."

She looks as if she's going to protest, but when she reads my face, she says, "I'll go in the other room."

"No. You have to leave the apartment."

"He's my father, too."

"True, but he's not your client. Go."

She scrutinizes my face again and nods. "I'll go talk to that cute marshal, Stevie. Let me know when you're done."

Holzner takes another sip of tea, and this time glances up.

I don't know why, but as Emily passes by me I put my arms around her and kiss her on the top of her head. I've never done that before. It hits me that Lovely Diamond's father, Ed, kisses his daughter that way. When Emily is out the door, I sit across from Holzner, retrieve my laptop, set it on the table, and wake it up. All this time, Holzner keeps his head down.

At last, the home screen comes up. I launch the audio file. When Holzner hears the first words on the recording, his body quavers so violently that he sloshes tea all over the table, fortunately missing the computer's keyboard.

"Shut if off!" he says.

I hit the pause button and then rewind back to the beginning. "We're going to listen to this together," I say. "And then you're going to tell me all of it. It's time."

The sleeve of his cotton shirt—the cotton shirt that I've loaned him—is drenched with tea.

"Oh, god, did you burn yourself?" I ask.

"It was lukewarm." He dabs at his sleeve with a paper napkin that can't possibly dry him off. "Play the damn thing if you're going to play it. Then I'll tell you what happened, and we'll decide what you're going to do."

—⚏—

Sedgwick: Hello?

Woman: Oh my god, Charlie, there's a bomb at the Playa Delta VA! Oh my god, I thought . . . Oh my god. Rachel did it. She put the bomb there. [Sobbing]

Sedgwick: Alicia? Chill out.

Alicia: Oh fuck, Charlie, what did I do? What did I do? Oh fuck.

Sedgwick: Calm down, Alicia. What do you mean Rachel's put the bomb—?

Alicia: She said she planted it in the restroom at the VA. I don't know what [inaudible].

Sedgwick: That's [inaudible]. Ian shit-canned the operation. Keep calm and don't worry. It's bullshit. You know how Rachel always [inaudible]. So just calm the fuck down.

Alicia: It's not bullshit. She [inaudible]. In the restroom.

Jerry Holzner [in the background]: What's wrong, Charlie. *What's wong, Chollie?*

Sedgwick: It's Alicia with some bullshit [inaudible].

Jerry Holzner: [Inaudible]

Sedgwick: Chill out, Alicia. Rachel can't build a fucking bomb.

Alicia: I did it, god damn it.

Sedgwick: Did what?

Alicia: I built the fucking bomb. She told me [inaudible]. I thought he fucking [inaudible]. The bitch told me [inaudible].

Sedgwick: [inaudible] [phone muffled] . . . Ian.

Jerry Holzner: [inaudible]

Sedgwick: The restroom?

Alicia: Yeah, yeah. Second floor. Oh fuck, Charlie. I never thought . . . I've got a son, Charlie. They'll take my baby away. Oh my God. [Hysterical sobbing]

Sedgwick: Just calm down. Ian will handle it.

———ᨈ———

With a surprisingly steady hand, I use the mouse to stop the recording.

"So it's true," I say. "I'm the son of the Playa Delta Bomber. The cops just have the wrong parent."

"Parker, it's not what you think."

"You're not seriously going to tell me that Alicia Bowers isn't my mother, are you? I'd know that voice anywhere."

"That's not what I was going to say," he says. "It's your turn to listen to me. Then you have a decision to make. The hardest of your life."

CHAPTER FORTY-EIGHT

"Sometimes kids with messed up parents do everything to seem normal," Holzner says. "Roles become reversed—the child becomes the parent."

"Tell me about it."

"Yeah, it's ironic that Alicia took care of her father, your grandfather. Pete Bowers was at the Battle of the Bulge during World War Two. He was one of about a hundred and fifty American soldiers captured by the Germans at a town in Belgium called Malmedy. The German SS opened fire on the prisoners and murdered eighty-four of the POWs. Pete Bowers was one of the survivors. I'm sure he considered it bad luck that he lived. Your grandmother was an alcoholic and heroin addict who got together with Pete because he handed over his veteran's benefits. She abandoned her husband and daughter before they moved into our neighborhood, where they lived in a one-room cheap motel that had a refrigerator and a hot plate. So now Pete was grieving for the loss of his wife—I say wife, but I don't even know if they were married."

"My grandmother. What was her name?"

"I . . ."

"It's a stupid question."

"It's exactly what you should be asking. I'm not sure I ever knew. I think you can understand why Alicia—it's been hard for me to call her *Harriet*—never told you anything."

"I don't understand any of this. Except that my mother is a murderer."

"Don't, Parker. Let me finish first." It's a command, but there's a gentleness in his tone that I've never heard before. Or maybe it's simply that I haven't recognized it. Maybe that's what Emily hears, what my brother, Dylan, heard.

"She was a sweet, quiet kid with no one to protect her, no one to teach her how to be a person, much less a girl or a woman," he says. "But somehow she managed. She was brilliant. Much smarter than I am. Do you know that, Parker?"

"Truthfully, I never thought about it. Your mother's IQ isn't very important when you're trying to avoid getting screamed at or slapped in the face or embarrassed that she's going to have sex with every male on a movie set who could advance my career."

He recoils, as if I've slapped *him* in the face, but like a child playing one parent against the other, I push forward. "You didn't know that about her, did you, Ian?"

"She needed someone on her side," he says. "I was that person, I guess. I stopped the kids from teasing her about her Goodwill clothes, about her hand-me-down shoes, about Pete riding around the city on that rusty bicycle and talking to himself and ranting about the demons that were after him. Do you know those asshole kids called her Boogie Bowers? To her face? She never reacted. When she got older, I stopped the creeps from touching her. I was stupid, because I should've known she'd fall in love with me. I laughed it off, thought it was a crush that would pass—she was like my little sister, for god's sake—but it didn't go away. The more I denied her, the more determined she got."

"That's Harriet."

"When people started to listen to my speeches against the war, when I became *somebody*—or, thought I was somebody—Alicia showed up, still infatuated. No, that's not fair, it was truly love. She wanted to be part of what I was doing, to be part of the revolutionary vanguard. I don't think she got any of it. Don't get me wrong, she understood the theory, but I think her acceptance of it was just a way to get close to me. Jesus, I sound like the arrogant bastard I was. Anyway, I told her to go away, said radical politics wasn't for her, that she was destined for better things." He places his hand on his forehead, almost slaps it like a cartoon character experiencing a light-bulb moment. "Jesus, why couldn't I see that if I was warning Alicia away from what I was doing, it must have been the wrong thing to do? If I truly, deep down had believed it was right, I would've welcomed her into it. How could I . . . ?" He gazes past me like an old man with fading vision who can't understand how his strong, youthful eyes didn't see the obvious.

"Alicia would not give up," he says. "Rachel O'Brien encouraged her. Alicia was jealous because Rachel and I were—I thought *I* was in love. That gave Rachel power over Alicia, because the unrequited suitor always wants to please the rival. Rachel kept telling me I should just . . . make love to Alicia and get it over with, that I was acting bourgeois with my middle-America gentlemanly attitude toward her. I thought Rachel was simply taunting Alicia and mocking me. She was a smart ass, always taunting other people."

That was true even in O'Brien's later years, because that's why she had Brandon bring me the tape recording—to taunt me, to let me know that my own mother was responsible for the deaths of four people. She waited until the only person whom she saw as a threat, Charles Sedgwick, was dead. She never thought Jerry would talk—and he didn't, until his last-ditch attempt to tell me the truth. She knew Ian wouldn't tell. And once I heard the tape, I'd have to choose between my parents. Whatever I decided would destroy them both.

"But I can't lay it on O'Brien," Holzner says. "Alicia finally convinced me that she truly believed in what I was doing. You know how? She reminded me of how the army had abandoned her father, how he drank Thunderbird that he got from Sam's Liquor and pedaled this old bicycle calling out, 'Where is she? Where is she?' You never knew if he meant Alicia or his wife. Alicia talked a perfect game, said she hated the government for what it did to her father, for what it had done to the boys in Vietnam. She talked about the rampant racism in this country. So I let her in. I think I was keeping her close so I wouldn't totally lose Playa Delta—even as I ranted against such middle-class attachments." He closes his eyes and whispers. "I . . . I taught Alicia how to make bombs."

I briefly wonder if I'm playing one of Poniard's nightmarish video games, in which Ian Holzner, Rachel O'Brien, Brandon Soloway, Moses Dworsky, and Belinda Hayes are the shadowy avatars who shoot bullets and sling deadly revelations directly at my heart, in which my own mother is the evil Boss of Bosses. A look at Holzner's pallid face drives home that it's all too real.

His words keep spewing out. He taught her because he never thought she could learn, but he soon found himself marveling at her facility and bravery. The shared danger was infused with eroticism, all the more so because they were the only ones with the courage and skill to do it. He finally did what she'd wanted him to do for years and slept with her. When she revealed that she was pregnant with me, he begged her to abort, but she wouldn't destroy a part of him. She vowed never to build a bomb again.

But she did build a bomb again.

He and O'Brien had planned to escalate their revolutionary activities, to do what the Weather Underground failed to do after the Greenwich Village townhouse explosion: assassinate the fascist enemies of the masses. They were going to target the Playa Delta VA precisely because it *was* in Holzner's hometown.

"My brother, Jerry, heard about it from Charlie," he says. "I think it was Charlie's way of trying to stop it without looking like a counterrevolutionary. And oh, did Jerry come at me. He told me to look at myself in the mirror, and I'd see that I had become as bad as the people I was fighting—worse. I listened to him. He really was my big brother. After I did that, I called it off. I made the mistake of telling Rachel O'Brien that I was a father now, and that the fact that I had a son—the fact that I had you, Parker—had changed me. I thought she'd scoff or go ballistic, even become violent, but she just nodded and said she respected my opinion. I should've known by that reaction what she was going to do." He inhales deeply. "My brother wasn't a stupid man. People thought he was, but he wasn't at all. Wisdom comes in many forms, but Jerry had it. I want you to know that about him."

"I know that."

"I didn't even get to see him again. I thought I'd at least get to say good-bye." I expect tears from him, but there are none. There's still something case-hardened about Ian Holzner.

"In early November nineteen seventy-five, I left the collective and went into hiding, as much from O'Brien as from the FBI. I hid from everyone. If I wasn't findable, O'Brien couldn't have her bomb. But I also abandoned Alicia and you. She was living in a two-bedroom apartment with six other people, working as a waitress in the MGM Studios commissary while I watched you, and then I was gone. Rachel struck like the queen cobra she was. She told Alicia that I'd gone into hiding because the pigs had turned up the heat. She said she had a message from me, that I wanted Alicia to build a bomb to be used to show the cops the power and ability we had to inflict damage. That we could kill if we wanted but chose not to. So the bomb would have to contain ball bearings and nails. Supposedly, the bomb was going to explode in the park at two in the morning when no one was around. And, as always, there would be a warning. Your mother refused at first, but Rachel told her that if she didn't comply, I'd consider it a betrayal of our love, that I'd never see her or you again. Alicia was twenty years old with the gullibility of an eager-to-please nine-year-old. She believed Rachel's bullshit." He pauses and inhales deeply several times, like a runner between wind sprints trying to catch his breath.

"How do you know this if you weren't there?" I ask.

I'm surprised that he seems surprised by the question. "Alicia told me."

"And you believed her?"

"She wouldn't lie to me."

"She'd lie to anyone."

"Not to me. Never."

Although my mother has built a life on thumbing her nose at the truth, I believe him. I've seen how she behaves around him.

"Rachel made it her business to tell Alicia what the bomb was really for—on the morning of the bombing," Holzner says. "More cruel taunting. She told Alicia it's what *I* wanted. She knew Alicia would never call the cops on me. So Alicia called Charlie. As it turned out, the

FBI was listening in, but this particular recording got garbled, so they didn't know about the bomb. Anyway, I went to the VA that morning to try to find the bomb and get rid of it."

"So it really *was* you whom Gladdie Giddens saw that morning."

He nods.

Contrary to what many believe, we lawyers like to be on the side of justice. If we attack an argument, an adversary, a third-party witness—especially a third-party witness—we hope the assault is merited. Discovering that I unjustly maligned an innocent person in a public forum, in this case a frail old woman, causes shame to grip my intestines and squeeze hard.

"Why in god's name didn't you disarm the damned bomb?" I ask. "Or call in a warning?"

"What happened, Parker, is that I fucked up again. I looked for the bomb in the women's restroom. That had always been Rachel's MO. She'd dress up like a young housewife, or a clerical worker, or a buttoned-down lawyer and leave the bomb in the women's restroom. So I went to VA and slipped into the ladies' room. There wasn't anything there. I searched and searched and had to hide in a stall when some women came in. I figured it was some hoax or misunderstanding, that Jerry and Charlie had gotten it wrong, that Rachel made it up because she was pissed and wanted to freak Alicia out. What I didn't realize is that Rachel put the bomb in the *men's* restroom. She'd never done that before. Why didn't I think to check the men's room?"

I'm sure he's asked himself that question ten thousand times.

"The earring that the cops found at the scene," I say. "My mother's."

"Either she dropped it when she was assembling the bomb and it caught in the pipe, or O'Brien planted it."

I try to think back whether my mother was ever fingerprinted. Despite all the drinking and drugs and violent tantrums on movie sets, I don't think so. Since the time she helped found the Church of the Sanctified Assembly, she's been as deep underground as Holzner.

"Why would you take the blame for her?" I ask. "She built an antipersonnel weapon to be used in the commission of a felony."

"Because Alicia wasn't responsible. Because she needed to be free to care for you."

"And what a great job she did."

"You turned out fine. Besides, what did it matter? The feds were after me anyway and would never have believed the story. We would've both gone to prison. What would've become of you?"

I stop myself from replying that I wish I'd had the chance to find out, but Holzner seems to divine my thoughts anyway. "I'm truly sorry about all of this, Parker."

In the ensuing silence—not true silence, but an ongoing conversation devoid of words—I think, well, at least I've finally learned the truth about my parents.

"I don't understand," I say. "After you left, she did everything she could to draw attention to herself. Putting me in show business, sleeping around, making a spectacle of herself. It doesn't make sense."

"I told her to hide in plain sight," he says. "Create a new persona and be brazen about it. Besides, she always wanted to be somebody important. When that bomb exploded, when I left her, she was a victim, too. No longer Alicia Bowers."

I could lash out at Holzner for defending my mother, for mentioning her in the same breath as those who died in the explosion, but all I can think of is my grandfather Peter Bowers pedaling around the town on his bicycle spouting gibberish. That sweet girl Alicia must have wondered what he'd been like before the fall—just as I now wonder about her.

"Why hire me as your lawyer?" I ask. "Wouldn't I be the last person you'd want?"

"You're the only attorney I could've hired. I hoped you'd find a way to defend me against these charges without learning the truth. But since you have learned the truth, you're the only lawyer in the world who has a reason to keep it to yourself."

"The jury—or some impartial jury—has to hear this tape, hear your explanation. After that, justice will be done."

"There's no justice to be done, Parker. That's what so many people don't understand. Sometimes there is no just resolution."

"Okay, we'll wait it out to see what Gibson does with the jury-misconduct issue. He has to declare a mistrial. We'll win the second time around."

As if these words were some kind of final punctuation mark for our conversation, he stands up and stretches. "Please go get Emily. I want to tell her good night."

CHAPTER
FORTY-NINE

Bombs—the concussive force of a perfectly timed explosion, the piercing payload of carpenter's nails and ball bearings, the shrieks of fear, the cries of agony, the yelps of submission, the silence of death. Then I awaken to Emily's shout.

"Parker, wake up! Parker!"

Emily is pounding on my door so hard that she'll wake the neighbors, too.

I get up and let her in. In her baby-blue sweats and without makeup, she looks like a child.

"Dad's missing."

"What do you mean?"

"I've looked everywhere."

"He must be in the—"

"No, no, he's not in the bathroom. Or in his bedroom or in the living room or outside on the balcony or in the kitchen. He's not anywhere."

I'm out of my room and down the hall in an instant, as if Emily could somehow fail to notice her father in a small bedroom. His bed is made, a meticulous job, as if he was an infantry recruit trying to impress the drill sergeant. Everything else is in its place. I'm about to check the closet and under the bed—why would he be under the bed?—when I see it. I'm reminded of the trial testimony about how as a kid Holzner took magic lessons—part of Reddick's *spoiled-brat* defense. The media joked about his forty-year disappearing act. Secretary Cracknamara, the obsessive-compulsive card shuffler, told me Ian Holzner was quite a magician himself. I didn't take him literally, but I should have. On the dresser is his ankle monitor. It's not severed, not obviously damaged in any way. There are no marshals at my door. I think back to the night I met Holzner, when he somehow broke into my locked condominium unit without causing damage and later vaulted over the balcony when Mariko Heim showed up.

Ian Holzner has fled, once again a fugitive from injustice.

Emily and I descend the stairs, nodding to the marshal who still thinks he's guarding against Holzner's escape. I walk up to him and say, "During the night, Ian Holzner escaped. His ankle monitor is on the dresser."

He looks at me as if I'm playing a practical joke, and then, when he understands that I'm serious, begins talking frantically into his radio. Emily and I start to walk away.

"Where are you going?" he shouts. "Stay right here."

"I'm going to court. I have to let the judge know what's going on."

"You can't leave the premises."

"I certainly can. I'm the defendant's lawyer. And in case you didn't realize it, I posted his bond. I stand to lose millions by this. I'm going to court, and Ms. Lansing is coming with me."

The wind from off the ocean is gelid, cutting through my gray, woolen suit. It's one of those rare days in LA that come around maybe once every three years when I wish I owned an overcoat. In my briefcase I'm carrying the original tape recording of Alicia Bowers's phone call, along with the flash drive containing the file that makes the conversation intelligible.

We pull out of my garage and take Lincoln Boulevard to the freeway. Fortunately, traffic is light. About ten minutes into the drive, Emily says, "Even if he is guilty, I'm glad he ran."

"He's not guilty," I say.

"How do you know?" When I don't answer, she says, "I'm sorry you're going to lose all that money. I mean, six million dollars. Will you be okay?"

"Yeah, I'll be fine," I lie.

"I'll be fine, too. I'm almost an adult." She's lying, too.

We're silent until I reach the Los Angeles Street off-ramp.

"What are you going to tell the judge?" she asks.

"The truth."

We park the car, walk to the courthouse, and pass through security. I don't expect many people to be in Judge Gibson's courtroom this morning. When I get off the elevator and turn down the corridor, I see a crowd at the courtroom entrance. They're not strangers, but regulars and reporters following our trial. As I approach, the doors open and everyone piles in, sputtering in excitement.

When Emily glances up at me for an explanation, I shake my head and hurry inside. The judge isn't on the bench, and Marilee Reddick isn't at the table.

A reporter comes up to me and says, "In-chambers hearings like this are unconstitutional. We all have our First Amendment lawyers coming down."

I don't ask what he knows about the hearing because I don't want to reveal my ignorance. I walk over to the clerk's desk, and before I can say a word, she says, "They're in chambers."

"Doing what?"

She turns a deep scarlet. When I start toward the chambers door, she says, "Mr. Stern, I'm not sure you should go in there."

I hurry inside anyway and walk past the judge's secretary and into the judge's office. Gibson is sitting at his desk, with Frantz and Diamond across from him to his left and Reddick to his right. Next to Lovely is the court reporter, manipulating the keys of her steno machine. This is an official hearing.

Lovely is doing the talking, and I can tell from her honed-steel voice that she's upset. The only words I catch are "... gross miscarriage of justice." When the judge sees me, he raises his hand to silence Lovely.

"I don't think Mr. Stern should be here," Frantz says.

"Oh, he absolutely *should* be here," Lovely says.

Harmon Cherry used to say that assumptions misshape perceptions. It was one of his least original observations but no less true because of its obviousness. I glare at Reddick, waiting for her to say something that will raise my hackles. Not until she fails to respond do I comprehend that it's Lovely Diamond and Lou Frantz who are on opposite sides of this argument.

"What's this about?" I ask.

"I don't know if I should let you argue, Mr. Stern," the judge says.

I'm still oblivious. "Your Honor, as Mr. Holzner's counsel—"

"That's just it," the judge says. "You're not Mr. Holzner's attorney anymore."

I know what it's about. They've discovered that Holzner ran, and now I'm no longer a lawyer but rather a sucker on the hook for six million dollars. There is, indeed, a conflict of interest.

"Your Honor, I came down to court to report Mr. Holzner's escape," I say. "I don't understand how it happened. I found his ankle monitor on—"

"It's not about that, Parker," Lovely says. "Ian showed up at our office this morning and asked us to represent him. He says that he's fired you and that he wants to retain Lou and plead guilty. He'll agree to life imprisonment in exchange for the government dropping its request for the death penalty. It's wrong. We have a good motion for a judgment of acquittal, and if that's not granted, an airtight appeal."

"It's a great deal for a murderer," Reddick says. "Everyone on that jury except the weird guy wants to see him fry."

"You're disgusting," Lovely says. "Parker, go talk to Ian. Stop him from doing this."

"You should correct this now, Your Honor," I say. "Judgment of acquittal, mistrial, something. There was jury misconduct."

"Yes, but by which juror?" the judge says. "I'm not going to be strong-armed into ruling. Tell Mr. Holzner to hold his horses until we get an investigation done."

"Mr. Holzner has instructed me that he will not do that and wants to accept the guilty plea," Frantz says.

"This can't happen, Your Honor," Lovely says.

Chaos doesn't have to be loud or disorganized or frantic. Chaos can be insidious, a slight deviation from the norm. These chambers are in chaos, and I don't think the judge can bring order to it.

"Your Honor, I think I can solve this," I say, reaching for my briefcase. "I've got . . .." And then I stop talking, because Holzner was wrong when he said I have a choice. It's his choice, and he's made it. I utter words I never thought I'd say. "It's Mr. Holzner's right to dismiss me as his lawyer and hire Mr. Frantz. It's Mr. Holzner's right to plead guilty if he so chooses. Though again, I'd ask Your Honor to do the right thing and avoid this. You should refuse to accept the plea and declare a mistrial immediately."

Lovely shakes her head so hard that some strands of hair come loose from her barrette. She looks at me with disappointment and confusion, but something in my expression stops her, and her eyes convey that though she doesn't understand, she accepts.

The judge glares at me, and says, "I'm not sure what I'm going to do, counsel. Don't you get it? We have a jury that came in with an eleven-to-one vote to convict and a bunch of extraneous events that really don't bear on what happened in nineteen seventy-five. I need to investigate this issue. Holzner is a smart *hombre*. He can avoid the death penalty. And for that reason, I'm going to accept the plea bargain."

How often do rules and procedures provide an excuse for someone to avoid doing the right thing?

After that, everything unfolds like a black-and-white silent movie sped up for effect. I return to the courtroom. Emily asks me what happened, and when I tell her, she buries her head in my chest, and this time it's natural for me to comfort her. Defying Frantz, Lovely joins Emily and me in the gallery rather than sitting with him at counsel table.

"I don't care if the son of a bitch fires me," Lovely says, and not in a soft voice. The truth is she cares a lot. Frantz has been good to her. He was the first to recognize her talent as a trial lawyer. Later, he adjusted her schedule so she could care for the ten-year-old son who was dropped on her doorstep. And not many lawyers get to study under a master like Frantz.

Holzner is brought into the courtroom, free of shackles. He doesn't look at Emily or at me. After taking the oath to tell the truth, he provides his name—Ian Holzner, not Martin Lansing—his age, and his highest level of education. He avers that he's not suffering from drug impairment or mental illness, that he's read and discussed the indictment with his lawyer, that he's satisfied with his attorney, that he comprehends the terms of the plea agreement and enters into it voluntarily, and that he understands the consequences of his plea—life imprisonment without the possibility of parole. He's giving up his right to appeal in exchange for avoiding the death penalty. I still hope that Judge Gibson will reconsider and refuse to accept the plea. It doesn't happen. And just like that, Ian Holzner is a convicted murderer.

When the marshals lead him away, he glances at me with what I recognize as a look not of sorrow but of gratitude. Emily, who's unsuccessfully trying to blink away tears, offers me her hand. When I take it, she squeezes hard, and if I let go, I'll start crying myself.

Lovely, Emily, and I wait until the room clears out, exit the courtroom, and are about to turn right toward the elevators when I notice a solitary figure standing at the far end of the corridor. She's here for me.

"You go ahead," I say to Emily and Lovely. "Meet me on the Main Street steps." They start to protest, but when they see where I'm going, they walk away. When I reach the woman, she almost recoils.

"He called me this morning," she says. "I told him to tell the whole truth. Or at least go through the legal process to see if he can get off. I didn't want him to do this."

"Then why did you let him, Mother?" For once, my tone isn't sarcastic or accusatory or cynical. She wants to talk, and I'm just giving her the chance.

"I'm frightened, Parky. I've always been so afraid. I was hoping that you'd tell the truth for me." Her eyes are muddied with fear; her shoulders are slumped, making her neck crane forward like an arthritic. She's knotted her fingers together in reflexive prayer. How strong her desire that I tell the true story; how overwhelming her fear that I will. I wish I could free both of my parents.

"Here's why I won't tell the truth for you, Mother," I say. "You're already in your own prison. I can't put you in another one. If I do, my father will never forgive me. I couldn't live with that."

CHAPTER FIFTY

In less than an hour, Ian Holzner, the Playa Delta Bomber, will be transported from the Los Angeles Metropolitan Detention Center to the United States Penitentiary in Atwater, California, located in the sweltering San Joaquin Valley, where he'll spend the rest of his life behind bars. This is the first time we've really had a chance to speak since his guilty plea three weeks ago. To avoid the obstructions of Plexiglas and intercoms and jail guards, I've come as his attorney. But that's not what I am, not who I am.

"Why didn't you wait for the judicial process to take its course?" I ask. "We would've won the next trial."

"There was no time."

"You waited forty years."

"Secrets have a way of percolating to the surface. You have the tape recording, and you obviously had someone listen to it to make it intelligible. The media knows about its existence. It's only a matter of time before someone unearths another copy and decodes it. I wasn't about to let that happen."

"It might happen anyway."

"The odds are greatly reduced with my guilty plea."

"Please reconsider this whole thing. Tell them that you weren't competent. The recording can't be enhanced by anyone but my people. I trust them to keep this secret."

"There's always someone else with the ability. Time is no longer on our side. I didn't want Alicia to go to prison then, and I don't want that to happen now." His smile is more poignant than a tear. "I still love her. With all her failings, I still love her, Parker. And I brought this on her."

"Even if they were to arrest her, she didn't plant the bomb, didn't know what was going to happen. She only built a device. It's not murder. The statute of limitations has probably run on whatever her crime was."

"They'll prosecute her for murder anyway."

"The tape recording is exculpatory evidence."

"That's not what the US Attorney would say, probably not what a jury would say. You're forgetting the earring. It has her fingerprint on it. No one would believe she didn't plant the bomb. And whatever the outcome, the publicity would destroy her. You know that."

He's right. Despite the trappings of wealth and power, despite her demigod-like status, Harriet Stern remains a fragile soul.

"Still, to let an innocent man go to prison," I say. "It goes against everything I've worked for as a lawyer. Everything that's right."

"I'm not an innocent man."

"I don't understand."

"I set it all in motion, Parker. I built the bombs, I set them off, I pontificated about murder in the name of a cause. I brought a naïve young woman into it and taught her how to make a killing machine. Oh, I'm guilty. There's nothing unjust about this."

"Neither of you is responsible. O'Brien was."

"She's dead, and the System has to be fed. As between me and anyone else alive, I'm the one who should be its meal." He stares down at the table for a long time. "There is something I'm going to ask of you. I've abandoned Emily like I abandoned you. Which means that you'll understand how much she needs someone now. She's only a kid."

"She doesn't feel abandoned. She thinks that the justice system failed you. And as you've always surmised, the feds were probably onto you anyway."

"Someday, she'll realize that I abandoned her. I turned myself in. After Dylan died, I played favorites, and my favorite was the dead child. But because of that I need you to . . . She's almost eighteen, smart, ready for college, and after that you can—"

"She'll need her brother after she turns eighteen and twenty-five and forty. And she'll have him."

He places his hand over mine. We speak not of terror and death but of life. We talk about his beloved wife, Jenny; of my brother, Dylan; of my sister, Emily, as a child; of his love of repairing cars; of my love for Lovely Diamond; of the exhilaration that comes from acting on a stage no matter how small the audience. When the guard says it's time, I put my arms around my father and kiss him good-bye, though it's against the rules.

ACKNOWLEDGMENTS

T hank you, Daco, Suzanne Ely, Allen Eskens, Karen Garver, Lynne Raimondo, Matthew Sharpe, John Whelpley, and Robert Wolff; Jill Marr, Sandra Dijkstra, Andrea Cavallaro, and Elise Capron of the Sandra Dijkstra Agency; and Dan Mayer, Jill Maxick, Cheryl Quimba, Jade Zora Scibilia, and Nicole Sommer-Lecht of Seventh Street Books.

ABOUT THE AUTHOR

R obert Rotstein, an entertainment attorney with over thirty years' experience in the industry, is the author of *Corrupt Practices* and *Reckless Disregard*, the first and second Parker Stern novels. His novel *Reckless Disregard* was named one of Kirkus's best thrillers of 2014. He has represented all of the major motion-picture studios and many well-known writers, producers, directors, and musicians. He lives in Los Angeles, California.

Visit him at his website, robertrotstein.com; or on Facebook, facebook.com/RobertRotstein1; or on Twitter, @rrotstein1.

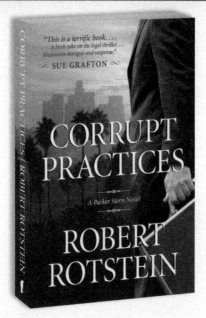
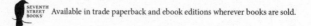

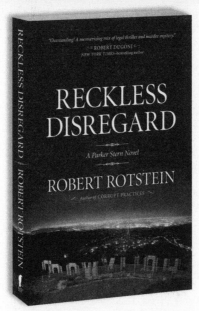
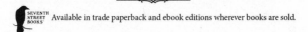